Now I'm Here

Now I'm Here

Jim Provenzano

Beautiful Dreamer Press

Beautiful Dreamer Press
309 Cross St.
Nevada City, CA 95959
U.S.A.
www.BeautifulDreamerPress.com
info@BeautifulDreamerPress.com

Lyrics to "Now I'm Here" by Brian May, copyright 1974 by EMI Beechwood Music OBO Queen Music Ltd.
Lyrics to "Bohemian Rhapsody" by Freddie Mercury, copyright 1975 by EMI Beechwood Music OBO Queen Music Ltd.

Paperback Edition
10 9 8 7 6 5 4 3 2
Printed in the United States of America

ISBN: 978-0-9981262-6-5
Library of Congress Control Number: 2018933831

Cover design by Tom Schmidt
Front and back photography by Dot
Author photo by Dot

for Don Amburgey

CONTENTS

Part 3

Now I'm Here

PROLOGUE

FACE A MAN with death, let him come out shining, and you
might call his bravery simple. Face a small town boy with fame,
love, and death, all before legal drinking age, and you will call it
anything but simple.

This is not my story. Lacking a family other than my mother,
I abide with ghosts. I have a spare bedroom in my apartment,
which Mama insists I should rent out to save money or, inadver-
tently, to find a good man.

But that room is for the boxes. The remnants of Joshua and
David, two boys who were my friends: boxes I still sometimes
browse, full of letters converted into blog posts, cassette recordings changed to mp3s, photos still to be scanned, to be
remembered, to share Joshua's gift and David's love and support
to the end. And that rickety old upright piano in the dining room
sits silently, reminding me.

After I escaped the local burden of working for my family's
small real estate company, I moved to Columbus's now-fashionable
German Village. I mourn the losses of my hometown's history from
a distance, occasionally escaping to Europe, where the ruins are
more attractive.

Last year they tore down the old high school and its echoing
gymnasium where Joshua Lee Evans once stunned the entire
school with his piano playing. That school should have been
placed on the historical preservation list, but you're lucky to find
your own driveway some winters in this ever-shifting sub-
suburban bliss known as Serene, Ohio.

My mother long ago accepted my distance, so I understand
why she likes to cling to some old ways in her days at the Serene
Senior Home. Despite her frailty, she has moved forward. Having a son like me, she had to. Despite her tendency for cynicism,
she is a decent woman, even at eighty-three. When some bigoted

resident at the home makes an unseemly statement about a non-white or non-heterosexual resident of our town, she sighs with a familiar phrase, "Honey, the South starts at Lake Erie."

It's people like Mama and me, I guess, who like to make the regular happenings in Serene—like what happened to Joshua and David—sound like myth. There are those who doubt the veracity of my words. But I know. I was there.

Not now, though; Columbus, where I now live, is a good forty-minute drive from Serene, where most of these events occurred. I return on weekends, and sometimes head up to Cleveland to visit friends or perform there.

My name is Eric Gottlund. When not performing as a guest harpist for the Columbus Symphony, I play piano in the front lounge section of Club Diversity on High Street, a little gay bar in Columbus, a city where every September farm boys in the form of college freshmen come to give away their beauty. We grow homosexuals here.

I play requests. Billy Joel, Sondheim, Spice Girls. I'm a pretty good tenor, but I like some help on those old show tunes, especially in harmony, if you can handle it.

When all the cute boys have moved on to the nearby dance club arm in arm with their friends, T-shirts soon to cling to their lithe forms with the sweat of their dancing, they leave the fat lounge singer with his tip jar. Oh, don't flatter me; I know I'm big as a house. It's my protection for a broken heart.

Each night's flock of boys will ask for Smashing Pumpkins, laughing at their joke, until I play it. Then The Cure, or even a lounge version of a Nine Inch Nails tune, until, surprised and mildly entertained, they find an excuse to go off and dance, be young and thin and deliriously happy.

But I prefer oldies, and I'm not just talking about music. I do prefer those as well: Billy Joel, Elton John, and Queen. Request a song by Queen and I'll feel a surge of melancholy that does not come from the drinks. Request a song by Queen and I might tell you a story, one you've heard before, or in parts. It is sad. They're all sad, eventually.

I knew Joshua and David, grew up with them. Class of '79. Go Mounties.

You go ahead and have your fun, with your faux-retro collectibles, salvaging pieces of my childhood as campy. But I remember it.

I watched these two boys from afar for years, being the sissy they rarely spoke to until later, after we'd each traveled down our own roads and then returned home. I am left behind to remember the beauties, when those two boys grew up to be men, then left a small legacy behind. I believe they're getting it right somewhere else. And as I forage through the boxes, I hope to get closer to the truth.

Part 1

Whatever comes of you and me
I love to leave my memory with you.

—Brian May, "Now I'm Here"

Chapter 1

WHO NEEDS YOU

JOSHUA LEE EVANS grew up scrawny, some say due to an illness as a toddler. But that fever sickness may have been what first drew him to the love of his life. His mother, Sara Evans, a healthy woman from San Francisco, got along well enough with her husband, Samuel Evans, an assistant manager at Serene's True Value hardware store.

His parents and various relatives did not eagerly anticipate Joshua Lee, the first of two children and the only boy of the family. Satisfied with one potential heir to his name and a daughter two years later, his father got a vasectomy, thereby avoiding the other, more cumbersome means of birth control that prevented him from loving his wife spontaneously. Despite his occasional lapses into silence, Samuel maintained a quiet passion for his wife and children.

So the lack of attention paid to the toddler Joshua was the same one that would disturb Joshua's life for years to come: a terrible case of bad timing.

Two years to the day after his birth, Joshua Lee Evans was taken to the Serene Valley General Hospital with a case of Scarlet Fever. It was early in the afternoon on November 22, 1963. According to his medical charts, remnants of which Sara Evans saved for decades, he was admitted at 1:07 pm.

While a nation reeled from the explosion of the first Catholic president's brain, equally chaotic events transpired on a local level, as if the nerve center of the country had unraveled. The pediatric ward of Serene Valley General Hospital endured some panic and confusion: although a scant two toddlers were being treated, the sole attending nurse, in shock over the news of the president's death, forgot to attend to Joshua Lee's most basic needs that day and fed only the other child instead, one Royce Jenkins.

Sedative treatments were all the rage in the early 1960s (several children born at the time with birth defects were not the product of inbreeding). However, Joshua Lee's mother, then pregnant with her second child, refused medication and remained in the waiting room. Exhausted by the events, she slept fitfully in chairs through the next two days. Upon waking, she was not told that she had a recovering healthy boy, but instead, "Oswald's dead."

In her drowsy state, she wondered why had her child died, and why had he been given such a strange new name?

Dazed by the explanation of the dual assassination, she turned her focus to the care of Joshua. Samuel Evans had spent the days secretively sipping whiskey in the hospital parking lot, a habit he gave up the day they brought the boy home. The two young parents huddled in the nursery and wept until Joshua's normal gurgles and crying brought them back to a sense of duty and cheerfulness. Children have a way of focusing the most overwhelmed of parents.

Joshua Lee's bout of Scarlet Fever left a scar on his brain that would heal in time, the doctors said. Doctors out in Serene were pretty smart back then, having to deal with the occasional farm animal as well.

But, due to the untimely nature of his near-death, Joshua Lee's birthdays came to be gloomy events, to say the least. Joy seemed false and forced. The papers were always filled with anniversary awfulness, since his birthday coincided with Kennedy's death. Anyone born on November 22, or December 7, or even April 4, can understand. If you don't know these dates, go look them up.

It is hard to tell Joshua and David's story because, you see, it is what could have been. What's left in the boxes barely tells what happened. A mere birthday tends to feel ever so small compared to such a morbid anniversary. "When's your birthday?" "Pearl Harbor Day, but I had nothing to do with it."

"I'm in Hawaii in my dreams," wrote Joshua in a diary he kept. He had finished adoring a *Travel and Leisure* photograph of a "POLYNESIAN" man in a straw hula. Joshua spelled Polynesian in capital letters, as if burning its magic into his memory. Joshua often talked about traveling, according to his mother. Years later, he would visit the city where his parents first met.

The people of Serene, Ohio hold fast to their heritage, or used to. Some farms and buildings in town go back more than a century, leaving any residents without an extensive local lineage always to be considered newcomers. Born of both local and California heritage, Joshua Evans's dual family tree bears telling.

A month into his hitch at Treasure Island Naval Base, Samuel Terrence Evans and Sara Catherine DiGiorno met on an April night in 1959. The two visited a dance hall popular with visiting sailors during Fleet Week. Too young to experience it but young enough to idealize the romantic films of World War II, the two were perhaps not as star-crossed as movie characters, yet they managed to become quite close.

Sara worked between college classes as a waitress at La Tomba, an unstylish North Beach bistro once owned by her father. Her politics, which rejected the conservative Catholic values of her parents, might have also rejected military personnel, but the forward sailor reminded her of Gene Kelly in *On the Town*, albeit less swift on his feet. With a plodding regularity that she found amusing, the twenty-five-year-old Sam Evans would call once a week to ask the twenty-two-year-old Sara to accompany him to dinner and a show. With two of his friends waiting outside, Sara always accepted the sailor's stuttered request.

They might have wed sooner, but the Navy interfered by

shipping him off to a six-month post at Naval Station Rota near the Strait of Gibraltar. He returned, as he said he would, half a year later. Sara went out for a date that very Saturday. She had already made a new dress and had marked her calendar in advance. When Sam's father became bedridden back in Ohio, he left again, vowing to return.

"I trusted this man," Sara said many times.

Her mother, Katherina DiGiorno, did not. Her only-slightly-wealthy husband, Leopold DiGiorno, once-owner of La Tomba, had died in the Korean War, leaving his wife and children with a small Victorian home in North Beach. I have a photo that features it. Being left to see to the betrothal of her only daughter (Sara has three brothers, whose stories will not be told in this account, since they did not respond to my inquiries), Katherina DiGiorno was disappointed not only by Sam's non-Catholic faith (Presbyterian), but also by the doleful demeanor and lanky frame of her daughter's non-Italian suitor. With nothing back in Ohio but a house and a cancer-ridden father waiting to die in it, young sailor Samuel seemed an unlikely, though handsome, choice. Sara's mother allowed her daughter this steadfast indulgence, for a time. At least she admired his dashing uniform.

Sam returned, only to beg Sara to come back with him and make a home. In a box with an engagement ring, he'd enclosed a snapshot of his house, nothing more. The photo convinced her.

Having been raised in a home with a back yard of jade plants, ginkgos, an evergreen, rose bushes, and dozens more plants, Sara wanted to see that bare lawn in the photo come alive. A long-distance escape from her perpetually arguing brothers held an added appeal. She agreed, only learning later that Ohio's total of sunny days averaged less than fifty-four a year. Even so, gardening would prove much easier than in a squat North Beach back yard. The two were engaged within the month.

News spread quickly. Sam wrote letters home, which my own mother read to Sam's ailing father during her days as a candy striper. It irritated the ailing senior Evans when other townsfolk began to call and congratulate the man on a betrothal that he had not approved. When Sam was finally granted family leave, his reunion with his father was less than cordial. Although not uncommon for a Serene bachelor to engage so quickly in the serious business of matrimony, to wed a girl from a faraway city like San Francisco, and a Catholic no less, led to gossip. Of course, we back in Serene—we being my parents and their friends and neighbors—were all shocked.

Sara's early arrival in Serene came the day of the funeral of her would-be father-in-law. Despite the morbid occasion, Sam supported her, introduced her at the wake and several gatherings. She charmed everyone so, with her then-exotic Italian dishes at the post-funeral gatherings in her new home. I remember my own mother's accounts as if I had been there.

Mother tells them at the home and tries to stir Sara's memory. I pay visits, fewer as the years go on. Along with my own mother, Sara has become one of those people I feel obliged to visit. There is the grieving part. I visit to become a sort of translator of the history of Joshua for her, years after it all, when she could talk more easily about him, before she began to forget so much.

"When I got here," Sara used to say, "I thought of myself as one of those pioneer women, but played by Merle Oberon." She gardened with fervor, one of her many skills. When my mother visited on a weekend day, she used to say, "Why, she just kept diggin' away like a gopher the whole time we chatted. I suspect she'll discover . . ." This is one my mother said so often even Joshua's mother repeated it to me as we joked at my mother's expense, ". . . she'll discover that gardening's much easier in this part of the country."

"I met him at a USO night at the town hall," Sara Evans once told Mrs. Humphries, one of three other wives who'd joined the League of Women Voters, in part because they all disagreed with their husbands about the impending 1972 election. None of the women trusted Nixon, who was up for reelection, and only a small minority in Serene could be counted on to vote for George McGovern. They also needed something to do with their thoughts and ideas that ironing and cooking never satisfied. Sara had taken classes at Beekam College only a few blocks away.

She liked the feeling of shaking things up in Serene, if only in a proper way, like in the League. Mrs. Humphries had been involved with it for a few years, as had my mother. Sara invited them over at least once a week for a time; they shared stories.

"He'd just started his training," Sara continued, "and I know you'll agree about the sight of a man in a uniform . . ."

"Oh, yes, my Harry was quite a sight."

"But even afterward, I remember something so calm and secure in that man's eyes."

Joshua sat off in the dining room, pretending to do homework while he eavesdropped on the women in the living room. Joshua knew what his mother meant when she spoke of his father's face, as honest as the cornfields on Route 93.

That didn't stop his father from worrying about the tenderness of the boy. It didn't help when Joshua's mother continued to refer to him as her "special child," as if he were a simpleton.

"He's jus' scrawny," his father would half-joke as he tousled his young son's hair, the boy's thin neck bobbing from the pressure. Kids his age had game plans, activities. They had futures. They cleaned their plates. Joshua seemed a little foggy, but he'd make out.

He often spent summer days lying on the expansive lawn of their home, watching the clouds roll by, imagining his name scrolling past with those of movie stars. Sunday mornings were spent enjoying big breakfasts, the *Columbus Dispatch* comics, and TV movies.

Theirs was not a religious family. Having abandoned her family's faith, Sara refused even to visit the nearest Catholic church in Columbus (not counting the tiny church in Lithopolis), much to the consternation of her mother, who continued to mail prayer cards to her grandchildren on their birthdays and holidays along with a ten or twenty dollar bill as a sort of presumed bribe. Sara did consent to the occasional holiday visit to Sam's less formal Presbyterian congregation, but she won out on Sunday school. Having suffered "more than enough being raised Catholic, and those nagging conversations with the Baptist biddies in this town," she declared, "Those bigoted yokels won't get their hands on my children."

In elementary school, Joshua did quite well, in fact. For a time, before his genius seemed to separate him from other children, we traded peeks at report cards. I always remember Joshua and I showing off our straight A's, then running from others to hide the embarrassment. Teachers often wrote in their report cards that Joshua had "plenty of intelligence and aptitude, but little motivation."

Our paths also collided outside of grade school, and I have a piano to thank for those brief encounters.

Joshua had a gift for music. After one of our Music Appreciation days where teachers ask the students to do unusual things like making up a song on the piano, Joshua's mother received a note from school that made her look at her son differently.

When it had been Joshua's turn to sit before the big black box with the white teeth which Mrs. Spears rolled in once a week (much too limited, as I recall, were the lessons in our small school), he proved himself more than smart.

I remember that day like the sweetest spring breeze that pushes its way in through windows, enticing children outside like a puppy with a ball in its teeth.

Joshua got up to the piano and, without having ever taken a lesson in his life, proceeded to play, improvising. Those little fingers barely hit a single sour note, and a song trickled out of that old box that started some of the kids humming.

I cannot recall the actual chords or notes he played, but I swear to you on a stack of Sondheim that this boy was an *idiot savant* without the *idiot*. He took to the piano with ease, and after several minutes, had to be asked to stop. Mrs. Spears nearly had to pry him from the piano bench. He was seven. I believe Mozart had already played before royalty by then. Would that we had kings worthy in Serene.

Culture wormed its way into the family through other means. Joshua's sister discarded her tomboy years one day after being called a "dirty brat" by a schoolmate and decided to take ballet lessons.

Joshua thought he deserved to move into the world of the arts as well. His mother kept the secret of his talent, fearing what her husband might think. That Christmas, though, the boy asked for nothing except a piano.

His father scoffed at the idea. "Where'd we put it?" he argued.

"Right there." Joshua pointed to the back wall of the dining room, as if his mother's china hutch had merely to dissolve to make room for his wish. Judging by his mother's smile, it did not seem to him like it would be a problem.

It would be 1974 before his dream came true. Pivotal years that might have separated Joshua from very good to great were thus lost. But what is time but water falling past us?

Despite their success and happiness, Joshua's family was not wealthy, and pianos had to be ordered from out of town. Nevertheless, fate assisted. One of his father's biggest accounts at True Value, Humerkeiser Construction, planned to demolish a block of old homes on Tremont Street to make way for a new Brethren church and its expansive parking lot. Among the debris of the abandoned houses—which in any more civilized city would have been deemed historical and preserved—sat a rickety upright piano, caked in layers of paint.

On a hot July day, Joshua's father had it loaded onto his pickup. Two men from the hardware store assisted as he backed the Ford right through the lawn and over his wife's pachysandras. (She recovered, as did the plants.)

The men wheeled it onto the porch with two planks and dragged it into the house, whereupon Sam handed Joshua cans of paint thinner, stain, and varnish.

"When you've got that thing lookin' as good as yer mother's furniture, we'll find the money for some lessons," his father said in lieu of announcing an early thirteenth-birthday present.

The boy had never taken to any of his father's carpentry skills but soon learned, breathing in the dizzying smells of the thinner like an addict. He stripped the ornate piano of its layers of brown, white, and, oddly enough, silver paint, revealing a beautiful framework of curlicues and trim that would soon face him for hours every week at his practice sessions.

He did not, however, wait for lessons before attacking the piano. He doodled, found chords, found notes, found music. Joshua had an ear. He also asked that it be tuned.

Sheet music, or "sticks and noodles," as he called them, meant little to him at first. He could see what they meant and how they mapped out where his fingers were supposed to go, but he had to hear a song, memorize the sound, and then play it over and over. Despite his small fingers, he had an aptitude others lacked. He kept going. If he made a mistake, he stayed on the beat, rather than crash back and start again, as if he were in a hurry to improve.

"That boy keeps bangin' on that thing like it means something," his father glared from behind his newspaper, his after-dinner cup of coffee growing tepid. Richard Nixon was on the television, resigning.

"Give him time, dear," his mother soothed. She tried not to squint as her "special" son hit another clinker on the worn keys.

Over the next four years, on each Thursday Joshua walked from our grade school to the home of his instructor, Mrs. Rose, usually needing more brushing up than he admitted, and suffering the light scolding of a small town piano teacher. Mrs. Rose hoped to sculpt her students' hands into wonderful articulate instruments. She was often disappointed. As one of her prize students, I worked hard. Joshua didn't have to.

Handing Joshua everything from "Swans on the Lake" to more intricate folk songs, Mrs. Rose watched, fascinated, as Joshua attempted to read notes, then asked her to play it once, and then, only then, did the boy play better. She knew some students had an ear and others had eyes. She liked to group them, if the other younger ones were even groupable. As one of Mrs. Rose's accomplished students, I managed with perfunctory if not inspired technique. I had eyes.

On long afternoons at home, Joshua would slip into the dining room to practice during the hours between school and his dad's return from the True Value. His father didn't dislike hearing the boy practice, but Joshua always felt more nervous when he listened, every note a penny plunked down, giving Dad his money's worth.

With the lumbering piano pushed against one wall, Joshua plunked away at yet another uninspiring tune, "The Water Mill." He wasn't sure why he persisted, but sitting before those eighty-eight keys offered an almost magical escape. Five of them, like bad teeth, were broken, the soft hammers and brittle wooden sticks cracked with age. He would open the ornate front panel of the piano and watch the hammers and wires flutter as he played.

Not to say that the boy remained devoted to his newly found art. As he stumbled into adolescence, other activities took priority. Like the piano, which still had patches of different colors here and there, he performed "shoddy work, but good playin'," as his father would say.

When he did have a mind to play, I imagine, like me, that he forgot everything else: the taunts at school, the strange feelings for other boys, the fear of wearing the wrong style of sneaker or showing up at school without his gym clothes. Sitting at the old upright, almost every key responded when he touched, so unlike anyone or anything else. That affinity, I believe, we shared.

18

But unlike me, Joshua felt destined for greatness of one sort or another.

I was there, and heard it the first time when Joshua played, before the school heard him. His lessons preceded mine for years. Once a week, we passed in the hallway of the Rose home. Each week I arrived earlier and earlier, most times content to sit on the Rose's porch or in the front room, from summer sun to winter freezes, hearing Joshua, knowing that merely being in the same room while he played, watching his small back hunch over the keys, his long brown hair shining in the afternoon light, would bring me to such distraction that I would fail even to find middle C.

But this took place before the unfortunate times. Mrs. Rose did not know whom she taught. She did not know how much it meant to Joshua to play well. She also did not know that the boy had yet to discover his true musical inspiration, a big-mouthed, mustachioed gentleman from England.

Chapter 2

TEAR IT UP

AS PARENTS, SAM and Sara Evans's next trial to endure after their son's bout of Scarlet Fever was what Joshua later came to call "The Feeling."

The sliver of scar tissue in his brain resulted in a few crossed neurological road signs. A few times a year, at odd moments, the boy's parents watched in terror as their child broke out in a sweat, eyes glazed, body twitching, his little chirping voice mumbling incoherently.

"It was as if he were fighting some invisible spirit," Sara described it to me on one of my many afternoon visits. I came to know Joshua's mother only in the last few years.

From the inside, the symptoms were the least of these seizures. To the five-year-old Joshua, the room would ignite in a series of horrifying sensory exaggerations that left him silent for days. The brown-orange carpet in the living room became a raging, moving brushfire. The television roared so loud as to be silent, the boy enveloped in its maw. Bodies of lamps wiggled like Disney cartoons, pink elephants on parade. The texture of plastic made him nauseous. Tinkling soda-glass ice cubes crashed like chandeliers. He once made mention of *The House of Usher*, how the character played by Vincent Price shuddered at any loud sound.

He remained a delicate creature. In earlier times, of course, such a handicap would result in commitment to an asylum or an exorcism. Sam Evans's upbringing at one time may have included either of these remedies, but Sara had been to college and had dated medical students. She knew better and trusted the world of pharmaceuticals and neurologists.

Through each episode, his mother would hold Joshua or sit close to him, watching attentively so that he wouldn't swallow his tongue. She would hold him tightly on a sofa that the boy feared would eat him. After a few visits to faraway towns like Dayton and Akron, the boy came to know the comfort of pre-scription drugs and EEG testing. He'd been taken several times to see a "brain doctor" in Dayton who prescribed chewable tri-angular pills known as Dilantin.

As the years of comparing his own life with his few friends continued, Joshua came to understand something else different about himself and his parents. Other kids seemed to dislike their mothers and fathers, spending their days in a frenzy of escape. Find a game, go to camp, join the Scouts, anything to get away from home. In most bird species, the natural instinct to flee the nest sets in before they grow feathers.

But Joshua liked staying at home, whether intently watching his father's face and hands as he repaired the lawn mower, quiz-zing him about the contents of a car as they toiled in the garage, or sitting quietly while his mother chattered away, entertaining a guest with more tales of far-away San Francisco. The boy loved his parents. He got along with his younger sister, although even as a toddler she distanced herself from him after his strange fe-vered episodes.

Joshua learned to hide his condition out of fear and a quiet shame. His attempts to befriend other boys often faced other barriers. When Mike Ebert from Cub Scouts invited Joshua over one Saturday to peek at his father's collection of *Playboys*, his assent hid confusion.

"Doesn't it make your dick hard?" Mike had asked Joshua.

"Sure," he mumbled, learning at age twelve how to lie to pro-tect himself. He'd see Mike in the halls, and wonder if that was just an excuse to show each other their dicks and get down to things, as it were.

Years later, the clarity of his attraction to other boys would coalesce in a form of joy in a least likely location: on a highway in a van en route to a rock concert. But that first boy kiss in a van was still a few years in the making.

Joshua's sister's birthday coincided with the school yearbook picture day. To celebrate this dual thrill, she threw a party. (You will forgive my not using her name, but Joshua Lee Evans's sister has threatened litigation should her name be included in this account, which, mind you, has been reimagined enough to avoid legal action.)

By the time they herded into the Evans house after school in a chattering cluster, the girls were still in their fine dresses and new braids, despite the school memo warning "No New Hairdos!" Sister didn't have to worry. She wore her hair long and straight with a band. Dory Jenkins's new curls were a little too much, but neither Sister nor any of her ten exclusively invited friends said so. After consulting the photos in the Serene Elementary High Yearbook, I must concur that Dory's new hairdo was a frightful one.

Throughout Friday afternoon, the girls filled the house with one perpetual giggle. Sister got a *Josie and the Pussycats* cartoon book, Barbie clothes, the *Mystery Date* board game, and more Barbie clothes. On their way upstairs to admire the Barbie collection, which Sister had conveniently arranged into a miniature showroom, the gaggle crossed paths with Joshua. He had been standing silent in his room, listening to their chirping conversation, and came out as they passed. The girls fell silent, ushered on by Sister like nuns.

The gap between girls and boys clearly defined, he retreated to his room and built a clay triceratops. He thought about making his GI Joes invade their party, but he didn't. That would make her mad and then she wouldn't let him put Ken's clothes on his three Joes. One had a real beard.

In art class at school, everyone had been given a new material to make art. One day they glued beans onto cardboard, then drew landscapes with colored chalk dipped in buttermilk. For Halloween they madly scribbled all kinds of colors with crayons, painted the cardboard over with black tempera paint, then scratched scenes of black cats, witches, and pumpkins. Joshua made a warlock, but had to explain it to Mrs. Belgrave, his teacher, who did not watch *Bewitched* as it was un-Christian.

That day, the project involved toothpicks and glue. While inconsistent when it came to academics (he'd been berated for using his fingers behind his back while counting multiplications), absent in athletics, and still unsure of music (the only kids at that time who took music classes were so odd Joshua felt afraid he'd become like them, bespectacled, sitting in a dark room sawing on a violin), in art Joshua felt secure.

He also developed a bit of competitive verve. When Don McAllister, the tallest boy in our class, made a replica of the Eiffel Tower, Joshua, whose log cabin had seemed fine enough until the oohs and ahhs of Don's tower made him jealous, decided on a radio tower, not unlike the one outside our town. The small log cabin became a studio, and he set to creating the spires of the tower. But as he neared the top, the rhythm of dipping the toothpicks in the glue and placing them began to take on a hypnotic effect. The three o' clock bell approached and he became determined to finish in a few minutes. He began to dip the sticks in the sticky glue tube and toss them up to the tower, making a spiky cluster on top.

"And what do we have here?" Mrs. Belgrave condescendingly queried.

"It's a radio station that's blowing up."

"Oh. Oh, my."

That week, Joshua also got in his first fight.

Violence rarely came his way, but when it did, Joshua refused to cower. He knew even at that age that something different burned in his small soul, and he felt his whole life might be spent fighting for his place. But even at a young age, he valued his hands. So he kicked.

After a field trip to the town cider mill, the busload of kids had been invited for Halloween cookies and a party at the home of Margie Silvanus. Her mother taught third grade, and was very popular. Kids told their parents to do whatever they could to get in "the cool class" where desks were arranged in small groups instead of tedious rows. Mrs. Silvanus's forte involved activities: magical afternoons with glue, paste and scissors that made the children almost regret the three o'clock bell.

Margie had preened about her expansive lawn, showing off their horse and a few swings while other kids hovered around the cookie table after a sing-a-long. Several of the boys had gone down to the small creek behind the barn to hunt crawdads, and chubby Brad Duffy had been talking about girls. I recall disappearing into a field to watch butterflies. I hid nearby, listening in on the conversation.

"Y'ever kiss a girl?" a boy asked nobody in particular.

"Sure," Brad Duffy said.

"Who?"

"Christine Malachik."

"What about you?" Brad nodded to Joshua.

"Sure."

"Who?"

"I ain't tellin'."

"Aw, he prob'ly don' even like girls."

"I do so!"

"You're a fag an' everybody knows it."

"Fuck you!"

Profanity served as a starting gun to violence. Drawn out of hiding, I witnessed the next events. Brad pushed Joshua into the water, whereupon the boy turned, sprang up from the bank, ripped off the husky boy's black-framed glasses, stomped them into the ground, and knocked Brad down. During the tussle, Joshua found himself twisted around with Brad Duffy's thick calf near his face, and in a decisive moment, having seen a Western movie where one man sucked the snake bite out of another man's leg, Joshua decided to chomp down on the Duffy boy's flesh.

This is how Joshua got his reputation for pugilism of the sissy sort. His kicks predated Bruce Lee, whose show, *The Green Hornet*, while only a few years absent from our TV screens, had been forgotten. Kicking was not yet fashionable, nor was the act of biting another boy.

Driven back to the school parking lot, where children were either picked up by parents or allowed to walk home, Joshua considered tossing the stern note from Mrs. Silvanus, but knew she would, as promised, call his mother about the fight. He sulked as he walked home, handed his mother the note upon arrival, endured a brief lecture, then retreated to his room.

Before dinner, Joshua talked with his sister, hoping to gain support. Her presents sat in a pile on her pink dressing table, the gift-wrapping and bows on another pile at the foot of her bed.

"You're in trouble," she scolded him.

Joshua changed topics. "I could have a party."

"Who would you invite?"

"My friends."

"What friends?"

"Oh, Mitch and Mike and . . . some others. Lots."

"What about Brent Carse?"

"Naw."

"Isn't he one of your friends?"

"Why?"

"He was standing with us on the playground and you went by and just nodded at me like you do."

"Well . . ."

"I mean, you don't even say hi."

"Sorry."

"He called you Fido. What's that mean?"

"Shut up, you idiot."

"Mom!"

"Aw, jeez."

Sara Evans tromped up the stairs, expecting to witness the remains of some bloody crime, but merely saw her two children at opposite ends of her daughter's room.

"Joshua got in a fight. He bit Brad Duffy!"

"I already know that," Sara replied.

"He bit him!"

Joshua tossed a bow as he ran from her room. "Shut up, you bitch!"

Sara followed him. "Joshua, where did you ever hear that word?"

"I dunno."

"You apologize to your sister. I have to get dinner ready." Not knowing what to make of the concerned phone call and the note Joshua brought home, his mother hoped his leg-biting days were over.

Joshua waited to approach his sister's room. With her door half open (a sign of truce), Joshua slowly battle-crawled his GI Joe doll down the carpeted hallway to her room.

"What is that little man doing creeping around like that?" she asked from her hyper pink Flower Power-stickered vanity table.

"He wants to play with Ken."

"In those clothes?"

"He wants to borrow some fun clothes and get out of uniform."

"How about the Hawaiian shirt and a pair of chinos?"

"Yeah." Joshua got up.

"What's the magic word?"

"Uh . . . macaroni and cheese?"

"No, silly."

"Uh . . . I'm sorry?"

She looked down at him and sighed, as if burdened, like a young princess, with the responsibility of either saving or beheading a ragged prisoner. "He's in the Dreamhouse playing records."

His combative day over, that night Joshua taped some songs off the radio, holding his cassette recorder to the speakers of his parents' old RCA stereo. He taped the Isley Brothers "Fight the Power," since they didn't have that in any of the stores in Serene. In those days, you had to go as far as Columbus for soul music. As my mother used to say, the South starts at Lake Erie.

Joshua's bite proved worse with his schoolmates' barks. He had been given the nickname Fido, and for days at recesses afterwards each call of the name brought him closer to repeating the near-cannibalistic act on his name-callers. It gave him a sense of bravery, and with it, a strange sense of daring.

He stopped taking his Dilantin.

For several weeks, considering himself too old for such safeguards, he hid them in a place in his room, sometimes even popping them in his mouth after dinner, only to hide them behind his teeth. He spat them out and added them to the growing sticky cluster wrapped in wax paper and hidden in a paper bag in a box of abandoned model plane parts.

For weeks, Joshua remained at the ready for any Fido comments. Fortunately, the attention span of grade schoolers is short, and his reputation dwindled.

But one boy remembered, and months later, he approached Joshua on the playground.

He was one of those taller boys who looked as if he should already be in high school, those whose homes you never see, the boys dragged in by the farm bus that picked up kids in a sleepy daze from having risen at dawn to milk cows. He was one of those boys many feared and lusted after; his blond hair approached a flaxen glow. He wore black T-shirts, baggy jeans and work boots to school.

He was David Koenig.

He stopped Joshua from running off with a few other boys who were going to see Brian Hansen dare some other boys to pee in the snow behind the bushes.

"Hey, Fido."

"Shut up." Joshua moved off the dark wet asphalt to the soft snow-covered field, as if preparing to be shoved to the ground, unwilling to take his gaze from the smirking blond boy.

There were not as many children on the playground since the older kids were in their classrooms, getting ready for the Christmas assembly in the gym. Joshua's mother had spent hours working on Sister's costume. She was playing an angel, a demanding role for her, Joshua thought. He thought about angels, looked up into the clouds, and was ignored, for a while.

The shine of the taunting boy's blond hair caught the corner of his eye, and Joshua faced the boy who would change his life forever.

"You the one 'at bit Brad Duffy?" David Koenig's blond hair shone almost as bright as the white yard of snow. Joshua walked away. He didn't want to look at the boy, who he knew lived out in the country, the target of equally stupid jokes, something to do with pumpkins. But this one—this one hurt to look at, he was so pretty.

"Hey, didja?"

"What about it?" Joshua snapped.

"Well, maybe he deserved it."

"Yeah."

"Yeah, bet you can't bite me." He grinned.

There weren't any other boys around. He wasn't showing off. Joshua knew this boy's name was David, but he could not look at him up close, the cold winter sun too bright.

"What?"

"Wanna try?"

"Go 'way."

"C'mon, Fido . . ."

"Lemme alone."

David's hand landed on Joshua's chest. He had to look up at the wispy blond bangs, the sleek nose, the blue button-like eyes, and the lips, thick and pale pink. Joshua did not know then that boys could kiss, that he could kiss a boy this beautiful. He wanted to, but couldn't, had been denied the basic concept. Rather, he desired the knowledge of having that desire.

So he punched him.

David was bigger and could have clobbered Joshua. David hadn't meant anything by it. It was just something boys did, part of the pecking order. His father ran a pumpkin farm and that made David popular even at a young age, particularly around Halloween, when other kids traveled with their parents to pick out their own pumpkins for making jack o' lanterns. David already had friends while Joshua was barely noticed.

The two did some obligatory scuffling, buffered by the snow. Urged on by the primal forces of violence voiced so clearly by children, they rolled on the ground, surrounded by a chanting circle of kids who appeared out of nowhere, eager for the sight of blood.

Being the larger of the two, David naturally ruled the fight, in which nary another punch was thrown, just a bit of clumsy tussling. Joshua threw no additional punches, having suddenly remembered the fragility and value of his hands.

David's blond hair practically gleamed in the recess sun. He straddled his unqualified opponent, who tossed his head in a sweaty rage. The kid was acting funny, mumbling and shivering.

Joshua was getting The Feeling.

From the outside, Joshua's seizures were not grand mals, but more furtive dream states in the midst of day. Funny what a simple nerve synapse can do to enhance one's oddball status.

From inside, this is how Joshua told me it felt. The bright sun scorched him. David's weight on his body almost squeezed his guts out of his chest. A sweat droplet fell from David's face and burned Joshua's skin like sweet acid. He screamed.

Shocked, David let go, then picked the boy up and hugged him tightly, holding him close with a tenderness he'd never felt before. "It's okay, it's okay," he soothed as he patted Joshua's back.

Not seeing the truce that had already been made, a teacher's huge hands pried them apart.

The two were trotted off to The Bench, a long bare wood seat comparable in sixth grade to a prison's death row. To be sent to The Bench meant an inevitable meeting with Principal Hudson, a wiry bespectacled man who brought dread and fear into the hearts and minds of every student at William Taft Elementary.

Joshua sat a few feet from David, who leaned back listlessly, expecting the worst and apparently not a bit frightened about the prospect of a paddling. The boys did not speak, but occasionally stole silent glares at each other in the empty hall. Joshua had recovered from his seizure but refused to mention it. He felt, however, that this boy who had saved him knew something. David spat on the floor, his saliva pooling at his lips and falling slowly to the floor in a glob. Joshua, impressed by the gesture, felt an erection in his pants.

The two grinned at each other, suddenly conspirators.

They had to sit as dozens of students in the school marched by, chairs in their arms, to the assembly. Joshua heard a rustling sound, then looked up to see his sister in line with a dozen others in choir robes, white wings flapping. Sister passed by, head held high, her older brother unworthy of her glance.

The boys were ushered into the office. Joshua worried that they might have to take down their pants for the whacking, then hoped it would happen, so he could see David's butt. It didn't happen.

Joshua felt no pain through the procedure. He just stared at the details: Mister Hudson's desk, the diplomas on the wall, the dank smell of the room. All was erased by the sight of the wooden paddle being taken from a filing cabinet, the sight of David Koenig being bent over. Joshua watched David's thick little fingers grip the edge of the desk as the paddle hit David's butt, feeling a combination of desire and admonition. David did not have good piano-playing fingers, he noted.

David stood and turned; his eyes were red and bleary, droplets of tears running down his face. When he saw David cry, his nose wet with snot, both of them barely boys, he did not even feel it as the principal whacked the back of his ass.

As the two boys were released into the empty echoing hallway, not more than ten feet from the closed door, David muttered, "If you ever tell anybody I cried, I'll pound you again."

Some part of Joshua, a part as yet to blossom deep inside, whispered that he was in love.

Chapter 3

SON AND DAUGHTER

BY THE TIME he began to grow hair between his legs, which fortunately coincided with his entry into junior high school, Joshua had also learned how to escape when he needed to get away from his family.

The compliments about his music began to irritate him. His "special" qualities had begun to embarrass him. When the great shift from elementary school to junior high school occurred, he lost friends. Boys who once never noticed his different interests now roughed it up at football practice, distancing themselves from boys who didn't go out for sports.

At the same time, Joshua felt at odds with the more feminine side of his nature. By pure necessity, Joshua began to distance himself from boys like me. Our passing in the halls of Warren G. Harding Junior High School were reduced to mere eyebrow nudges and nods. I do not blame Joshua for this distance. It was a matter of survival. I understand and forgive. They were horrible years.

That first year in seventh grade pained us all. With the many surprise eruptions on faces and in groins—and for girls, their breasts—merely showing up at school (with the appropriate nickname War on G. Hardons) became a ritual that each of us should have been rewarded for merely enduring. For some, the facade of popularity guarded the fear. For others, well, those others just got hung out to dry.

It might have been a Sunday afternoon when they met. Joshua never could remember, exactly. He did remember that he met

Kelly sometime around Easter, because that is when he also found a new affection for his own name.

In Ohio, one of the television stations always played *The Ten Commandments* on Easter Sunday. Not being in a religious family, Joshua didn't think much of the film at first.

Then he found his namesake in a black-haired beautiful man who wore sandals and had a tight crazed stare in his dark eyes: actor John Derek at his most handsome. Captured and tied up by Vincent Price, his bare chest glistening, he certainly got Joshua's attention. He sat in the living room watching, hoping for more of "Joshua," but was disappointed.

He tore himself away when Sam Evans asked him to get dressed and help with some gardening, digging a trench for his mother's new shrubs. Joshua liked helping his dad with yard work. They talked.

"What was going to church like when you grew up?"

"Boring, but it was good for me."

"Why did you name me Joshua?"

"Your grandfather had a brother. He was in the Navy, too."

"I know." He also knew that his great-uncle Joshua had died in a war.

"Why didn't you name me after Grandpa?"

"Would you want to be named Horace?"

They laughed as the dirt crumbled beneath their hands.

"I guess I just wonder about stuff."

"Well, that's good. It's good to wonder about things, like what you wanna do with your life."

Joshua thought about John Derek in those robes and sandals. He wanted to stand on a mountaintop and do something noble like him, or do something less noble to him.

When they finished planting the shrubs, Joshua asked his father to look at the chain on his bike, which his father reminded him should be taken off and cleaned, but Joshua forgot about things like that. His father sprayed some WD40 on the gears, which helped.

"Whyncha go take off. Back before six. Dinner'll be on."

"Oh. Okay."

Joshua wanted to ask about his father's sailor uncle, but it never seemed like the right time.

Joshua felt a secret joy as he rode through parts of town his father warned him about, exploring the dirty warehouse district of town near the railroad tracks. It was his own safe way of misbehaving.

A small rock pinged against his front wheel with a clarity that he knew was not from running over a pebble. He shot a glare sideways and saw a girl.

She did not exactly look like a girl, though. Her short hair and faded jeans were not at all girlish, but the round push of her breasts against a black Harley Davidson T-shirt assured her gender. Joshua screeched his bike to a halt.

"What do you think you're doin' throwing rocks at me?"

"Aw, cool your jets."

Joshua looked at her, and then tried to pick up a rock without unstraddling his bike.

"Don't even try it. Here, have a cigarette." Joshua's ears perked up. He had never done that.

The girl, Kelly Seifering, a classmate Joshua had hardly noticed, was usually truant.

"What are you doin' riding out here?" Kelly asked.

"Nothin'. You?"

"Work. At the Pizza Hut."

"Savin' up for a car?" he asked.

"Nah. A motorcycle. That or a guitar."

"I got a piano. Varnished it myself."

By this time, the summer before his sophomore year, Joshua had become more accomplished at the piano. The girl remained unimpressed.

"What kinda music you like?"

"Kiss. Aerosmith. Judas Priest."

"Oh, cool." Joshua had heard them on the radio, but was afraid to buy their records. He would not ever consider asking for that kind of music for Christmas or his birthday.

"What are *you* doing out here?" he asked as he learned how to smoke. He felt as if his head were about to burst. He coughed, but not excessively.

"Been walking," the girl said. "Sometimes I hitch."

"Where do you live?"

"Out on Township 57, next to the big antenna."

Joshua whistled. That was at least five miles from town, a winding country road that lay on the other side of Serene. "Why ya walkin' so far?" he asked.

"My foster parents. They make me wanna buy a gun."

"Why?"

"You hear about *The Orin and Mabel Show*?"

"That Christian radio thing?" Serene was littered with churches.

"None other."

"No shit."

"Well, they're my parents. My foster parents."

"Bummer."

"Tell me about it. They sent me off to a brainwash camp, tried to make me normal. It didn't take."

Her foster parents were none other than the born-again radio talk show hosts who had been in the papers at the time. Several truckers had complained that their Biblical ranting interfered with more serious broadcasts. Despite their Christian proselytizing, their only child, a foster child, had become less than angelic.

"You like your parents?" Kelly asked.

"I guess so. Dad works at the True Value. Mom's a Bohemian."

"Whassat?"

"She's artistic and does 'projects.'"

"Mine ain't nuthin' like that."

"Are they mean?" Joshua asked.

"Aw, they whup me a bit, but I always get away. Besides, if I act up they'll just send me off again. I figure I got about the weirdest couple this time. Can't get no worse, so why not stick it out until I get my bike." Kelly wanted a Harley. She wanted to ride to San Francisco and she explained why. "I like girls."

Joshua sat on his bike, confused. In his own search for identity he'd spent many an afternoon in the local library looking through the H section of dictionaries and encyclopedias. Magazine searches for any documentation on homosexuality revealed a few mentions of lesbians, but he had failed to find any visual references.

There had been such examples for his gender, though. His mother had pointed out Truman Capote on *The Merv Griffin Show*, even Paul Lynde in his central Hollywood Square, and said with a nervous honesty only reserved when her husband was still at work; "He's gay, you know." This was after she tried to explain a joke Paul Lynde had told. Peter Marshall asked, "Why do men who ride motorcycles wear leather chaps?" Paul Lynde responded, "Because chiffon wrinkles."

Sara knew about her son, as most mothers do in their psychic way, and her unsubtle clue was meant to allow him a burgeoning sense of identity. For Joshua, it seemed more of a twisted future fate, as if the next step of his growth progress could only culminate in becoming a wickedly funny television celebrity.

But Joshua had never seen anyone like Kelly on television— well, perhaps on *Police Woman*.

They smoked a few more cigarettes until Joshua became nauseated. He said he had to go.

"I like you, Josh boy."

"Yeah?"

"Yeah, you don't have that sex look in your eyes the way other guys do."

He blushed, then shyly admitted, "Oh, I do, it's just not for ladies."

"Well, I'll be damned. The two youngest town queers finally meet."

"You mean there's more?" he gulped.

"All over the world, kiddo. All over the world."

"But not here in Serene."

"Kid," she said like a sage in a teenager's body, "the future's got nothing to do with Serene."

Unfortunately, social restrictions being what they were, Joshua never saw much more of Kelly. She lived out in the country while his house was in a nice section of quaint homes in the upper middle income Morgan Avenue set.

He wouldn't hear much about her or see her until yet another playground fight. But before he graduated, through an act of the God her parents so abrasively advertised, the entire town and millions more would hear about Kelly Seifering. Joshua, in his own way, would tell them.

Chapter 4

FLICK OF THE WRIST

"NO, MOM, BELL bottoms are out!"

Convinced that from then on he would have to do his own clothes shopping, Joshua persuaded his mother to give him the money to buy new school clothes for his seventeenth year. For that, he loved her.

By 1978, the summer before his senior year in high school, he thoroughly realized, like his strange friend Kelly, his romantic inclinations were not to be discussed in public. A final examination by the neurologist in Dayton assured them that the seizures were probably over, and the Dilantin could be discontinued. Joshua felt like he might finally be growing up. He kept the cluster of stuck-together pills in his model plane box, though, just in case someday it happened again.

He had been plodding through the usual crises of small town boys: the pressure to date girls, the too frequent eruptions of his skin, and the occasional accidental bathroom intrusion. His father caught him masturbating in the garage once, but instead of retreating, merely stopped, then stood while the boy replaced himself into his jeans. His father then took his hammer from the bench and walked out, trying to stifle his proud laughter.

It wasn't until that year that he discovered, hidden away in a box behind his father's worn-out work boots, a stack of *Playboy* magazines.

The few moments he had alone in the house began the moment his mother's car pulled out of the driveway, taking his sister off to ballet, while his father was still away at work for another hour and a half. He crawled down under his father's dangling shirts and pants, breathed in the smell of his belts and ties and dry-cleaned gray work shirts, and delicately deconstructed the pile of shoes and extracted the box.

He did not stay long on the centerfolds. Once he discovered that the buxom amazons enjoyed kittens and Boz Skaggs, his disinterest increased. He flipped mentally to the memorized pages: the movie pictures of Richard Roundtree in the shower in a scene from *Shaft*, the shot of Burt Reynolds lying on a rug, wearing only a shirt, his hairy butt right there for him to see, the full frontal image of Jan-Michael Vincent and the completely, beautiful furry naked form of Harry Reems, who, he learned, was some kind of porno star.

But he could not take those precious pages out. Some scared superstition told him that his father, on some secret days, looked back at these magazines. Why else would he keep them?

The first time he spurted at the foot of his father's closet, afterward meticulously wiping the floor for sperm droplets, Joshua felt a sense of communion with his father.

Other times, he crept into his own room with one or two magazines, the pages opened out to his beautiful Hollywood men. He'd nearly gotten caught on a few occasions. Once, having fallen asleep, he was jolted awake by the sound of his mother slamming the front door. He rushed, pants around his ankles, to toss the magazines and the box back in place, then swiftly crept back into his lair to clean up before heading downstairs.

"You look like you've got a fever," his mother exclaimed as she scanned his flushed cheeks.

Refuge lay in his room. He had made it into the usual shrine of rock stars, monsters, and superheroes. The only exception was the slick Hurrell portrait of Gary Cooper that he had ripped out of a movie magazine. It hung on the inside door of his closet, just above his small full-length mirror. He liked to feel dashing when he dressed to go out, even if only in a T-shirt and jeans.

Joshua had a reason to be nervous. He had a dream.

As a nearly silent member of the student council (he'd run for it that September on a dare, as did I. We were both elected), Joshua grew a plan to work on the Senior Prom, which would take place in the spring of 1979. Being a large affair, plans began as soon as the previous fall.

Joshua liked (and quickly learned to play by ear) Elton John and his version of "Lucy in the Sky With Diamonds." He wanted that song to fill the gymnasium for one night. Maybe Matty Clark, one of the many boys he secretly adored, would like it. They had discussed a mutual admiration for the outlandish singer at a school dance the previous year when Matty, as DJ, brought in his impressive record collection.

Joshua had made sketches, plans, and schematics, but didn't tell anyone, until he saw Gretchen Olson.

"So, are you running for anything?"

"Well, I wanna be on Decorations Committee."

"Oh, me too. I'll nominate you."

"Does that mean that I'm supposed to . . ."

"Oh, no, Margie'll nominate me."

"Right."

The nominations and elections were held in the auditorium while the rest of the school sat in morning homeroom. While the elite student council discussed balloons versus crepe paper, everyone else had to listen to Drew Bowers, one of the Speech Team kids, announce the fall sports events over the room speakers, and hear the principal lecture about the evils of tobacco.

Spared from such doldrums, the Student Council meeting got underway, including the election of officials for the Prom Committee. Several friends of friends nominated each other to the ranks of status.

Elected council president, Karla Fitch, while not quite popular, was the daughter of Serene's most respected pastor. As Youth Leader of the notorious Teens for Christ, she was feared more than liked, and led the meeting with a presumed air of authority.

When they got to the Decorations Committee, Margie nominated Gretchen. Gretchen then nominated Joshua. There were no other nominees.

Satisfied with their propulsion into office, Gretchen and Joshua were told by the Student Council advisor, Mr. Haas, to make a suggestion box that would be placed in the Principal's office, and in addition to the notes stuffed into the box, they were allowed to make suggestions.

Joshua already had his idea fully drawn and conceptualized on the pages of his Grumbacher pad at home. I have viewed these drawings on several occasions.

The meeting broke up quickly after that, as Mr. Haas noted that the bell had rung for first period. The cheerful assembly of twenty elite young politicians filed out.

Gretchen caught up to Joshua, her glee mixed with a glance of what he construed as flirtation. It made him uncomfortable, not in the way that seeing boys naked in gym class showers did, but more like when a perfume-clouded aunt leaned too close to kiss him and he saw her bra.

He ducked into the boy's restroom to pee, thinking that since it was during classes he would be alone.

He was wrong.

Ensconced in a cloud of smoke, David Koenig sat on the sink counter, glancing up for a moment in fear, then upon seeing Joshua, relaxed and resumed puffing. The two barely exchanged a grunt of "Hey."

Before walking to the urinal next to the sink (he barely managed to pee with David watching) Joshua glanced at David, who wore a faded black Queen T-shirt with the emblem from the *Night at the Opera* album, the one with the swans. Young muscles pushed out at David's arms and chest. If David was gorgeous at the time of their snowy tussle in sixth grade, then, like a saddle, he was a bit more worn at seventeen, but still handsome and sturdy-looking.

Rather than escape in his usual fashion, Joshua relaxed instead and imagined David wanted to hear him piss. The tingling through his dick never felt so relaxed. "Got a smoke?"

David shook his pack at him. One cigarette pointed at Joshua's outstretched hand as he finished peeing. Joshua knew if he smoked he would become dizzy, but the cigarette was an excuse to finally speak to this boy again.

"Skipping class?" David asked as he offered his lighter.

"No, uh, Student Council meeting."

David snorted. "Make any new rules?"

"No, we had some elections. I'm on Decorations Committee for the prom."

David stifled a laugh.

Joshua stood nervously and puffed lightly, held back from coughing. He glanced in the mirror to look at David's back. He was rumored to have a tattoo. Joshua wondered where.

"Really? What's it gonna be this year? *Saturday Night Fever*?" David smirked in a way that assured his disapproval of the film.

"Oh, gross," Joshua blew smoke ceilingward. "No way." The two struck a chord of agreement as Joshua zipped up. "Actually, I was already thinkin' about a theme."

"Yeah?"

"You know that song, 'Lucy in the Sky with Diamonds?'" Joshua asked.

"That old Beatles song?"

"Jeez, you don't know how great it is to know somebody else who knows it isn't an Elton John song."

Joshua probably said that in the way any boy of his age would, a boy who believes that entire cultural icons are speaking to them, as an inside joke among friends. He thought he heard David jokingly say, "So, do you wanna go to the Prom?" until he said "What?" and David repeated, "You wanna do the prom theme about that song?"

"Yeah, why not?" Joshua noticed the way David's butt hugged the sink counter as he leaned against it. For the second time in his life he was alone with David, yet he merely grinned in a sly pose as his heart thudded.

"Pretty cool. Plasticine porters . . ."

". . . with looking glass ties."

"Trippy."

"Yeah, it is, right? Have you got the *Beatles Illustrated Lyrics–*"

Another classmate, Chuck Seelig, walked in. David nodded to him. The boy stepped into a stall.

David should have said something, but he watched Joshua get lost looking at his body, the casual way his jeans frayed out over his Adidas sneakers, the way they stretched tight across his thick thighs, the bump between his legs, his lean chest muscles pressing against the Queen logo on his T-shirt.

"Where'd ya get that?" Joshua asked, making a quick excuse for his caught glance.

"Mail order in *Creem.*"

They both stood taller and their hair was quite a bit longer than the last time they were alone together. David's had darkened, but retained a trace of the golden shimmer of his childhood. David slid his bangs behind his ears, a gesture he would perform a thousand times, one that Joshua would never tire of seeing.

"Brian May's great."

"Yeah. Which song's your favorite?" David asked.

"Um, I dunno, 'Bohemian Rhapsody?'"

"You gotta hear 'Brighton Rock.'" Chuck in the stall.

"Ya got the first album?"

"Naw," Joshua shrugged.

"You gotta hear it. They're gonna be here." Chuck again.

"Who?"

"Queen. At the Coliseum."

An immense gathering space of rock bands, Richfield Coliseum lay north in the suburbs of Cleveland. Joshua had never been to a rock concert.

The toilet flushed. Chuck stepped out, zipping up, held out a hand, then yanked it back, muttering, "You know where that's been."

"Yeah, they're gonna be here," David said. "You should come with us."

Us. Joshua became simultaneously relaxed and excited. His stomach fluttered. He had been invited, asked on a date, by a guy.

"Sure. That'd be cool," he said, knowing that this moment signaled his entrance into an entirely new world. "When is it?"

"Coupla months."

"November twenty-fifth," Chuck said.

"You got tickets?" Joshua asked.

"They go on sale next week at the mall. Ed's gonna drive, if his van's outta the shop."

Ed Wallenbeck was one of David's friends. Joshua had seen them hang out after school. Taller than David, Ed wore glasses and had a very large nose, the only features that protruded beyond his long brown hair.

"Catch ya later," Chuck said with a look to David. It seemed something was supposed to have happened between them, but Joshua's presence prevented it.

"Ya wanna go with me to get the tickets?" David asked after Chuck left.

A date before the date, Joshua thought. *Thank you, Lord, for this piss, even if I did mess up his possible drug deal.*

"You need money?"

"Naw, later."

"Cool." Joshua pretended to finger comb his hair in the smudged mirror, when he was actually glancing at the slight V of David's back. "I gotta go anyway to get some things."

"What things?"

"Aw, my mom wants me to get new clothes."

"Shit, nobody notices that crap." David dampened his cigarette butt under the faucet, tossed it in a trash can. Joshua repeated his move.

"Yeah, but she already gave me the money. She says living in the boonies is no excuse to dress like a hick."

"Well, as long as she gives you the money, I guess that's cool."

"Yeah, I guess." He wanted to get a pair of tight jeans like David's, but his mom would want a nice respectable pair of corduroys. Maybe he could just get tight corduroys.

"Where ya headed?" David stood.

"Back to Biology."

"Ugh. Ja dissect a frog yet?"

"Yeah, that's the fun part."

"The only fun part."

Their bond re-established, Joshua nurtured the fire in his heart that had until then been a mere pilot light.

That night he thought of David, knees weak in the shower, his own seed mixed in with soapsuds. Pure Prairie League's "Amy" squeaked through the small bathroom radio.

On Saturday he scraped together all his savings, plus begging a few extra dollars from his dad in exchange for more chores, and bought Queen's fourth, fifth and sixth albums. He played them all that weekend, *A Night at the Opera*, *A Day at the Races* and *News of the World*, placing them carefully in order in his growing record collection. He wanted to hear more, to have all the songs memorized in time for the concert, and after warming up on his practice drills, he realized he no longer wanted only to hear them.

He wanted to play them.

Joshua's mother certainly questioned the activity when seeing her son unload the stereo from his bedroom into the dining room, but soon relented when she heard the improvement in his playing while listening to the rock music on headphones. She also noticed that the piano would have to be tuned again or she would be driven to filicide.

As he listened on his headphones, Joshua started learning Queen songs with piano parts, then more Elton John songs, then the particularly haunting Pink Floyd piano riff on "Great Gig in the Sky." He played for hours in the afternoons then for a while after dinner until his sister would storm up to her room, the door closed, as she dove into homework or called her growing clique of friends, who inspired her to join them for informal get-togethers, feigned study sessions, or movies out—anything to get away from Joshua's piano-playing. She should have thanked him for inspiring her to become more socially popular among her classmates.

Joshua's parents remained more patient and proud. As he plunked away, they turned the TV off and read in the living room, newspapers for Sam, books for Sara, or sometime snuck up to their bedroom for private time.

One night, as Joshua's repeated attempts to play along to a difficult passage of "Funeral for a Friend/Love Lies Bleeding" became a bit annoying, Sam Evans approached Joshua at the piano. He pulled down his headphones.

"Sorry, Dad. Too loud?"

"No, it's just . . . don't they have sheet music for these songs?"

Joshua shrugged. "Yeah, they have songbooks downtown at the music store, and at the mall. But Mrs. Rose wants me to learn some basics. I'm just doing these for fun."

"What if you did some chores and used the money to buy some of those songbooks?"

"Great."

And so, after cleaning the basement, and the garage, and raking leaves, Joshua rode his bicycle downtown and walked into Mr. Beene's Music Emporium, ready to spend the cash his father gave him. He glanced at the shelves of playbooks and sheet music. The elderly gentleman prepared to point out a nice Beethoven sonata, but when Joshua asked if they had any Pink Floyd, the old man sighed in disappointment, pushed back his spectacles to read *The Serene Journal,* and pointed to the back of the store.

Lined along an entire wall were music songbooks, each brightly colored in the same designs as his record collection; well, parts of it. He had no Barry Manilow or Paul Anka. It was the other section, with Boston, the Allman Brothers, Kansas, Aerosmith, and even Kiss, in full album form, that amused him, but not enough to buy them.

He saw an entire collection of Beatles albums, grabbed an anthology of 100 songs, and then found Pink Floyd's *Animals,* Elton John's *Goodbye Yellow Brick Road* and Queen's *A Night at the Opera, A Day at the Races* and *News of the World.* Unskilled in making shopping decisions at that age, he bought them all and asked Mr. Beene to order the other Queen songbooks.

Music began to fill his head with a new enthusiasm. He sometimes passed the hours of boring classes by silently fingering the parts on his desk. He loved it all, but something differed about Queen's music, aside from him thinking about David when he listened. They possessed an artistry, a sense of humor, a flair, and a regal quality that no other bands could match. Of course, the voice of Freddie Mercury, whose range soared beyond the crackle of Joshua's own, rang true for him. He sounded like the silliest queerest entertainer. He was a queen, and it was the biggest joke, like a huge billboard that only he could see. The promise of seeing them perform filled him with anticipation, as much as the promise of David.

Chapter 5

TIE YOUR MOTHER DOWN

"THE BIG MAC Pumpkin is a member of the Cucurbitaceae family and is part of the species Cucurbita maxima. They are not usually used for eating or as jack o' lanterns, but are prized in weigh-in competitions at county fairs. Big Macs are derived from seeds developed by farmer William Warnock whose 1893 record of a pumpkin weighing 365 pounds remained unbeaten for decades."

This excerpt from David Koenig's report for his Future Farmers of America chapter, along with a clipping from the local newspaper documenting his Third Place win at the Serene County Fair Pumpkin Weigh-in the year he turned fifteen, serve as a record of a momentous year for the boy, who, because of a pumpkin, lost his virginity. Later that season, his mother left, never to return.

Three years before he invited Joshua to a rock concert, David had no expectations of any momentous events the day he carefully hauled the giant ochre gourd onto his father's truck and drove all the way to the county fairgrounds. Into one of the many warehouses, close to tables of prize-winning canned fruits and vegetables, they brought the giant pumpkin and set it delicately on a low platform with nearly a dozen others.

The contest drew a few photographers, among them Brent Carse, then a sophomore like David. He took a few basic shots of the trio of winners until David noticed his camera focusing on himself more than the others.

Carse struck up a conversation, introduced himself. "I want to get some photos of farm kids like you for the yearbook. How 'bout I come by your place and get some photos in a field?"

"Sure," David replied, already sensing an ulterior motive from his classmate. "Can you get out to my farm?"

"Oh, yeah. Just got my driver's license," he grinned.

That Saturday, Brent arrived in his parents' car with his camera in hand. They walked out to the somewhat sparse pumpkin patch, where he directed David into a series of innocuous poses.

"How about one by a tractor. You got one somewhere, right?"

"It's in the barn."

"Let's go."

Another stroll, where Brent asked David a series of naïve questions about farming.

After a few shots inside the barn with David leaning against the John Deere tractor, the door slung open to let in light, David offered to drive the tractor outside.

"No, no, this is fine. How about you take your shirt off?"

"What?"

"I dunno, I just thought it'd be cute."

"Fine."

With the air on his slightly sweaty bare chest, David felt a surge in his groin, suddenly realizing Brent's intention as he moved closer, adjusting David's pose.

"Put your hat back on."

A touch, then another, toward the visible bulges in their pants, and the two of them quickly shifted to an abrupt fumbled pumping session, tugging each other to too-quick orgasms with their pants barely undone.

While Brent offered mumbled apologies, David felt a sense of relief. Yes, he'd wanted to do that, and he felt fine, if a bit flushed.

"We should do that again," he said with an air of bravado.

"What, now?" Brent seemed shocked.

"No, I mean, some other time."

"Yeah, okay."

They did, with Brent visiting infrequently, the two managing some basic, quick, and unemotional blowjobs and jerkoff sessions in the barn, until one day they got a bit reckless and left the barn door half opened.

"What the goddam hell are you two doin'?"

Brent yanked himself away from David, who jolted up from kneeling before him and turned to see his father's fire-red face charging toward them.

"You, boy! What's your name?"

Brent didn't offer it, but managed to dodge Roland Koenig's grasp, race out to the driveway to his car, and speed off down the road.

"You think I'll let some faggity-ass shit go on in my barn?"

David tried to run, but his pants got caught. Grabbed by the back of his neck, he struggled, endured a few hits to his back, a yank on his arm.

"Get away from me!"

"You little shit!"

He started toward the house, for what, he didn't know. Would his mother defend him?

Was she even home? He had thought they were both gone. That had been his mistake. Instead, he stalked off behind the house and across the field, his father shouting after him, but not following.

David felt hurt and confused, panicked. He walked to the far edge of the farm property, kicked a fence post, then walked over to the small woods between his family and his uncle's land. The darkness wasn't a problem. He'd snuck out on many a night to explore the quiet solitude of a cornfield or the pumpkin patch.

After several hours, his growling stomach forced him to decide. He could ask to stay at his uncle's, but explaining why he needed to would surely stun them.

Time to face the music, he resolved, and walked back to the house.

As expected, despite the late hour, his father sat in his usual chair, the TV volume low, Johnny Carson telling a joke. David foraged in the refrigerator for something quick to eat before he'd get beaten again.

"Get in here." Quiet.

He obeyed, stood at the far end of the living room. He could always outrun his father.

A long stare, sullen, a head shake. "I could be within my rights to kick you out of this house for good."

David waited, wondering if he even had a suitcase to use. His parents had only taken that trip to Texas when he was a kid.

"But I'm gonna cut you some slack, for bein' stupid and reckless."

David nodded, a sort of consent, a slight gesture of subservience.

"But I catch you ever doin' something that sick . . ."

The sentence didn't complete. The threat lingered, open with possibilities.

"Get to bed. I can't stand to look at you."

Being confronted so abruptly while having sex opened the question of what exactly he was doing. David didn't even know how to ask another guy about sex, and Brent Carse, when they would later meet at school, turned into a denying sort of apologetic weasel. David found himself no longer attracted to guys, or at least not Brent.

Maybe I'm one of those bisexuals, he thought after he heard the term on TV one night. *Maybe I'm just horny.*

He'd wanted to ask his mother about it. Helen Koenig had never been one to mince words. He usually took her side when she fought with his father, or else just walked out of the house to stroll through the fields to get away from their fights over money or other things he didn't want to hear about.

51

He'd wanted to have that difficult conversation with her. A few days later, when his father had left for a bar in town after yet another argument, obviously about him, he tentatively walked into their bedroom only to find his mother packing a suitcase.

"Honey, we have to talk," she patted the bed. He sat.

"You making me leave?"

"What? Oh, no, sweetie. No."

"Then what?"

"You're old enough now. You can take care of yourself, but it's me that's leavin.' I have to get out."

"What?"

"Listen, please. I stayed because of you, to protect you. But you're grown up now. Your father and I . . . it's over. I'm so sorry." Her once bright blonde hair appeared dingy, her eyes tired.

"But, you can't!"

She drew him into a tight long hug. "It'll be alright," she cooed with a drained unconvincing resolve. "This isn't about you and your . . . friend."

"But where are you going?"

"It's better you not know yet. He'll just come after me."

A phone call later, a man David had never seen before, younger than his father, helped Helen Koenig with her two suit-cases and waited outside as she said her goodbyes. He sobbed like a baby, even more when he saw that she wasn't. Something inside her had already died.

"I'll write to you as soon as I can."

She did, but infrequently. For those next few years, David hardened, closing himself off, enduring his father's rages at their loss while keeping his distance.

Farm work became a refuge. He could dig his hands in soil, grip the steering wheel of the tractor, or the broken down Ford truck his father begrudgingly gave him when he got a new one. The man could be kind one day, but angry the next. David learned to gauge his questions or complaints, especially after his father, probably a bit drunk, fell off the tractor one day.

Through the weeks of hospitalization and recovery, David's father called upon his brother-in-law Joe Kemp to take over supervising the summer planting, then eventually leased several acres as well. The upshot was that David's uncle started paying him for his work.

But as his father became more housebound, permanently on disability for his never-fully healed back, he became more angry and bitter as he slouched in a chair doing little more than watching TV and complaining about the Cleveland Indians or the Browns.

David's desire to have any sort of conversation about sex seemed out of the question. A few of his farmer schoolmates in FFA did offer an escape, mostly with a few beers, a joint on occasion, and weekend prattle about sex with girls.

Aside from a few dates with Brenda Kruger, where David went through the motions of lust and happiness, he didn't even grasp a ghost of the idea of love.

Until he met Joshua again, three years later. His impulse to invite a near stranger to see Queen came from almost nowhere. As they had talked in the boys' room, he'd maintained a cool air. But he knew if Chuck Seelig hadn't also been pissing near them, David would have reached over and impulsively kissed Joshua.

Remembering that playground fight when he'd held him in his arms, he felt a soft surge of affection, not just a sexual urge like the abrupt encounters with Brent Carse.

Joshua's eyes, big and wide, his soft features, brought up a longing in him he'd never felt, or perhaps one that had long been inside him and only just then cracked open.

David determined to keep it friendly, test the waters, figure out why the boy stirred something inside himself he couldn't define. After all, he'd only invited him to a rock concert. No big deal.

Chapter 6

DON'T LOSE YOUR HEAD

AS OFTEN HAPPENED on school playgrounds, fights continued to break out, little bursts of testosterone and turf establishment. Like packs of small dogs, teenagers could not resist the urge to repeatedly establish the pecking order of supremacy in the ranks of school bullies and victims.

What was so unusual about the fight Joshua observed one day was at its epicenter stood a short-haired, defiant girl, Kelly Seifering.

At first, Joshua saw only the gathering swarm and didn't see Kelly until the circle opened up as a boy's arm swung down upon her, missed, then shoved. Why it had started was lost to the frenzy of the crowd. Joshua didn't recognize Kelly's attacker. He glared as David Koenig inserted himself into the fumbling brawl, swiftly chopped his hand away, and shoved him to the ground. The mob parted and the circle expanded to an oblong as one of their teachers approached, Mr. Heinz, who was apparently in no hurry to stop the action.

Kelly shouted at David, "I'll fight my own fights!"

Joshua saw the disdain of the teacher, the way he deliberately held back to let the fight progress. He came to understand that slow response as evil disguised as tolerance. With his mere presence, though, the fight dispersed. Joshua felt as if he should play the diplomat, introduce David to Kelly, since he knew them both.

David and Kelly separated, leaving Joshua and a few other students standing around the scene, which was quickly abandoned. Out of a sort of duty to refill the vacuum the truncated fight had caused, and as sort of an afterthought, a squat-faced boy made a crack about Joshua's rayon Hawaiian print shirt. Prominently displayed at the mall's Chess King, it seemed worthy of derision by a greasy-haired Pete Wink. Joshua was forced to defend his dignity and fashion sense.

Freshly enamored of the late Bruce Lee—a poster of the shirtless beauty over his bed, muscles taut and glistening— Joshua made the stylistic mistake of attempting a karate kick on the noonday playground. On top of being branded afterward a sissy for kicking, he flung his fashionable Tom McCann two-tone platform shoe a good twenty yards.

Then the boy blurted out the word that burned into Joshua with shame.

"Faggit."

The boy walked on so swiftly Joshua didn't have a moment to respond. But he burned inside and felt sweaty and weak. He wanted to be home, safe, where he could taunt his sister if he wanted to. He wanted to sneak into his dad's closet and take that *Playboy*, the one with the "Sex in Cinema" layout, and gaze lovingly at that small picture of Harry Reems, standing naked in a green forest. He wanted to live in that forest, where waterfalls hissed forever and men never wore clothes.

Instead, he sized up Pete Wink's back, and remembered a flying kick he had seen performed by Bruce Lee. He thought he should try again, but lacking a shoe, he stood alone as the bored kids dispersed.

"You okay?" David returned, still flushed from the brief fight.

"Yeah, just . . . " He wanted to tell David, share his revulsion over Pete Wink's arrogance, knowing that David would come to his defense, but he stopped. "You seen my shoe?"

As the day wore on, the scuffles were almost forgotten. Joshua's one school pleasure awaited. On Tuesdays and Thursdays, for sixth and seventh period, he had Music Theory and Stage Band.

Theory, in which the Gregorian chant was that week's topic of discussion, half-inspired Joshua to scrawl out his own version of a song, more to prove the simplicity of the style. But Joshua also secretly worked on his one-piano and a cappella choir arrangement of "Bohemian Rhapsody."

His playing became an addiction. He could not pass a piano without touching it, hearing its age, and pressing his fingers onto its keys. With Mr. Rose (his piano teacher's husband) late to band practice again, Joshua, approached the rehearsal room piano and casually trilled the opening of the Styx song, "Sailing Away."

A few boys jumped to standing, winging out the first bars in parody, then a few more hummed or sang along. Mr. Rose's entrance cut them short, but the kids sang a few more lines. Joshua took his place at the smaller electronic keyboard near the back of the room.

"It seems one of our own was in a tussle today."

The band burst into laughter. With few upcoming concert shows until Christmas, everyone was more casual, including Mr. Rose.

"Don't go breaking those hands, young man." Then, practice commenced.

In the days before their trip to the mall together, Joshua felt distractions he hadn't known. Other boys left him clouded in a reverie of their muscular butts in stolen locker rooms glances, but with David, it went deeper. David talked to him. David seemed to want him for himself, not just because they'd met again.

That Saturday, with what he secretly called his date with David looming in a matter of a few hours, Joshua could not hold still. His weekends usually consisted of practicing and doing chores around the house. Samuel Evans, home on a rare day off, looked on in near-amazement as his son volunteered not only to rake leaves, but also to wash his father's pick-up and his mother's car, a dingy brown Plymouth Fury.

His father worked on a leak in the kitchen dishwasher while his mother labored in the basement, doing laundry or clay pottery, or both (Sara Evans sometimes displayed her work at the annual County Fair, even took a few prizes). Joshua took a pair of English muffins out of the fridge and spooned out spaghetti sauce and some Kraft Romano cheese, put them in the toaster oven, and read a *People* magazine at the kitchen while they cooked.

His father told him if he did enough chores they would soon be able to buy something special. Sara wanted new screens on the porch. Joshua wanted a new piano. A used one would do, actually, but one with all working keys. Joshua kept a list of his chores by the key rack in the kitchen on a chart he had made himself. He had actually gone to the only store in town that sold pianos and priced each one.

Joshua hosed down the car, his hands wet and chilled in the October air despite the sun. He left one door open as he scrubbed and played the radio at a low enough volume that neighbors wouldn't complain.

As he was enjoying his time alone, Sister strolled down the driveway to invade it.

She had been boasting about her newfound popularity since being chosen for the cheerleading squad. She practiced a few moves on the lawn near her brother, but talking with Joshua had another purpose.

"I know something," she said coyly.

"You want a medal or a chest to pin it on?"

"Lame Award!"

Joshua tried to ignore her, but she persisted. "You're not gonna get a new piano."

"Why?" Hadn't he been working hard enough? Didn't they give you extra credit for living through high school?

"Mom and Dad are poor now. We can't afford it."

"That's bullshit."

"Don't swear or I'm tellin'."

"It is bullshit."

"Is not. Dad says it's Jimmy Carter's fault."

"We'll see about that."

Sister sauntered back to the far side of the lawn for more practice moves, then ran into the house when the phone rang. Finally, he was alone again.

"Baker Street" played on the car radio, a song that seemed strange to him, not at all like his rock songs or trippy head music. The wailing saxophone sent a rush of melancholy through him. The afternoon sun died in golden glints behind the garage and the neighbors' trees behind that. He kept waiting for someone to come by and see him doing this most simple and glorious act, washing the car. He knew it was silly, but as the saxophone pealed again from the car radio, he felt an untouchable rush, a sense of length in time, as if he felt the end of his childhood, that amazing and terrible things were going to happen, and for these things he could hardly wait.

Then David Koenig's rumbling old red Ford truck rolled up the driveway.

Chapter 7

LAZING ON A SUNDAY AFTERNOON

THE BOYS DROVE half an hour to Lancaster while listening to David's tape of Queen's *News of the World*. The radio barely worked, so he'd attached the cassette player himself. As they pulled into the crowded parking lot to the squat palace-shaped River Valley Mall, afternoon sunlight glared on the tops of the rows of cars.

"Wait," David said. "Before we go in." He opened what appeared to be a secret sleeve in the glove compartment, and extracted a joint.

"We're gonna get stoned at the mall?" Joshua whispered incredulously, looking around the parking lot as if a police car might be lurking.

"Sure, why not?" David flicked his lighter.

"During the day?"

"C'mon, Joshie. It's not like anyone's gonna know." Joshua wondered when David had turned into a bad kid, and he wondered if he was about to become one too.

David lit the joint, sucked in, then handed it to Joshua. The truck cab became filled with smoke, a sweet smell that he would learn to love. He sucked down hard and slow, careful not to choke.

A woman with a stroller passed by, eyeing the boys. Joshua held the joint low, looked over at David. "Blah blah blah, I'm just sitting here chatting with my bud, not breaking federal laws." He felt the cannabis invade his lungs, and felt higher with every exchange of the joint, their fingers touching. Joshua remembered the day when he had seen those same little fingers gripping the desk of a principal. He longed to describe the memory to David but choked on the escaping smoke.

David coughed up his held toke, choking in laughter. The woman passed, but Joshua still ducked down. They didn't even finish the joint.

"Must be the confined space what done it," David joked as they looked back at the truck, still clouded inside as if it were on fire. The two boys fumbled with their jackets, making an exaggerated show of sprucing themselves up before their entrance.

The wash of noise from the crowd, the fountain in the center of the enclosed mall, and the addition of his first dose of pot made Joshua giggle and forget to close his mouth.

"This is a lot better."

"Than what?" David asked.

"Then what?"

"When what?"

"No, than, this thing I had. I used to get seizures."

"Oh, yeah."

"Made me feel things weird."

"So that's it."

"What's it?"

"When you . . . Remember when we had that fight?"

"Duh, no shit." He was just thinking of that!

"You flipped out. I thought you were gonna turn blue or something."

"Well, did I?"

"No, but you scared me. Does that happen anymore?"

"Nope. Dope."

"So pot feels like that?"

"No, not at all. We decided to be this way. That makes all the difference."

He looked into David's eyes. Beneath the pink glaze, he found reassurance. They would get away with it.

They made silly puns as they wandered the mall, intoxicated by the smells of new clothing, food, and women's perfume.

After buying the Queen concert tickets, they spent an inordinate amount of time in the record store, since all the clothes, jewelry and shoe stores suddenly looked quite goofy. Joshua pointed out all the Queen records and songbooks he'd bought. They had nine dollars left between the two of them. They twice nabbed samples of sausage from the Cheese Barn. David enjoyed flirting with the girl, who squirted extra Cheese-Do on some crackers.

Between the crackers and a sudden attack of dry mouth, Joshua couldn't speak. He could never remember where the drinking fountains were. Maybe he could just cheat back to the hissing decorative fountain in the middle plaza and take a sip while pretending to toss in a penny.

But David diverted their path and found a place with fifty-cent soda and a kid who gave them extra larges "by mistake" and winked. David later explained that the boy had been at a party David had recently attended. They sat at a booth, holding back occasional giggles at passersby.

Eager to ask a question, a dozen questions, all about David's life, his friends, Joshua held back his curiosity, tinged with a surge of jealousy. He wanted to spend every moment with David from then on, which he knew might be impossible.

"So. Pumpkins."

"What about 'em?" David slurped from his straw.

"Are they hard to grow?"

"Naw, they just sit there. The huge ones, the Big Macs, those are a bitch to load. Dad's, well, my Uncle Joe, he hires a coupla Mexican guys; they're cool. But the pumpkins crack sometimes, get dropped. Worse is the Indian corn and the pig corn."

"Pig corn?"

David shifted in the seat. "Man, you townies. Feed, for animals. We don't grow sweet corn. That's people corn."

"Oh."

"Remember that summer we had the locusts? Back in '74?"

"Cicadas. Yeah." Joshua recalled the whirring sound in trees all over town. Kids would pick off the discarded shells still clinging to trees, attach them to their shirts like prizes or try to scare girls by putting them in their hair.

"They were everywhere. We lost half a crop." David then leaned forward, lowered his voice. "But you know what I really wanna grow?"

"What?"

"Don't tell or I'll whoop ya."

"Promise."

David's eye lit up. "Flowers. All kinds, petunias and zinnias. I wanna build a greenhouse behind the barn, but Dad says it's a bad investment. 'Too fragile,' he said. I mean, who doesn't love pansies?" He chuckled, and Joshua thought he got the joke.

After they finished the sodas while muttering jokes about every arguing family and whining kid and geeky bespectacled or braced kid that passed by, the two boys tossed their cups and went to Mellow Yellow.

Several Christian types had boycotted the mall specifically because of Mellow Yellow. The local papers called it a "head shop." David called it "cool."

Grateful Dead T-shirts, concert posters, Farrah Fawcett posters, incense in dozens of scents and mysterious sexy board games For Adults lined the cluttered shelves. Wacky gag shot glasses and breast-shaped alarm clocks, penis-shaped windup toys caught the embarrassed giggles of kids and adults. But even worse, according to local authorities, were the pipes and rolling papers sold under the counter, which is what led to the shop's eventual closing. To this day, even paraphernalia is illegal in Serene.

But back then, things were bucolic, and sweet, and available.

The boys walked to the back of the store, flipped through the racks of psychedelic posters, tigers in black velvet, African lovers, heavy metal bands. A smaller bin of rolled up posters sat next to the racks. Those were the ones people bought. Toward the end of the racks, more risqué posters tempted them, busty babes in wet T-shirts. David smirked. Then they both saw it: Burt Reynolds, standing with his back turned, wearing nothing but a football jersey.

"He's got a hairy butt," David said.

"Know who that is?"

"Yeah. Burt Reynolds."

Joshua didn't mention the *Playboy* magazines, that he'd already enjoyed the sight of the actor's butt. "You seen any of his movies?"

"Yeah. *Smokey and the Bandit*. He's cool."

"He's the one that got naked in *Cosmo*." Joshua felt embarrassed by his admission, but at least he didn't tell David he filled out those stupid quizzes in the magazine. That made Sister mad when he didn't use a pencil so she could erase it.

"Really? Do they show his dick?" David grinned, holding the rack wide open, both of them standing before a nearly naked movie star, ignoring the guy who stared at them.

"Uh, no." Joshua gulped and adjusted the pressure in his pants. He turned away, embarrassed.

"Hunh." David sort of grunted at the poster, then smirked. "You see the pipes they got?"

"No, where are they?"

"Under the glass case. Go look."

Joshua left him to see the pipes. His mouth was suddenly dry again.

They wandered around the mall, agreed that they were bored, and walked outside. Their ears relaxed as they escaped the rush of noise inside the mall.

As David started to sit down in the driver's seat of his car, he stopped, turning his back. Joshua watched as a rolled poster slipped out of the back of David's coat. Joshua sat, pulled off the plastic covering, and unrolled it, expecting Led Zeppelin or one of the busty babes. He wasn't surprised that David had stolen it. He was surprised by the subject: the Burt Reynolds poster.

"Got it for you," David blurted.

"You mean you stole it."

"Same difference." He hit the ignition while Joshua fumed in a cloud of embarrassment and joy.

Driving in silence a while, Joshua fought back the panic in his heart enough to ask David a question.

"Why'd you get that for me?"

"You wanted it, dincha?"

"Let's stop at Wendy's. I got the munchies."

"Thought it must be tough to get jack off material."

"Thanks. You mind?"

"What?"

"Me bein'. . ."

"If I did, you wouldn't be goin' to see Queen with me, wouldja?"

"Guess not."

"Besides, he's a big fag, too, y'know. Freddie Mercury."

"Thought so."

"No offense. They're still a great band."

"Yeah." His mouth still dry, inside Joshua felt better. What he imagined as a large earthquake was just the rumbling muffler of David's truck.

That afternoon, Joshua waited for a quiet moment in the house to sneak into his closet where he had hidden the Burt Reynolds poster. He thought of playing with himself, but then pushed it back behind his sweaters and shoved his erection up in his pants so nobody would see it.

The attic, lit by a naked bulb hanging from the angled ceiling beams, held the stuffy air of treasures neatly packed away. He'd gone up there to play every now and then, just to see his Match Box collection or feel the hard edges in a box of Legos. He had opened his sister's Barbie suitcases to feel the tiny clothes. They still smelled of girl perfume. The tiny plastic hangers in red, yellow, and blue poked out of the piles of tiny sweaters, gowns, and shoes. He snuck a hot pink sweater onto his GI Joe doll once, figuring that's what a fag looked like, not that he wanted to dress like that.

His mother never threw books away. Piles of paperbacks and novels lay neatly stacked in boxes, the remnants of the cultured life she left behind in San Francisco. He pried open a trunk filled with school drawings, papers, and report cards. His old scrapbooks of Cub Scout checklists and bug drawings recalled childhood memories.

Under the papers lay yearbooks all the way back to the first grade. Each of the elementary schools had their own sections, and all the faces grinned like little mush-faced puppies. Almost all the boys had buzz cuts, and their ears stuck out like cup handles, their facial features almost too big for their heads, their eyes bugging out in a constant state of wonderment.

Carefully looking through the years, Joshua opened each book, and after finding his own image and those of a few kids he liked, he lay each year open in sequence, from first grade up to his junior year in high school. Listening that no one was coming upstairs, he loosened his pants and let himself free in the musty air, rubbing himself as he scanned the one face he'd found in each book, from the bright little cherub to the scowling shaggy-haired boy called David Koenig.

He made silent solitary love to all the years he had hardly known David as if making up for lost time. He aimed away from the yearbooks at the last moment. The dry wood floor soaked up the rivulets of his sperm. For the first time, he didn't even bother to wipe it up.

When he took the yearbooks downstairs, he thought about

cutting out the pictures of David and putting them somewhere, but then thought Sister would get upset and tell, since some of the yearbooks were hers.

So he snuck out of the house with a backpack full of them and walked to the Beekam College library, where he pretended to scan the shelves until there were no people near the copy machine.

He knew the routine from copying a few books and magazines with pictures of nearly naked men in them. They were artistic, too. He liked that, the secrecy, that even in a small town like Serene, the college library could hold such treasures. If the Christians ever found out, he figured they would burn the place down.

But this time his copies were more innocent. He gathered the pages from the yearbooks, splayed open to a moment from each year of their school lives. He dropped a nickel in for every year, and feeling like a spy, copied each page with David's face.

On the way home, so elated by the idea of being in love with David, of being in love with a boy, or maybe even just having a friend who didn't mind, Joshua walked home through the music building, which he'd never had the bravery to investigate.

He found ten practice rooms, half of them empty, each one with a different piano. With a quiet joy, he padded out the first two chords of Foreigner's "Cold as Ice."

He played song after song for three hours, undisturbed until hunger pangs and near darkness drew him away.

Home again, he put the yearbooks back on a shelf in his room, carefully cut out each of David's faces from the copies, and taped them together in a little accordion file. He folded them up and put them in a tiny envelope from an invitation he had saved from a cousin's wedding in Chillicothe.

"Joshua! Dinner!" His father called, and Joshua began to salivate. Roast beef, must be, since it was Sunday.

He had homework after dinner. *Butch Cassidy and the Sundance Kid* was on TV, though. After that, he would retreat to his room, where almost a dozen pictures of David waited for him, forever smiling.

He watched the news for a while as his mother made coffee for herself and his dad. Jimmy Carter gave a speech, something about fundamentalist Muslims in Iran. Things were very scary over there. Images of women in long black dresses with their faces covered filled the TV. Joshua figured if the Christians in his town had their way, women in Ohio would dress the same way, only their dresses would be floral prints.

He lay on the floor gazing over the newspaper, when, before a picture distracted him, he leaned back, and announced, "Oh, I don't need a new piano now."

"Why? You're not giving it up, are you?"

"No," he assured his mother. "There's all these practice rooms at the college."

"Oh," she said.

"Good," his father said, snapping his newspaper. "Thank you, son. It's a smart thing you've done. Now make sure you're allowed to play there."

"Yes, sir."

Joshua felt proud, good, and full of life. He read the newspaper, but his eyes could only look at pictures. He glanced at the movie showings. Some movie called *Butterflies* was showing at the Drive In. He figured it wasn't about insects.

The mere thought of the Drive-In made him quiver. It lay out on Route 33, between the mall and Serene. He had wanted to drive into it on that cold fall dusk with David, pass through its decaying drive-thru booth.

The Drive-In had fallen into a bit of financial trouble when the eight-screen movie theatre opened at the mall. While every night of its first summer screenings sold out with movies like *Star Wars*, the Drive-In now showed mostly adult films. One of them, showing that night, the local newspaper ad read, costarred Harry Reems.

The mere thought of finally seeing the man whose *Playboy* image he had gazed at lovingly actually moving filled Joshua with a nervous joy. He would rip the ad out the paper, but only after it lay in the garbage for the evening.

His impossible plan to take his mother's car out to the Drive-In on a cold October night was distracted by the television. On TV, two people sat behind a desk, the Cleveland news anchors from Channel Five. Accompanied by urgent news music, the man said, "In our lead story, a police sting operation in a Circleville public men's room leads to multiple arrests."

The other anchor, a woman with a stern look, continued. "Circleville police have released the names of seventeen men caught in a weeks-long sting at a rest stop in Marion State Park, among them a pastor at nearby Ohio Christian University. Reporter Sean Nalley is on the scene."

The TV cut to a man standing near an outdoor rest stop. As he spoke, Joshua couldn't hide the fact that he'd jolted his head up from the floor. His father and sister sat rapt, staring at the screen through the entire segment until a Jell-O commercial broke their gaze. Joshua turned around to see them both look down at him, as if awaiting his response, as if he knew more than they did, or wanted to know. The silence was broken when the telephone rang. Sara answered it.

"Joshua, it's for you."

Expecting David, he jumped to retrieve the receiver. But his mother covered the mouthpiece and whispered, "It's a girl," with a curious expectancy. Her son's face twisted into a puzzle of confusion. "Don't be long. I want to call your grandmother."

"Hello?" he said quietly, turning away from the sound of his father evenly stating the obvious time difference between Serene and San Francisco.

Feeling the whole family listening to him, he ducked deep into the darkened kitchen, the phone cord taut.

"Guess who likes you," a girl's voice teased over the phone.

"What?"

"Someone likes you."

"Who is this?" He heard giggles and a plastic wrapper. He could imagine a slumber party in a girl's bedroom at the other end of the line, all in pink pajamas, half a dozen of them, their hair in curlers, their faces done up in wild exaggerations of sophisticated makeup, not unlike the Barbie dolls that probably littered that room. Somewhere on a girl's bed, among freshly painted nails, he imagined a bag of Cheetos and an abandoned board game of *Mystery Date*.

"Someone likes you. Guess who?"

"Amy Carter."

"No, silly."

"How do you know she doesn't like me?"

"It's someone at school," the voice pressed, as if explaining the rules.

It wasn't David, and even if it was, he did not expect the girl on the phone to tell him, so he quickly tired of the game. "Well, since she doesn't have the guts to tell me, I really don't care." He put his finger gently on the hook, then pretended to talk to the dead line, making up flirtatious responses that could be heard by his family. Finished with the charade after a few moments, he hung up and returned to his place on the floor below the television.

"Who was that, dear?" his mother asked.

"Just some kids from school."

The silent response ended any discussion. Besides, *Butch Cassidy and the Sundance Kid,* the ABC Movie of the Week, had begun.

He pretended to do his homework during commercials, then went to his bedroom and slipped the envelope out of the secret compartment in his wallet. He gazed at the succession of David faces and went to bed dreaming of shootouts with him. He imagined himself as Paul Newman and David as Robert Redford.

Before turning off his bedside light, he carefully returned the pictures of David to his wallet. He imagined himself being tragically hit by a speeding car, whereupon a medic in a dashing white uniform would search him for identification, find the pictures, and profoundly say, "Why, this must be his long-lost partner in crime."

Chapter 8

DREAMER'S BALL

LIKE MANY IN Serene, the Evans home, built in the post-War 1940s, had a good foundation, a sturdy frame, and a large front porch. But the earth in the valley is soft, long ago gouged out by a slow-moving glacier, and some buildings in the county had a tendency to slump. Years later, that would become a problem when I brokered its sale.

Joshua often sat on the front porch when anticipating the arrival of David's truck, even in cold weather. Joshua's parents avoided critiquing his eccentricity, although they had asked David inside the first few times, as if requiring a visual and social inspection of Joshua's new friend.

The boys had begun hanging out together a lot since their trippy journey through the mall. Joshua kept the poster rolled up, hidden in the dark recesses of his closet when the attic proved too cold and conspicuous a hiding place.

On days when he went to the college music department to practice, he often imagined David sitting behind him, listening, touching, and smiling. He was completely in love, and it served to inspire him.

Joshua had a ritual for getting dressed to go out with David. QFM96, one of the Columbus radio stations, played a three-song tribute to the weekend that included "Friday on My Mind," "Cleveland Rocks," and "Born To Run." Joshua would prance around in his fresh jeans to get the stiffness out, recheck his face in the bathroom, and then, only at the last moments, when he knew he could avoid one last trip to the fridge for leftovers, he would brush his teeth, smiling wide. *Just like the UltraWite guy*, he would say to himself.

The UltraWite commercial featured a man wearing only a white towel around his waist, his body shining with water, his hair gleaming. The actor would smile so sweet and bright that Joshua once thought of him when he jerked off over the bathroom sink. That last secret smile to himself became his own personal send-off.

His fluttering stomach awaiting David on those nights became tinged with frustration on those days when he didn't see David, who sometimes skipped school without telling him. The joy of seeing David in school had to be muted, especially when he hung out with some of his larger, scragglier friends.

Those fellows would be Ed Wallenbeck (who now lives in Cleveland, has a family, and still plays with an amateur band), Hank Cushnak, nicknamed Crusher, and Don Wiley, his thinner counterpart. Neither Hank or Don were available for interviews for this account, being dead (Hank), and in Lompoc Federal Prison for a drug arrest (Don). Funny that Kelly Dienstberger didn't mention that in last year's class reunion newsletter.

But when he visited inside Joshua's home, David was ever the gentleman. He had them fooled.

So after a while, his parents grew tolerant of Joshua's lone vigils on the porch, peering out the living room drapes at their son anticipating David's arrival.

"Is he late?" His mother's voice startled him.

"No, Mom. Just . . . no."

"You could invite him over if you like."

"What?" Joshua looked into his mother's eyes for a moment, as if she were X-raying him. Invite David over to hear his father fart? To endure his mother quizzing David until she had him pegged, while she introduced him to PBS and cheese fondue? Then what, off to sleep as their son's bed springs squeaked?

"For dinner."

"Okay." Maybe she was just trying to be nice. Headlights rounded the bend of their small street. "See ya."

He leaped off the porch. David pulled his truck only halfway up the driveway before Joshua opened the passenger door and hopped in.

"Evening, dude. Ready for a night of debauchery?"

"Sure thing." David's cassette player pumped a Rush tape.

"Put on 'Cygnus.'"

"Not yet," David teased as he eased out of Joshua's neighborhood. The song held a special significance, meant only for late-night-getting-stoned moments on back farm roads when they drank beer and smoked. Joshua knew that, but wanted to hear the song.

"Been busy?" Halloween was less than a week away.

"Haulin' punkins on overtime," David sighed.

"Missed you at school a few days."

"Yeah, Uncle Joe's got me excused. It'll slow down November first."

They drove out to Margie Silvanus's farm on Route 29. A week before Halloween, Margie had clarified in her invitations the party's theme for her eighteenth birthday: "No Costumes!" She'd invited the entire marching and stage bands. Even though the weather had already begun to turn chilly for Ohio that fall, the "pool party" aspect remained optional.

Some had joked about Margie's party being a dud since the word had been spread that her parents would be present. This demoted Margie's party to pre-party status, meaning, the "nice" party before another party with beer or pot for those so inclined.

Joshua and David didn't mind, since they usually imbibed in private before such social events. Those joints were the primers, David used to say.

Margie Silvanus had risen to popular ranks through her baton twirling, a status not as honored as cheerleader, but one that required a great deal of skill. She performed at every football game intermission with her partner, Brenda Kruger, David's sometime girlfriend.

At games and pep rallies, Brenda and Margie were quite a sight. They worked very hard on their routines. At halftime shows, they wore spangled outfits in the school's colors, blue and white, and flesh-colored tights, sometimes two layers on colder nights late in the season. They inspired cheers when they flawlessly accomplished the much talked-about feat of twirling fire batons. Margie even dyed her hair blonde to match Brenda's natural color.

Brenda Kruger later attested to the fact that she and David Koenig did maintain an infrequent sexual relationship, which explains her years-later dismissal regarding the nature of David and Joshua's relationship.

The Silvanus home, a ranch house in the middle of farms outside of town, wasn't too far for nearly all the members of the marching band and a few jocks from the football team to attend.

As they drove to the party, Joshua commandeered the cassette deck, which flipped back to radio while he changed cassettes. Joshua turned the dial, searching for some music, hard to come by on AM in Serene, other than country and talk shows. A distinct pealing burst out of the speaker.

". . . so sayeth the Baptist, John 1:23, I am the voice of—"

"Turn that shit off."

"Just a minute."

The preaching stopped as he shoved in Queen's *News of the World* to the foot-stomping "We Will Rock You."

Through a bit of nagging to Mr. Rose, the anthem had been quickly added to the cheering repertoire of the marching band. The cheerleaders had reluctantly agreed to assist in leading what they considered a thudding cheer, their talents honed to other multi-rhythmed routines.

"Brenda wants you to go on a double date with us," David said over the music.

Thinking he meant just the three of them, Joshua quickly agreed. He rarely went out with David when he was with Brenda. David either dated her, went out with a bunch of guys or just with Joshua. David sort of hopped company each weekend night.

David explained, "Your date's Gretchen Olson."

Joshua felt a bit confused. Gretchen Olson played clarinet, and although pretty of face with a voice as sweet as her instrument, she had a figure more akin to a cello.

"Oh." Although he continued to air-piano a song on the dashboard, his face dropped to a studious non-emotion.

"She's real sweet," David added as they swung off Route 410 and onto a familiar county road.

"Yeah, I know."

"Why doncha ask her tonight?" David said, as if instructing him under the cheery tone. Brenda had probably demanded it of him, but David, though he shared secrets, would never admit that.

"Sure, I'll ask her," Joshua nodded, finishing up the solo and retrieving a stick of Big Red from his coat pocket, always handy to disguise cigarette or pot breath when in social situations chaperoned by adults. Joshua tried to pretend that it didn't hurt to have the boy he loved tell him he had to date a girl.

"Matty Clark's havin' a sort of Halloween party next week, so we'll go out the Saturday after that. I'll drive."

"Okay, Davey." Joshua nodded, lowering his head like the cartoon dog from the animated kid's show *Davey and Goliath*. At some point in their budding friendship, the two had made a joke of the Claymation series, where in each episode Davey learned a valuable Christian lesson after committing a minor sin.

"Don't worry," David grinned. "She won't know. Nobody knows."

"Yet."

For Joshua, Margie Silvanus's home held a special sliver of dread, now almost forgotten, in the memory of his fight with

Brad Duffy. Approaching the ranch house brought back a feeling of awkwardness. But then he remembered that had it not been for Brad Duffy's leg, he would never have met David.

Margie's mother was a tall country woman, still remembered fondly by many of the kids as their favorite third-grade teacher. Her home was decorated in the latest magazine trends. Red checkered cloth covered a picnic table of snacks adorned with all the proper *Redbook* extras: glazed cookies, healthy dips and carrot sticks, fresh popcorn and chips, surrounded a huge punch bowl of liquid tinted a bright and unnatural fluorescent orange.

"Isn't this sweet," David joked as he stuffed several snacks into his mouth. It was certainly nothing like the beer blasts with older guys they had weaseled their way into; not a speck of illicit substances anywhere.

They must have been bored with such company. I recall attempting some chitchat where the boys were quite cordial, despite the absence of herbal or alcoholic amusements, except perhaps in David's truck or neatly pre-rolled in his FFA jacket pocket.

Kids stood around outside, awkwardly chatting by the warm fire of the barbecue, loudly berating each other with inside jokes and classroom foibles. It was acknowledged that Kim Ralston and Brian Nestle were indeed dating. It was revealed that Rod Hershler had loosened the screws in Mrs. Postle's English class stool. It was exposed that Russell Taylor had received only one detention for rushing the lunchtime DJ radio room to commandeer the microphone and, to the pleasure of all listeners at third period lunch, had issued a loud fart.

"What's that blinking light?" someone pointed to the south field.

"That's her neighbors, those crazy born-agains. The ones with the radio show."

"It's *The Orin and Mabel Show*," someone else mocked. I remember laughing too loudly at that comment. One of the Christians among the students glared at me.

"Is that what we heard coming here?" Joshua asked David.

"It hogs up half the dial, being so close," Margie complained.

"Why should you worry," someone else said. "You've got more records than they have at the mall." Everyone laughed while Margie's face turned crimson.

Someone changed the record in the house. A silence followed through which one could drive a slow tractor.

"Who's going in the pool?" Brenda called out coyly. Despite the season, the Indian Summer had proved to be a warm one.

"It's heated," Margie reminded us. The pool's cover had been pulled back to expose the lit glimmering water.

In a county where swimming holes were few, a heated pool was a true luxury. Although an invitation to swim had been extended by Mrs. Silvanus, no offers had yet been taken. Most of the kids had seen each other in bathing suits at the city pool and at less formal ponds out of town all of their lives, but on this unusually warm night and in this party setting, it seemed awkward and daring. The erotic sparks flew in erratic patterns, and there was no alcohol, drugs, or loud rock and roll to dull or enhance their libidos.

"C'mon, Margie, give us a birthday dive!" David hooted as he stood beside Brenda, his arm around her. Joshua brooded nearby, glaring once at his fate, Gretchen Olson, who briefly met his glance with a prepared smile.

"Oh, you first, guys!" Margie called back. David didn't hesitate.

"C'mon," he tugged at Joshua.

They had brought their Speedos but left them in the truck. The pattern set, several other guys retreated to the small barn to change while Margie escorted some girls into her house.

Since I hadn't been so much as shirtless in public in years, swimming was unthinkable. Even then I was overweight. Instead, I stood by the snack table pretending to enjoy Bill Meisler's recreation of an entire *Saturday Night Live* skit, one about those wild and crazy guys, and chatted with Alison Wodjik, who played the tuba.

I had never seen a pool at night, and a steaming one no less. There was something special about that night. I do not know if there is some Greek myth about two warriors or lovers who arise out of a pool, or dive in to claim immortal glory, but on that night some of us saw Joshua and David, what was between them, and what would become of the two of them.

David stood beside his truck at the far end of the driveway. Hidden by the door, he casually pulled his shirt off, dropped his pants and then sat on the seat to slip off his boots.

Joshua had followed and stood by him, stripping down. Due to their separate gym classes, Joshua had never seen David naked, a limitation that possibly increased his affection. For a moment in the darkness, their pale figures lit by the dashboard light, the two stood completely naked, stealing glances at each other, giggling.

The smoothness of David's skin first stunned Joshua, how the line of bareness from his chest down the side to the rounded buttocks and down his thick legs all glowed pale in the low light. Joshua enjoyed the moment, but as he darted down to see David's pubic patch and the dangling penis and balls, David caught his look, glanced downward at Joshua as well, and their eyes met. Other boys would have joked, but the moment lasted a bit too long for levity.

They quickly pulled on their Speedos, dumping their clothes on the truck seat. David closed the door. They stood in the dark, the glow of the far-off pool catching in David's eye.

"Better not get our clothes stolen," he mused.

"Yikes," Joshua softly cursed as, barefoot, they padded lightly over the gravel driveway and onto the lawn. He walked back with David, almost naked. He could have felt ashamed and small, like he had those times when other boys called him a fag. But with this crowd, although many knew it or thought it, they were polite. It was the envious kids who blurted out the truth. It was the kids who had not learned how to lie who said the words. But they had not been invited. Besides, he was with David, and anybody with half a brain knew you did not mess with David's friends.

A few kids were already bobbing about tentatively in the pool. David let out a "Yeee-hah!" and dove into the water. Joshua followed with much less drama.

Kids splashed about, swam lengths, made water bombs, and engaged in flirtatious sexy comments. Some, like myself, more afraid of revealing themselves, stood back, clothed under the excuse of having forgotten swim suits. David taunted us with water sprays and we shrank back, laughing loud. I will remember this night forever.

So of course, when I saw David and Joshua's bodies, wet and slippery and steaming as they dove around that pool, I felt as if I were given a splash of that water to awaken my sensibilities. I was just hiding behind that extra seventy-five pounds, hiding from my potential for such love.

But this is not about me. This night between David and Joshua, they talked lovingly about it for years afterward. It was the first night they truly touched. That was how Joshua put it. David always said, "Hell, that was the first night I smacked his bare butt." We always laughed when David said that, because love is funny, too.

Margie and Brenda, another girl, and a couple of boys all swam around in the small pool, lit with bright turquoise lamps. Their shadows bounced off the walls of the Silvanus home.

"C'mon, you two, let's do some water ballet." Brenda instructed David in a lift, and soon she was flying up boldly into David's upstretching arms, while Joshua fumbled about lifting Margie. They collapsed back down in the water to the amusement of us onlookers.

"Esther Williams," Joshua yelped. I recall laughing loudly at that joke, catching Joshua's sly glance. His look said, we have so much in common.

"Who?" Margie asked.

"Never mind."

A sensual drama ensued in the pool, one that rent hearts and stirred desires. For a moment, Joshua shared an awkward look with Margie as David and Brenda kissed, their heads bobbing in the deep end. Sensing a mutual dread of being forced to imitate, Margie and Joshua pulled apart, feigning exhaustion with the frolics.

Two boys jumped in, avoiding embarrassment by swimming in cutoffs. Some roughhousing ensued, the girls retreated to a corner and, for several moments, David swam underneath like a lurking shark, striking up at guys, spilling them over. At one point David's blurry form appeared between Joshua's legs, and while he stood still, accepting anything from him, he allowed his friend to quickly shuck off his Speedos.

"Aww, he's naked! Oooh, look!" David emerged, his arm swinging triumphantly with Joshua's bathing suit. Joshua dove after him, and despite a bit of resistance, Joshua managed to pull down David's Speedo, his one hand distracted by making a quick grab for David's bobbing gonads. For a brief, almost miniscule underwater moment, Joshua managed to plant his face directly into David's crotch, catching his bobbing cock in his mouth before David retreated.

Upon rising, another silent mutual glare passed between the two boys. They pulled back, eyes just above the water, each other's suits in opposite hands. Others splashed about, but they swirled clockwise like sharks about to mate. It was a decisive moment, and Joshua pressed closer. David glared at him, sultry in a way only a teenage boy can be. The motion had been accepted.

"Getcher suits on!" Margie hissed from beside the pool, a towel wrapped around her shoulders. Hearing the cries of amused nudity, Mrs. Silvanus emerged from her house.

Joshua looked back to David, who sensibly pulled his legs into Joshua's suit. He did the same, tickled at the prospect. Would he someday wear his jeans as well, his favorite T-shirt?

"Okay, I think that's enough now, boys," Mrs. Silvanus herded them out, offering a stack of freshly folded beach towels. "There's plenty more hot dogs and hamburgs to cook. Get changed and you can dig in."

David slapped Joshua's butt once and ran off. Brenda wrapped a towel around her waist by a lawn chair, where Gretchen Olson sat sipping a cup of punch. Joshua grabbed a towel and approached, figuring he'd get his impending torture out of the way.

"You guys are ridiculous," Brenda teased.

Joshua shivered under the towel. Gretchen watched silently.

"She said we could hang out and have fun."

"Yeah, right."

They chatted more until Brenda propitiously excused herself to get dressed, leaving Joshua conveniently alone with Gretchen. A mesh-wrapped glass candle flickered on the white metal table beside her. Sitting further away on a lawn chair, I pretending to listen to some other student's prattle, but my eyes kept darting back to Joshua, his lithe frame. I had never seen him so nearly naked, and knew I might never have this opportunity again. I stared, my lips pressed closed. I watched him shiver under that towel as he stood by the Olson girl, preparing himself for a thin lie. I wanted to jump up and hold him, warn him, stop him.

"So, uh, why didn't you swim?" he asked her.

"It's too cold."

"Yeah, I guess," he shivered.

"Besides, I don't look good in a swim suit."

"Aw, that's probably not true," he lied.

"It is."

"Well, anyway, um, Dave and Brenda kind of want to know if we wanna . . ."

"I know."

"Yeah, well, um, it's Saturday. I mean, ya wanna go out next Saturday with them?"

"Sure. You mean in two weeks, right?"

"Oh, yeah, right." They could have planned to go possum skinning for all she knew, but still she agreed. "Well, um, Dave's driving, so I'll call when we'll pick you up."

"Sure."

"Cool." He retreated to the darkness, preferring to have kept David's swimsuit.

"The deed is done," he confessed as he redressed on the other side of the truck. David had sprouted a semi-erection that they both couldn't help but notice and smirk about.

"Ja ask her?"

"Yup."

"What'd she say?"

He shrugged, braggadocio. "What do you think she said?"

"Alright, Fido!"

"Hey." He mock-glared at David. "Don't start, or I'll have to beat you up again."

After David and Joshua bid the girls and the rest of us good-night—Brenda, Gretchen, and a select group were sleeping over at Margie's—they drove along the back roads while sipping beers. That night was one of many weekend evenings Joshua spent with David, merely driving, or driving to find a place to be alone. Some say they had sexual relations all of those times, but they told me their courtship inched along more gradually.

David drove to a high hill off Route 410, looking over the entirety of Serene: a mere collection of grounded stars. He pulled a joint from his pocket. Joshua lit it while the precious Rush tape was slotted into the cassette deck. Joshua could have driven with David all night, but as the song faded, David shut the engine off, left the music on, and got out. Joshua obediently followed. They pissed, then stood, and watched the star-clustered night with stoned rapture.

"We should go to the Drive-In," Joshua suggested.

"What for?"

"They're showin' a porno movie."

"What? You mean you never seen one?"

"Nope."

"You don't got ID."

"Do they check?"

"I think so."

"Oh." Joshua zipped up, stealing another glance at David's piss stream, following it up to his zipper.

"Course we could drive around the back road."

As they returned to the truck, David explained that a dirt road ran along the back of the Drive-In, but sometimes cops chased cars out.

"It's worth a shot."

They drove.

"How's the piano going?"

"Good. I'm gonna do 'Bohemian Rhapsody' for my recital in May."

"No shit!"

"Yeah. Mrs. Rose is cool, when she's not gabbing her head off."

"Do me a favor."

"Anything, Davey," Joshua slurred in Goliath's dog voice.

"Don't forget me when you're a famous rock star."

"Forget you? Never. You're too much a pain in the ass."

David slowed to turn down the tiny dirt road behind the Drive-In. He switched off the headlights, they parked, and from inside the truck peered over the ratty fence. Harry Reems sat in a living room with a woman kneeling before him. Joshua was so hard he almost asked David if he minded if they jacked off together, but then a pair of headlights flashed them blind.

"Shit! Cops." David blinked his headlights on and backed up, passing the police car while the search beam followed them. The cops never stopped them, but they were half-panicked nevertheless. Once they got out back on the highway, David hooted. "Well, shit, at least you can't say I didn't try, good buddy."

"Well, thanks, anyway."

They drove on, listening to Aerosmith.

"God, I'm all sweaty," Joshua said.

"What, from that? Think we'd end up in the clinker?"

"I dunno what."

David reached out his hand and felt the back of Joshua's neck.

"Man, you're all poured out with embarrassment juice."

"What?"

"You know, when you suddenly get flushed and all of a sudden you're soaked?"

"That's it, alright."

They rode on a while. David gazed for a dangerously long time at Joshua, his right arm still up on the back of the seat, still close to Joshua's neck, so close he could almost graze it with a few fingers, and could sense Joshua wanting him to do that. "Josh. You like me?"

Joshua waited. What was he supposed to say? "Sure, Dave."

"No, I mean, you really like me, don't you?"

If he hadn't been slightly high and slightly drunk, he would have never have had the guts to say anything. He would have said that yes, he would drive all night with him, anywhere, and only ask to share the cramped air in his beat-up old truck, crank his tunes, gulp from his beer can, smoke his cigarettes, if only he could just stand to be near him without touching. "Yeah, I really . . . really like you."

"I thought so." David pulled out a cigarette from his pack on the seat. Joshua lit it for him.

"Bother you?" Joshua lit one himself.

"Huh?"

"Does it bother you?"

Up ahead, the tiny lights of Serene glowed in the valley.

David looked at him a moment in the darkness, then turned to the road back to town, hands on the wheel, steady. "You never bother me."

Chapter 9

DOING ALL RIGHT

"NOW, GERSHWIN WAS said to have very large hands. That's why he played a ninth . . . and a tenth, and an eleventh. But you, my dear—" Ellen Rose leaned close, examining Joshua's left outspread palm like a scientist "—will do quite well with an eighth for now."

Her remark during his lessons had not bothered Joshua, except for the second and third time she said it. The limitation of his hands had no longer mattered for the boy, however, for he had set his sights on playing rock and roll, and with a hard eighth in the left (one octave span from his pinky to his thumb) or a solid fifth, and a mere three keys of a chord at a time in his right, he knew there wouldn't be a problem, except for his hunger to learn more rock songs.

Armed with the stack of new music books, at his next lesson he asked Mrs. Rose which song he could learn next. She scanned the titles of the Beatles album with pleasant recognition, looked slightly aghast at the strange photos and lengthy score to Pink Floyd's *Animals*, but looked curiously at the selections from the white book with the pleasantly elegant logo of a swan.

Mrs. Rose liked swans. She had several glass sculptures of them on her mantelpiece.

"Let's give this one a look, shall we?" And with a little bumpy stalling, he played a passable version of "Seaside Rendezvous."

"Well, you've got your work cut out for you, I'll say that. Which one did you have in mind?"

Joshua politely took the book and flipped to the last song.

"Oh." Mrs. Rose peered closer. "Well, maybe in little bits. But how about a simpler Beatles song to start off with."

"Okay." He chose "Eleanor Rigby." That already sounded classical. She would like that, he thought.

Every Wednesday, Joshua walked to the Rose home during sixth period. He tried to get his study hall on last period so he could leave school for seventh and be gone all day, but there was only one geometry class, which he'd avoided taking until his senior year, and it was last period. He had no intention of trying for anything above a C, but at least he got some good doodling done then.

He'd slipped his score of Pink Floyd's *Animals* to Ed Wallenbeck once, but nearly had it taken away by Mrs. Portmouth, the geometry teacher. He couldn't concentrate on proofs and graphs, especially on piano lesson days, when he'd get excited about learning the riff from Bruce Springsteen's "She's the One," or better yet, Queen's "Melancholy Blues." Nothing else gave him such a combination of dread and joy. He wanted to see how much he'd improved, wanted to learn more, but aside from his occasional lax rehearsal discipline, one problem remained.

Except for myself, Joshua was Mrs. Rose's only student over the age of thirteen. Struck by our civility, instead of her usual stern finger-pointing demeanor, she chatted away while we sat, hands poised over the keys, waiting to be permitted to play.

This connected Joshua and myself that year, our mutual complaints about our piano teacher. With only this one topic to discuss, our conversations were limited. However, I speak from authority about the nature of Mrs. Rose's lessons, which encouraged but didn't demand enough discipline.

"You know, you shouldn't worry about how you sound now, for you are preparing for later," she would say. And then, with the predictability of her metronome, she often said, "We must look every day into the future."

Practicing at home, Joshua felt everyone in the house listening. It was better in one of the tiny rehearsal rooms at Beekam College where the pianos all had functional keys. There Joshua had more than a dozen pianos to choose from, each with its own private room, like an acoustic buffet.

One day he would hammer away on a sharp and easy Yamaha, then on another day play on the heavy old Steinway to develop his muscles. He hopped rooms for hours sometimes, until he was exhausted by his musical limits, fatigued by the repetitive comfort of hammering out "Because the Night," or the jaunty melody of "Martha, My Dear." Notes were fine for hard stuff, but with the buoys of chord letters right above the lyrics, he could play, really play between them, differently each time.

Then one day a strange man interrupted his privacy between songs with a polite tap on the door.

"I've been listening to your music. You play very hard." He wore a dark mottled sweater and had a large belly. His glasses slid from his nose. His hair frayed out from both sides of his head.

"Thank you, I think," Joshua stuttered.

"No, I mean, there are many ways to play, and I think it would be just as satisfying to play softly as banging away on those rock tunes."

"I'm pretty much happy right now with banging." That came out wrong. "If that's all right with you. I mean, I could go somewhere else."

"Oh no, I can barely hear you in the other studio. I'm all the way down the hall. I just wanted to stop in and see who it was." He entered all the way and closed the door.

"Now if you let me tell you about some other composers, you may want to expand your . . . range. Are you a music student?"

"Yes, but not here. I'm still in high school."

"Oh. Well, I don't see the worry. As long as there's a vacant studio for others."

Joshua felt a bit uncomfortable. The man smelled like butter.

Sure, he might know more about classical stuff, but he didn't know what convulsions and giggles Joshua could stir up at a talent show rehearsal by simply tinkling the opening riff from "Get Down Make Love," or just the first few chords from Styx's "I'm Sailing Away." Deceptively simple songs they were, but adults nearby never knew the siren-like meaning since they didn't know the lyrics. They did not know the power of pop.

The fussy man leaned a bit too close for Joshua's comfort. "Anytime you want to play together, you just come by. I'm in studio every day from four to six."

"Uh, sure." Joshua had never heard the term *in studio*.

Joshua practiced at home more often after that, or snuck into the college music department at different times. He didn't want to see the older guy, but not because he seemed a bit creepy. Joshua didn't want to lead the guy on. That's how he put it.

I began to see Joshua outside of school at the practice rooms. We were both advanced. Sometimes, I would peek around the little windows and try to get a studio next to him, either at the college or in one of the three much smaller rooms at the high school. He had begun pounding away at "I Am the Eggman," and I had wanted to introduce him to a fellow orchestra class-mate who played cello and loved The Beatles.

Anyway, had that happened, everything might have turned out differently.

I don't know about those things they say about Joshua running off to California and allegedly "bringing AIDS back to Serene," as the town gossips put it. I would say there were a few other transmission outlets. Of the five other known homosexuals from our class, and a few classes before and after, not one lives. And they never left Ohio.

Perhaps that is what saved them for a time, my boys. No rest stop trucker action or miserable cop bait bar scene for these two. They grew new fields to plow each other every year. These boys were like rural versions of those Riace warriors. They deserve to be set in bronze, Castor and Pollux. Gay sexuality was all around us in that small town, some of it different, much of it a mystery. Perhaps it could have happened in a small college practice room, or in a barn or a truck. If we are to imagine a romantic monogamy, it requires the complete absence of truth.

Home again, Joshua flipped through his bedroom's growing record collection: Aerosmith, Foghat, Yes, ELO, Neil Young, Boston, Elton John? No, Queen. Only Queen would do. When it was too late at night to practice, he air-guitared and air-pianoed in front of his mirror, sometimes donning a flowing bathrobe or wrapping a T-shirt over his head like an Egyptian headdress, imagining himself in one of Elton or Freddie's more flamboyant costumes.

Little dramas worked through his head. The posters looked down, sage icons spurring him on, helping him, guiding him, Bruce Lee protecting. Exhausted later, he began another bit of self-love. He could play for what seemed hours, naked in his bed or while gazing out the window, standing before his closet door mirror to see his lithe body, check a few muscles and marvel at the stiff thing between his legs, inspect its red flushed flesh, wondering if David were doing the same thing somewhere, miles away, in his own bedroom.

Still energized, he stopped playing with himself and put on a pair of sweatpants and a baggy shirt. He barely heard the knock on the door and his father walked in on him swaying while playing air-piano to a Yes song with his headphones on.

"Telephone." The door shut.

He put down the headphones, shut off his cassette player, then crept into his parents' room to pick up the upstairs extension. He lay on his parents' bed and smelled his mother's perfume.

"Joshua."

"Davey." Joshua hid his joy. It seemed all he had to do was think of David and he called.

"Game plan."

"Do tell."

"We still got our big double date next week."

"Yeah, yeah."

"But this Saturday night, you and me. Matty Clark's havin' a sort-of Halloween party."

"Cool."

"Pick you up."

"Yeah."

Back to his room, not daring to go downstairs even to bear walking by his father's face hidden behind a newspaper, Joshua returned to his sanctuary, lay in bed and promptly shot a wad of pure seventeen-year-old virgin spunk.

Finished, he felt oddly energized, as if it were a starting gun. Usually the act released him into a dream world of half-grazed thoughts and fluttering imagery so fantastically comforting he had a difficult time waking.

He clicked on his study lamp atop the desk his father had re-stained and varnished for him. An odd Christmas present one year, it took two rolls of wrapping paper. Joshua had been disap-pointed when it wasn't a new stereo. Desks were like socks, purely functional, only larger.

His father, however, took a quiet pride in discovering his son hunched over it, scratching away on a textbook with a pencil. He watched him, undetected, for a few minutes.

"Studying?"

"Sort of." Joshua didn't turn around. His father took in the wall full of posters: strange fancy dressed men sweating into microphones and guitars, a poster of the moon.

"Your mother tells me you're doing pretty good."

"When I'm not too bored. Geometry is completely pointless."

"Actually, isn't it all points?" his father deadpanned.

Joshua smirked, erased the penciled notes of some student from the previous year. Kids never owned schoolbooks in Se-rene. Joshua wiped away the scrawlings of the previous user, as if to cleanse the path for his own thoughts.

"You going out with David again?"

"Why?" He brushed a mound of eraser crumbs into a small pile beside the book.

"No reason. Just glad to know you've got a friend."

"Oh."

"You don't drink, do you?"

"Sometimes." Joshua did not feel the need to lie.

"I want you to be careful."

"David likes his truck." Joshua faced his father. "And he likes his driver's license."

"Just want you to get home safe, you know."

"I know."

"I don't want you hurt."

"I'm very safe in David's ar— car, truck." He had almost said "arms." "He's my best friend. I never had a best friend, Dad. Please don't—"

"I had a good buddy in the service."

A story. This is different, Joshua thought. His father continued. "We went out a lot. Did some real wild things. That was before I met your mother in San Francisco."

Did he ever call her by her name anymore? Joshua had never heard him address his wife by anything other than "Hon." That was something Joshua would never do. He would always call David David, or occasionally, Davey.

"The thing is, I want you to know that there will come a time when you'll go your different ways."

"Separate."

"Yes, well . . . the thing is, you'll be off to college, and he might get a job or move or get married."

"He has a job. He works on his farm for his dad's brother-in-law. And he's not getting married."

"He said that?"

"I know that. I'm not either."

"Okay." His father fingered a small suede and stick teepee, a gift for his son on a trip to the Indian mounds in Chillicothe when he was twelve.

"I'll see you in the morning." He left quietly to the sound of his son's eraser rubbing against paper.

Chapter 10

THE MILLIONAIRE'S WALTZ

HIS HAIR HAD smushed over to one side from lying down, so Joshua stuck his head halfway under the faucet, got it wet, and combed it out again. He leaned in close to check for any poppable zits, then adoringly grazed his fingers over the few sprouts of facial hair. He only had to shave every other day. Besides, it was cool to show off some stubble in school.

He heard David ring the doorbell, being welcomed in downstairs and chatting with his parents. They liked him, or acted as if they did, since Joshua had not invited anyone else over in years.

Joshua dawdled in his bedroom, adjusting his flannel shirt collar for no reason. His mother had made a comment about his change in dressing habits a few days earlier, and seemed shocked when he bought a few used shirts at the Goodwill, which she considered a dumping ground. He had even seen some of his own outgrown clothes among the bins. But she begrudgingly accepted his change, seeing it as just an assertion of his maturity, if not his questionable taste as well. I remember this shift in Joshua's attire when he and David began to dress alike, the way couples or people and their pets grow to resemble each other.

His sister caught him making a few last-minute inspections in the mirror by the open bathroom door and as she sauntered by carped, "Off on another date with your *boy*friend?"

He didn't deny it, didn't even reply.

Clomping down the stairs, Joshua suppressed a flush of warmth to see David sitting on the sofa. In greeting, both their faces lit up, as if their days apart had been years, or they were about to set out on a secret mission. In a way, they were.

David's blue corduroy Future Farmers of America jacket seemed almost regal against the sofa's faded brown tint. Joshua not only knew that his father liked David, but that he approved of his friendship. His parents didn't know about the wilder things they got up to, at least not at the time, but Joshua's mother would later admit to denying to herself what she felt as a strong affection between the boys. The few times that Joshua spoke to her, in between his practicing piano and running off with his new friend, he didn't speak much about David after blushing and realizing he'd been talking about him too much. Then he'd abruptly switch to discussing music with her, which might lead to another trip to the library, one of few things they still did together other than eat dinner.

"How's your fall crop comin'?" Samuel Evans attempted a bit of "banter." That's what he called it.

"Pretty good, sir," David smirked. "The pumpkins have been harvested and sold. We've still got lots of acorn squash and Indian corn to sell off, probably wholesale. If we get another rain, all the leftovers'll wash down to Zanesville."

As they laughed, Joshua smiled at David's ease with adults. Where he might stutter, his friend knew how to behave respectfully with adults, speak more clearly, sit upright.

With his dad warning of the midnight curfew (usually obeyed), the two climbed into David's truck and set out, waiting a few blocks to light up cigarettes and blast some Foghat.

"So, are we getting costumes?" Joshua asked.

"Huh?"

"You said Matty's having a Halloween party."

"Aw, no. It's more of an anti-Halloween party. Don't sweat it. His dad's gone for the weekend, again."

"How convenient."

Since he'd been running around with David, there always

seemed to be a party. Every Friday or Saturday seemed to promise another welcome invitation by yet another high school or college guy with absent parents. In some circles, the 1970s had spawned a flood of single-parent children grooming themselves to become amateur party hosts.

The houses they visited were usually run-down homes on the north side of town, rented by college students or recently graduated local factory workers, their loose connection to the occupant being a younger brother or an acquaintance of David's. Sometimes they'd get an invite to one of the rich kids who lived near the Country Club, like tonight.

On their way to get beer, David suddenly smacked his hand against his head in an "I coulda had a V8" gesture.

"What?" Joshua asked.

"I forgot my fake ID."

"So?"

"So we gotta bring some beer."

"But Matty's gotta have plenty of booze."

"It's rude to show up without something." Despite his seemingly reckless behavior, David had often taught Joshua such little points of social behavior: how to pass a joint, what to bring to parties, when to show up, when to leave.

"Shit."

"What's the problem?"

"The old man's prob'ly gettin' home soon. Maybe if we hurry." David slowed, veered off the road and pulled a U-turn.

"What, you embarrassed for me to meet him?"

"Goddamit, no, it's not— I'm just— You don't understand."

"What? Tell me."

"Nothing." Now in the opposite lane, David floored the gas pedal.

"What is it? I tell you my problems. What's the matter?"

"He's just— Look, he drinks, okay? Not like we do. Ever since my mom left us, he hates me."

"Your dad hates you?"

"Look Josh, not everybody has the happy little home life like you. Some of us— The farm is fucked up. My dad went on this rant last fall with a couple of the hands, and they quit. I gotta supervise this old drunk who's been dad's friend for like, forever. I been late to school more, 'n not 'cause I'm sleepin' late. This old guy has to be told what to do every day. I keep tellin' my dad I'm not doin' crew work next year, and he better hire one, but he won't. He's like, I owe him room and board, so I gotta work."

"I'm sorry."

"Don't be sorry. Just, if he's home, be careful, alright?"

David slowed as they headed south out of town with a slight feeling of dread. They drove under the highway overpass and the bar that served as the town bus stop. As they passed more fields in darkness, Joshua felt the actual distance match his own from David.

Pulling into his driveway, David seemed relieved. "Well, his truck's not here. That's a good sign. C'mon."

Joshua was scared. He didn't want to be. He'd never been to David's house before. He'd wanted to, but David always shrugged it off. Joshua wanted this to be special, like when newlyweds enter their first home. It wasn't anything like that.

He followed David up creaking steps to a weathered porch and into a rundown house. A grey barn sat further back near the U-shaped driveway. The house smelled funny inside, like oatmeal and cigarettes. The living room was almost bare, with a sagging sofa, a beat-up coffee table, two chairs with the kind of Western wood frame Joshua thought only poor people had. Faded wallpaper repeated almost unrecognizable patterns of cabins and colonial people.

Then he realized David *was* poor. It hurt him, all the comments he'd made about white trash. David had laughed, but here it was, right in front of him. A large tacky painting on the otherwise bare wall loomed over a television, a boring landscape of trees and horses by a river. Joshua wondered who would buy such a picture. Did they come with houses like this? It seemed like something that people put on a wall just to fill space.

"C'mon."

David led him up the stairs. Joshua felt a small thrill in knowing he was going to see David's room. He was secretly charmed when David flicked on the light. He knew they were in a rush, so he scanned it quickly, wanting to memorize every detail. The wallpaper, repeating patterns of deer and hunters in a dank faded brown, reached up to the arched ceiling above his bed. The curtains were a drab, darker brown. Posters on the wall included Cheap Trick, Pink Floyd, and Aerosmith. For Joshua it was like a shopping list. He wanted to make his own room exactly like David's so he could lie in his room and imagine himself here every night.

He noticed a starfish in a plastic box, and a small framed photo of a boyish David standing by an ocean, hugging close to a taller similar-looking teenage boy: a brother? A cousin? Standing near them, a young woman smiled. About to ask about it, David said, "Be back in a sec," and left for the bathroom.

Joshua quickly stole a moment and lay on the bed, his bed, breathing in the smells. He wanted to take something, steal a dirty sock or a T-shirt, but David's footsteps jolted him to standing. He looked again at the framed photo on David's dresser.

"Oh, that's from a million years ago, my mom and my cousin Curt. He's down in Texas."

"Where's your mom now?"

He shrugged.

Downstairs, the front door slammed. Joshua heard creaking and footsteps, a shifting in the very walls of the house. "Getcher fuckin' truck outta my way," a voice yelled.

David gritted his teeth and glared at Joshua. "Don't say anything more than hello." He jammed his ID into his wallet and led Joshua down the stairs.

The television was already on, blaring light and sound into the living room. A large scrubby man pounded in from the kitchen, a six-pack in one hand, and a bag of potato chips in the other. He did not seem interested in meeting his son's friend.

"Ya hear me, boy?"

"I'm leaving now."

"You know you're supposed to park that heap by the barn."

David cowered, his shoulder sinking. All the strength and solid maturity Joshua admired in David had suddenly drained out of him.

"I was just coming in for a minute."

"Well, here," his father tossed something at the boy. David flinched, then picked up a set of keys. "Pull mine out, then put it back."

"Alright." He headed out the door. David's father watched them leave. Joshua turned back, thinking it would be polite to say goodnight or something, but the large man merely glared at him as if he were a stray dog, then shook his head, as if he'd witnessed a sight too sorry for words.

The two boys retreated out the door as the man plopped himself down on the sofa.

"Fucker," David seethed. "Here," he handed Joshua the keys. "Back mine out by the barn."

Honored by the small responsibility, Joshua silently obeyed as David moved his father's truck, preceding Joshua out the driveway, then pulling it back in. He ran into the house with the keys. Joshua heard raised voices, then saw David slam the door and return. Joshua scooted over to the passenger seat. David sat behind the wheel, gripped it, then let out a little sigh, and gave Joshua a look that said, "Well, there you have it," then yanked the truck into reverse and onto the county road. They sped away.

"You're lucky we caught him sober. I'll prob'ly spend Thanksgiving at my uncle's again. Last year, he was passed out on the couch."

"Is he always like that?"

"On a good day."

"Family ties . . ." Joshua said, cueing David.

". . . In fact I don't think I ever heard a single little civil word from those guys." Joshua laughed at David's deliberate hitting on the S's, just like Freddie Mercury.

By the time they reached the Mini-Mart Drive-Thru, the tunes and small talk cheered them a bit, and Joshua insisted on paying for the beer. They remained upbeat all the way to Matty's house, but for Joshua, the night had already given him more than he expected. Seeing such a sad part of David's life made him love the boy even more.

You're probably wondering why these young men, who obviously wanted each other, who would eventually grow a home and a marvelous pumpkin farm, and even host a hoe-down benefit in their barn for a neighbor's hospital bills, waited so long to consummate their love. Why could they not even figure out that their mutual desire had developed a scent, a cloud almost palpable to others? How did they breathe at the sight of each other? Many girls and a few boys had a crush on one of them at some point.

And why, since others could tell something special vibrated between them, could they not find the wherewithal to do the deed? Lacking the right to sleep together, location was a persistent problem, even the possibility of inquiring in a romantic if not even abruptly sexual manner.

Years later, David refrained from telling too many details about his love life with Joshua. David became very stoic in his latter years. Owning land that quadruples its value in ten years can do that to a man, make him feel more conservative about other things.

So why did David not take a cue from his abrupt few incidents with Brent Carse, and just make an advance? Because boys are the most fearful creatures on the Goddess's green earth. We fear everything: for our penises, for our property, for our totems. The mere idea of actually pressing your thigh deliberately against one of the other four guys packed into a friend's Camaro on the way to a bonfire (for example) was alternately performed with homoerotic silliness (like the pool party) or avoided completely.

The night of Matty Clark's party could have been one of those opportunities for love, but instead it became a narrowly missed trap.

David and Joshua drove to another part of town closer to Joshua's home, but distant in other ways. Turning off a stretch of tree-lined road, they entered what was simply known as Club Town. Set apart by high poplars and hedges turned deep ochre or shedding in the autumn chill, the winding small roads had no sidewalks, but the expansive lawns belied the true reason. It was not a neighborhood that welcomed strolling visitors.

For a town of 20,000 or so, the few dozen that could afford to live in the secluded area across the road from the Country Club and its golf course (thus the name Club Town) flaunted it. A few plantation style mansions loomed, other discreet mock Tudor homes hidden in darkness intrigued.

Matty Clark's father owned one of the modern homes, squared off in imitation of Frank Lloyd Wright, made of dark wood, nestled in a cluster of thin birch trees, with its own small creek. It was the sort of modern dream house Joshua desired, so unlike the rest of town, more like something in a magazine.

Several cars had already parked in the driveway and on the street. A few guys stood outside near the front door with cheap plastic Halloween masks pushed above their faces as they smoked. Like many others they attended, it was a strictly boys-only party. Girls either had not been invited, or knew better than to show up. Joshua didn't mind.

"Hey, he's finally here!" A familiar voice called out on the darkened porch. The boys walked into the shadows. Ed Wallenbeck's face glowed as he took a drag from a cigarette. He slid a plastic werewolf mask back down over his face. "Boo." He then nodded toward a trio of jack o' lantern pumpkins on the porch, their toothy grimaces lit by sputtering candles inside. "Yours?"

"Better be. Where's our intrepid host?" David approached, with Joshua following.

"Probably passed out somewhere inside." Ed nodded and smiled. "Josh."

"So soon?"

"His dad's been gone all weekend. He started early."

After they hung their coats on a hall rack, Joshua followed David inside, surprised by the size of the house. The ceilings were unusually high, and each room had a feeling of enormity. Music echoed throughout with hidden speakers installed everywhere, it seemed.

The fireplace was lit and burning. Above it hung a huge scribble of an abstract painting. Bottles of liquor and soda crowded the expansive kitchen counter. Instead of a separate room, the counter divided the living room from the kitchen. Joshua had seen such homes on TV. He thought it was neat.

Sitting on the living room sofa, Matty passed a red plastic bong around in a circle with Rick Taggart, Bill Stumbaugh, and a few others boys. The night the Music Club decided to hold an Elton John dance, Matty had walked up to Joshua and bragged, "I have every Elton John album ever made." From that day, Joshua had admired Matty Clark from afar. Their night in the DJ booth reigned as the high moment of his year.

Matty greeted him like a long-lost cousin. "C'mon, dudes. You got a lot of catchin' up to do!"

Along with a few other Halloween masks, which Matty or someone had bought as a joke, a few bowls of snacks lay on the coffee table. Sitting down, Joshua and David shared an awkward moment. There was a chair far over by a wall, but only one space on the sofa. Joshua wanted to sit next to David, but he had to get the chair, then pull up next to him, although there was more room at the other end of the circle near Bill.

While getting high with David and his friends, Joshua made sure to sit on David's left. According to courtesy or some ancient rite, shared tokes usually always went clockwise, and Joshua wanted David's fresh spit on the bong. It was what he secretly called "a tube kiss."

The conversation ran from the inane to the totally stupid, but the pot was good, and Joshua let his mind wander as he gazed at the strange paintings.

"I wanna get a Camaro, man," Taggart said. "With a button-down cockpit."

"Or a cock down your button pit," David said.

"What?"

The room exploded in laughter. Between the spurted beer and choked tokes, David grinned awkwardly at Joshua, as if he'd been momentarily caught with his slip showing. Then Joshua felt it, the air in the room, the heat stirred up by their funk and bravado, this horde of boys, talking of sex but not inviting girls, yakking and guffawing and catcalling while they tried on different masks.

He was one of them. He'd been led into the inner sanctum of coolness and found nothing more daunting than a pack of horny drunken stoned boys with the same rocks in their pants and shaggy hair covering their too-wide eyes. He had a crazy thought for a moment, that maybe all of them were gay, that it was only the awkward fear that kept them from being themselves. He put it aside when the talk returned to the body parts of women, but still it lingered in the haze of cigarettes and pot.

Bill Stumbaugh drank too much liquor and ended up barfing into the toilet. A couple of the boys carried him from the bathroom and dumped him into one of the bedrooms while the rest of the boys told jokes about other bodily functions. In the kitchen, three boys were munching anything and everything, the fridge door open. They hunched over a small radio on the counter. The Top 100 Countdown was down to number one. The boys cringed and flew away from the radio as the box blared, "Love, love will keep us together. . ."

The evening seemed a strange waste, and every time David engaged in a conversation, Joshua tried to keep up. But the talk turned to cars and sports, and he felt left out. He backed away, distracted. He wanted to see more of the strange and wonderful home.

He wandered down a hallway past the bathroom and peeked into the darkness of Matty's bedroom. A warm familiar smell greeted him. Then Matty swayed around the corner and grinned.

"C'mere."

Matty flipped a light on and showed him his model airplanes hovering on almost invisible strings, with model cars along a low shelf next to his stereo, which played the same music out into the den through two extra speakers. Along the shelf, filed neatly with little alphabetical tabs, was an immense record collection.

"Just don't get 'em out of order."

"No way." Joshua crouched to marvel at Matty's collection. He saw all his favorites, then a lot of others, even some classical and jazz albums. Longing to say something cool, near the J's he saw every Elton John record ever made.

"Wow."

"Yeah. He's the best."

"I still remember that dance you DJ'ed."

Matty nodded.

Joshua wanted to mention the *People* magazine article where the rock star had said he was bisexual, but he didn't. Matty sat on his bed, then slumped back to lying down. His eyes were rather glazed. Joshua stood and looked at him. Their eyes met.

"Ya wanna get high?"

Joshua had expected something else. "I am high."

"Oh. Okay." Then Matty closed his eyes, rubbed his stomach and left his shirt halfway shucked up, exposing his pale stomach and tight little belly button. Joshua wanted to lie down next to him, not really get sexy with him, although he was cute. His jeans bunched up in all the right places and clung tight around the thighs. Matty seemed more as if he just needed to be held in someone's arms for a long time.

But Joshua thought he shouldn't make an advance on his host, since he was there with David, his date of sorts, so he stood looking at Matty as long as he could stand, then silently stepped out and told David he was tired and wanted to go home. Luckily, David agreed.

Chapter 11

ALL DEAD, ALL DEAD

BY MONDAY, THE rumor had spread from teenager to teenager faster than a bout of mononucleosis.

About a half hour after David and Joshua left, Matty's neighbors had called the police. Matty's father had been called from wherever he was, and all the boys had been sent home with police escorts.

Matty Clark had been sent to The Seed.

Usually the last resort of desperate poor families, just the name of the place drew fear in the hearts of kids, like Room 101 in *1984*, which we read in English that year. Supposedly housed in some old barracks about an hour north, The Seed served as a rehabilitation institute for kids on drugs or with delinquency problems. No matter what their problem, they all disappeared for a few weeks, sometimes a month or more, then came back looking like extras from *Invasion of the Body Snatchers*. They dressed conservatively; the boys wore ties and closely cropped hair, and the girls who'd been known for tight jeans and tube tops suddenly wore long dresses and no makeup. They spoke to no one except others who'd also endured the forced rehab.

Secrecy swirled around the topic. Although school officials appeared complicit with the program, there had never been any classroom discussions, no pamphlets handed out. Kids disappeared, and returned as model—if not nearly silent—students.

It seemed an odd decision on the part of Matty Clark's father, Ralph Clark, who owned the largest car dealership in the county. Along the western road out of town, every driver passed the expansive lot, festooned with flapping plastic banners and posters announced one terrific deal after another on "100% American Made Autos!" Joshua, who achieved A's in English by default, often shared a running joke with his mother on their trips mall-ward: "What American?" They had a hard time explaining to Joshua's father the difference a hyphen could make.

The rumor-spreading seemed to make sense. Matty's father, while no grammar ace, was also divorced, had never had time for his only son, a spoiled brat who dealt pot and had crashed two Camaros by the time he was seventeen. Matty always threw great parties and never asked for gas money among those privileged to enjoy his reckless driving skills.

Joshua, who held a quiet affection for him, was already missing Matty as if he were dead.

"I heard it's up near Canton, like a concentration camp, and they shave their heads first thing."

"I heard they scream at you and make you cry and it's all religious too and they turn you into a God Squad type."

Joshua overheard two kids talking about it on the cafeteria line. He did not mention that he had been at Matty's party. They would surely pump him for more gossip. Besides, they were not the types to be invited to such a party. Joshua figured it was a good time to shut up about the fact that he had become that type.

But as he pocketed his change for his tray of Salisbury steak, canned corn, Apple Brown Betty and milk, Joshua noticed his own thinking. Only a few months ago, he would not have been the type to be invited to such a party. What had happened to him since he had become David's friend? Hell, get real, he told himself, since he had fallen in love with David?

He ate his lunch in silence, not bothering to go through the ordeal of finding some half-friend to eat with. He had practically dropped the few friends he had. David ate during the other lunch period, and Josh's old friends from stage band did not see him much anymore outside of practice. The kids in stage band—well, they were fun, but something had happened to Joshua. The silly gabbing and joking didn't mean much anymore. Repeating the best punch lines from the previous weekend's sitcoms no longer made him laugh. He now had private jokes with David, things he did not share, except with Ed or David's other friends.

He hadn't really become a hood. He did get drunk and high, but he didn't go out and buy the stuff. It was just there all the time with these new friends. He'd admitted a bit of that to his father. Would his parents be upset if they knew more? Would they send him away if he got out of control?

He had not been practicing enough lately, Mrs. Rose said recently. She was right in a way, but she did not know that he had begun writing songs, doodling and improvising in ways he never thought he could. Those years of listening to music had come back out in creative ways, and he had begun to pile up a secret stash of scribbled chord patterns and lyrics. One song was even about David, but carefully worded with no "he," only "you."

Moreover, getting high had changed him. Weekend mornings, he'd begun to sleep in later, and all day he felt so much more relaxed, saw strange ironies in television commercials, and found a new simple joy in just lying in his room, thinking about things and watching dust motes swirl in the afternoon sun. He felt tingly and relaxed at the same time, excited and exhausted. He could still feel remnants of the buzz even up to the next school day.

But the pleasant buzz faded that morning. The tale of Matty Clark's disappearance was not all that disturbed him. Joshua finished his lunch and dumped off the tray on a conveyer belt. A large kitchen worker with her hair in a bun took it away and tossed it on a rack by the huge metal washing machine. He thought of Germans, the roads out in the county where the Amish families lived, and then he remembered one particular girl of German and Swedish extraction. He had a date with Gretchen Olson on Saturday.

"You heard?"

"Yeah."

David grabbed Joshua from behind, scooted him to a side hallway under some stairs. They glanced like conspirators at passing kids.

"Your parents know?"

Joshua shrugged. "Your dad?"

David's glare said, *Don't even ask.* "Don't tell your parents we were there. We'll be okay."

"All right."

"Still on for Saturday? Gretchen?"

"Uh, yeah. Listen, I don't—"

"A favor for me, okay?"

"Okay."

"Besides, you might like it." David smiled, patted Joshua on the back. He felt a warm burn where David's palm had touched him, held it, tried to memorize the smell of David as he passed, the pattern of a freckle cluster on his neck.

He had expected to go further, not through any hint of desire on Gretchen's part, but from the smooching sounds coming from the front seat of Brenda's car, which David drove after having parked his truck at her house. That he maintained an erection while fondling Gretchen had less to do with her shy responsive clutching at his shoulder than the sounds coming from the front seat, little wet slurps that he knew were made by David's tongue along parts of Brenda's body. He could nearly smell David through Gretchen's cloud of Love's Baby Soft and tightened his embrace.

But he would have performed better had he not encountered Brent Carse the previous day. Brent had caught Joshua's eye when he nearly bumped into him way down at the gym end of the school.

"Oh, hey," Brent said as he stepped out of a door. Beyond it, all Joshua could see was a dark red light.

"Whatcha doin'?" Joshua asked.

"Oh, just gettin' some shots for the yearbook. I got a lot of shots. Got some of you."

"What from?"

"That honor roll thing last month. Candid shots."

"Oh yeah?" Joshua had already forgotten that achievement, although his mother had the Harrison-gram attached to the refrigerator with a magnet.

"You should come by the darkroom sometime. Pick up some shots. I can make you prints."

"Oh yeah? That'd be great."

When he got to the darkroom after the three o'clock bell, Brent welcomed him in like a secret agent. He showed him the picture of himself.

"It's neat. Thanks."

"You like it?"

"Yeah, it's . . . natural."

"I like to capture people when they're just themselves."

Joshua liked that. The only pictures he had of himself were yearbook portraits and corny posed Instamatic and Polaroid shots at birthday parties and barbecues. This picture, a grainy black and white print, was of Joshua sitting in English class raising his hand. Brent had taken it through the little glass window in the classroom door.

"You spend a lot of time in here?" Joshua asked.

"Sometimes I just forget about going home and print for hours."

"Hmm."

"Just work on stuff and jack off."

"What?"

"I jack off in here. Ya wanna?" Joshua's gut did a double half-gainer as a surge of blood rushed to his groin.

"No way." Brent was really cute, but Joshua knew that he couldn't jack off with a guy. Then everyone would know he was a fag. Brent could not be a fag. He was on the baseball team.

"S'okay," Brent shrugged. "Maybe some other time."

"Yeah, right." His erection prevented walking comfortably, so Joshua stayed in the darkroom with Brent for a while watching him print photos. Had he really jacked off in here? Was that just a fake-out? Would he ask again? If he had, Joshua might have agreed. It was dark, and Brent did have a key. The door was locked.

But Brent seemed to take his rebuffed proposal in stride and gave Joshua a print of the photo.

After leaving Brent to his darkroom "activities," Joshua was two blocks from walking home when he realized he'd forgotten his books, but by then he didn't care. So dismayed was he as he remembered the impending date with Gretchen that he almost thought to bail out of it. Nevertheless, with this blood-rushing Brent-trauma of frustration behind him, he forged on with fair Gretchen in the back seat of the car.

"No," she whispered as she removed his hand from her breast. Was he supposed to be demanding?

He wasn't, but said, "Let's go take a walk."

She looked at him suspiciously. "No tricks."

"Alright." He reached over her lap to open the car door for her.

"Where you guys goin'?" David's head popped up over the front seat like a Sesame Street muppet. His hair was disheveled, his face flushed.

"We need some air, and you need some privacy."

"Don't go tippin' any cows."

"Get bent."

Walking out into the night, Joshua felt the cool breeze against his skin, smelled the odor of cow manure and rotting corn furrows. A low rumble echoed across the horizon. Immense thunderclouds loomed over the night.

"Look at the sky," he said. "Isn't that a beautiful Beethoven sky?"

"Beethoven sky?" Gretchen asked.

"Yeah, doncha think it looks like a Beethoven symphony, all dark and brooding but clear?"

"I suppose so," she said. "You're really into music, aren't you?"

"Yeah, but not classical. I wanna be in a rock band someday. You?"

"Oh, I'm just in stage band for the fun of it."

"But don't you wanna do something with it? All those years of study?"

"Not really."

Joshua did not know how to respond to that, how she could not have a vision, have wild hopes. Gretchen suddenly seemed to him a blank slate. Maybe she just wanted to have a family. He realized that he might be even more different from his classmates, how truly unusual were his desires, beyond just kissing boys.

He took her hand as they watched the purple sky and the clusters of stars, holding it as a gesture of friendship, knowing that she could deduce more, if she cared to. Far off, I-70 hummed with the distant rumble of semi trucks. Joshua considered placing another kiss on Gretchen, just to show an air of persistence. He was saved from any further heterosexual impersonations by a large loud *crack!* from across the field.

Joshua had seen lightning smack down violently on country fields before, but never so close. Gretchen jumped out of his hand, and emitted a small "Oh!" which, at the time, made him think of Dorothy Gale at the moment her house landed in Munchkinland.

The jolt had spat out its line of white electricity just over the hill, and after the two recovered from the shock of its proximity, they noticed a small cloud of smoke. It curled up into the sky near Margie Silvanus's house, or rather, closer to the antenna of that oddball Christian family with the radio show.

Chapter 12

ANOTHER ONE BITES THE DUST

THE TOWN OF Serene, Ohio had never seen much controversy. That is, of course, until the night God fried Kelly Seifering.

Alarmed by the lightning flash, David had driven them toward it, a small billowing black cloud, and on the far ground, a contorted body, blackened and still smoking. Only David dared to step closer, as the other three clung together by the roadside.

Brenda and Gretchen were a mess. Joshua had never seen a girl cry so hard, and he held her close, holding back his own shock while David returned and talked softly with Brenda, wiping her face occasionally with his hand.

"What do we do?" Joshua asked.

"The house is dark. I could break in to call an ambulance, but . . . it's too late. Josh, c'mere." He led Joshua away from the girls, who returned to the car.

"I think it's that girl in the fight, remember?"

"Kelly?"

"I think so."

Joshua wanted to rush to the body, but his fear took over. "She said they had a radio show. This must be it." He looked up at the twenty-foot steel and wire apparatus.

Eventually, Mabel and Orin Seifering came home from a revival meeting at their local Baptist Church. They seemed almost defensive about the presence of the four teenagers, until David explained the lightning flash. After rushing to the prone body of their step-daughter, the Seiferings retreated into their house, Orin Seifering comforting his wife as she muttered a few quiet sobs.

He returned to walk across the yard. "Please come in and pray with us."

"We're fine," David said, looking toward the car. "We really oughtta—"

"Well, thank you, then. I must go in." Before walking off, Orin Seifering offered David and Joshua a concerned glance.

An ambulance arrived, and closely behind it, a few cars. One of them had a photographer, but not from the police, who were there as well. It was a reporter from *The Serene Gazette*, one of three that arrived.

"Oh, thank you for coming," Orin Seifering said.

Joshua was not sure why the man said that, but then he realized something that cut off his tears as quick as a drought. Kelly's stepfather had called the newspaper. What kind of parent would do such a thing?

Fighting back tears, Mabel found the strength for a few brief words with a local news reporter. "It's just God's will to take her away so young. It's a message from Him. That's all I can say."

Despite the family tragedy, Mabel vowed to go on spreading the Gospel through her words. Orin announced that his show would be making calls for a fundraiser to get them a functional lightning rod for their antenna just as soon as possible.

"We will not let God's taking away our dear foster-daughter keep us from giving out God's message." The reporter offered a perplexed stare, but kept writing on a notepad.

They didn't hear much else after the police told them to get back in Brenda's car. Date night was pretty much finished.

They dropped Gretchen off at her family's ranch house, where the porch light flicked on at their arrival and a parent swept her back inside, thus eliminating Joshua's need to apply a goodnight kiss to her prim lips. It didn't seem right to kiss a girl goodnight after she had seen her first dead body. Joshua didn't feel so good either.

David dropped Brenda off with little fanfare, they switched to his truck, which he'd left on the street near her house, and Joshua took the shotgun seat. He felt relieved by the familiar gurgle of the truck's old engine, the scent of David and dirt.

The two boys drove back out into the country in silence, as if radar had honed their instincts to a certain spot. Despite or because of that night's tragedy, neither of them was eager to get home and relay the evening's events.

Once parked, David flicked off the motor but pushed the key back. They could not speak in the silence of his old truck. The tape deck lit up again, and David put in a slow dirging piece of music, something by Merle Haggard. Joshua never liked country music, but at the time it seemed just right. Their minds unleashed with the aid of cannabis, they talked while, in hundreds of nearby homes, people would soon sit fascinated by the local news told on the radio or TV.

There had been teen deaths before. A year earlier, a young Roy Stitzel, working weekends in the town's pipe factory, had fallen into a bit of machinery and been chopped to pieces. A few farm accidents had occurred, and no less than three drunk driving fatalities in the last ten years. Each event was treated with an appalling sense of dread, the empty desk haunting their classrooms for weeks afterward. No kid would sit in that seat unless forced to. Dead kids become mythologized in these parts.

Kelly's death made front-page news in Serene, as did any fatality. Talk accompanied it over dinner in every house. By the next school day, the desks Kelly sat in each period were avoided by wary eyes. I sat precariously near one such desk. Although she had been absent for weeks, suddenly other students had compelling and intimate stories to tell. I considered them all rubbish.

Even the news articles were suspicious, as was the County Coroner's report. The investigation lasted all of five minutes, since the cause of death was deemed accidental electrocution. No authority questioned Mabel and Orin Seifering any further beyond getting the voltage of their radio tower and the personal details about the incinerated girl.

Did anyone ask to verify the whereabouts of the foster parents? No, because they, of course, were, and still are, God-fearing Christians, on their way back from church when they had car trouble.

Well, all I can say is, *How convenient.*

Chapter 13

IN THE LAP OF THE GODS

"THE ADDAMS FAMILY."

"What?"

"This place is like the Addams Family."

David's whispered comment would have made Joshua laugh were it not for the fact that they were at the Donn Funeral Home with Kelly's body lying in a closed coffin in the other room. With their ties nearly choking them, it felt even more uncomfortable.

Since Kelly was not a popular girl, not even known well enough to be unpopular, there was no rush to attend her funeral, a quick affair that took place that Monday afternoon, unlike the funeral of cheerleader Debbie Schantz, who had died in one of many drunk-driving accidents in Serene County. Debbie had been a popular girl, even more so in death, and had attracted students in droves to grieve for their "dear departed friend."

But David and Joshua were the only students at Kelly's funeral. The rest were devotees of Orin and Mabel Seifering's radio program and church services, squat women and stolid men thickened by the smugness of their beliefs. They listened with rapt attention as Orin Seifering took the podium. "Gawwd works in mysterious ways."

"Here it comes," David whispered.

"And it is such a mysterious way that he called our young Kelly to Him, to be by His side," Seifering continued. "True, she was no angel, and I cannot help but fear for her soul, knowing that she must now be standing before the angel Gabriel to answer for her many sins."

David coughed, but just barely verbalized through it the word "bullshit." It came out "Brrshtt!"

"She was a good Christian girl who loved her parents dearly," Orin said.

"No she didn't. She hated you all," Joshua muttered to himself. A large woman turned in the pew in front of him, peeved at his outburst. Joshua had made the foolish decision to join David in a pre-funeral joint.

Orin Seifering spoke clearly and without trembling, as if this were merely a grand opportunity for him to preach before a live audience, unlike his endless radio blatherings.

"Sin—"

"Oh, man," David whispered.

"—can take a life worth living and make it misery. We tried to help Kelly, and considered it our Christian duty to take her in and straighten her out. Unfortunately, God had a different plan, and took her from us in this most unfortunate way, perhaps as a message to our youth. A warning about the corruption and drugs that threaten to turn our fair town into a den of malicious evil and craven behavior . . ."

David rolled his eyes at Joshua, then whispered, "What's being toasted have to do with getting toasted?"

Joshua erupted in a burst of barely controlled laughter, which he quickly converted to a faked sneeze-choke of grief. He could not cry then and there, and for a moment felt insincere, but then he realized Kelly would have been proud of him and David.

At home, his mother asked about the service. She thought it was appropriate that the boys go unescorted, although it was a serious affair. She felt proud when he returned from the church without losing his tie.

But the topic was never discussed again. It never broke the silence of their afternoons together. Sara Evans was no longer Joshua's confessor. He had found his own secrets too heavy for afternoon chats before Dad came home. Joshua could not face his mother. The combination of grief, morbidity, and hypocrisy from Orin Seifering made him want to swear and laugh at the same time. Having gotten stoned with David beforehand had made it both worse and better at the same time.

But days later, when the weekend came, he spilled his anger in a two-beer rage while coasting up Route 410 with David. They drove to the newer mall to see a movie.

They had already smoked a joint earlier, then cooled out. David never drove when he was high. That is a point that people who like to place blame often forget. Some people can handle their highs. David was good at that. The truth, however, does not get around in Serene. Never did, especially between the pews. Joshua knew that.

"She showed me scars from where they beat her," Joshua seethed.

"C'mon," David soothed, putting his arm around Joshua's shoulder.

"She killed herself!" he blurted.

But even Joshua could not know that to be entirely true. His stomach blocked it, felt sour in his gut.

As for the others, the town was not in total shock. It became a bit of a joke, actually. While awaiting the repairs on their radio tower, Orin and Mabel continued in their persistent industrial manner. They went to cable access.

The Beekam College student television station was offering enterprising locals a chance to produce their own shows. Somehow, arms had been twisted enough to offer free airtime to Orin and Mabel's show, since they were a non-profit religious organization, all donations tax-deductible.

The couple began each broadcast by showing only one image: Kelly's junior class portrait. People watched it sometimes like a poor Our Lady of Guadalupe: holy on the same level that a televised fireplace was warm. So the townspeople forgot about Kelly's death—until people from outside turned a hungry gaze their way. What had been the unfortunate death of a young girl became a crusade, a curiosity repeated on a few Columbus newscasts that sculpted her into a posthumous saint, though there was no local Catholic congregation to canonize her. Baptists, Presbyterians, even Methodists had their flocks—and the Amish, of course, but they didn't count since they all lived so far from town and didn't own televisions.

At first, Joshua didn't come forward with his information and did not feel compelled to. It was his silent secret, held among himself and David and the girls from date night until a swarm of locusts invaded, the kind with cameras and microphones.

Among the media stringers who had latched onto the tale from the larger regional paper was Garrett Glass of *Cleveland Today*, a "news magazine" broadcast on a Northern Ohio CBS affiliate. Eager to stretch his touching five-minute human-interest story into ten, he decided to quiz the youth of the town, since he was an admirer of youthful talent.

Girls who'd never met Kelly cried on cue in front of the camera, claiming to be her best friend and how they missed her. The taping was done at the local mini-mall with a JC Penney, not the newer bigger mall in Lancaster. Yet the girls lined up like novices at a *Star Search* audition. Glass's last interview was with Joshua, who had no intention of talking to a TV crew.

The smaller mall's musical instrument store had advertised a sale, including electric organs and baby grand pianos. David had to work on the farm that Saturday, so under the guise of shopping early for Christmas gifts for his parents and sister (for Dad, a sweater; a small owl sculpture for Mom, who collected them; and earrings for his sister, all of which took less than an hour to find), Joshua then headed for the music shop, knowing a purchase would be impossible but a visit would be fun.

Thanksgiving had yet to take place, but holiday carols echoed through the mall's sound system, and giant plastic candy canes hung over walkways. Joshua briskly passed a giant lit tree and a small "Closed" Santa village carpeted with puffy fake snow.

Outside the music shop's entrance, a shiny black baby grand Yamaha piano had been pushed out into the walkway. Next to it, green and red garland wrapped around a sign declaring Low Monthly Payments.

The TV crew drew a small cluster of curious people on the other side of a group of benches. Joshua avoided them and headed inside, waited until he caught the attention of an older balding salesman in a red and green sweater vest.

"Sir, may I play that?" He pointed to the Yamaha.

"Are you any good?"

Feeling cocky, he replied, "Want to find out?"

The salesman smirked, waved him permission.

Taking off his jacket, he thought to lay it on the ground, then folded it on the bench beside him. He looked around, wishing David had been there to cheer him on. But then, realizing he knew no one nearby, he relaxed.

Nothing really matters.

He hadn't finished his arrangement of "Bohemian Rhapsody," having yet to decide how to transfer the guitar-heavy parts and the melody, but he didn't care. If it wasn't a holiday-themed song, nobody would notice. The echo from the first chords made him think few would pay attention anyway. He sang it in his head, then luxuriated in the piano parts between lyrics, humming a bit. Was someone behind him singing softly? He kept playing.

Gotta leave you all behind and face the truth . . .

By the phrases of "Thunderbolt and lightning," he felt an audience had grown. Don't look up, he told himself, or you'll lose your place, which he did, twice. As he reached the banging finale, though, he softened, tried to find a more delicate version, and yes, people were singing, standing still, paying rapt attention until the last andante ending.

There. Done it.

As the onlookers applauded, Joshua saw the TV camera had been aimed at him.

The reporter, a microphone in his hand, approached, waving the cameraman along, who fumbled with a tripod.

"That was amazing!" he beamed.

"Thank you."

"Garrett Glass, of *Cleveland Today*. Can we do a quick interview?"

"Um, okay." Joshua noticed that the man had a tan or make-up on his face while his neck was pale.

"Your playing, I'll have to get that to a producer. We didn't get it all. We're actually here doing interviews about the recent tragedy."

"Which one?"

"Did you know Kelly Seifering?"

"Yes." Joshua felt a small surge of suspicion.

"What kind of girl was she?"

"A hood."

"What's that?"

"You know, she partied."

"How did you hear of her death?"

"We were on a date, my friend, er, with girls, and we heard the crash, um, we thought it was lightning, then we drove to it and saw her, and anyway, she wasn't the kind of girl everybody's makin' her out to be."

"How do you mean?"

"She was— Can you turn that light off a minute?"

"Oh, sure. Manny." The light went off.

He told Glass about the Kelly he knew. The man's eyes bulged. Garrett Glass looked around the mall, as if waiting for the man who left the attaché case with twenty thousand dollars to reclaim it before he snatched it up.

"Listen, what's your name?"

"Joshua Lee Evans."

"Josh, boy, this is bigger than just what we're doing, do you get what I'm saying?"

"Oh, Gary, not again," the cameraman moaned.

"Shut up, Manny." He leaned close to the boy and handed him a card. "We'd like to call you in a few days and bring you up to Cleveland to do a TV spot. Maybe play that Queen song again in the studio."

"Uh, I dunno if I can."

"Never mind. We'll talk details later. Give me your address and phone number. We'll be calling you very soon. Okay?"

"Sure." Joshua did not believe him, but he gave him his information anyway.

The music shop's salesman approached, patted Joshua on a shoulder, and told him he could come by and play any time he liked.

As he watched the TV men pack up and leave for another location shot, he felt assured that somehow something was going to happen, and it was going to help things, or at least rip some things wide open. Then again, the guy would probably forget all about him. He was probably some pervert.

Joshua drove home along the four-lane road that gutted through the town ever since the new mall was built. He reasoned that he could handle a bit of fame. That was not the problem.

He figured it would be the best way to get his mom and dad's attention. Sure, he could sit by them in the living room, talking as he went over his homework or banged away at the piano, but their eyes would usually remain on the tube, asking him to help out with the next round of *Jeopardy*. He liked the show, thought Alex Trebek was handsome, and enjoyed trying to one-up his sister on answers. It was good for homework, history and stuff, but he did not feel they were listening.

He could spend nights giggling away to *Rhoda* or *M*A*S*H* or whatever was on, and tell the best jokes in school the next day to a few of his other quiet, non-athletic friends. He could listen half-interestedly over his Cream of Wheat each morning and enjoy current events as told by an early morning Barbara Walters while his mother planned her day. That, and talks after school before dinner, used to be their time together, even if most of that chat was about filling him in on the latest story, his father's newest hardware debacle, his mother's latest art project.

But he felt he couldn't really just talk to them anymore, except to ask for things: a ride to school, some money, PTA attendance, more money, sheet music, and more money. He wanted to be able to honestly say, "Mom, Dad, I'm in love with David and we're going to be married."

But then he realized perhaps even David didn't want to hear that.

Going on TV seemed the only logical step to take.

Chapter 14

MY FAIRY KING

THE QUARTET OF boy-men rode in Ed Wallenbeck's van to witness the rock and roll theatrics of the world's foremost British post-glam rock group one November Saturday night, two days after Thanksgiving. Ed drove his Chevy van at a cool sixty miles per hour, Ed's friend Chris Harpster sat up front, while Joshua sat on the carpeted floor in the back with David.

Joshua kept stealing glances at David's recently cut blond hair, more accurately, his newly exposed neck, his marble blue eyes, his stubby nose and just about the most beautiful, pouting red lips a guy could have. He became flushed just sitting in back with David in the van's warmth. David frequently lay back, a hint of his belly exposed when his Queen T-shirt rode up as he lay atop his coat. Not having the steering wheel of David's truck to distance them left Joshua feeling awkwardly close, as if with any bump he might land in David's lap. The frequently passed joints filled the van with a dense cloud of sweet smoke, until Chris cracked the window.

David got tired of passing the joint to the front. Chris dropped it twice on the plastic cup holder between him and Ed who, being the designated driver, took only one hit.

"I wonder how they're gonna do 'Bohemian Rhapsody,'" Chris said.

"I heard they use a tape for part of it," Ed said.

"They wouldn't," Joshua said.

"How they gonna get all them voices? They overdub that stuff on the album."

"That's cheatin'," Chris declared. "They use a tape, I want my money back." Chris was a sometime stoner who'd graduated the year before. He had a hearing problem, which made him talk loudly.

"Yeah, right." Ed said. "You gonna go to the manager?"

"Well. I'll complain."

"C'mon," David nudged Joshua, and they headed back to the dark end of the van near the back door.

"Sounds better, huh?" he nudged toward the speakers installed in the walls of the van. WMMS played a nonstop tribute to Queen, especially for concert-goers, but also for those unable to attend.

"Yup," Joshua added in his most convincing Gary Cooper. Thrilled to be close to David, and pretty much out of sight of Ed and Chris, he glanced back as they watched the road. The music pumped loudly as David popped another beer, took a swig and offered it to Joshua. He took pleasure in gulping from the can to taste David's spit along with the beer. From the look of David's sly grins, he knew it.

David lay back again, relit a joint and took a long toke, then exhaled. He sat up and gave it to Joshua. It was moist with more of his spit. Joshua was getting a hard on.

As he handed the joint back, David did something Joshua had never done but had seen before, said, "Shotgun." He put the joint in his mouth backwards, then pulled Joshua close to him, as if to kiss him. Instinctively Joshua puckered his own lips and brought them within an inch of David's. The smoke exuded from his lips in a thin trail. He sucked in slowly, letting the smoke seep into his lungs.

The reefer high sang through his body as the radio pumped "Fat-Bottomed Girls," not his favorite, although Ed and Chris were singing along with joy. David took the joint out of his lips and glanced down at Joshua's crotch.

Did he notice? David looked up and smiled, then his brow

furrowed with concern as the joint coal sputtered to a halt. He sucked the last of it into his mouth and leaned toward Joshua again. They puckered up, drawing in the smoke. There was no rolling paper between them this time.

The moment David exhaled the last of the smoke into Joshua's mouth, the van hit a bump. David fell toward him slightly and their lips met. Finally, those thick full lips pressed to him. They closed their eyes. He felt David's tongue seep past his lips and touch his own.

Before he knew it, David's arm wrapped around him and pressed him to the floor. The warm rumblings of the van vibrated below. Their tongues dug into each other, licking and pushing. He pressed his palm against Joshua's crotch, kneading his jutting dick under denim. Joshua reached up to grab David's crotch, which was equally hard.

Chris said something up front. The two boys looked up. Fortunately, Chris had not looked back. They pulled apart, sat up and stared at each other, shocked with lust.

Then they both broke up laughing and David fell on top of Joshua.

"Hey, what are you guys doin' back there?" Chris called out.

"Rasslin'!" yelled David as he groped under Joshua's crotch at the hard dent in his jeans. He wrapped his other arm around his friend and they laughed, rolling around together.

They did not speak again for a while, but with sly grins and a string of exchanged glances, Joshua knew David was just starting. Cross-legged, their knees nudging together, David secretly grazed his fingers up inside the back of Joshua's shirt.

"Why now?" Joshua leaned close.

"Why not? 'Cause I'm high, and feelin' good, and, well, I been too chicken to do it before."

"But when did you think . . . ?"

"That day in the boy's room; you couldn't stop starin' at me." He nudged Joshua, grinned.

Finally. It didn't matter that he was still dating Brenda. All those months of getting to know each other, talking around it, didn't matter. That they laughed it off didn't matter, because they both knew.

"Almost there," Ed announced. Up ahead on the highway turnoff, cars slowed to line up. Joshua and David broke their intimate huddle, crawled forward to lean over the seats and look out the windshield. Before them loomed the gauntlet, the palace, the tower: Richfield Coliseum.

"Here we go," said Chris.

They joined the trail of red taillights that glowed in the night like a twinkling necklace of rubies.

The stomping began, for real this time.

The *boom, boom, clap!* had been led by cheerleaders at basketball games the previous winter. But they'd never heard it in such a large space, this great dark arena littered with the flames of a thousand lighters in a massive cloud of cigarette and marijuana smoke. Joshua truly rushed, stomped along. He felt aligned in tremors of anticipation with the entire audience as he stood between David and Ed, with Chris on the aisle seat.

The band took the stage.

Preening like a rowdy nancy boy, Freddie Mercury became a virtual echo of Joshua's pent-up queer rage. He screamed with every high note, singing every line of every song with absolute devotion. Stage lights flared green, red, and yellow, with Mercury prancing with pride, calming for the acoustic sections, then, as the more rousing songs were played, dancing more on a sleek metal unit of stairs, each lit by a row of lights. It was the *Jazz* tour, and Joshua stomped loudly, feeling an anticipation of his own imagined fame.

During the concert, David stood next to him, pressing his side against him, secretively grazing his hand, or openly wrapping an arm around his shoulder. Through David's persistence in getting the tickets the day they became available, the four had snagged choice seats on the stadium floor only twenty rows from the stage. But few people on the arena floor sat down.

Joshua felt incredibly close to David, their bodies almost connected. David's body pressed against his. He felt a slight nudge and David's thick hand holding on to his waist, his breath on the side of his neck as he sang to him, an excuse to lean close.

They watched Freddie Mercury prance about, belting out notes with precise beauty, even if some of them were sung in a lower range than the recorded versions. Eventually shirtless, with a red tie and tight black leather pants, Mercury's stylish look made Joshua laugh at first.

Brian May's guitar solos curled about the songs with a rococo flair, and induced by both his sudden passion for David and the pot haze, it seemed to Joshua that May's flowing sleeves floated like wings. The two boys were entranced and sang along with the audience, full and loud to every song, through the rousing call and response break in "Now I'm Here."

After "Keep Yourself Alive," the band left the stage, but the audience knew what lay ahead, the encore, the big one, the song that pushed the boundaries of rock music and radio, and every one of their lives, especially Joshua's. His voice already hoarse, he hooted and screamed and stomped with the others, demanding it, requiring it: the operetta, the signature.

Lights went up on the stage again, and the crowd's hoots soared into a victorious cheer then simmered down as Freddie Mercury sat at the piano, the men resumed their positions, singing in the sweetest harmony.

"Is this the real life? Is this just fantasy . . ."

The boys sang along to "Bohemian Rhapsody," the crowd did as well, and all were entranced. Joshua saw only Mercury's head over the piano, but he knew where Freddie's fingers were going, the delicate layer of chords.

But then, as they approached the strange and beautiful vocal section, the middle operatic break, the stage lights went black, and blue spots whirled about the arena. People screamed and hooted appreciation, but Joshua frowned in confusion, scanning the darkened stage. Where were they? No one stood at the microphones. They weren't even playing, let alone singing. This section was on tape.

By the time the smoke exploded and Freddie once again pranced about while Brian May whirled into the final section's chords, Joshua felt a bit more of the joy of the great song. But inside, he felt betrayed and disappointed. They made that music. Why couldn't they play it live? How could they cop out on their greatest song?

But after a short break, and a lot of foot stomping in the crowd, the band returned and brought the energy back with five more songs, including a revved up version of "We Will Rock You" and "We Are the Champions," during which most people waved their hands. The recorded "God Save the Queen" closer signaled the end of the concert.

As the dull arena lights snapped on, signaling the end of the encores, the boys shuffled back up the aisles and stairways amid the subdued throng. Joshua reached up to his head. The muffled sound made him think someone had put a cap over his ears.

David smiled. "Wait till you get outside."

"Huh?"

He smiled knowingly at Ed, who grinned, then stuck his fingers in his ears, as if he could pick out the ringing.

Even though the wait was several minutes, they had to piss. David and Joshua stood next to each other in the crammed men's room line, then shared a stall and peed together. Joshua felt dizzy and weak, yet purged, and strengthened somehow. The ringing in his ears persisted.

"Now you know."

"Jeez, it's like there's a doorbell in there and it's stuck."

"Yeah," David said.

"They didn't even play 'God Save the Queen' live."

"Yeah, well, whaddaya gonna do."

Joshua's disappointment slid away as he watched David unbutton his fly. They fell silent as they tried to relax enough to pee, but they both got half-erections and almost couldn't manage it. Finished, David stuffed his cock into his fly, embarrassed.

"Jeez, I gotta get together with you real soon." David said as they finished up. Joshua reached for the stall door, but David pushed his hand aside and stole a wet kiss.

In the parking lot, guys were holding up bootleg T-shirts for sale. Joshua found one with the swan logo on it, not as good as David's, but he bought it anyway, since it was only ten dollars.

Driving home was awkward, almost sullen, as they waited for a long time in the snaking line of red tail lights out of the parking lot. Chris kept bitching about the show, and only Joshua agreed about the taped section.

"And what was with the leather shit? Mercury is such a fag."

"Shut up!" Joshua blasted.

"What's your problem?"

"Of course he's a fag!" Joshua defended. "What do you think the name of the group means?"

"What? They're British."

"Josh . . ." David held his arm, but Joshua leaned forward in the van, getting closer to Chris, too close to Ed, who was trying to drive.

"A queen is a fag. Jesus, you are so dumb."

"What?"

But Joshua fell back in the van, brooding. How could he explain that he knew what the leather meant? That it all was so obvious but he couldn't tell them?

"I think you oughtta let the fag here walk home," Chris said to Ed.

"I think you better shut the fuck up," David shouted.

"Let's all shut the fuck up," Ed said. "Or else you're gonna

130

make me wreck this thing." Ed snapped on the radio. An Eric Clapton guitar solo cut their anger. No one spoke for quite a while.

Both David and Joshua longed to be alone, to huddle somewhere, anywhere, but Joshua's parents expected him home. And David's father? Probably drunk and asleep, but David lived far from town and had to keep his ride with Ed.

"Hey, tomorrow's Sunday. I'll see you in a few hours."

Home; soundless, but for the ticking of the living room wall clock.

As he cautiously crept in, Joshua's father sat under a single lamp, reading a newspaper, or pretending to, in his pajamas and a dark blue robe.

"You didn't drink, did you?"

"A few beers."

"Did Dave drink?"

"Yes, but he didn't drive. Ed did. I told you."

"Did Ed drink?"

"No, Dad. Ed never drinks when he's driving. He still has to pay off his van. He's not about to wreck that thing. He just put in new carpeting and speakers."

Joshua's father folded his newspaper, stood. "I'm very good with you, aren't I, letting you do this? There's a responsibility that comes with it."

"I know, and I appreciate it. It meant a lot for me to see this concert."

"Well, get to bed. Your mother wants us to get started on the Christmas tree in the garage tomorrow. Bright and early, you're gonna trim it and set it up."

"Yes, sir."

His father headed up the stairs. Joshua peeled off his coat. The T-shirt he had bought in the parking lot after the concert fell to the floor.

How was he supposed to care about a Christmas tree when he was in love with his best friend? The T-shirt would guide him. He could wear it proudly in school on Monday. His T-shirt, his royal seal, his swan, would guard him from any interference, serve as his silent declaration.

I got this the night David kissed me.

Chapter 15

YOU'RE MY BEST FRIEND

THE DAY JOSHUA almost got suspended with David, the boys visited the school darkroom at the invitation of Brent Carse. David and Joshua sometimes snuck a cigarette in the photo lab at lunch. The darkroom had a motorized ventilator that helped mask the smell, but also Brent seemed like a flirt. Greg Dellerba also showed up once and brought a joint, but only he and David got high, and Greg did not flirt. Joshua knew he would explode in giggles if he got high before school was out.

"And then you put it in the fixer," Brent narrated his process of printing a photo, again. "Smell this."

"What?" Joshua feigned disgust.

"No, c'mon, smell it."

Joshua sniffed the wet strip of film and the silver canister; a cool bubbly soapy smell, almost sweet.

"That's Photoflo."

"What's it do?" David sat on the other side of the lab atop a counter.

"Washes the chemicals off so it stops developing."

"Huh."

"I took a picture of my dick once."

"Really?"

"Hard."

Joshua snapped. "You think I'm gay or something? Do I look gay?"

"I don't know. What would you look like straight?"

The room felt stuffy all of a sudden. The bell rang.

"Gotta go," Brent said. "Don't forget to lock the door."

"Okay, see you at lunch, maybe."

The two sat up on the black marble tabletop. Joshua waited, a bit nervous, since the subject had been so stupidly blurted out. Privacy was theirs, but not bravery. They kissed for a few minutes, but held back from peeling off any clothes.

"You think he knows about us?"

"I think he's got an idea."

"Huh." Joshua wondered if David knew more about Brent but changed the subject. "We should celebrate, show off, somehow, without really—"

"Hold hands?"

"Too easy. I heard some of the college frat guys streaked naked at the college."

David shrugged. "Okay."

"What if you get caught?"

"Who cares? I get suspended a few days. We're graduating this year. I will streak the halls naked if you will . . . get high and blow me in the middle of a school day."

"Easy," Joshua grinned.

"In the school."

"But—"

David pressed on. "And not in the photo lab, a rest room, or the parking lot."

"Shit." Joshua paused a moment. "You're on."

"It's a bet."

"Where are we gonna do it?" Joshua asked.

"What?"

"Get high."

"I dunno. Someplace . . . someplace cool."

William Henry Harrison High School was built in the 1920s first as a theater, then with the school built around it a few decades later. Our local historical society has a collection of vintage programs and photographs of the then-famous opera singers and "decent" Vaudevillian performers who graced The Serene Theater's sizable stage. After World War II, the town size expanded with the increase in post-war children, and the small school-houses that dotted the town and outskirts couldn't match the need, so schoolrooms and a gymnasium were built around the theatre.

That explains the clash of styles between hallways and the auditorium. The orchestra pit, where I sat many nights playing the harp, glockenspiel, and other assorted instruments through our school's mediocre productions of Rodgers and Hammerstein musicals, offers an unusual angle up to the rafters of the theater, whose catwalk and roof, for some odd reason, became Joshua's daring location for their adventure.

"I'm scared," Joshua giggled as they ascended the ladder that led them to the dust-laden heights above the stage floor.

"This was your bet," David whispered as he found an uneasy foothold on the metal grid above it all. He helped Joshua up the last rung of the ladder. "You never seemed too scared."

"You don't think I'm scared other times?"

"Like when?"

He huffed, a bit exhausted. The air was stuffy, so close to the ceiling.

"Like with you. Driving around, wondering' when I'm gonna be able to . . . wondering when you're gonna dump me out the car when we go drivin'. When you're gonna get sick of me."

"Why would I do that?"

"I dunno. Just c'mon."

"I can't."

"Just don't look down."

"C'mon, let's go back."

"No, we're gonna go up on the roof," Joshua declared.

"Now *I'm* scared."

"C'mon, Davey," Joshua taunted in his Goliath voice. "We

can be scared together. I play on your terms all the time. This is
my turf, it's my turn." He found a strange surge of bravado, began jumping, darting about between beams like Gene Kelly
hopping rain puddles.

"Stop that."

"C'mon." He hopped back to David, enjoying this feeling of
power, superiority over his love, now frightened out of his wits.
Joshua took his hand and led him over. They wobbled a moment
on the large beam. David grabbed for Joshua, his arms around
him. He would have swooned, but he was too busy trying to
remember this smell, the dust mixed with David's sweat.

Joshua leaned against a column, and David leaned toward
him. Their lips sort of fell together again, despite their every
effort to avoid its inevitability.

Joshua fought the dizziness in his chest and head. The salty
taste of David's mouth wasn't at all like Gretchen's, whose thin
little lips had felt waxy with lip gloss. He preferred the taste of
David, accidental, messy, sudden.

Fortunately, despite their passionate clutching embrace, neither boy fell between the beams.

It was a chilly afternoon in the first week of December, about
2:30. Both had carefully arranged excuses, Joshua's being a fic-
tional extra piano lesson, David's a new shipment of fertilizer to
unload on his farm. Both shared the skill of imitating adult
handwriting and stealing the proper stationary. It was only one
period, but still, it felt as if they had accomplished a great caper.

"This way."

They found the escape hatch to the roof, crawled through it,
and stood imperiously atop their own school. Being such an ar-
chitectural relic, the top of the building was unadorned, flat, yet
trimmed around the edges with crests and crenellated like a castle. Gravel not stuck to the tar roof crunched under their feet with
glassy bits of ice and snow. David stepped to the edge and pulled
off his shirt. Joshua noticed his waist was slim, his nipples small

and dark pink. He was like a young princeling atop his father's estate.

"You're gonna freeze," Joshua shivered.

"No, I won't."

Their hands were all over each other, and before they knew it, their lips met, wet and messy. David pulled his pants down and let his dick swing free, then he did the same for Joshua. They nudged up against one another, then David crouched down, licking a trail downward, and put his mouth around Joshua's erection.

He stopped after a few furtive minutes, just before Joshua exploded, as if he could feel when it was going to happen. They crouched down and had to pull their pants up so their bare butts wouldn't get all over the gravel and ice. Joshua dug his hands deep into David's pants while he figured out how to fit David's erection in his mouth. David guided his head softly, thrusting his hips up until he quivered, burst, gasped, groaned and pulled back.

Joshua wanted to get it all, but gobs of it fell on the tar. He almost managed to swallow all of him, not that he could bear to look down. His eyes were shut tightly, and only once did he open them, to look high up at the cloudy sky, David's head tilted back. He felt a drop run down his neck, already cold.

Standing again, David smacked his lips, tasting Joshua on him. As they zipped up and David pulled his shirt on, it seemed as if no man could harm him, so Joshua thought he deserved a taunting poke.

He did not know then how his playful dare would harm his teen lover. He wanted to forget the game, and wrap him in his arms, confessing his love. Yet, a burst of bravado filled his chest, fighting off the warm joy of the taste of David on his lips. He let out a whoop, started again, until David covered his mouth with a hand and leaned in for a quieting kiss.

Chapter 16

GET DOWN, MAKE LOVE

HIS GREAT SECRET catapulted him from bed each morning. It composed silly tunes in his head as he dressed. It pushed a spring in his booted steps through snowy fields and cracked sidewalks, as if the very ground were one large air hockey board.

Joshua had hoped to spend every day of Christmas break with David, but his father had found him a short-term job at a neighbor's dairy farm. Up at dawn to feed and assist in milking the cows, then shoveling dung and hay for hours, David often grew tired. Early evening make-out sessions in his truck more often left Joshua huddling close as David nodded off to sleep.

When school resumed in January, interrupted by occasional snow days, they found moments to be together between classes. Their secret shoved Joshua's pencil through classes and whisked him through the tedious planes of geometry. It guided him through clouds of teacher lectures and lengthy family dinner conversations at home. Occasionally, in the brief moments he actually shared with David in the halls, it re-ignited with such a force that Joshua felt the entirety of NASA could not have held him on an orbital leash.

Through those cold nights David lay in his little room in that farmhouse on the other side of town, his half of the great secret, nestled beside him on his pillow every night. Joshua lay too, imagining David's hair in his face, his back to his belly, David's butt to his groin, his arm over the hip of his . . .

". . . boyfriend." Joshua whispered for only the pillow to hear.

But they didn't let all that mushy love stuff stand in the way of their secret passion. They pretended to go to movies and the mall on weekend nights (and even some days if they found a remote parking spot), fumbling about in David's truck, the windows coated in steam. Or when the weather blustered through a freezing night, David drove Joshua back to his farm to help attach the slightly cracked canopy to the truck's flatbed. Under its cover, they jostled atop blankets while parked on some township road or back field outside of town. David seemed to know the secret places between farmhouses where not a single light exposed them except the occasional moon.

For weeks through the winter, with the night sky their chilly canopy, they lay together, nuzzled, stroked, licked, and dozed arm in arm. On a few daring afternoons in the muddy wooded back end of his father's land, they leaned against trees, pants down, shirts up, never fully naked, but skin pressed together, lips flushed and wet, arms entangled.

One sleet-filled night when a snowstorm turned into more of a thick rain, as their heat defied the damp outside, they shuffled under a blanket, the padding below them not exactly comfortable. Satiated from simultaneous blowjobs and a little butt-fingering David had taught him, Joshua rearranged himself and nestled close, his head against David's chest.

"What'll we do after school's done?"

"How do you mean?" David brushed his fingers through Joshua's hair.

"I mean, we could move, live together somewhere?"

"Where?"

"I dunno. Columbus?"

"Oh, great."

"Anywhere, you know, where there are people like us."

David heaved a sigh, making Joshua's head rise and fall. "I ain't goin' nowhere. Some day, the farm's gonna be mine."

"But don't you ever think about leaving?"

"All the time."

"So then, why stay?"

"Because I'm part of the land, you know? It's gonna be mine. And yours, if you want it."

"But—"

"You can go be a rock star, and play in a band, do whatever with your music, and I'll be yours when you get back."

"Really?"

"Yup. I broke up with Brenda."

"So, are you, like both?"

"I dunno. It was different, just fun and easier. She's nice and all, but you're . . ." He perked his head up, waited for Joshua to meet his gaze. "You're mine and I'm yours, as long as you want me."

As the weather finally warmed over those bucolic months, the quiet fields just outside of Serene continued to serve as their playground. Any thoughts about their future were set aside for their nights together, the days spent waiting, impatient yet content, thinking nothing would interfere as long as they kept their secret.

"Feel like dancin', dancin', dance the night away," David sang, his pants at his ankles, playfully jutting his hips as his dick and balls flapped about. Hidden away after dusk in another remote field, they had finished a bit abruptly after David's fumbled attempt at a standing unlubricated hump against, and briefly into, Joshua's backside, until he asked David to stop.

"Hey, that reminds me. You still gotta streak." Joshua wiped the dribbles of David's jism from his butt before pulling his pants up.

"This ain't good enough?" David turned, wiggling his butt.

"You promised; at school."

"Alright, if you insist." David shucked his pants on.

It was one promise he should have broken.

Chapter 17

SHEER HEART ATTACK

THEY TIMED THE dare for Tuesday, April 1, during the fitful tidal wave of the three o'clock bell. The plan was simple: from one end of a crowded school hallway, David would run naked in nothing but sneakers and a ski mask with eyeholes to disguise him.

They each forged similar notes for the same excuses. They learned that school administrators are easily fooled by regular patterns. Joshua and David would meet ten minutes before the bell in one of the piano rehearsal rooms.

There, David would quickly strip down to his sneakers and the ski mask. He would take off half a minute before the bell so that mid-streak he would be dashing through the main hallway the moment students poured out of classrooms. Joshua would run across the school lawn, David's clothes in his gym bag, and the two would meet at the other end of the school outside the horticulture back yard, since all the FFA kids got out last period to go work on farms, and David had swiped a key to the greenhouse.

David would dress at the other end of the school, where he had parked his truck, and the two would then drive calmly away and wait until the next day to enjoy the second-hand gossip about their feat.

Moments before the bell, David stood in the small rehearsal room stripped down to nothing but socks and sneakers. Joshua felt a need to play something slow. He also wanted to get on his knees and get David hard as a rock, but figured that would be going too far.

They thought they were alone when they kissed. They did not know that some boys also hid out in music rooms, boys like myself.

Joshua moved his mouth to David's ear, nibbling his lobe. I will never forget that day, that glorious day that David Koenig displayed his perfect body for the entire school to see.

The boys caressed and kissed, and David's short yellow strands of hair must have smelled like the honeysuckle stamens in Joshua's mother's back yard. He wanted to say what it smelled like, but only stuttered, "Sweet."

"Yours too."

"Herbal Essence."

David giggled. "Really? You fag."

"Steal it from my sister. She always complains."

David pulled away before he got too excited.

"Well, here goes." He shucked the black ski mask over his head, leaned in, and gave Joshua a quick peck on the lips. The ski mask brushed Joshua's face.

Joshua stepped out and watched his nude buddy dash off through the hall, his bare butt flexing, turning in midair once, giving Joshua one last beautiful view of his form, his cock bobbing up as he jumped. Then David's feet landed and he was gone.

Joshua sped outside across the schoolyard, but was stopped midstream as he ran into Gretchen Olson full blast, knocking her books in the air. She fell to the sidewalk. He stopped, panicking a moment. He could not stop.

"Uh, sorry, Gretch."

She let out an "Ooooh!" that only truly pissed off girls can do, a sort of low rumble with a sense of humor. Joshua wanted to stop, then did, and helped her up.

By the time he got to the FFA greenhouse, there was no one there. He went back in the exit, and saw David's bare butt flanked by two big teachers, Mr. Hendricks and the Vice-Principal Conway. One pushed him off into a room while the other shooed kids away from the door. Girls screamed and whispered to each other. Guys stared around, asking who it was.

Joshua ran back outside and tried to find the window to the side room where Mr. Hendricks had dragged David. He clutched his gym bag full of David's clothes, and listened near the high window. He could not see, but heard a loud smack.

"You think you're smart, huh?" *Smack.* "You think you're hot stuff, eh? I'll show you what's hot stuff, you little puke." *Smack. Smack.* Joshua heard a slight whimper, followed by the clank of a man's belt buckle.

He did not know whether to run up to the teacher and get David his clothes, or run off and pretend nothing happened. What would David want?

He thought by then the best thing was to fess up and at least get David dressed, even if it meant a whole week of suspension. He could make up the class work.

But as he returned to the door, he found a teacher blocking his way.

"Where are you going? We have a situation going on."

"Back to my locker. I forgot something."

"All right."

The school grounds seemed flooded with kids. They had all been rushed out, and the criminal apprehended and ushered into the principal's office.

Joshua tried to listen nearby, but the glare from the principal's secretary Mrs. Marble shooed him off. He went to his locker, then pretended to get a book, shut the door, and crept back to the office. All was quiet, except the tap of a typewriter in the back office.

Mrs. Marble saw Joshua again, and did not smile.

"Yes, Joshua?"

"Um, did they get Dave?"

"I'm not at liberty to discuss that, young man. What do you need?"

"I . . . wanna give him back his clothes."

"You—? Oh."

Joshua held out the gym bag like an offering. The great se-cret, splayed open like a dissected frog, hung from his hands. Mrs. Marble stood and took the bag, placing it behind her desk.

"I'll make sure he gets them. Now get on home before you get in trouble."

"But, I need to see him—"

"Get home now, you hear?"

Joshua turned and left slowly in a fit of silent fury.

He waited outside the school at the edge of the parking lot. He picked at strands of tall grass, and kicked flattened soda cans and bits of trash. But after half an hour, David did not come out.

A familiar-looking truck did show up, and parked out front, where a very large man in jeans and a worn jacket got out and went into the building. It was David's father.

Minutes later, a police car showed up, and two uniformed cops went into the school. Another half-hour passed before David's father, the two policemen, and David, fully dressed, came out. They stood by David's truck, opened a door, and searched it, took something from the glove compartment. David's father got in his truck without David, who was pushed into the back of the police car. They drove past the silent Joshua, who stood unafraid of being seen. In the back of the car, David did not turn to look back.

Chapter 18

GREAT KING RAT

UNLIKE THE BENEVOLENT and gentle grade school principal Mr. Hudson, who so lightly whacked the boys' butts as mere children, Roland Crumrine, the high school principal, resorted to more drastic measures of punishment. He had called his younger brother Elwood, the Serene County Sheriff.

What Principal Crumrine found upon investigating David's clothes and gym bag was a small bag of pot in the pocket of David's jeans. It was this small plastic wrapped herb, more than the boy's nudity, that worried Mr. Crumrine, and greatly concerned the Serene County Sheriff's Department as well. They'd searched his truck and found a larger bag of pot, not even an eighth of an ounce, but enough for a possible arrest.

The thing that got to David, everyone says so politely these years later, now that they can choose to recreate what they had said about him, was the guilt. Would David, shall we say, *requested* by the police, and without the benefit of a lawyer or a father who gave a fuck what happened to him, draw up a list of every boy and girl from whom he had bought pot, smoked pot, given pot, or sold it, perhaps?

Joshua had been understandably nervous and sleepless all night. He'd refused to share any details of his failed prank with his parents. Even calling Ed Wallenbeck might raise suspicion. Instead, he silently chastised his own foolishness.

By the next day, he tried to ignore the chattering gossip, walked away when those who knew he was David's friend tried to pry any information from him.

He arrived at his last class, stage band practice, early, but Mr. Rose, the band director, hadn't emerged from his office. His memory of where he'd been, what he'd been taught, even what he'd eaten at lunch—the entire day escaped him until he found himself uncoiling cable to set up the electric keyboard.

As more stage band members entered the practice room, Charlie Funch, a saxophone player, tried goading Joshua to play Styx's "I'm Sailing Away."

"No."

"Play 'Cold as Ice.'"

"No."

"Aw, whassamatter. You sad 'cause they took yer boyfriend?"

Joshua turned, heard gasps and the sound of chairs being knocked over before he opened his eyes. His fist was raised—a defensive gesture while turning, actually, but Charlie had thought it was a sucker punch. He had suckered, falling backward.

A few silent moments ensued, sides taken among the student musicians as they hovered nervously or turned away to fuss over their instruments.

Mr. Rose swooped in with an air of fatherly concern, looking surprised to see him.

"Joshua, you seem upset."

"Oh, I—"

"Mr. Rose," Charlie called.

"Just a minute."

"Mr. Rose!" Charlie, hushed by a gesture from his teacher, scowled.

Rose led Joshua back behind the grand piano. "I understand you may have been part of that little prank yesterday."

"Well, not—"

"You know, a great artist needs to focus and be disciplined."

"Please sir, I don't care about—"

146

"You have another arrangement ready?"

"What?"

"That Beatles song."

Joshua had written a stage band score of "Savoy Truffle" with an amazing saxophone solo which would have totally rocked. But that solo would have gone to Charlie, so none of that mattered to Joshua at the moment. David was missing. "I scrapped it," he lied.

Mr. Rose patted a hand on Joshua's shoulder, huddling with him as his classmates filed in, warily eying this private talk.

"Now this pop stuff you play. It is amusing, and great for the repertory, but you're much better than that. To really get an idea of composition, you should focus on the classics, and learn what they did to become so articulate. I should ask my wife to give you some Ravel and Debussy. You could handle it."

Joshua nodded briskly. But at that moment, he did not want to think about music. Nothing sounded like music.

"Um, sir?" He pointed to the insistently hand-waving saxophonist behind him. "Charlie thinks I punched him. I missed."

If his parents knew about David's fate, they didn't let on. He didn't tell them about the dare, the streaking, David's arrest. He waited until a day later, with the house empty, to make a few calls. Joshua phoned another Koenig listed in the small county phone book.

"Ah, that's muh cousin's kid." A woman gave him another number of a cousin, who knew nothing of David's fate.

Finally, he dared to call David's home.

"He can't talk to anyone, 'specially not you." David's father hung up.

Back in school, his silence did not stop the rumors from whirling around him.

"Didja hear?"

"Dave Koenig got sent to The Seed."

Joshua overheard it, dashed to a rehearsal room to cry. It didn't happen. He tried to feel anger at the school, at the cops, at David's father. But what he felt was regret, incredible regret that they hadn't made love sooner, more often, and in better places than in David's truck or in cold muddy fields and forests. Why hadn't they arranged a night in an actual bed when his parents weren't home? And that first time, anywhere but up on the roof of that awful school that got him in so much trouble. They'd had a few months of joy, and now this.

It was over, past. He could not stop thinking about all those years with the little pictures of boyhood David from his wallet lying beside him on his pillow. He felt an aching loss as big and as long as the years between each one of those photographs. For the first time, he cried himself to sleep over the fate of another.

Part 2

There are eighty-eight keys on a piano, and within that, an entire universe.

—James Rhodes

Chapter 19

STONE COLD CRAZY

if you don't let me out of here stop that goddam another
movie why do they want me to stop thinking about sex
when they keep showing me these goddam movies if they
only took the straps off once in a while my fuckin hands are
so fuckin sore oh daddy why did you do this to me why do
you hate me why did I do these things where the fuck is
this place why won't they tell me why won't they just let me
write a letter to Josh I can't even remember his address I
remembered it a while ago it's these fuckin meetings and
the shouting and hell I've had worse these are just so
boring I'm lost in a cloud and then they sharpen you up if I
have to make one more fucking speech in front of those
thiefs and acid heads I think I'll puke that's what I'll do I'll
just puke in front of them all and get sent back to medical
for a while that worked the last time when I pretended to
get sick the food sucks I feel so awful they won't even let a
guy play some hoop once in a while and not even a
moment alone to think about Joshie little Joshie where are
you come and get me out of here get a gun buddy where's
my truck god so many times with him so much kissing and
everything in it fuck dad probably sold it or burned it I
wanna see that whole fuckin school burn to the ground I
wanna see that fuckin meeting leader hung up by his balls
and doused in gasoline and get sick from the smell of his
rotting farty old flesh burning in a corn field and then I'll
jab a railroad spike into his eyes while he screams in pain

and I'm wearing a fireproof suit and he doesn't even know who I am and then the moment before he dies I'll take off the goggles and spit in his mouth and say here I hope that puts out the fire you fucking waste of sperm the other kid who's a homo gets shipped off the way far end of the other wing the day I got here as if we'll start suckin dick in the cafeteria or something if I have to pray out loud one more time I'm gonna start believing it fuck they don't even let you shit alone they don't trust you to piss the one kid told me to start gettin with the program like I was bringin the whole group down and we'd never get out if I kept up with the bad boy act this ain't no act fuckface this is me where am I little me I want to see you god I wish I didn't love Joshie more than anyone but I can't help it I know there's a shrink out there who agrees I read about them in the library or a magazine or something if they'd just let me have a beer I'd be so relaxed I could even talk to some of these kids about what not to do I always knew how to control it that fuckin brainwash cult leader just got me holding and man that fuckin old man is gonna get it if I ever get out of here they can't keep me forever it's illegal it's against the law to hold an adult for this long I'm 18 but they don't show no calendars here and you can't even have a watch oh no not the quiz again if they

cant finish gotta go Love, Davey

This is the only letter David ever wrote to Joshua. He would later tell me how he tried to sneak it out in the mail through a series of bribes at The Seed but failed. He did save it, hidden away in a sock or a pocket, a slat behind a shelf in a supply closet, for weeks.

You're probably wondering how I knew all these details, admittedly somewhat embellished. Aside from knowing these boys then, only a whiff of this incredible friendship passed me by, as did so many beautiful boys. But later, when they came back, I knew them better. And years later, when my family's real estate company handled the sale of Joshua's mother's house, I kept on remembering them.

We did not deal in farm properties so we did not handle David's inheritance after his father died. I don't know if I've spoiled any drama by mentioning that, but men like David's father always died in their fifties then: smoking, drinking, no women. Even most of the gay people found some way to live longer.

No, we only handled Joshua's mother's estate, not the entire neighborhood of houses that were snapped up by Beekam College and turned into a parking lot that's empty four months of the year.

They call them "nail houses," the dwellings of those few stubborn holdouts when developers loom. You've probably seen pictures of them online: the stub of land jutting out amid an excavation site in China, the Seattle elderly woman whose cute little house is dwarfed by high-rises on three sides. Sara Evans's situation was less historic or successful. It was not covered by any media except locally, where the tone was less sympathetic. *The Serene Gazette*'s largest advertiser was Beekam College. Editorials predictably supported every new project. Those who refused to sell were castigated for hampering the college from achieving its manifest destiny.

Yet Sara Evens was one of a few holdouts, and damned if I did not feel so proud of her for sticking it out for so long.

The whole thing stunk from the beginning. When my own family admitted they had bid on the project, I quit working for our real estate company and found myself abroad again.

After returning, I found so much about these boys, held on to all that remained: the recordings, the sheet music, their photos— for I am the sole archivist of this romance, this affair, this love between two boys who became men.

However, before those years, the boys seemed compelled by other forces to part ways and lose each other for a while. It would be years before I saw them again. Graduating that May, I spent more time at college and little time wondering about what became of any high school acquaintances. Such was my loss.

For years David refused to discuss his time at The Seed with me. But when he did, those weeks sounded bleak.

Rising from their cots, detainees, called Seedlings, would be shepherded into the showers, boys and girls separated. They were never left alone. Older residents, dubbed Seeders, who'd achieved a level of seniority, monitored their every move.

The day would continue with a mostly silent breakfast of re-constituted eggs, oatmeal, or dry cereal with watered-down milk, served in the cafeteria of what had once been a small low-security prison hidden away in a fenced-in tract of land outside of Canton.

"We're going to do some more intake, explore what we've done wrong," announced their group leader, Stan, a burly bearded man in baggy pants and an oversize flannel shirt.

Sitting in a circle of chairs for hours, Stan pressured each Seedling to recount their crimes: drug use, drug sales, thievery, sex, drinking, rebelling. The other kids, most of them Black or Latino from Cleveland, Columbus, or other cities, told their tales of skipping school, hitting back when their mothers smacked them, running away, shoplifting.

"You really fucked up. Admit it," Stan would interrupt. The basic pattern of an Alcoholics Anonymous meeting veered off into repetitive attacks meant to break them all.

One Black boy, thin and soft-spoken, dared to say, "My mother wasn't there so I—"

"Stop it. You're blaming others for your mistakes," an older kid blurted.

"Conning," a few repeated.

The young man apologized, stuttered, recanted, re-phrased his actions as his own.

"Okay, Farm Boy. Your turn."

That was David's new nickname. He sat up, tried not to scowl, and began again confessing, carefully gauging his words.

"I smoked pot, gave it to others, bought it, brought it to school. I drank, went to rock concerts, cursed at my dad, and . . ." He stopped.

"The sex, admit it," Stan commanded.

He would not betray him, not name him aloud, not here.

"I had sex with Brenda half a dozen times, risked my life and hers. I could be a father right now if I weren't more careful."

"You weren't careful! You were stupid! Get out of your head!" Stan's voice echoed through the room. Heads nodded in agreement.

"I was stupid," David repeated.

"Farm Boy, stand up."

He obeyed.

Stan sauntered around outside the circle of chairs.

"How many of you girls would date Farm Boy, with his pot stench and his lying?"

No hands raised.

"Any guys?"

None.

"You fucked guys, too. Right, Farm Boy?"

David nodded.

"Maybe a farm animal?"

Laughter.

David stood, pressed his lips together. Don't react. That's what they want.

Stan pointed. "What we have here is a slow-witted user, who betrayed his father, pulled a stupid prank, got caught with his precious drugs, fucked guys and girls, and still blames others. You've got a lot of work to do, Farm Boy."

David could have snapped, told him his farm didn't have any livestock. He remained cowed, silenced, and finally was allowed

155

to sit. He learned the game quickly. He pretended to listen to the others confess and get berated. He almost nodded off until a girl sitting next to him elbowed him.

After a few hours, the confession session ended and the call and response repeated like chanting.

"God grant me the serenity to accept the things I cannot change, the courage to change the things I can, and the wisdom to know the difference."

Stan clapped his hands once. "Okay. Pee breaks. Line up. Everyone outside until lunch."

David sat on a bench, avoiding others, talking politely when they pushed him into a conversation, more of a retread of the meetings. He stared at the fence.

The slow, quiet pain wasn't that he was trapped. The painful truth was, he could leave. But where would he go? Home? His father would just send him back, or he'd have to face a drug sentence in an actual prison.

No, the torture of The Seed lay in its options. He could abandon this odd cult-like punishment, but should he, an even worse fate awaited.

So he sat quietly, waiting for lunch, then another meeting, then chores, then a few hours of school lessons, barely enough for them to catch up or get a GED upon their return. Evenings were filled with an awful sing-along, almost worse than the meetings. The repeated programming switched from a day full of berating and accusations to a false joyful repetition of caring, "Love you!" "We're here for you!" followed by a round of hugs. David grew to hate those hugs. Every touch was a lie.

Although he resisted, the constant put-downs sunk in. David refused to name his love, even in his head, except in that letter. He felt the endless meetings, day after day, beating him down to the point where he couldn't even think about— No, don't say his name, even in your head. Hide it, tighten it, make it smaller and smaller.

The husk of memory in his head wove itself into the new truth that was drummed into him. He had hurt him, used him, exploited his innocence, taken his virginity, goddammit. David was unworthy, a stoner low-class farm boy. He didn't deserve love. It wasn't love, but lust. He would change. He would improve, survive, endure.

Chapter 20

LIAR

AFTER HE PARKED the tank and strapped the machine gun to his chest, Joshua prepared to scale the walls of the castle to save David, who knew of the escape plan via secret messages sent in a pack of cigarettes. With his camouflage makeup smeared over his face and his G.I. Joe sweater with the patches sewed on the elbows and shoulders pressing against his sweaty torso, Joshua swung the steel-clawed hook on a thick-corded rope. It almost caught, but missed the building's precipice, and began falling down, down toward his face.

"Dinner time."

Joshua started up from his bed with a bolt. His father stood in his doorway. "Wash your face, sleepyhead." He left the door open.

Joshua had been sleeping a lot. He usually fell asleep every day after school as soon as he finished masturbating to the stolen *Playboy* pictures under his bed. He didn't care anymore if Mom or Dad or Sister found out. He'd pump off into a sock while looking at Harry Reems or Jan-Michael Vincent, trying not to think about David, then toss the papers and moist sock under his bed and doze off in his clothes, his fly undone.

Being awakened from this ritual nearly every day to eat didn't help his appetite. But he sullenly made his way down the stairs to sit at the table and endure the chattering about his sister's latest upcoming ballet recital, or his father's disgruntled customers, or his mother's latest encounter with an octogenarian at Meals on Wheels.

"Add to the conversation, dear," his mother said.

My boyfriend's in a fake jail and I hate everyone. "The pork chops are dry."

"Smart mouth."

"Can I have some more applesauce?" his sister asked cheerily.

The phone rang. Joshua's father did not quite understand why his son nearly choked on his mashed potatoes and jumped from the room to answer it, but it bothered him.

"I told you, we don't take calls at dinner. Tell them you'll call back."

"Dad, it's okay."

Expecting to hear from David, or from someone who knew David, he was oddly disappointed yet intrigued to hear the voice of Robert Something, Executive Producer for the *Cleveland Today* show, from all the way up in Cleveland. He wasn't ready for this.

"Joshua?"

"Yes."

"How are you?"

"Fine."

"Did you talk to your parents about doing the show?"

"Yeah."

"And?"

"They're still discussing it."

"Oh, can you put them on the line?"

"Um, that's not a good idea right now."

"Oh, I'm sorry. Is there something wrong?"

"No, I'm fine, they want to, I just— Hey, do I get a school day off?"

"Maybe one. We will shoot on a weekday. How's next Tuesday?"

"Oh."

"How about you just discuss it with your parents, and when you're ready—"

"No, no, I'm ready."

"Let me give you a number. Got a pen?"

Joshua scrambled in the jumbled drawer full of jigsaw puzzle parts, mismatched playing cards, rulers, protractors, compasses, half-used erasers, safety pins, Band-Aids, A&P coupons, anything but a pen.

He considered his situation. His boyfriend incarcerated, kids at school gossiping, wondering about Joshua's friendship with David, his dead acquaintance Kelly Seifering on her way to local sainthood.

He stepped back into the kitchen, tugging the telephone cord like casting a line, and reached over the dining room table to the royal amusement of his sister and mother and extracted a pen from his father's pocket.

As he turned his back on their laughter, he heard Robert calling, "Are you there?"

"Sure, I'm here."

He scribbled an address and phone number, then returned to the table.

"And who was that?" His father, obviously peeved.

"Robert Something-or-other."

"Who?"

"From the TV show."

"Really?" Joshua's mother's face brightened. "Oh, I can't wait to tell everyone at—"

"Hon, can we, can we . . ." His father pecked at her accolades like a woodpecker. Joshua always admired his father's patience when his mother's voice reached such pitches and decibels. He understood.

"I think we ought to discuss this a little further," said his father.

"Oh, I'm sorry, dear. Didn't I tell you? He met a reporter at the mall who, what is it, Joshua?"

"Executive Producer. They want me to play the piano, the Queen song."

"Yes, one of those talk shows. I'm always out then. I never watched, but he's got all these controversial people on, and visiting celebrities, intellectuals, and family therapists, and you know a friend of my mother's was on that show."

"Mike Douglas?" his father asked.

"No, not that one."

"Anyway—"

"We could visit a museum."

"What?"

"When we go with him."

"Where?"

"To Cleveland. Let's have a little vacation."

Samuel Evans relented. "Fine. I'll take a day off. I've got one due."

"Really?" Joshua's sister's voice approached a squeak.

"Sure, let's do it."

And while his parents hugged, Joshua and his sister had already traded glances. He had upstaged her big time, and he would eventually pay for it.

On Thursday, he had already laid out the suit he would perform in the next week. Antsy all through the next school day, he barely noticed Brent call out to him.

"Hey, Josh. I got those pictures developed."

"Yeah?"

"And um, . . . I got some pictures of Dave, too."

"Really?" They whispered suddenly, as if conspiring in some banned act.

"C'mon down to the darkroom."

Confused and distracted, the thought of being alone in a dark room with the boy sounded good.

In the red darkness of the photo lab, Brent took out the photos of Joshua that he'd told him about.

"Here ya go." He handed him two pictures, one of David, shirtless and brooding, not smiling, but just looking. The other was a far shot of David standing proudly in a field.

"Wow. That's pretty cool." Joshua pushed down a surge of jealousy. Why had David taken his shirt off?

"Neat, huh? I get to decide what we'll remember ten, twenty years from now. J'ever think about that, Josh? Ten, twenty years from now?"

"I'm jus' tryin' to get through this week."

"Them takin' Dave's pretty bad, huh?"

"Yeah. J'ever meet his dad?"

"What? Naw," Brent lied.

"Total creep, lemme tell ya. If my dad was like that—"

"What, hated you for something?"

"Yeah, well, even, if he acted like that."

Brent moved in behind Joshua, putting his arms around the other boy's waist.

"You know, you're not alone. Joshua, c'mon." Brent bent in close and barely kissed the back of Joshua's neck. "Let's mess around."

He pulled away. "Stop it, stop makin' fun of me." He was shocked by Brent's sudden advance, unlike David, who'd grown on him all his life, it seemed. Brent moved closer.

"I'm not. I'm serious. Dave said he liked you a lot."

"What did he say? You mean, you and him . . . ?"

"Well, sure."

Brent tried to kiss him but Joshua pulled away. How could he feel jealous of the boy he'd sent to jail? Nevertheless he did, and a flood of rage swept through him. He wanted Brent sexually, but it would be like cheating on David. But he never knew when he'd see David again. And Brent's smile was there in front of him.

But worst of all, he realized that Brent had gotten to David first. That ripped his little ego to shreds like a sixth grade Valentine's Day box that gets last place.

"C'mon, Josh. Let's make some nice memories." Brent reached for Joshua's belt. Below it, his erection pushed out from his jeans.

"No, goddamit! Jesus, fuck. Shit." He pulled away and went for the door as he fumbled with the bulge in his pants. "I don't need you, or him, or any of you!"

Had he stayed, and had he loved David a little less, he might have spent himself in Brent's playful embrace and loosened up enough to get through his senior year with some comfort, knowing that Brent could serve a good second best at least. But at eighteen, Joshua didn't understand, and his little head couldn't see beyond tomorrow. He slammed the door and walked out, leaving Brent in the darkroom.

Despite the rumored horrors that surrounded those who were sent to The Seed, the camp's "Seedlings" were all released, eventually.

They returned in button-down shirts and ties for the boys, while the girls wore prim skirts below the knee. No more denim. No more concert T-shirts. It seemed as if they concurred that the very garb of a hood—T-shirts and jeans—naturally led to the road of damnation and drug habits. So they returned, silent and docile.

It was between periods that Joshua saw David standing alone at his locker. He didn't recognize him at first. His hair cut short again, his posture rigid, he spoke to no one, ignored the double takes, the whispers. He wasn't Davey the hood anymore, but shorn like a young ram.

Without looking at him, having sensed his approach, David muttered, "I can't talk to you."

Joshua couldn't speak anyway. The shock of David's beauty made so bald, so white and bristled, opened up a new form of adoration. Everyone felt it.

"I'm not supposed to talk to my old friends."

"I'm not your old friend. I'm me! It's Joshua! I'm, I'm your . . ." He wanted to say "boyfriend," but the word caught in his throat. He wanted a cigarette, but David was the one with the smokes. Used to be. But this way, with him looking so blank with his ears sticking out, he couldn't find the words.

Then he felt his wallet in his pocket.

"Look. Look at this." He searched behind the fourteen dollars, his library card, social security card, and driver's license. There. He found it.

David watched him open a small envelope, too tiny for mailing. Joshua unfolded the worn accordioned collection of faces, all of them David's, from first grade to junior year.

"I keep this with me all the time. I look at it every night, almost."

David's face winced, as if he were being forced to watch a cat drown. He started to walk away, but Joshua grabbed his shoulder.

"Brent Carse? Really?"

"That . . . was a long time ago. Before you." He turned away, stiffly walking down the hall, his back tight, awaiting an attack.

Joshua couldn't follow him, but he stared at the back of David's head. He spent the rest of the day in a blur, watching teachers' hands move across chalk boards, scrawling symbols, letters and lines, talking about cosines and Emily Dickinson and Theodore Roosevelt. It was all ancient, dry history that had nothing to do with the real world, the world of terror and rage and his torn passion. His pen ripped through pages of his notebook as he gouged angry, angular lined doodles in complete silence.

He did try to talk again at lunch. David sat with other Seed kids in the cafeteria. Empty chairs bracketed them. Nobody wanted to sit near them. But Joshua sidled right down next to David. The other three boys, Matty Clark, Sam Humerkouser, and Russell McAllan, gave him a wary skittish glance. Shelly Andreas never looked up.

"Hey guys, how's it going?" Joshua forced a smile as he crumbled saltines over his bowl of tomato soup.

They ate in silence.

"Nice to have you all back."

More silence. Then Sam spoke. "We can't talk to you."

"Why not? You're all better now, aren't you?" He wanted to get David alone, just talk to him, at least tell him about Cleveland, about being on television, to warn him, to confess, to share a secret. They had so many secrets. Where did they go?

"We're not supposed to."

"My old friends are a bad influence." David's eyes never left his plate. His spoon lay in the bowl of blood red soup. Then he looked up at Joshua. "Please go away."

"Christ! Like you weren't the one that got me stoned or taught me about blowjobs!"

Dozens of cafeteria eyes darted at them. Joshua wanted to fling his tray at them, get some reaction out of them, but he just left his lunch on the table and stormed down to the rehearsal studios. He closed the door and banged away on a piano. He stayed late, pounding into his favorite songs with anger, fumbling over chords with a determination to race through the melodies until he felt he had stored up a form of energy or power to conjure an audible form of revenge.

Chapter 21

UNDER PRESSURE

WHEN HE STOOD in front of the lights before the taping, the heat felt like a toaster oven. Joshua couldn't stop sweating. He didn't know he could sweat so much. The collar of his shirt felt like a hot rag.

He never knew a TV studio was so crowded, like a small messy laboratory, with thick black cables snaking like entrails from the pair of giant cameras on wheeled stands.

While his parents and sister waited in a line outside the studio with other audience members, Joshua tried out the piano, set in a bare corner of the set with a simple curtain behind it. Next to that, the small talk show set appeared unimpressive. A center chair between two short sofas sat on a raised carpeted platform in front of what, upon a closer scan, proved to be a flat painted series of boards and a large backdrop of the Cleveland skyline.

Joshua tested the piano, a black Steinway grand worn around the edges. The pitch seemed a bit off, but the studio's acoustics weren't very good either. A technician fiddled with a microphone on a stand aimed inside the open lid. After the make-up woman approved of his "coloring," she pointed toward a big door to the left. He almost tripped over some cables, got lost twice until someone else told him to stay in the green room, where two other people, a young woman and an older man, sat waiting. The small yet stocky Black girl seemed to be avoiding the man, who read silently from a bible in a corner chair. Joshua figured it would better to sit next to the girl.

A large television in the green room had the station's channel on, Joshua realized, since a few minutes before the show they saw a promo with Garrett Glass saying, "Coming up on *Cleveland Today*, teen rehabilitation camps: success or abuse?"

The girl leaned toward him, whispered, "You went to The Seed, too?"

"Oh, no, I have a . . . friend who went there. A couple of kids from our school."

She nodded her head. "I can't wait to tell the truth."

The three of them watched the monitor as the show began.

Recorded theme music played and a camera showed Garrett sitting, then a close-up.

"Teenagers in trouble, and a controversial program that claims to help them get straight. We've got guests, one who defends it, another who was in such a program, and a special musical guest." Glass introduced a videotaped segment with a short introduction, then, "Representatives from The Seed declined our offer to appear on the show, but sent this statement. 'The Seed Rehabilitation Initiative has been approved by numerous school boards throughout Ohio, and has a proven record of success. Our retraining is rigorous and tough, but our participants have overwhelmingly, through our group sessions, found their way to sobriety, free from drugs, alcohol, and promiscuity, and returned to complete their educations. Many of our counselors are also former trainees.'"

Glass paused, then looked up. "However, investigative reporter Karen Listerly found a different story. Here's her report."

Joshua and the two other guests watched a videotaped segment. With her voiceover narration, a few far shots revealed a fenced-in flat building and an almost creepy tone pervaded. Interviews with a few teenagers told of late night "meetings" where "Seedlings" or inmates were forced to undergo hours-long berating from other group members.

"You're never allowed any privacy," said one, his face blurred. "Even to use the bathroom."

"They didn't hit us, but they scream at you," said another. "They call you a liar for not 'coming clean.' They made us march around all day. And the food was the worst."

The reporter's voiceover again: "But others who underwent this controversial treatment offered praise."

The tape cut to a wiry Black teenager, his hair clipped short, in a shirt and tie. "I was doin' drugs, dealin' too, and hurtin' my family. Working out my problems with The Seed saved me. I'm gonna graduate high school."

After the video summed up, the monitor returned to Glass on the set.

"Coming up: two different sides to this story."

The clipboard headset guy entered the green room. "Miss Washington? Mister Haybert?"

"Reverend Haybert."

"Yes, right. We're ready for you. Joshua, right?"

Joshua sat up.

"You'll be up in ten minutes."

As they left, Joshua watched the commercials on the monitor. When they ended, the two guests debated the merits of "juvenile rehabilitation." The Reverend maintained a smug condescending tone, heaping praise on the program, while the girl repeated the abuse accusations others in the taped segment claimed. More than a few times, Glass stopped a bit of crosstalk between them before it became a louder argument. Then he spoke to the camera, "Up next, a song that operatically captures youth in turmoil."

The man with the headset returned and led Joshua back out to the studio. The audience sat on bleachers, uncomfortably close, waiting, demanding entertainment even before the floodlights glared. He squinted, scanned the small crowd for his family. His mother waved briefly and smiled.

Seated before the piano, Joshua waited as Glass, standing nearly in front of him, introduced him to some applause. Joshua played "Bohemian Rhapsody," not his best performance, but a passable one. He lost his place at the polyrhythmic break before the "So you think you can stone me and spit in my eye" section, but made up for it by milking the glissandos before the ending.

Led to the couch during the commercial break, clipboard-headset guy hastily attached a small microphone to his tie. The girl smiled and patted his back while the Reverend, on the opposite sofa, sat immobile, refusing so much as to glance at him.

"We're here with our guests," Glass repeated their names and summed up the show's theme succinctly, glancing between cue cards off-camera and a few note cards in his hand. "So, Joshua, you had a rather unusual experience with the daughter of a pastor in your own home town of Serene, is that right?"

"Yes." A pause.

Glass filled in for him. "Kelly Seifering, the girl who was tragically electrocuted on a radio tower?"

"Yes. I met her before she died."

"And you believe that Kelly killed herself out of grief for the treatment she was getting from her foster parents?"

"Yeah, they're real Born Agains. They beat her. Sometimes they locked her in the basement."

"And you say that she didn't want to go to The Seed, is that right?"

"Yes, she called it a brain-washing camp where they send kids who are stoners."

"Excuse me, you said 'stoners'?"

"You know, kids that get high a lot, on pot."

The Washington girl nodded. Nervous laughter crept up from the audience. Joshua couldn't tell what angle it came from, at him or with him, but he smiled, realizing that he was giving his grin a little effect, as if he were faking being embarrassed about the mention of drugs. He was acting, as if just being himself weren't good enough, and some part of him knew it, and took over, and hammered it up a bit.

"And you said that she shared some personal information with you?"

"Oh, yeah. She told me she was a lesbi—uh, gay, you know. And we talked about that."

"About being gay?"

"Yeah. We did."

A stunned silence followed until the Reverend interrupted. "This is why these children in sin need this kind of rehabilitation! That *song* encourages murder and suicide! It even references a demon!" He spouted some bible passage, kept talking despite Glass's attempts to stop him. The girl looked over at Joshua, rolled her eyes.

Joshua felt a new sheen of sweat pooling under his shirt. He wiped his upper lip, wet with a residue of makeup.

"Thank you. Sir." Glass's upheld "stop" hand pushed a bit too close to the Reverend. "Joshua, do you know other teens who were sent to The Seed?"

"Yeah, my best friend David. He got caught with some pot, see, and he . . ." Something told him not to mention the streaking episode. He didn't want them to laugh now. "They just took him off. No court, no trial, nothin'. His dad doesn't care about him. It was like, 'Take him off my hands,' and then he was gone. And since he came back, he can't talk to me."

"A difficult subject and one that remains controversial." Glass turned away from Joshua in a move that looked too practiced, and faced the camera. "I want to thank my guests. Tomorrow on *Cleveland Today*, we'll have recipes with a popular local chef, and adoptable puppies. Stay tuned for a new episode of *Guiding Light*."

The clipboard guy behind a cameraman waved his arms, and the audience started clapping as the recorded theme music echoed from a distant monitor.

As they finished, the audience was herded out, a few of the studios lights clacked off, and Joshua forgot to take off his microphone, the cord yanking him back in his attempt to catch up to his family. Headset-clipboard guy helped him while he fidgeted a bit. He nodded at the girl. The Reverend talked with someone else, so avoiding him was easy. He shook the girl's hand.

"That was some nice playing," she smiled.

"That was some smart talking. You were very brave."

"I'm just glad I got to speak my piece." Her mother, in a Sunday-best jacket and matching skirt, approached, warily allowed a brief introduction before leaving with her daughter.

Where were his parents and sister? The studio people, busy shoving the set piece and piano off through a large open doorway, were no help.

Glass approached, shook his hand, then offered an awkward half hug.

"You were terrific! I really want to thank you for being on the program."

"Well, thanks. I messed up the break a bit."

"No, you were great. You've really got some talent there, and I want to thank you for discussing this." He leaned in with an almost whispered voice. "I got a lot of flack about even approaching this topic, but if it does any good, then it's worth it."

He left it open, gazing at Joshua with a sort of admiration that seemed more than professional.

"Anyway. I think your parents are in the lobby. But keep in touch. Here's my card."

He walked out of the studio and down a hallway where he found them: his father stunned, his sister furious, his mother abruptly turning on a cheerful yet weak smile.

Silence filled the car as his father drove south for a good twenty minutes, not even the radio, then only a few words. It seemed the museum visit had been cancelled.

"I wish you'd told us." Sam Evans's callused palms gripped the steering wheel.

Joshua stuttered. "I didn't know he was going to do that, that it was all about that."

"I just hope no one at school finds out. This is so horrific!" Sister had a flair for the dramatic.

"I swear, just when I thought I had a handle on you. Now I suppose your sister wants to be Marie Osmond."

"I don't think so!" More flair.

"Well, I think he was terrific," Sara Evans interjected. "Are we hungry?"

They stopped at a Denny's near Akron. His father couldn't make eye contact through the entire meal, becoming suddenly interested in restaurant decor. Joshua didn't mind so much. He'd had his say and played well enough. It was for them to figure out.

Somewhere in the middle of more silence homeward, his father simply stated, "In the future, Joshua, you should talk to your mother and me before you announce your problems on TV. Okay?"

"Okay."

Although *Cleveland Today* aired during the school day, Joshua expected some sort of enthusiastic reaction from students who may have at least heard about it, perhaps to offer congratulations. Instead, he got stares, and a strange array of responses from strangers and people he knew, or thought he knew.

The TV show might have been forgotten had it not been for a subsequent article in *The Serene Gazette*. To call it slanted would be an understatement. As the paper's Religion columnist, Pastor Arnold Dullahan extolled the virtues of "rehabilitating our wayward youth," and while not naming Joshua, excoriated "willful accusations and lies" about "worthy attempts to save our children from sin."

On a smaller scale, more personal journalistic efforts were unsuccessful. Joshua, attempting to remain unnoticed at his locker, cringed to see Brent Carse approach.

"Hey, wait. Josh. Listen, I tried to get the school paper to do something about The Seed, and your TV show, and—"

"Brent, don't."

"No, people need to know. Dave cut me off, too, man. It sucks. But our advisor Mrs. Kenney refused to let me do a story on it. Could you—"

He could have communed with Brent, asked for more photos of David, even had sex with him as a distraction. But his resentment and anger took over.

"Brent? Fuck off."

Lunch with Ed Wallenbeck became his sole refuge. When two other boys, Randy McCallister and Gary Corson, sauntered by, Gary blurted, "Hey, Evans. Why'd you have to say you're a fag on TV? Everyone knows."

Ed snapped back. "Hey, Corson. Why'd you have to prove you're an asshole? Everyone knows."

Muttered threats ensued, but the two boys left.

Ed pushed his tray aside. "Man, this sucks."

"You didn't have to do that."

"I did, man. Dave's my friend, too. Or he was. So are you."

"Thanks."

At home, while his father remained puzzled, his sister complained about the gossip that shifted her way until their mother had a few words with her. When Joshua told his mother what had been going on at school, she made a decision.

"I think you ought to take a few days off."

"What?"

She leaned in, placed her palm against his forehead. "Yes, definitely a fever."

"I'm not sick, Mom."

"No, hon. You're not the one. But the school doesn't need to know that."

With one phone call, Sara Evans relieved her son of a few

days of school. She encouraged him to play as loud and as long as he liked on the old piano in the dining room, and he occasionally accompanied her on errands.

"I think the boy's touched in the head."

Joshua heard Marion LaCorte responding to Darlene Hotchkiss's comment as she pretended to browse the shelves at the A&P. Their gossip lay silent only a moment, a house of hens merely visited by the returning fox.

"Did you see him on the show?" Darlene Hotchkiss asked.

"No, but Elsa Bennett did and she told me all about it."

Joshua stared back, momentarily shaming the women into silence.

And when he'd returned to school, Gretchen approached him after English class.

"You know, I never told you, but I'm so sorry about everything that happened."

"Thanks, yeah. Sorry I never called for another date."

She shook her head, dismissing the issue. "You understand of course, that since you missed two meetings, we couldn't keep you on as Decorations Co-chair of the prom committee."

"Oh, sure. I understand."

"Don McAllister's doing his best."

"Don McAllister?" The Eiffel Tower toothpick king.

"Oh, and uh, the theme isn't that 'Lucy in the Sky' thing anymore."

"What?"

"Karla Fitch says that her church group said that the song was about drugs and that it wasn't appropriate for our school to do a prom about it, so they changed it."

"To what?"

"We're doing a tribute to *The Love Boat*."

Joshua's burst of laughter rang in Gretchen's ears as he walked away.

Mrs. Rose, already singed by the flames of gossip, greeted Joshua with a combination of shock and sympathy, as if her long lost golden retriever had returned, albeit with a grenade strapped to his collar.

"I'm sorry I missed last week."

"That's okay."

"I know all this is different," he explained as she led him inside. "But I still want to perform at the recital."

Mrs. Rose's face flushed. She was more concerned about her busybody neighbor Carolyn Yost peeking out her side window and seeing "that boy who'd been on TV and said he was queer."

"Of course, you're still going to play at the recital. Did you want to take lessons this summer, too?"

"Yes, please, ma'am."

"Well, I can see how you'd want to get back to things again, but—"

"Mrs. Rose?"

"Yes, dear?"

"How many of the composers I studied were gay?"

"What?" Her swanlike neck seemed to dart back, leaving her head bobbing.

"If that's what's bothering you, I think you ought to realize that's the only reason I ever wanted to study piano. Because it's for sissies. There's nothing wrong with sissy music for me. I like sissy music. I think Mozart was a sissy. I think Schubert was a real sissy. That's why I like them. Do you understand?"

"I think so, Joshua."

"Thank you, Mrs. Rose. We must look every day into the future, right?"

"I suppose so."

"And the lessons are still ten dollars an hour?"

"Yes, dear, of course, but—"

"Here's thirty." He handed over a check his mother had written.

"Oh, Joshua dear, you don't have to—"

"Yes, I do, Mrs. Rose, I have to keep playing. I have to get better."

"Well, alright dear, you got it." Nosy neighbors be damned.

As they sat down, Joshua at the piano, his teacher beside him, the boy struck a C-Major chord for emphasis. "Let's face it, Mrs. Rose. The future's got nothing to do with Serene."

After his lesson, when he found me waiting patiently on the porch, I offered a few words of encouragement. Joshua muttered a shy thank you. I longed to say more, but he rushed off, being understandably distracted.

Chapter 22

KEEP YOURSELF ALIVE

DAVID STOOD BY the road downhill from his home and waited for the school bus. Since his release from The Seed, he wasn't allowed to drive his truck. No pot, of course; his father and a Seeder senior had rifled through his room, interrogated him over any hiding places, and only found a hidden half-empty pack of stale cigarettes which, oddly, were permitted.

Missing after-school events like corny pep rallies and assemblies didn't bother him. He was allowed to stay a few days late for his Future Farmers of America classes in the greenhouse behind the school, which sometimes lasted longer than last period.

On his meeting days, Larry, one of the more annoying senior Seeds, poured on an extra dose of lecturing before the meetings as David sat trapped in the passenger seat of Larry's smelly cramped Honda Civic.

He could stand these intrusions. He'd had any concept of privacy ripped from him, along with the pervasive threat of "re-entry" drilled into his cowed being. Daily after-school meetings had been reduced to a few times a week. He could not imagine a world without the profanity-spewing Seed seniors hovering over his shoulder in his mind.

His father acted differently, smug, even benevolent at times, like a man who had found an abandoned puppy and finally house-trained it. He'd sip a beer in the living room, silently taunting him, smacking his lips with each guzzle as he watched some sports program.

But the bus was the lowest.

Since every other farm boy his age had their own car or truck, David had to catch a yellow school bus for the grade school four blocks from the high school. Seated with chirping preteenagers, he remained silent as they loud-whispered questions about him, until he returned a solemn glare.

He'd managed to avoid Joshua at school except that one time.

His nights had become fraught with worry and guilt. Even touching himself had become ruined, the hours of scold sessions from group meetings seeping into his mind. "Filth! Wasting your life energy!"

After-school group sessions in the basement of the Baptist church on Center Street maintained the Alcoholics Anonymous-rip-off structure that comprised The Seed's format, but with their own vocabulary and a more terse form of encouragement. "Love ya!," the oft-repeated greeting in closing, took on sinister undertones. "Love ya," unless you are a lying cheating druggie, which you are deep down, you loser.

A pair of cawing crows flew overhead, rousing David. The bus arrived down the road between his Uncle Joe Kemp's field, just starting to sprout a new crop of alfalfa, and on the other side his father's, where rows had been tilled for the pumpkin seed planting in July.

The bus stopped, the driver nodded as David stepped up and took an empty seat.

A boy who'd once asked him if he was one of the "slow kids" only to get a glare quickly shifted to a seat behind David, bounced on it a bit, perhaps to get his attention.

It worked. David turned, about to quiet the kid. But the boy's little round face, his short crew cut, and a gap where he'd proudly lost a baby tooth, made David smirk.

"Are you, are you David Coning? Keith said you live on the pumpkin farm."

"That I do."

David offered his hand, which the boy shook awkwardly.

"I'm Toby Findley. My real name's Tobias, after my grampa, but everybody calls me Toby."

"Nice to meet ya. David Koenig, son of a pumpkin farmer."

Toby didn't exactly get David's joke. "That's cool. One time, one time, one time, I carved out a pumpkin and pulled out the guts and my arm went all the way in!"

"Musta been a big one."

"It was! It was so big!"

"You gonna get some more this fall?"

"Well, sure. Can we get them at your farm?"

"Usually we ship them to the supermarkets, but I'll save some just for you."

"Cool. So, so one time, Mom took the seeds and washed off the guts and she baked 'em and put salt on 'em and we ate 'em. J'ever do that?"

"Every harvest."

"I wanna grow pumpkins. Dad won't let us. We raise chickens, but I don't like 'em. Chicken poo stinks!" He laughed at his naughty remark and David did, too. "Dad says he wants to sell 'em to the chicken farm over in Zanesville so we can move to Florida. He says it's 'cause of the 'conomy."

"Yup, it's a tough business, farming. But maybe when you're older, you can come work with me."

"Really? Cool."

They sat in silence for a while as the bus rode into town until Toby resumed. "So, so, Keith says you have to take the bus 'cause you were bad."

"Keith sure talks a lot. Which one's he?"

Toby pointed toward a taller boy seated further back, who, once spotted, scowled and turned away to stare out the window.

"So, were you?" Toby insisted.

"That's debatable."

With a puzzled look, Toby asked, "What's bedate-able?"

David chuckled again. Toby reminded him of his younger self, sneaking out on chilly fall nights to sit in the pumpkin field like his childhood hero, Linus, awaiting the Great Pumpkin.

Cheered by his new little friend, he had a good day at school. Nobody stared at him, his Seed "friends" didn't over-share their gripes at lunch, he stayed alert, possibly due to his newfound appreciation of a morning cup of coffee, which had been served too frequently at the facility. It almost felt as if his absence had been a blip, a forgotten dream.

Before Larry picked him up for another hours-long after-school meeting, he quietly worked on a cross-pollination project with a few of his fellow FFA students. The greenhouse had become a sort of refuge. The guys knew better than to mention David's "time off," and knew all too well the problem of difficult parents, particularly when so many independent farms were losing money. Zack Huber told of his father's bankruptcy, Ethan Butterick bragged about acquiring some tools at a recent auction, and others pondered their own futures.

As he walked toward the parking lot to search out Larry's Honda, a familiar voice made his heart jump.

Blurting out in a doleful voice of Goliath the Dog, Joshua moaned, "Davey, I waited for you."

David's shoulders stiffened, then relaxed. He turned, still ashamed, afraid. Of what? The boy who loved him?

"You can't just go. C'mon, David," Joshua said.

"I'm not supposed to—"

"We're not supposed to do a lot of things, but that never stopped you."

David's pained face contorted in so many positions, any but the one facing Joshua. He saw Larry's car approaching.

"It's—"

"What happened? Please, Dave, please. I—"

"It can't be like it was."

"What?"

"You still want me to—"

Larry's car pulled up next to him, honked loudly. David switched to a tone, officious, so Larry could hear it, but more so Joshua could understand that this was a lie he had to tell. "I'm sorry I got you into drugs and hurt you and took advantage of you."

"Davey, this is us." He made a gesture, the air between them. "You're mine and I'm yours. Nothing they did to you's gonna stop that."

"I gotta go."

David turned away and got in Larry's car.

"Who was that?" Larry shoved a pile of fast food wrappers off the seat.

And he was back in Seed mode. "Just another loser."

In David's boyhood, spring filled him with anticipation, the satisfying repetition of planting and a sense of pride in running the tractor, which he first drove as a ten-year-old.

After his return, his Uncle Joe never brought up his internment, merely offered work and an escape from it all. He shoveled manure, parsed seeds, cleaned out the baler, scraped rust off the thresher, whacked nails into errant planks on the barn's walls; anything for a distraction, all the while knowing at least he was saving some money.

Every grasp of soil or metal pushed aside the guilt-ridden thoughts, the blaming accusations repeated at The Seed, that his pot smoking and "fornication" were somehow his friends' fault. How could that sweet little guy, who kissed so softly, who played piano so passionately, how could any of this have been Joshua's fault?

Deep breaths, he told himself, one of the repeated lessons he found useful, neutral even. One day at a time. And tomorrow, he told himself, I'll wait for a bus full of children, and start again. Hopefully, Toby would be on the bus to cheer him up.

But still, in the back of his mind, and moving forward more often, the fact remained. He was soon to graduate high school. He was eighteen, an adult, legally. And that meant he could escape from the farm, from Serene, from ever hurting Joshua again.

Chapter 23

DON'T STOP ME NOW

SHEET MUSIC IN his hand, Joshua walked down the small aisle between two groups of folding chairs in his piano teacher's living room. Heads turned expectantly, as if at a wedding, among them his parents'. He approached the piano. Once so comforting, familiar and warm, Mrs. Rose's living room now seemed oddly foreign.

Mrs. Rose's recitals traditionally started with the youngest students, some eight or nine, plinking out a simple melody, moving upward to more accomplished kids, but none of them performing anything memorable.

Joshua played "Bohemian Rhapsody" quite well and with an energy that occasionally cracked at the loss of a few notes, but the rhythm never faltered.

The other kids were relegated to the back patio; a few softly sang along. Joshua turned to see their curious faces peeking from around the hall as he bowed. They cheered, frightening a few mothers who didn't quite understand why their children were so excited about such an odd piece of music, singing about not wanting to be born at all.

Joshua returned to the kids' area on the patio like a small hero. Kids giggled and stared. John Needham, a fellow piano student, shook his hand. He was short and muscular with a pug face that beamed admiration.

"That was excellent, man."

"Thanks. Thanks a lot."

My own Bach solo, while technically more difficult and the last piece that day, proved to have been thoroughly upstaged. Though I was resentful at the time, I've since learned to forgive.

After the recital, cookies and punch were enjoyed on the patio and in the back yard. Mr. Rose approached Joshua, parting a cluster of admiring students. He seemed about seven feet tall, his face big and almost rubbery. "That was a very unusual piece, Josh." He shook Joshua's small hand in his big palm.

"Well, yeah, it's kind of my favorite."

"I could tell. It seems very popular with the kids."

"Oh, yeah, definitely."

"C'mere a sec. I wanna ask you something." He guided him out past the porch away from the fawning mothers and kids hovering around the cookies and lemonade.

"It's too late for the talent show, but we've got an assembly coming up at the end of the month, before graduation. I was wondering if you wanted to play that song."

"At the assembly?"

"Sure. You've performed enough before other people, even on TV, I heard tell. How 'bout it?"

"In front of the whole school?"

"Yes, in the gym. We're giving out end-of-the-year awards and things. Thought it might be a good change of pace. We'll put you on after the orchestra."

"Uh, okay. Can I do it with a guitarist and a drummer?"

"Sure."

Feeling more than unprepared, he later called the only student who still spoke to him.

"Ed?"

"Yah."

"This is Joshua."

"Hey, man, where ya been?"

"Layin' low since my bit of TV fame."

"Oh yeah. Don't let those jackwads at lunch get to ya."

Joshua sighed. He had another friend left in the world. He may be a stoner hood, but he was a friend.

"You don't mind?"

"About what?"

"What I said, that I'm . . ."

"Fuck no. Same thing I told Dave once. Just don't go pokin' yer dick at me and we'll get along fine."

"Wouldn't think of it. Besides, you're not my type."

"No problem, dude."

"We gotta talk."

"Sure, man. You allowed out?"

"Uh, I am out."

"Huh? Oh. Extra cool. I'll pick you up. We'll get some brewskies, smoke a bit, eh?"

He needed that, an escape. But he also needed a friend who knew about David and would understand his stunned reaction to a second rejection. Getting lost in music with a bong hit or two would help, too.

Word got around that Joshua had rocked his piano recital and was playing for the school assembly, and people started talking to him. He didn't say much until Brent Carse invited him, walking up as bold as anything, and said, "I'm havin' a party on Saturday. My mom's got a baby grand. You wanna come?"

Brent sure wasn't David, but he was there.

"You're not mad at me for telling you to fuck off?"

"I'd be upset, too. It's cool."

His parents seemed relieved that he still had some friends, and his father didn't even warn him about a curfew. "You need to borrow my car?"

"No, Brent lives just ten blocks away."

He walked in the night along quiet sidewalks, wondering if the invitation was some kind of prank.

There was a lot of chatting around the kitchen. There was no beer. Brent's parents were still home, somewhat hidden away in their den. Ed, Joshua, and Brent joked about being trained while they furtively smoked a joint in the garage.

"So man, you, uh, would you play it here tonight?" Brent asked.

Joshua still felt as if he was being dared or set up, but Brent smiled. "You can do it."

"Just lemme listen to it once, first. You know, I'm still high."

"Cool man. Got some boss headphones in my room."

Ed waved them off, and Joshua got to spend a few moments with Brent in his room. He seemed ready for something more, but Brent left him alone to listen to "Bohemian Rhapsody."

He played it later, imagining a full orchestra accompanying him, and the guys at the party clapped, and then someone asked for more, so Joshua played the easy favorites, Foreigner's "Cold as Ice," Toto's "Hold the Line," and some people sang along, and then the strangest thing happened.

Joshua felt loved again. He also figured that if he could play drunk and stoned, performing sober in front of the entire high school would be a piece of cake.

The echo alone scared him. In the gymnasium where he'd a hundred times been proven worthless, where his presence amounted to little more than a pesky bump in Phys Ed, here he would play his song.

The work crew had wheeled the piano into the gym and were setting up platforms behind it for the student orchestra. A lectern and microphone stood to the side.

"Can I try out the piano?" he asked one of the men, whose name he never learned but whose face was familiar at every assembly.

"Are you the one 'at's playing this?"

"Yeah."

"Well, I guess it's okay."

"Thank you." He sat on the stool, opened the lid and ran his fingers softly over the keys. It wasn't the best piano in the school. The action was a bit muddy and a few crucial keys, middle C and E, stuck a bit. But he'd figure it out. He'd hammer through it and make a complete fool of himself.

A rush of queasy fear swept through him. He softly marked through the song, trying to ignore the few dozen people walking about, moving chairs, pulling out the wall of bleachers from each side. It was good that they made noise. It comforted him, hiding his tentative run-through.

Herded into homeroom for last period, when most school assemblies took place, Joshua sat at his desk, alphabetically placed between Theresa Eisel in front and Tim Foster behind. He'd put his books in his locker between bells and sat with his hands before him, wriggling them slowly. He figured he'd file in with the rest of the class, but then his homeroom teacher called out his name and told him to report to the gym.

"Brown nose," he heard coming from the direction of Tim Foster. He tried to ignore it, but a few kids giggled. He walked out into the suddenly empty halls. His footsteps echoed solemnly. He passed each door, peeking in briefly at the rows of faces waiting to be sent to the gym.

The risers set up, the microphones tested, a few other custodians busied themselves about the place, making themselves look overworked.

"There you are," Mr. Rose saw him across the wide expanse. Joshua crossed a painted line in the wooden floor, the same line that he'd stood at twice a week in Phys Ed, only to hear a fresh new joke tossed his way by the pig-faced gym teacher. He crossed that line now, standing between Matt Crodach's drum kit and Ed Wallenbeck's guitar amp.

"Is the piano mic'ed?"

"Oh yes, just like you asked."

"Great. Sir, could you do me favor?"

"Sure."

"Can you turn the piano around?"

"Well, I don't know if we can."

"Sir? It would mean a lot."

"I'll see what I can do."

I played harp with the orchestra in the first part of the assembly, a "Music Appreciation Day," it was called. That segued into some mid-concert announcements by the principal, which was really just patter until the students in the orchestra returned to the bleachers. Then the annual awards were doled out for the students voted Best This and Most That. It's actually astounding that they allowed such things, awards for Most Funny, Best Jock, Best Body, and a few prank awards to teachers.

At a cue from Mr. Rose, Joshua, drummer Matt Crodach, and guitarist Ed Wallenbeck walked up to their instruments set up in front of our abandoned music stands. I remember the feeling of comfort Joshua gave us, smiling as we left the gym floor and they entered. As a member of the orchestra, I was one of those kids who really knew how it felt, the accomplished pride in performing music. It was as if we were all merely working musicians. I would do the same later when we all became friends again over a piano, remembering these little moments.

Other than the wave of joy they brought the school that day, Brent Carse may have been the spark that got Joshua even more attention. Yes, his photo appeared in the student newspaper the next week: an image of the three of them playing in the gym. Framed through the piano's raised lid, with Joshua's head momentarily upraised in sharp focus and Ed Wallenbeck's hand sweeping across his guitar, a rapt bleacher full of students off in the distance watch attentively.

Years later, Brent told me he'd sent prints to *The Plain Dealer* in a rushed application for a summer internship. When they hired him, for some reason they published that one photo. Otherwise the concert might have remained a memory, a local story, not a day that would soon send Joshua off to the other side of the country.

If my description seems a bit florid, perhaps it's because, other than that photo, it wasn't recorded. No one thought to ask the AV club or anyone with even a cassette recorder to capture a mere school assembly.

"You seen him?" Joshua asked Ed, not having to explain, David.

"Naw, the Seed kids are excused. They go to their meetings after school."

Joshua scanned the bleachers, hoping anyway. Surely David had heard, knew?

Unlike our playing, backs to one wall, a basketball hoop above us, facing the assembly, Joshua had managed to have the piano placed so that he would turn his back on the school as he played. And did they notice? Did they care? Either way, it was that staging that led to the now famous photo.

Principal Crumrine picked up the next card. Anticipation banged off the walls of the gymnasium, off the bleachers, and back into Crumrine's microphone, where it erupted in a brief piercing shriek of feedback. Crumrine furled his brow at the AV teacher manning the controls.

"And now we have a special surprise, something a bit more contemporary, I'm told." He grinned over at Mr. Rose, as if to say, *This is your gamble, not mine.* "With Ed Wallenbeck playing guitar, and Matt Crodach on drums, here's Joshua Lee Evans performing his own piano arrangement of a song called 'The Bohemian Rhapsody.'"

A smattering of applause barely covered the rumble of chatter, accented by a few whistles. Joshua stood by the piano and sort of half-bowed as Ed stood holding his guitar. Matt beamed, confident as ever. The three exchanged a smirking nervous glance.

"The moment of truth, dudes," Matt muttered.

Ed replied out of the side of his mouth, "Let's knock their fuckin' socks off."

The space between his bench and the piano seemed to stretch out as Joshua impulsively stepped away from it. Ceiling flood-lights glared on the shiny gym floor. The smattering of applause faded as he walked to the principal's microphone. He held a hand up, signaling a moment. Ed and Matt's confused silence strained. He actually heard the lights humming.

A voice yelled out, "Rock and Roll!" The tension broke with clusters of laughter. He'd made it to the other side. Ed's amp let out a short rip of static.

Joshua stood at the microphone and scanned the crowd to si-lence. He saw Mr. Rose from the corner of his eye, his arms crossed nervously, possibly regretting his decision. Joshua wanted to look up, but instead simply pictured the roof above him.

"This is for Kelly." Joshua's soft voice echoed the assembly to silence. He wanted to add "and David," but instead said, "You're all welcome to sing, because we're not gonna."

Returning to the piano, he sat, took a long breath, looked up at Ed, who nodded once, his guitar shining. Matt twirled his drumsticks and grinned, more than ready. Joshua stretched his fingers and softly pressed down to the first tight cluster of notes.

He didn't hear what he was playing. The internal voice of Freddie Mercury sang through him. He didn't notice it at first, but a few students began to do just that, mumbling the lyrics along with him, softly at first, and then, as the piece rolled with the playful split sections, certain groups of kids started waving their hands together, or popping up for certain parts ("Galileo!" "Galileo!" "Let him goooo!"). The teachers could not control them and so gave up and sheepishly clapped along.

But that moment, oh, when the boys played, with everybody swaying along to that odd tragic tiny operetta of a song, the song that demanded your attention in a car, demanded to be turned up, demanded that a gang of kids turn themselves instantly into a portable choir, taking parts high, low, battling over notes, celebrating tragedy as the guitar and piano trilled and pounded along, that moment energized our small school of kids as nothing ever had, not even the bonfire years back when the mascot almost caught on fire.

It is the day they most talked about afterward. It is the day that burdens a surviving friend, being forced to remember, to tell it again.

Their voices became louder, until we heard them over the boys' playing with more clarity and familiarity and devotion than any patriotic trumpeting of a national anthem in any country, because this was a country of children torn down. These children, this age of mine, all sang to the music of a grand queen, interpreted by a little prince.

By the time Josh reached the last tinkling chords, he felt the impact of what he had done. I did. I was proud to shed tears. So were others, even boys. It was an act of revolution, delivered in a most elegant and precise span of six minutes. The teachers felt it overtake them as the students roared in applause. This was not the stuff of cheerleaders, jocks, or academic valor, but the quiet dark bedroom agony inside each of these near-adults brought forth and aired out in the bright afternoon of their lives, and for a moment, it was truly dangerous.

"Nothing really matters to me," the students' voices faded as perfectly as a trained choir's. The gymnasium grew still as Joshua finished the last few chords, Ed following up with the final curling notes as we sang so softly, "Any way the wind blows," and Matt gracefully struck one last time on his cymbals.

Joshua stood, bowed, a grin spreading across his face despite his fear. He glanced at Mr. Rose, looked back at the cheering, hooting, clapping crowd, bowed, and walked off, wishing for a moment more to enjoy it. The applause continued until well after he sat back down in the bleachers, where hands of people who'd never spoken to him patted his shoulder like old friends. Ed and Matt followed. They shook hands, then hugged. Joshua fought back tears as he said to them both, "Well, I guess we showed them."

Matt grinned even wider. "We showed them plenty."

Chapter 24

I WANT TO BREAK FREE

HE COULD NOT get the smell of blood off his fingers. His moment of glory two months in the past, Joshua lost himself amid fryer grease and frozen hamburger patties.

Why was such a talented young man flipping burgers? Along with the rapid deflation of his brief celebrity status, it came down to a family argument shortly after graduation. Joshua, not playing the piano, moping around the house, refused to work for his father at the hardware store. His father threatened to withhold his college tuition money. Joshua admitted that he wasn't sure he even wanted to enroll, even though locals got a tuition discount at Beekam College.

When his father, standing over him in the living room, dared to bring up David as the reason for his "personal problems," Joshua just hauled off and shoved his father out of the way before storming out of the house.

Years afterward, Joshua refused to talk with me about that fight. His mother has forgotten it all. With his father now dead and his sister refusing to speak to me, it remains a puzzlement.

He scanned the local Help Wanted ads. He returned to the music store at the mall to see about a job, but some lady, snooping nearby while pretending to shop for an organ, recognized him. He saw the woman's pointed finger as he left, her gossiping over his shoulder. By the next day, the manager called back saying the job had been taken. The only place that would hire him was a Burger Chef off I-70. Clayton Briggs, the manager, didn't seem to care about his reputation, and since the customers didn't see him, neither did they.

Briggs did *know* about him, though, but he didn't tell him so in so many words. "Rookie, I need them grills cleaned out by midnight," he'd bark, his wide torso barely fitting through the thin passage between the oven and the white tile wall.

Standing before the grill, an immense steel machine, Joshua flapped out frozen patties, separated by thin slices of paper that stuck to anything. He flopped the patties on a rolling chain that dragged the circles of beef through the flaming oven. They plopped out the other end like turds, but he had to catch them on the bun or they'd fall into a puddle of grease.

At the same time he had to run a pair of buns through a similar smaller machine for toasting, except the timing was different, so there was always a wait. Condiments he didn't mind. If the customers had been served their sandwiches open-faced, they would have probably enjoyed the artistic swirls Joshua made with mustard, ketchup, and a pickle-eyed smiley face.

He hated this job, his first, more than life itself. The first day, Clayton told him to clean the women's rest room. What he hadn't told him was that someone had had a diarrheic fit and missed the toilet by about two feet.

After he'd recovered from nearly vomiting and cleaned the mess away, he washed his hands three times and fumed silently while the other employees glanced and the girls at the counter giggled from across the slatted metal rows for burgers and chicken sandwiches. He didn't care about life on the other side of the fryer. He rarely spoke at all.

The work tired him, the polyester uniform itched, and even at night, in bed, his hands still smelled of burnt blood and grease. But it made him forget. At least he thought so.

Once he had to pay for a new nametag when he left it pinned to his shit-brown polyester tunic. It came out of the dryer with his nametag warped like a noodle. It read Jcsspch.

194

He took the manager's criticisms to heart at first. But one night after closing when the night manager had already locked up and Joshua was heading home in his mother's borrowed car, he suddenly felt hungry. The free meal hours were long gone, so he wheeled around on the highway and headed back toward the QuikMart 24. He ended up driving, once again, by the rest stop he'd heard about.

The idea of toilet sex burned in him. Was it a joke, scoffed at between laughs by some school kids or one of the workers? He wasn't sure, but he did have to take a piss anyway.

What stopped him though was the green Pinto. His boss's green Pinto parked in the lot. And he hadn't even worked that night.

He saved the piss for home, but made it to the QuikMart for a bag of chips before his bladder burst.

After that, he took Clayton's gripes with a smirk. None of it mattered anymore, and he seemed to smile more after getting work done, even pretended to flirt with the girls. At least he wasn't doing *that*. At least he'd had David in his arms, for a while.

By late July, Ed finally showed up, just walked in and ordered a double cheeseburger. Joshua didn't know how to react, even though he'd told Ed weeks before where he was working. Ed waved and pointed, exaggerated, like he'd spotted a monkey at the zoo.

Joshua begged for a break, and after some steaming, Briggs relented. He sat as Ed wolfed down the burger.

"How is it?"

"Terrible."

"Good."

"What are you doing here, man?"

"Paying the rent."

"Way out here? Your mom was embarrassed to tell me."

"Well, there's some other things she's embarrassed about, too. But I guess you know what they are, and that's why I can only get a job out here where the trash don't have TVs and they can't get *The Orin and Mabel Show* on the radio."

"I'm gettin' you out, at least for a day. Next Saturday. The World Series of Rock. Aerosmith, Journey, AC/DC, Thin Lizzy, a few others. It's like an all-day festival."

The bands were far from his favorites. "Cleveland Stadium? Yeah, I heard about it on the radio. Gotta work."

"You gotta come with. Chris Harpster and Ken Schinsky, you and me."

"They know about me?"

"They don't give a fuck. They're so stoned all the time they wouldn't even care if you blew 'em."

Joshua knew that wasn't exactly true, but he also knew there was someone missing from the cast of characters.

"You seen Dave?"

"Naw."

Nothing. Joshua chewed on that, and a French fry.

"Heard he's just holed up at his ole man's place."

"Oh."

Thud.

"He's done with The Seed?"

"Yup."

Located. Target in sight.

Joshua stood outside with him for a smoke break, letting Doug, his "not at all an asshole" co-worker, take his place at the burger machine. After hours by the fry grill, Doug liked to hang out in the walk-in freezer. The only customers were a couple of kids or commuters from the highway. It was eleven at night, inside a tiny burger hut by a highway.

"So, when's the concert again?"

"Saturday. Already got you a ticket."

"I'm gettin' off."

"And high, dude." Ed discreetly handed over a small bag of pot.

"Dude. I don't even have a bong."

"Go buy papers, or get an apple."

"A what now?"

Ed sighed. "You cut two holes in an apple, like a pipe. Forget it. Here."

Ed covertly handed him a small packet of rolling papers. Joshua stuffed them in the pocket of his polyester shit-brown uniform. He had to remember to put it in his gym bag so it wouldn't melt into his pants in the laundry.

"What time you guys heading out?"

"Like, noon. It's an all-day show."

"You're a lifesaver."

Ed patted his back, walked across the parking lot to his van.

David was back. He had to go to the concert, or Joshua could use inviting him as an excuse to call him, or even visit his farm.

Of course Clayton, his barrel-chested manager, had a hissy fit when Joshua asked for the day off.

"That's our busiest day," he huffed in the tiny office that barely fit Joshua, his girth, and the cluttered desk. Worksheets loomed on the wall. Joshua saw his name filling six days for the next three weeks.

"You know, I know who you are," Briggs said.

Found out.

"Now, don't get all upset. I hired you because I understand your problem and I thought I'd give you a chance."

Then it hit him. The manager was not married, and he did kind of swish, like that guy in the practice room at the college.

Suddenly Joshua realized that there were people like him in Serene and nearby, and some of them stayed there. But he didn't want to become one of them.

He didn't tell his boss about his plans, but instead worked up to the day before the concert. As a soft summer rain came down, Joshua clocked out, and shoved open the always-sticking metal back door. Briggs was out back, smoking a cigarette. He timed it right.

"I wanna thank you for giving me a chance," he said as he unzipped the polyester tunic that made his skin crawl. "Maybe I'm like you in one way, but I am not gonna stay here and rot in all this grease just because of it."

He tossed the tunic at Briggs, who made a failed attempt to catch it. The shirt dropped to the asphalt. Joshua drove home in his worn undershirt, barely nodded a greeting to his mother in the kitchen, did not respond to her, "You're home early," trod upstairs to the bathroom, showered off the grease and blood for the last time, fell to his bed and slept, thinking about the concert on Saturday and how stoned he was going to get, how his ears would ring again for days afterward, and how it would be so great if David were going too.

He dared to call David the next day but got no answer. So he waited for Ed's van to pull up, told his mother he was going to a concert, didn't even wait for her astonished reply, nor did he wait more than a few miles on the highway to ask for help rolling a joint.

He should have enjoyed it, an arena full of devoted fans, waving hands, flicking lighters by the thousands, and his being higher than he'd been in months. But their seats were too far away and hard on his butt. Ken suggested they migrate to the open field, but the idea of standing amid a crowd with a blocked view held no appeal. He spent most of Ted Nugent's set waiting in one line for a toilet stall to hide in, then another for an overpriced hot dog and a soda.

By the start of the last act, Aerosmith, he relented and followed Ed, Chris, and Ken down the stairs, where they jockeyed for any sort of view. He could almost see the chords in his mind, how he would play the keyboard parts in his imaginary version of "Train Kept a Rollin'." Perhaps the cannabis was to blame, but he also saw outside himself, a mere dot in the crowd.

By the time the stage lights darkened and the stadium lights went up he was tired and dehydrated but somewhat lifted by the music as he and his friends joined the calm exodus out of the stadium.

Over the next days, he contemplated his situation between scolding lectures from his father about tuition costs. He'd saved money by eating at work and not really living. He'd gotten a short haircut for a job he no longer had. His skin recovered after he stopped eating mostly fried food. He wasn't the beautiful shaggy-haired boy who spilled his guts on TV. He wasn't anybody, for a while.

When his savings reached more than four hundred dollars, he felt it growing like a lump that had to be digested. With David still a zombie and a few miles away, a high school diploma and college to look forward to (or dread) in September, he didn't feel anything until he got a call.

"Joshua?"

"Yes."

"This is Garrett Glass."

"Who?"

"From *Cleveland Today*, the show you were on."

"Oh, hi. Oh, hi!" His father at work, his mother out in her garden, and his sister off attending a teen cheerleading camp in Wadsworth, he felt a sudden solitary expectation.

"How are you?"

"Good. You?"

"Great. I'm actually out in Hollywood. Well, near Hollywood."

"Oh, wow."

"Yes, I'm working on a completely different show, a few actually, in development, and somewhere in my forwarded mail I got your letter and the clipping about your school performance. Looks like you had a bigger audience than in our little studio."

"Huh, yeah, it went pretty well." Except David wasn't there.

"I wanted to call, because I actually have you to thank for my moving out here, in a way."

"How so?"

"Why? Well, as you recall, your segment got a lot of attention. Not much of it good, I'll have to say. Those Bible-thumpers started a phone campaign to get me fired, and it worked."

"I'm sorry to hear that. Yeah, I got some reactions here, too."

"Understandable. But for me, it all turned out good. I sent my reel around—you know, that's a videotape of my best work—and your show was one of them. I got a job offer out here in LA, and there's a kind of talent show competition I think would be perfect for you."

"A what now?"

"Kind of a take on *Star Search*, but different. It's a limited summer show. I could set you up for a visit for a few days, see how it goes. You're eighteen, right?"

"Yes, my birthday was back in November."

"Good! Good! So, let me know when you'd like to come out. Do you need to talk it over with your parents? You need plane fare?"

"Um, maybe. Yes."

Just gotta get out. Just gotta get right out of here.

Goodbye, burger blood. Goodbye, cornfields. Goodbye, Serene. Goodbye, David.

Chapter 25

SPREAD YOUR WINGS

CLOUDS COVERED THE squared patches of land over the Midwest. People and cars became tiny dots, but the higher the plane rose, the giddier he became. His ears popped. He borrowed chewing gum from a woman seated next to him.

He saw the Grand Canyon from above. The land looked beautiful. Trying simply to enjoy the flight and the strange luxury of eating food above clouds, he tried not to think about David and the whole mess at home. But that was what had propelled him into the sky and across the country, to tell his story. He thought back and tried to relive his life without any of the mistakes, with only he and David being happy together.

He tried to understand why he was in love with such a brave loser. How could he be in love after only doing it with him once on a rooftop, a few times in a truck or in fields, and not even sleeping together? That was what he had always wanted, to lie in a bed with David, to hold him after making love, see his breath move up and down inside his smooth chest. So often he'd touched himself, breathing shallow, pretending it was David he touched, David he caressed, and not his own skin or his own pillow.

It wasn't until the plane lowered toward Los Angeles that he began to realize what he had gotten himself into. Everybody seemed eager to rush off, like they all had important meetings with famous people. He did too, but he wasn't sure he would make it. What if they forgot about him?

His fears were calmed, then heightened for a moment when he saw a man in a black suit standing solemnly with a card that read J L EVANS.

"Are you waiting for me, sir?"

"Are you the Evans boy?"

"Yes."

"Let's go."

The driver took his luggage, opened and shut the door for him, then pulled off to an on-ramp to the highway.

"You want the sunroof open?"

"The what now?"

"Here. Enjoy."

A blast of air and bright light swept into the cushioned room on wheels. Joshua hadn't noticed the tiny bar and television in the back seat. He shyly lifted his hand up to feel the air through the roof and almost touched the palm trees that seemed to lean down in benevolent homage to his passage.

He was in Los Angeles.

"Your first time?" The driver half-turned back from the steering wheel.

"Um, yes."

"Lemme point out a few landmarks."

An informed chap who seemed to enjoy sharing his knowledge of the sprawling city, the chauffeur pointed out hedges behind which he said famous movie stars lived, restaurants where famous food was served, and buildings where infamous crimes happened. Joshua peered through the one-way window at cars on either side. A young girl in the back seat of a convertible, no older than Joshua, stuck her tongue out at what she assumed was an impossibly rich old fart behind the tinted glass.

After passing through busy streets, their drive slowed as traffic became quieter, more residential. The car swirled silently up the curved driveway of a mansion that to Joshua looked like Rebecca's Sunnybrook Farm sliced up and rearranged in the wrong order. It was modern and ancient, and it was huge. The car stopped and the driver opened his door. Joshua stepped out and saw the wide front door swing open.

Standing in the doorway, in white shorts and a green polo shirt, Garrett Glass held his arms out in a welcoming benevolent pose. Two tiny dogs snapped at his feet, their push-faced snouts sniffing at him.

"Welcome to LA, doll!"

"Is this all yours?" Joshua asked as they entered the mansion with the dogs circling their feet.

"Oh, no, hon. I'm just house-sitting for a producer friend." Garrett mentioned a name Joshua didn't know. "He's off in Tunisia filming another over-budget epic. I have a little place in we hoe."

"Where?"

"WeHo. West Hollywood. I'll give you a tour soon." Garrett led him upstairs to a guest room, where he put his suitcase and overnight bag.

"Now, we have so many people for you to meet that we just thought we'd have a little party in your honor after the taping. Nothing fancy, just a few friends. We want to show you how we gay people can live free and openly. Just to give you a little boost after your big premiere. Oh, I feel like the mother of a debutante. Now. The first thing we have to do is get you some decent clothes. Did you bring a dress suit?"

A bit stunned by Garrett's almost prissy demeanor, nothing like his more officious tone back in Cleveland, Joshua hesitated. "Uh, well, I have one I brought."

"Let me see." Glass pulled down the zipper of the boy's overnight bag and made a sour face. "No, too funereal. We'll have to go shopping. Come on!"

Garrett led him across the hall to a larger bedroom, one of five.

"Let's see. Most of my clothes are a little large for you." Garrett foraged in a closet the size of a small room. "We'll have to get you a tux for the show, make it look classical and classy. In the meantime," he tossed clothes out of the walk-in closet, "try this on."

Of course Joshua had no idea how expensive the clothes were. He only noticed that, when he put on the sunglasses Garret handed him, things didn't look nearly as foggy as they did when he wore his pair from K-Mart.

"Hop in the shower and you'll be ready for Rodeo Drive."

As he stripped himself, Joshua noticed a telephone by the toilet. He dropped his pants, sat down, and before he finished, had already dialed home.

"Where are you?" His mother's concerned tone hurt.

"Los Angeles."

"Have you run away?"

"No, I'll be back soon."

"How did you get to the airport?"

"Ed drove me."

"Why are you there?"

"I'm gonna be on a TV show. I had to sneak out 'cause I knew you wouldn't let me."

"How do you know that?"

"Okay. Mom, can I go to California and be on TV?"

"What for?"

He gave her the gist of the show, that he didn't know when it would air, explaining little, wanting to tell her everything. At least he let her know where he was. That made him feel relieved.

He heard his mother's voice quavering. "It's just so sudden, but you are eighteen, after all. When are you coming back?" In her way, he had been forgiven and was free to enjoy this new and strange adventure.

"I'm not sure."

He said goodbye, kept calm until the hot shower released something inside him and his brief jagged burst of sobs and tears swirled down the shower drain.

After another drive where Garrett talked nonstop about the shows he was working on, they parked on Santa Monica Boulevard amid rows of fancy shops and restaurants. What he had sought so desperately in David's eyes now spilled over on the streets as men looked openly at him with flirting glances. He blushed from the ease with which these men carried it. They passed a jewelry shop.

"Oh, I wanna get my ear pierced."

"Are you sure?"

"Yeah. What kind should I get?"

"Well, you have to start with a post."

Joshua imagined a large railroad spike jutting out of his ear. "Oh, uh, okay."

They went in.

"Not that ear. The other."

"What's the difference?"

"A lot, dear. A lot."

Garrett bought him a few shirts and pants, they found a rental store for a tuxedo that almost fit. The salesman fussed over him, and he and Garrett exchanged quizzical glances as Joshua sat in a chair, posing as if playing the piano. The elbows were a bit tight, but he didn't complain.

"So, rehearsal's tomorrow, then the taping the day after. Feel free to practice on the piano. Don't let the dogs outside, and make yourself at home."

With his new and rented clothes, Garrett left him alone at the mansion-ette for a few hours to go to "take a meeting." People seemed to do that a lot in Los Angeles.

Wandering around the absent film producer's home that night, Joshua crept down to the den, a dark and warm room at the level of the back yard and swimming pool. Knick-knacks in porcelain and silver crowded tables and shelves. A shelf stuffed with oversized art books, another stacked with bound copies of . . . He pulled one out: screenplays, dozens of them, a few whose titles he recognized.

Above an empty fireplace, a framed poster-sized black and white photo of a young nude Gary Cooper sitting on the bank of a pond loomed like an erotic sentinel. Was it real?

He padded silently about the room, feeling like a stranger. The sliding glass door opened with a whoosh. Raised in a home where the air conditioning battled stifling humidity all summer and the heater fought freezing cold all winter, Joshua felt somewhat exposed. He had never been in a home where the temperature inside was the same as it was outside. It felt strangely seductive, as if the walls were breathing. There were no boundaries between inside and out.

He couldn't avoid his infatuation with the photograph. He shucked down his pants and undershorts, knelt, and briskly tugged himself while gazing adoringly at the Gary Cooper photo. He tried his very best not to think of David, and for a few moments, it worked.

The studio resembled a giant warehouse with a huge antenna atop its roof. After Garrett drove through the gate and flashed an ID badge to a chubby guard who sat silently in a small booth, they drove past a long line of people waiting to get in.

"Are they the audience?" Joshua nervously clutched a folder with a photocopy of his solo arrangement of "Bohemian Rhapsody," even though he had it memorized.

"Not ours. One of the game shows tapes today."

He saw people in the crowd staring at them, hoping for someone famous. When they proved otherwise, people turned away, disappointed.

Garrett parked on a more private side of the studio, led him inside and down a long hallway with several doors, most of them open. In each one, he heard and saw singers warming up, girl gymnasts stretching, a man juggling orange balls.

"And here. Why don't you warm up and I'll introduce you to the other producers. Just a sec."

A young woman stood by the side of the piano, glanced up, returned to a score, hummed a bit. Joshua approached her.

"Are you my accompanist?"

"Um, no. I'm in the show."

"Oh. Sorry. Katie. Katie Crystal." She held out a hand.

"Joshua Evans."

"Sorry, I'm still waiting for an accompanist. Do you play?"

"Actually, I do."

"Do you mind?"

She handed him her music, which he glanced at, saying, "I'm not the best sight-reader," but fumbled through as the girl shout-sang her rendition of "Before the Parade Passes By." Her ending blast of notes was met with a smattering of applause as three men entered the room. Katie took a bow as Joshua remained seated.

"Thank you, dear," said one of the men. "Could you give us the room? Thanks."

As Garrett introduced the two other producers, Ken and Andrew, Katie offered a thumbs-up to Joshua and a silent thank you as she shuffled out.

"So." Ken or Andrew said as he and the others took chairs in front of a wall of mirrors. "You're going to play that Queen song, am I right?"

"Yes, sir."

"How about you give us a spin?"

"Oh, play it now?"

"You got it."

"Okay."

"It doesn't have to be full out, just give us a taste."

Garrett offered a slightly nervous grin of support, and Joshua began playing, the copied sheet music atop the piano. But just before he passed the second verse and was about to dive into the operatic break, a voice stopped him.

"That's great, just great, Josh," Andrew said. "Can you give us a minute?" He nodded toward the door.

"Okay." Joshua stepped outside, heard the men talking, a voice raised, then quieted. Garrett opened the door. "Slight change."

Joshua stepped in, not knowing if he should sit at the piano, but Andrew stood and gestured for him to take his seat.

"Josh, we have a one-hour show and a lot of acts, and while it is a classic, I know, we do have a strict time limit. I'm gonna bring in Arnie, our musical director, and he's gonna help you make some cuts, okay? Now we have to go see the rest of our contestants, so we'll see you tomorrow bright and early for the taping, okay?"

After more handshakes, the two men left, leaving Joshua stunned.

"I'm so, so sorry," Garrett said, "but this is gonna be fine."

Another man, older with a graying beard, was introduced, and he and Joshua sat at the piano.

"Now, let's see. I know you won't like this, but here, may I?" He held a pencil to the sheet music.

"I guess."

"We cut the second verse," Arnie crossed out half a page, "and jump to the break," another slash, "shorten the instrumental," slash, "and jump to the end. Give it a go."

"Now?"

Arnie nodded. He knew the song almost backwards and forwards, and plunked through the abbreviated version with a studious scowl.

Joshua simmered in disappointment. He waited for Garrett in a hallway for almost two hours. People kept walking by, some in almost-orange make-up, others in costumes, most of them just ordinarily-dressed people with headphones and clipboards, all busy, busy.

Joshua sat in silence as they left. Garrett patted his shoulder then led him to the car.

"It'll be great. Besides, people won't know the difference."

"I will."

"This is Hollywood. Ya gotta make a little sacrifice every now and then."

"What did they do to the juggler, make him use just two balls?"

Garrett, stunned at first, saw that Joshua was kidding and grinned. "Kid, you're gonna move on to bigger things. I can tell."

The stage, enormous and shiny, with glittering set pieces that seemed half a football field away, dwarfed the piano, which, Joshua was relieved to see, was a finely tuned black grand Yamaha. His sense of assurance waned as the show began. With other contestants crowding the large greenroom, he could only stretch his fingers and wait.

He'd spent the morning rehearsing the truncated version of the song. His attempts to air-play it in the green room, interrupted by half a dozen singers warming up, sipping drinks, and chatting, became useless. He thought having performed it on the Cleveland show and at school would make him more at ease. But the monitor kept cutting to shots of a much larger audience, hundreds of people, clapping and whistling for an act with a man in a green jacket and his tiny dog dressed in a vest and hat. The dog stood on its hind legs, jumped through hoops and balanced on a plank. Where did they come from, these people who cheered? Who would spend hours waiting in line in the Los Angeles sun to watch a talent show?

"Wish me luck?" Katie, the singer he'd met, offered a meek glance. He stood, gave her a brief hug, his tuxedo almost catching on a few rhinestones of her shiny blouse.

Joshua then watched as the young woman sang, cracked a high note, but kept on singing. She returned to the green room, shaking her head. He wanted to offer a word of comfort, but someone called his name and he was led out through a hallway, behind the enormous set, and out to the piano during a surprisingly quiet moment when it seemed the cameras weren't rolling. Crew members guided him to the piano, where he sat.

"No. Stand and wait for the red light, then take a bow. It'll be better."

He followed the instructions, waited for the host to introduce him, bowed abruptly, then sat, waiting for the applause to settle.

Racing through the song's shortened version, his mind was distracted by the lights, someone in the audience leaving, a camera sweeping around on the other side of the piano. He almost halted at the edit points, but continued, then slowed for the legato final bars.

The surge of applause stunned him. A flush swept over him, the sweat seeping through his shirt and into the jacket. He bowed, smiling in appreciation, but also oddly wondering if he'd have to pay for dry cleaning before returning the tux.

"A dog. A goddamned dog."

Katie Crystal slumped into a chair in the green room after the show's taping. "Well, I think I'm done with Hollywood. How about you?"

"Um, I'm staying for a while. Garrett has a few small gigs set up for me, I think."

"Wow, you had an in with a producer and you still didn't win."

"It's not like that."

"Whatever it is, it's back to Fresno for me."

"Fresno?"

"Yeah, well, we can't all hang around and wait to be famous. I've been living in my car."

Joshua wanted to offer Katie a hug, but Garrett rushed into the green room, hugging him as if he'd won.

"You did great, kid! I'm so proud of you." He nodded to Katie. "Great vocals, my dear."

Katie nodded but walked out with sad resignation.

"I didn't win."

"Don't worry about that. This is just a start."

The start of what, Joshua wondered.

Chapter 26

KILLER QUEEN

THE ARRIVAL OF Giannis Bacchus reminded Joshua of those old British movies where the staff lines up outside the estate door as a lord's carriage arrives.

"How long do we have to wait?" he asked Garrett as a uniformed maid and butler lounged by the front door. Garrett had dressed Joshua in a crème shirt, blue tie, and black dress pants.

"He called from the airport. Shouldn't be long."

"Will I have to leave?"

"Probably not."

With Garrett a guest of the film producer, and Joshua a guest of the guest, he figured he was on thin ice.

"But if he hits on you, lie and tell him we're dating. That should hold him off for a while."

Joshua blanched.

"I'm kidding. Sort of."

A black stretch limo pulled up, its underside briefly scraping the uphill driveway. The staff snapped to attention, the maid squelched a cigarette into a planter.

"Dahlings!" A rotund man in a blousy multi-colored shirt, white pants, and sandals emerged from the limo.

Joshua couldn't tell who were the "darlings" until the maid opened the front door and let the two small dogs out. They yapped and leapt at the large man, who struggled to bend over and scoop them up.

"Garrett, my dear." Two air kisses. "And who, who is this?"

"Joshua Evans. I told you about him. He was on my talent show."

"Did you win?" The man peeled off his wide sunglasses to inspect the boy. "You're not an actor, I hope."

"No, sir. I play piano."

"Oh! I love a cute peenist!" Close kisses on either cheek were accompanied by a groping hug that concluded with a grab at Joshua's butt.

"Consuela." Giannis held the dogs out and the maid dutifully took them. "What have you got cooked up for lunch?"

"Shrimp salad, fettuccini, and a Beaujolais."

"Excellent!" He turned back to Joshua. "Come, come! You will play for me and at my party. Are you the classical type, Rachmaninoff? The jazzy type?"

"Um, a little more rock type."

Giannis' face soured. "Oh. Well, you will play at my party and we shall see."

As the entourage followed him in, carrying his luggage and dogs, Giannis Bacchus began a lengthy tale of his filmmaking exploits, his temperamental actors, his unruly technicians, the hordes of indolent extras, and a horse that died.

Garrett and Joshua sat at the lengthy dining room table eating the delicious meal as Giannis talked and talked, his mouth half full of food, until he stopped abruptly.

"So! Garrett. You found this boy where? I didn't know you had such an Adonis!"

"Back in Ohio. He actually has a very fascinating story."

Giannis' eyes dulled. He waved his hand. Consuela appeared and cleared the dishes.

"You tell me yourself, my boy. Go put on some swim trunks and let an old queen gaze upon your beauty by the pool. I should be jetlagged, but I suddenly have such energy!"

Apparently, they were excused.

As Joshua hesitantly changed into a pair of swim trunks, Garret knocked and entered the bedroom.

"He likes you. That's good. But he's a little jazzed up. He may offer you cocaine. Decline."

"Um, yeah."

Having changed into a flowing orange and pink caftan, his dogs nestled on his ample lap, Giannis Bacchus sipped another glass of wine as Joshua slowly swam laps in the sparkling pool under a Hollywood sun. Beckoned to the film producer's side, he rose from the pool and picked up a folded towel on a beach chair beside Giannis.

"Such beauty."

"Thanks?"

"You are not used to admiration?"

"Um, not exactly."

He was not going to lie about Garrett, nor reveal anything private, particularly about David or his family. No, he was determined not to. But another glass of wine later, he had told a bit too much. Giannis seemed to have heard enough.

"This is a very sad story."

"I'm sorry."

"No. Would make a good movie, you know? A small movie."

"I never thought of that."

"But this is what I do, my dear boy. I take people's little lives and tragedies and turn them into magic."

"It seems to have done well for you."

"This?" Giannis waved his hand. "This is all a dream, a glorious web I have spun. You think I am some kind of royalty? My parents were poor immigrants. They worked in a shoe factory in Trenton and paid for my college courses in cinema, my trips back to Greece to learn about my culture. Then, I paid for their new house in Montclair."

"That's nice of you."

"But enough about me. Go, go practice. You've played on my piano?"

"Yes, sir. It's great."

"Good. Be my muse. Let me hear your music while I rest."

And so Joshua played as his host slept and perhaps dreamed of the story of a young boy from Ohio.

Garrett decided to cheer Joshua by giving him a taste of Hollywood's scene—and get out of Giannis's way. The producer awakened from his nap sunburned and cranky. He spent most of the afternoon shouting over the phone in his office.

After an early dinner, Garrett took him to a small nightclub to hear throaty cabaret tunes crooned by a man in a red lamé bustier, feather boa, and too much eye makeup. Joshua tried to stay awake.

"Alice Cooper wears less," he joked to Glass.

"Who?"

"Alice Cooper."

"Oh, that rock star. Had him."

"Had him what?"

"On a show I produced. Plays golf with Groucho Marx, you know."

"Really?"

Glass brought his lips tightly together and sipped his drink.

"Let's go to the party, dear. I promise we'll make a quick exit. There are just a few people who want to meet you."

"I'll bet," Joshua said. Only a few days of LA had burned him just enough to grow an unrefined sarcasm.

He and Glass barely spoke on the drive to the hills of Brentwood. Glass seemed to know each groove in the wooded curving streets. Joshua tried not to marvel at the homes hidden away under green camouflage and luxury.

The night of the show's airing two weeks later, Joshua was to perform and be "introduced" at Giannis Bacchus' welcome back party. Glass tried to impress upon Joshua's mushy head the importance of this evening. The incredible launch into whatever his potential oblivion craved at the moment was laid out before him in the svelte bodies of the wealthy, handsome, over-tanned men and women he was about to meet. It was like the party scene in *Laugh-In*, only it never stopped and he didn't get the jokes. It was a career buffet, one that the boy, had he a semblance of ambition, should have devoured. Instead, he felt like the meal.

"Does he know any Cole Porter?" one man queried, as if Glass were his trainer.

"You're cute," quipped another. "That'll help."

At about ten o'clock, Giannis told Garrett to bring Joshua to the piano, and shouted as he wafted through room after room in another flowing long shirt, white pants and sandals, "Come along, everyone! Performance! Performance time!"

After most everyone had gathered in the large front room around the piano on chairs and sofas or standing in the back, Garrett started to introduce Joshua. Giannis cut him off.

"As you all know, I recently returned from Tunisia, where my latest epic was completed, and I have only the—familiar to some of you—excruciating task of chopping my vision into little pieces for the studio's taste!"

Laughter ensued, followed by more of Giannis' comments. He finally got to the point.

"Thanks to my associate Garrett, who discovered this little Orpheus, I was brought back from the hell of filming. No heads turned, although he has turned a few heads tonight!" More laughter. "It gives me great pleasure to introduce to you a new 'rock lounge' sensation, Joshua Evans!"

Still more applause. Emboldened by a quickly downed glass of champagne, Joshua called out, "I heard there might be some talented singers here tonight."

Giggles bubbled through the room as a curly-haired young man and a lithe young woman in a slinky black evening gown were shoved forward.

"You can sing along, since you might know the words."

Taking Garrett's advice, he started big, with "Bohemian Rhapsody." The woman and man caught on and sang after the first lyrics, thanks to Garrett having prepped them in advance.

Joshua almost fumbled, the edited version still confusing him, but the singers kept him to his goal, looking back to him and performing with him in sudden rapport.

After shouts and applause and the clinking of glasses, the singers conferred with Joshua and he launched into another song ("Killer Queen") and another ("I'm in Love with My Car") and still another.

By the sixth number, Giannis stepped forward, still a mask of mirth although Joshua immediately understood the problem. Giannis was no longer the center of attention.

"Come, now we dance! Desserts and party favors by the pool!"

A few people remained by the piano, and the sassy queens who'd dished the boy now marveled at his playing. He was handed business cards. "You must play for my birthday party!" "I know just the right music producer for you." Compliments, promises, adoration, and champagne flowed.

After several introductions and warm handshakes with yet another designer, producer, or television executive's assistant, Joshua felt a bit sweaty, and with a third glass of champagne down his gullet, he walked outside. As some danced, Giannis held court by a table and two young men even stripped down to swim naked in the pool. A disco beat he'd heard on TV began to pulse and a high-pitched woman began to sing.

"What is that music?" he asked a tall handsome man who offered and lit a joint with a magician's flair.

"That is God. That is Sylvester."

"Oh."

"He is divine."

"That's a man?"

"Well, that's a debatable point, but still . . ."

"Hmm." Joshua was getting his confident buzz, and the man

217

was familiar and handsome with a ruddy look and a cleft chin. "What's your name?"

"Oh, I'm so sorry." He shook hands. "Terry. You're Joshua."

"How'd you . . . ? Oh, duh."

It seemed only a short time that the man and the boy talked together. People came in and out, one even whined, "Oh, excuse *meee*. I didn't know we were doing a scene." Joshua asked what that meant.

Terry half grinned. "Nothing, much."

Hours later, Garrett bid most of the guests goodnight except Terry. Giannis had retreated to his bedroom with both of the naked swimmers.

Terry stayed, fixed a last drink, and returned to the now quiet poolside. Joshua had a soda.

"You did very well, little man." Terry scruffed his hair and took a sip, looking away from the boy to enjoy the view of LA's grid of lights. Joshua gazed up at him. He looked familiar, like one of his history teachers, only more interesting.

"Thanks. Say, uh, are you . . . ?" *Garrett's boyfriend?*

"An actor? Yes."

"Um, no, I mean . . ."

"UltraWite."

"Huh?"

"UltraWite. The commercial."

It was then that Joshua recognized him. "Oh! Yeah! That's you!" He wanted to say, *But you look thinner*, but his manners prevented it.

"Yeah," Terry smirked. "That's me. For now."

"Do you wanna be something else?"

"Of course. I can't just barge into town like you and take Hollywood by storm."

"Oh."

"That was a joke."

"Sorry."

"I did a few soap operas. The best I can hope for is more TV, then, then . . ." He sighed. "See, you got a big break, but it's the wrong kind. You're news."

"Oh, you mean the show back in Cleveland?"

"Yep. Garrett showed me a tape."

"News of the World."

"Yeah, well, syndication, at least, which is great. But actors, well, we have to be very careful about such . . . things."

"Really? It seems like everybody I meet who works here is gay." It felt good to just say it so casually.

Terry shrugged. "Yes, well, that makes it even worse."

"What do you mean?"

"Oh, let's just say it makes the piranha more familiar with the taste of rumor."

"You're losing me."

"That's okay, Josh. You'll understand someday. For now, just be happy you got to do what you did. You reached a lot of people. Garrett said the ratings about the talent show were pretty good."

"You know, even though it was great to tell my story, I feel like it didn't work."

"Why?"

He told Terry what he knew about Kelly from his private talks with her.

"Really? Did you tell Garrett?"

"Yeah, on the other show."

"Tell Garrett what?" They both turned. Glass strolled onto the porch, cigarette smoke trailing. "We should be getting to bed, boys."

Joshua didn't know if that was a dismissal or an invitation.

Glass bid Terry goodnight, kissing him lovingly on the cheek. After Glass sighed, "Well . . ." two or three times, a silence fell. Joshua felt like he wasn't going to be sleeping in his bed.

"Is he, Terry, your boyfriend?"

Glass gasped. "Why, child, no. Whatever made you think that?"

"I dunno. The way you . . . care for each other."

"Joshua, that beautiful creature who just left is my sister."

"Huh?"

"We used to 'date.' Now we're pals. 'Buddies,' I think they still call them back in Ohio."

"Oh. How come?"

"What?"

"How come you're not boyfriends?"

Glass sighed. "Joshua dear, there is something you might as well learn now. It is more important to maintain a friendship with a man like that than to have him. That way they come back."

"Oh."

"Besides, for someone in my position, getting a boyfriend in this town is as easy as picking up laundry. Boyfriend material clings like moss if you don't keep moving. Friends, however, must be cultivated."

"Huh. Like plants."

"Yes. Now, aren't you exhausted?"

"Yeah. Can I just sit here for a while?"

"Of course." He looked down at the boy. "Goodnight. Try not to let all this stuff go to your head."

For a few days, despite his loss on the talent show, a sense of pride surged into him. Scanning the array of papers and magazines, including *Variety,* which noted that his show netted an 18 share, which was "very good" according to Garrett, Joshua felt a part of something great.

He leafed through an issue of *People* magazine, where one of the men from the party was interviewed, posing with a woman, his "girlfriend." Joshua had definitely seen him embracing another man at the party. But judging by the way Glass talked, and the snippy comments he made about certain movie and TV stars, what he read in the magazines didn't have anything to do with reality.

Except maybe his own story. It was strange, the way what was once so mysterious seemed so dead, final, confined to those columns of words in newsprint. Would David ever find out about his performance?

Garrett, serving as an informal agent, made a few reminder calls and got Joshua booked at a few parties over the next few weeks. None of them were as grand as Giannis's, but they paid a few hundred dollars, people flirted and admired him, sang along, or more often ignored him as mere background music.

There came a day when Garrett informed Joshua that Giannis had invited a few of his latest "protégés" to stay with him. Despite the extra bedrooms, it seemed the two had overstayed their welcome.

"I called the guy who's subletting, another actor-waiter. He'll be out tomorrow."

"Oh. So, do you think I could get on any more TV shows?"

"Well, dear, it's not like there's more to your story than what we used."

Hurt by the dismissal, he still had to ask, "Can I stay with you?"

"Well, sure dear, for a few days, until you get settled. Maybe we can even get you a job as an usher or something. You don't have a car, of course."

"No."

"Tricky. Damned impossible in LA."

Garrett's bungalow-style apartment in West Hollywood, while small, had a cozy atmosphere, with arty prints on the walls and throw pillows nearly filling a sofa.

"So, I'll just take my things and put 'em in the guest room."

"Um, Josh dear?"

"Yup?"

"It's only a one-bedroom, and you can sleep on the couch. But my bed's quite large, and I don't snore, so if you don't mind . . ."

"Oh, that's okay." He cautiously moved a few pillows and sat on the sofa.

"Of course. Fine. Now, go get cleaned up and we'll get something to eat."

At first, Joshua slept on the couch. After a few weeks, Garrett stopped asking him to tag along at any of his parties. So he stayed in, read a few of Garrett's books, and watched TV.

As a show of appreciation, one morning Joshua tried to cook, but the eggs were overdone. They sat, the sound of English muffins crunching in their mouths. Joshua broke it with a question that had been waiting to come out since before he'd arrived. "So, how's the UltraWite guy?"

"Terry? Oh, he . . . he's sick. He got pneumonia."

"Huh? What, was he frozen somewhere?"

"No, it wasn't like that. Actually, it was very sudden. He had been sick a few times, but then, he just . . . collapsed."

"Oh, that's too bad. He get better?"

"Hopefully."

"I'm sorry."

"That's all right."

"It's pretty strange, a young guy getting pneumonia."

"Well, dear, there's something you have to watch out for in our circles. Boys like to play a lot, and nobody gets out of it without a bout of something every now and then."

"Oh."

"Well, anyway, thanks for breakfast."

That night, what he knew would happen happened. It wasn't as bad as he thought it would be, but it was still awkward, despite the strong margaritas Garrett made.

The sex wasn't bad, considering he didn't want it. Garrett fawned over him. He could close his eyes and just enjoy the sucking sounds and the warm wet feeling on his cock, his belly, and even his butt. Garrett actually had a nice body, but the sex felt like payment.

Garrett's skin had a perfumed smell, like a department store. He puffed and preened, and when he lowered his large, slightly chunky form over Joshua's smaller body, the boy felt something slick come off the man's face. It was makeup.

At least he didn't insist too much when Joshua couldn't take his large erection in his butt, but then the boy had never had anything sizable up there. Garrett lubed him up with a few fingers, but it still hurt. The margaritas made the boy sleepy, too sleepy even to wait for Garrett to finish himself off.

One thing Joshua had learned was to play the innocent. He knew his time with Glass was limited. He didn't pretend to love the man, and refused to feign affection during and after the sex. And so he failed the audition for the role of live-in boy toy.

A few days later, Garrett announced that he'd found Joshua a lovely shared apartment further up the hill off Fountain Avenue with one of the production assistants, Margaret something. Garrett drove him to his new home and handed him an envelope with several hundred dollars in it.

"Here, dear," he said. "Do take care of yourself, and don't fall for any old queen that comes along."

Chapter 27

LEAVING HOME AIN'T EASY

"COFFEE?"

Slouched on the sofa, the television din tired him. Bed was calling. David had to be up at six the next morning.

"No, thanks," he responded as his father sauntered off to the kitchen and returned with a cup.

He glanced up as his father switched channels to the latest crop of violence in Iran, narrated by Dan Rather, then settled behind a newspaper.

"Well, I'm gonna head off to bed," he announced.

"G'nite," his dad said from behind the paper.

The truce with his father maintained a quiet, uneasy balance. Content to have an obedient son, there was no need even to mention that a single phone call could send him back to The Seed or jail. His father merely gave instructions about house and farm work, as if this was how things should be.

David trod up to his room, stripped down to underwear, and slid under the thick layer of sheets, blankets, and knitted afghans. Gifts from his aunt in Texas, they littered the furniture and beds of the house.

Tomorrow he would once again face the yawning acreage of the farm, the sputtering gas fumes of the tractor. It was late in the season and few workers stayed on. The two Mexican migrant workers, Hector and Ezequiel (whom everyone called Zeke), had left to find work further south. He hoped they'd return in the spring as they had for the past five years. David missed their steadfast efforts, their chuckles at his fumbled Spanish, and the occasional shared joint.

The only coworker left was Old Bob. The red-nosed geezer clung to any job that would keep him. David's tolerance had reached a limit, his annoyance softened only by the charm of another worker, the blond dusty-voiced Dennis Simmons.

But no, he realized in the darkness, Dennis wouldn't be there. He'd just gotten a winter job at the water treatment plant. Never again to have Dennis's company to distract him, his tales of Vietnam passing the hours. Never again to have the opportunity to attempt the moment alone.

Dennis reminded him of his cousin, Curt Hildebrandt. Before his family left Serene in 1972, the two cousins had often played together, even though David was ten years younger. Curt had imprinted a sort of image about the kind of man David admired and desired: odd, cool, and slightly tough. He had served in Vietnam and come back only slightly scarred. A letter from the Hildebrands from their new Texas home said that Curt was living with his parents, recuperating from the wounds of grown-up life. He'd had a problem with drinking, wrecked his car, and survived that as well.

David wasn't sure how long he'd last at home. If only he'd worked on a wheat farm. Then he could fall neatly into a combine like Neil Staller, that guy in high school. Sliced like lunch meat, dead in a minute. It was difficult to get yourself killed on a pumpkin farm. Sharp equipment was hard to come by, save clippers for the vines. Perhaps a concussion from a poorly tossed Big Mac. Not likely. Zeke, Hector, and Dennis's loading technique was too polished, and David, the smallest, climbed atop the gargantuan gourds, stacking them and the smaller ones carefully in the big rental truck. The labor honed into his muscles with medicine ball regularity.

His boss, Joe Kemp, his father's brother-in-law, a stern-faced yet nice enough man with a wife and three kids, appreciated him.

Unlike his uncle's other employees, David shaved regularly and could form complete sentences. This once again merited his promotion into the lucrative world of produce sales.

Dropped off at a roadside stand in the parking lot at a busy intersection in town, David took pride in his artistic arrangement of the homegrown and imported fruits and vegetables on the ten-by-five foot wooden trailer. The summer days passed as he bagged corn and tomatoes and hauled Georgia watermelons into car trunks.

Daily donning his John Deere cap, a white T-shirt, jeans, and Red Wing work boots, no customer would know he was into guys, at least not from looking at him. He had the definitive farmer's tan, pale above the bicep and below the shirt collar, but his face had grown ruddy in the daily sun. Several times the tips of his ears had dried to a crisp.

It was only when some wizened older man would quiz him on whether the peaches were from Georgia or North Carolina, or if a snippy housewife asked if the muskmelons were fresh that he'd ignore them or point to a sign. Whether they bought the damn stuff didn't matter too much to him. If it went bad, it'd just get hauled back and dumped in the ravine by a creek at the back end of Joe's cornfield. If customers cheated and took fourteen ears of corn to the dozen, David wasn't about to make an accusation.

David just wanted to get through the job and figure out what the hell to do with his life. The Seed meetings had come to an end. He was allegedly better, fine, sober. He told himself he wasn't thinking about Joshua—except when a car would pass, its window rolled down, and a Queen song blasted across the road.

It got to be a bitch every now and then, getting razzed by impatient shoppers, or having to deal with Depression-era survivors who elevated price-haggling to a sport.

Housewives clouded in perfume emerged from their air-conditioned Chryslers in floral-print blouses that shone brilliantly in the sun, wondering why bees attacked them and not him, who smelled of corn husks, dirt, and sweat.

"Well, Ma'am," he imagined saying, "you wouldn't have that problem if you didn't come out here dressed like a five-foot petunia."

David waited for a slow moment to walk back behind the printing shop that rented the bit of parking lot to Joe Kemp. He was allowed toilet privileges, and the few moments in the ink-smelling, cold office gave him a brief reprieve. But he went instead to the back faucet and filled a bucket with cold water.

He returned, relieved to see no waiting customers. He stood atop the wagon, pouring water over the sweet corn and peaches. Some girls in their daddy's car on their way to the mall hooted at the presumably dopey hunk. A trucker honked his horn, coaxing David to his cab window for a quick toss of a cantaloupe for a buck. The trucker winked and smiled. David smiled back, extra wide.

By mid-October, his hands had grown so callused his nights of self-abuse were like shaking hands with a stranger. So much for staying pure.

Loading and unloading trucks of pumpkins made his arms and chest tight with muscles. It was real work for dirt pay and it felt good, but what was left of his ambition had curdled to a quiet resentment, almost dormant, still waiting to strike.

What kept him from bolting was the calm pride in knowing that he had touched nearly every pumpkin on the farm. On Halloween night, having finally been given driving privileges again, he drove all through the town, admiring the candlelit flickers inside every porch Jack o' Lantern. He had helped turn half the state of Ohio into glowing grins for one night. Giddy children in kitchens had gutted the cool, seedy slime of a thousand gourds. He figured the Great Pumpkin owed him a favor.

He traveled with his uncle to several shopping malls throughout the county, wheeling crates of pumpkins, tomatoes, squash, and corn to sit nicely atop folding tables provided by the mall's maintenance crew. Joe would often leave him for the day and return well after nightfall. He was thankful to be indoors for a change, able to stand and watch the mostly women shoppers and children gawk and marvel at the piles of produce, some proudly picked by himself.

He even made some stilted chitchat with the occasional neighboring Amish folk, whose simple baked goods, cider, and brown sugar candies sold at a steady pace.

"You had a good season?" a young Amish man asked, admiring the stacks of vegetables and bags of Macintosh apples Uncle Joe had bought wholesale from a nearby orchard.

"Yup," David nodded, trying to meet the gaze of the strong-jawed man, whose black hair and wide shoulders stirred a hint of lust in him. He was young like David, probably nineteen or twenty. He hadn't yet grown the noble beard of his elders. Talking was difficult, but not through any language barrier. David wanted to get to know him, but wondered if an honest talk would result in a torrent of Biblical quotes. Amish couldn't be gay, could they?

He might as well have joined their sect since his sexual possibilities at home were so remote. Was there even a gay bar within fifty miles? He'd heard there were a few in Columbus.

He'd also heard something about a high school teacher getting caught with another man at a nearby rest stop, but he had no idea which man, which teacher, or—most crucial—which rest stop.

David scanned the passing faces in the mall. Joe had gone to get some auto parts at Sears. He itched to roam the mall, see the pockets of shops and clothing stores, just to see if he could find someone, anyone that might help him get out of all this for a while. Just being in the mall reminded him of that silly first "date" with Joshua when they bought the Queen concert tickets.

Joe used old newspapers to wrap the corn, had bundles of

them he got through one of his workers who collected trash as a second job. A few pages remained uncrumpled, and he glanced at a photo that caught his eye.

Local Pianist Performs
on Hollywood Talent Show

Serene High School graduate Joshua Lee Evans performed on *It's Entertaining!*, a talent show broadcast on NBC last week. Evans came in third place after second place contestant Griffin Smythe, a tap dancing Marine veteran. Sandy Cathwell and his dog Chippie, from Encino, California, took first prize. Evans performed a solo version of the popular song by Queen, "Bohemian Rhapsody." In an interview with the host, Evans said that he had moved to Los Angeles to pursue a music career.

David stopped reading, checked the newspaper's date: July, four months ago. Had it even been shown on local TV? He rarely watched, and when he did, his father dictated their viewing, usually football or news. Was Joshua in town? Still playing? The clocklike mechanism still lurking in his mind from The Seed became cracked.

Joshua. *You loved him, you idiot.*

"You ready for a break?" Joe appeared behind him and lifted the lid of the metal cash box.

"Oh, sure." Startled, David grabbed the section of the newspaper, folded it into his pocket, adjusting his hat. He'd forgotten how hungry he was. That might have explained the dizzy feeling in his head.

"Looks like we're doin' good." Joe pocketed the twenties and handed one to David, winking. "Whyncha go get a bite and see a movie. They got one a them octopus, octoplexes, eight movies down a ways there. Don't worry 'bout me. I'll hold the fort."

"Thanks, Joe." David scooted out from behind the tables, tucked in his shirt and headed out.

Flattered by the extra money, he strolled the mall's space station atmosphere, ignoring the tinny rush of water fountains and Muzak. He knew he was different there, a dirty alien. His boots clomped loudly. Shop girls glared at him, fearing he might possibly soil their neatly folded sweaters and discounted slacks.

Joshua. Gone.

He passed the Chess King, glanced at other men, and stopped at Wendy's for a double-cheese-tomato-lettuce-mayo-large-fries-medium-Frosty-for-here.

His gut satiated, he strolled on to Waldenbooks, where the glossy periodicals tempted him, especially a few muscle magazines. He'd have a hard time explaining those to Joe. Instead he walked on.

From a long distance he saw the poster. As he drew closer, it grew larger. The image pulled him toward the movie theater. It was not only the man he wanted, but the sort of man he was at that moment sorely attempting to impersonate. Stepping to the box office, he discovered that *Smokey and the Bandit II* was about to begin in three minutes.

The silly road movie became a cathartic experience for the boy. He'd sweated, gritted for months in fields, suffered the mindless repetitions of a thousand crabby customers, and woken up sore every dawn since June that year. He wondered if Joshua still had that poster of the actor showing off his fuzzy butt.

Seeing the film, in which he surely enjoyed Burt Reynolds' reckless machismo, eradicated the pesky goals and whimpering doubt of where he should go, what he should do, and when he should do it. The images of high-flying car chases lodged into his brain. An entire program of desire had been formatted, awaiting his input.

Just gotta get out, just gotta get right out of here.

"Enjoy yer' movie?" Joe asked. The piles of produce around the man had dwindled a bit. At the next table down, a bonneted Amish wife nodded silently at his return.

"Oh yeah, definitely," David said.

"Good, 'cause I gotta take a leak."

Dark thoughts settled into David as he resumed, on the outside, the placid role of cheerful farmhand, ready to bag corn for suburbanites. He weighed green beans, made change, and nodded thank-you's while the cinematic flash of Burt Reynolds' thigh pressing toward a gas pedal zooming down a dusty road reminded him of a desert by an ocean.

The next week, David quit. The sun was annoyingly bright, although it was cold for early November. With Halloween a week gone, pumpkin sales had understandably plummeted. Skies at dusk grew fiery in the chill.

His Uncle Joe needed only a few men to clean up the farm and keep things going until first snow. David was determined to hold off making decisions until absolutely necessary, yet every day the urge to quit came to him.

Slogging through three inches of ice-laced mud, David helped Old Bob load a wagon of overripe butternut squash away from the barn and out to the ravine near the creek.

The other workers had left weeks before and the constant company of the old drunk repelled him. Bob had been fired twice, only to come back begging for the ten-dollar-an-hour work. David never admitted that he'd long ago received a two-dollar raise, and he seethed while the bloated man told more jokes about "dogs fuckin' to beat all" and "niggers makin' chitlins' to puke," and "Hoo doggie! Weren't that a funny one," belching and farting with the regularity of a time clock. David had to laugh, or pretend to laugh, otherwise the old bastard would tell the jokes twice. "Whazzat'? All that maryjane makin' ya' deef?"

Old Bob proved to be doubly annoying in Dennis's absence. Being older, he often assumed control. David wanted the man to simply die or get so drunk he couldn't come to work. Then maybe he and Dennis could have snuck up to the barn and fucked in the hay.

"Lemme drive the tractor, Bob."

David tried to prevent Old Bob from mounting the rusty John Deere. He resented his taking the wheel. Driving the chugging monster was one of the true pleasures David got, driving it high and low, mastering all twelve gears, brake and clutch, trekking over the short expanse of Route 410 between Joe Kemp's north and south acres, making all traffic slow to a halt or risk passing. He wasn't sure if the bleary-eyed old man could handle the machine, but as he tried to tug him down, the overpowering whiff of alcohol forced him away.

"Naw, I got it, boy! I got it!"

Old Bob hauled his paunchy body up and plunked himself into the metal driver's seat. His eyes blurred in a pink haze, his chapped hands peeked from the sleeves of his overcoat, quivering a bit as he gripped the wheel. The engine started with a sputter and then fell to a purring chug, belching a puff of blue smoke.

"Wahl, come on, boy," Old Bob bellowed from the throne of the muddy tractor. "Lez' git' goin'!"

It was Old Bob's idea to back the wagon further down the ravine so the rotting rinds and squash would just fall away and David wouldn't have to work so hard at scraping them off the bed. But in his inebriated condition, Old Bob misjudged the distance. Before David could turn around, the wagon backed into him, nearly knocking him over.

"Fuckin' shit!"

The back wheel ran over his foot, squishing his boot deep into the mud. A corner post ripped at his thigh, scraping it to the skin and ripping his jeans in a V-shape.

"You fuckin' drunk!" David screamed.

Old Bob slammed the brakes on as the wagon dropped lower. The tractor lurched back another foot. David pulled away, but the tractor pushed back against the wagon, bending the rusted steel yoke at an odd angle.

"You fuckin' broke it!"

"Well, you were 'sposed to direct me!" the man bellowed back. He wobbled atop the tractor, afraid to get down. The entire machine threatened to topple into the ravine.

David's rage dropped a moment, then he bent over, scooped up a handful of mud, and flung it at Old Bob, missing his neck by a foot. Brown droplets spattered his face.

"You little faggit!"

"I ain't helpin' ya!" David stormed off, limping and holding his bleeding thigh as he shook the mud from his hand. He stepped over row after row of dying pumpkin vines and bumpy furrows.

"And tell Joe I quit!" he yelled over his shoulder. "I ain't workin' with no alkie fuckhead!" He stomped off toward the road.

The pain in his cut gone, David stopped limping and walked down Route 410 at a good pace. His sulking prevented him from seeing the beautiful autumn countryside. The setting sun drained in long golden arcs over the fields. Bleeding leaves blended in with the bright sky. But David looked down and only saw the edge of the asphalt highway and the tops of his Red Wing boots, one with a muddy wagon tire tread crossing it, the other without. With, without. With, without.

An occasional whoosh of passing cars inspired thoughts of inducing a hit and run, but he came to the fringe of his senses and merely contemplated his father's angry reaction at home.

It took three honks of Dennis Simmons's horn to bring David's eyes up from his boots.

"Where ya goin', my man?"

Dennis hung his arm out the window of his truck, a dopey grin under his blond mustache. His truck faced in the opposite direction that David was headed. The two conversed across the small two-lane road as if they were chatting from either end of a living room.

"Home, my man."

David put his hands in his pockets, chilled. He remembered he'd left his lunch box in Uncle Joe's barn near the time clock. He hadn't clocked out.

"You quit?" Dennis took a drag of his perpetually lit Marlboro.

"Yup. Old Bob ran the tractor in the ravine. I'm sick of it."

David did not want Dennis to coax him out of quitting, as he'd done before.

A blue Honda, waiting behind Dennis's truck, honked once.

"Hang on," Dennis said to either David or the Honda.

Dennis drove up to the next driveway, let the car pass, then pulled back and turned around to meet David, who stood watching with a deceptive apathy. His heart pumped a bit faster, from the walk, from quitting, from his crush on Dennis. David always imagined his knight in shining in armor was bound to show up in a dirty pickup.

"Hop in."

David had already opened the door.

Dennis handed him a cigarette as if he had asked for one. He put it in his mouth, then took his lighter from Dennis' hand, lit his cigarette and boldly reached over, dropping it back in Dennis's breast pocket.

"You really gonna quit?" he asked the boy.

David took in his look, the warm smell in the cab of the pickup, the twang of Conway Twitty on the AM radio and the rush of his first long drag on a cigarette in three days. The combination of elements, served over the gurgling rumble of the engine, calmed him. He rolled down the window to touch the breeze. "I already did."

"Well, hot damn. Ya' finally did it!" Dennis reached over and patted David's shoulder, letting his palm rest a moment. "Good for you. You shouldn't feel bad. Joe's nearly got everything wrapped up. I was jus' gonna get muh' last paycheck."

"He's still got the gourds and Indian corn to sell."

"Aw, folks just waste that for porch decorations. He'll get by. Doncha worry 'bout him. Jus' give 'im a call tonight."

"Yeah. I guess I should. My dad's gonna have a shit fit."

David pulled open the flap of his torn jeans to inspect his wound.

"Aw, fuck yer old man. Hey, thassa' mean one."

Dennis reached over and put his hand on the young man's thigh, which gave David a surge of blood a few inches above his injury. "Gonna need stitches?"

"Huh? Naw. Don' think so."

As Dennis returned his hand to the steering wheel, David resisted his impulse to scoot back and hide the growing bulge between his legs. Instead, quivering with a nervous energy, he pushed his legs wider, showing it off. Dennis glanced back down a moment, then back to the road.

Dennis looked a lot like his cousin Curt. He too was a strawberry blonde with a roughened face, and he'd also been to Vietnam.

"Well, before ya' go, I gotta' buy ya' a farewell drink."

"Sounds good."

C and C, he thought: Crown and Cola. That's what Curt once told him he drank.

Dennis pulled into the small parking lot of the Evergreen Tavern, a dinky saloon near the I-70 overpass. A few cars and trucks were grouped in the gravel parking lot. David briefly wondered if he'd encounter any former high school acquaintances, then wondered again if this was Dennis' way of seducing him.

He'd held off, had rarely even thought about sex, had tried not to think about Joshua, but there it was, the possibility, a distraction, a substitute, a final breaking of The Seed's brainwashing.

He didn't recognize anyone among the half dozen thick-faced men in the small tavern. A jukebox against one wall, some posters on another, and a small bar with some tables and booths; that was about all there was. He wouldn't have to bump into some successful high school buddy and hear the question, "What have you been up to?" only to respond, "Up to my ass in pumpkins."

He tried to relax at the booth, smoking cigarettes, drinking beer and talking with Dennis, but he spent more time listening, avoiding telling too much about himself. Dennis seemed to need an audience, and they sat close, huddled, talking low. Their feet crossed a few times under the table. He stared into Dennis's eyes, watched his lips wipe the beer from his dingy yellow mustache, stole glances at his thick fingers as they clutched a bottle. David brushed his leg under the table against Dennis' and kept it there. Dennis didn't seem to mind. Patsy Cline was singing on the jukebox about walkin' after midnight.

Dennis talked about his new job at the water treatment plant, then rambled a bit about Danang, which sounded creepy, but through Dennis's lips, the war also sounded exotic and sexy.

David didn't exactly have to lie conversationally until Dennis said something about pussy. "J'ever fuck an Oriental chick?"

David hesitated, wondering how far he could take it, how far he could bring Dennis into the truth. He saw the road he'd followed so many times before, the comfortable lie. He didn't want to take that road, but the other one was still under construction.

"Nope."

"Wahl, it's diff'runt, I'll tell ya that. Better'n those high school girls you prob'ly broke yer' nut on."

They laughed loud and strong. David pressed his lower leg forward, then back in disappointment; what he had thought was Dennis's receptive ankle had actually been the table stand.

What could have ended in a simple blowjob and a kiss goodbye petered out to a drunken farewell as Dennis dropped David off at his house with a bleary-eyed handshake. If Dennis had only considered doing that, David may have been merely thrilled at the experience, then scared, then relieved enough to get on with his life, keep his father happy. Dennis would still have been straight and David would still be out of a job. Neither would meet again and they would move on to the next stage of their lives.

But the conversation was too heavily littered with girlfriends and hunting knives. David began to see how different Dennis was from Curt, despite their similar war experiences and shaggy blonde hair. Curt had known David was different, even as a kid. Curt held him, hugged him, before he'd become damaged by the war.

David began to miss Curt with a long silent pang of hunger. A simple, ignorant person can inspire an emotional twister in a frail soul. Did Dennis even have a clue? David would pine away for days wondering about that, but not from home. He had a place that needed visiting. It made no sense to go back, no sense at all. Somehow that complete lack of logic became quite appealing.

A warmed-over dinner awaited him in the oven, two slices of meat loaf with mashed potatoes and gravy, green beans, and some peach pie for dessert.

After eating, he dropped the plates into the sink, washed the dishes, watched some TV in the living room with his father, who read the paper with the television on.

Waiting for a shout, a smack to the head, a twisted arm, even a tossed beer can, David expected Uncle Joe had called out of concern for his absence, at least. But it seemed the fight had been drained from his father, who simply waited for a commercial break on the TV to state quietly, "Tomorrow morning you're going to Joe's place, apologize, and ask for your job back. There's still work to do, and he's startin' up his Christmas wreath sellin'. We ain't goin' to their house for Thanksgiving next week with this hangin' over our heads."

"Yes, sir."

He trundled off to bed, stripped off the dirt-coated clothing, crawled under the covers. He was too tired for anything more, not that he wasn't thinking of Dennis and his pink lips under that blond mustache.

He awoke at three in the morning with a sense of lucid dread. The nearly full moon spilled though his bedroom window. Maybe it was Dennis's not noticing him, or how Dennis reminded him of Curt, or the thought of facing his uncle. Perhaps it was nothing but wanderlust. Whatever it was, it pulled him from bed.

He became efficient in the dark silence, as he had often done when sneaking home after high school weekends of carousing. He stuffed a pile of clean clothes in a canvas duffel bag. He put on a clean pair of jeans, a T-shirt and a sweatshirt with WOOSTER in red varsity block letters. He pulled on socks and laced up his boots, still clotted with the dried soil of Joe Kemp's land that had once been his grandfather's. He crept down the stairs, mindful of creaks in the wood flooring.

A Hefty trash bag held a random bundle of pilfered food from the refrigerator, breadbox, and cabinet. He accomplished all this in near-darkness, a creature suddenly imbued with night vision. The fridge light briefly blazed against the kitchen ceiling.

A set of keys hung on a wall rack redundantly carved in the shape of an enlarged key. Slipping on his John Deere cap and his old Carhartt jacket as though he were stealing it, he slowly pulled the back door open, a bag in each hand, the keys between his teeth. He felt a kinship with thieves and outlaws.

Dormant near the barn, his old truck slumped in the darkness. A light frost coated the windows in an icy cocoon.

Dropping the two bags softly onto the seat, he scooted in on the driver's side, rubbing his hands against the cold steering wheel. A rumble, then a sputter, then nothing. He tried again. His father would be sleeping, hopefully too deeply to tell that this was one of theirs choking to life. For a brief moment he hoped he would stir, hoped he would stop him, keep him home, prevent him from running, but it didn't happen.

The truck started. He shifted into drive, pulled away from the barn and the house without looking back and drove south on the county road to the off-ramp by the truck stop to I-70.

He zoomed around Columbus, then south on I-71, cutting a swath through Ohio and Kentucky, stopping only to sleep, eat, shit, piss, and stretch. He picked up a hitchhiker, a cute Army boy who got him stoned and nearly made him miss a turnoff, but didn't once hint of sex. He was stopped in Tennessee by a cop who pointed out that his left headlight was out.

He drove while a song by Journey told a tale of lovers leaving on a midnight train, it goes on and on and on and on. He sang aloud to Joni Mitchell when she was unfettered and alive, and to product jingles, and then to anything that would stay tuned-in. He parked at rest stops expecting trucker orgies, but instead found rows of silent toilets reeking of cleanser, sexy as a crate of Ajax.

A day after leaving, he politely phoned his irate father from the middle of nowhere to say that yes, he had taken his truck. Yes, he was all right. Yes, he had enough money. No, he wasn't sure where he was going. Texas, maybe. "No, I'm not doing this to punish you. This has nothing . . . this has nothing to do with you. Yes, I'll be careful."

His father gave him the number of his aunt in Texas, just in case he felt like taking a left turn. It seemed odd for his father to be so understanding, but he'd been obedient for so long, perhaps it surprised him too much to get upset.

Until the calm of his saying it chilled him.

"You know when you get back, I'm gonna beat you senseless."

"Yes, sir."

The whole thing seemed a bit ruined, but at least he could travel easier now. Hell, did Billy the Kid ever write home to ask which bank he should rob? He looked at his greasy reflection in a metal slat of the telephone booth. Someone had scrawled a word with a knife. PRAY.

He kept four hundred dollars folded in a wad in his right boot, the cash nestled between his foot and the gas pedal. He kept his John Deere hat on at every gas station. It wasn't until the truck finally began to trail smoke in southern Mississippi that he even looked under the hood. A mechanic pointed to a tube bloated like a fresh-fed snake and said, "Sir, I'd like to introduce you to your engine."

The part cost six dollars to replace. He felt rich since he'd seen fields full with Black migrant workers actually picking cotton.

He went further south until he hit the Gulf, bounced right like a pinball, spent a day in New Orleans in search of debauchery, didn't find it, veered right again.

A yawning, expansive, zoom-along-as-fast-as-you-fucking-can-we-don't-give-a-damn state, Texas swallowed him whole. Red Rider's "Lunatic Fringe" repeated on the radio. The broad sky burned in violent reds and purples as the sun set behind the jutting crystalline viper skyline of Dallas. He rolled down his window, screamed long and loud. Nobody minded.

Twisting through a mess of off-ramp underpass traffic, he found a spot under the airport take-off signal and watched planes roar overhead. He stopped in a pool hall with fifty green tables and a hundred men and women leaning over with the concentration of monks.

I could stay here or leave. I could get a job or get a gun, get a life or rob a bank.

Unshaven, hungry and tired, he resembled a crazed psychotic. He drove and drove and went to an adult bookstore, overloaded by the selection of hardcore fuck books, his dick rigid from the sights. Only brave enough to buy a *Blueboy*, he pulled it from the brown bag in the secrecy of the parking lot. Included among the nude spreads was a series of color Quaintance paintings featuring, of all things, cowboys.

He spotted a cheap-looking motel. Panicked when asked for a credit card, he took off his boot and paid cash, two days in advance.

He took a two-hour bath and was happy to discover a complete shaving kit with his room's Complimentary Travel Pack. He lay under the ticking bathroom sunlamp and began to play with himself, then stopped. He hadn't driven a thousand miles just to masturbate in a hotel bathroom.

He watched the TV with the sound off: same news, different heads. He picked up the phone and watched himself in the mirror while using his erection as a towel rack.

"Operator."

"Yeah, uh, can you give me the number of any gay bars?"

"Excuse me, sir?" It occurred to him that she might be a born-again Christian.

"Well, if you don't know, put someone on the line who does."

His voice was clear. His mind was lucid. Another operator gave him the number of a gay switchboard, where a very cordial and very gay voice gave him a complete rundown of the types of bars he had to choose from, their phone numbers and locations. He chose the most Western-sounding bar, The Corral.

"Do you think you'll go back?"

Noel reentered his bedroom doorway with a tray of coffee and muffins for two. The first to buy him a drink, teach him a little two-stepping, and really listen as they'd sat on bar stools, David didn't have a second to doubt what he hoped would be this stranger's expertise in bed. He seemed authentic. As they'd pulled apart from their first kiss in Noel's car that night, David had mumbled, "Thank you, Great Pumpkin."

What had originally looked like a guy straight off a ranch turned out to be a clothing designer with an apartment decorated like a hair salon. Authenticity was hard to come by. But David had had enough of authenticity. His Red Wing boots were still crusted with it.

"Back to what, Ohio?"

David heard a car backing up outside the window and wondered if his truck, parked down the street, might get towed.

"Of course. Milk?"

"I'm not sure. Yes."

"You're not sure if you want milk?" Noel held the creamer over David's mug.

"Oh, yes. Yes, please. No, I'm sorry."

Noel's bathrobe fell open as he leaned over the bed to pour. Seeing once again the muscular hairy body he'd enjoyed for hours the night before sent a warm flush through his insides.

"I might visit some family friends," David said.

"Where are they?"

"One's down in Baytown."

"Would you want to stay here?"

"Maybe."

"So, are you going to look for work, or do you just rob a 7-11 every now and then?" Noel sat beside him. David grinned.

"A job would be nice."

"What kind of experience do you have?"

"Pumpkins, mostly."

"Well, we don't have much call for that kind of work down here."

"Oh, then I guess I could work in a restaurant," he shrugged, "or something."

Noel sipped his coffee slowly. "You don't look like the waiter type."

"I don't really look like what I am just yet."

He scanned the strange bedroom, the rumpled sheets, scattered clothes strewn about like the debris of a plane crash.

Chapter 28

SOUL BROTHER

THE MOMENT HE saw his cousin Karen's face at the door, he remembered someone else, the man he'd really come to see.

Years before, Curt had accompanied Karen, their parents, David, his mother, and his father on a two-family trip to South Padre Island. The Hildebrands had recently moved to Baytown and invited David's family to Texas for a most unconventional Christmas. Curt had invited a high school buddy, Timothy, who took to David so quickly that he fell a little bit in love.

Leaner and shorter than Curt, Timothy's dark hair and perpetual beard stubble made him seem older, yet he took to David's younger energy in the simplest of activities.

For that week's vacation, he and Timothy were inseparable, and on a few occasions, David, then ten, got to play with him alone, the others out of sight. They dug a hole in the sand, went swimming, and chased sand crabs. Once, on a run around the northern end of the beach, David spotted Timothy walking alone atop a dune. He seemed so tall then, his dark hair tossing in the wind. The little boy caught up with him and the two watched the water. Timothy had his hand on David's shoulders. David had leaned back against the young man, who seemed so grown up, but was only nineteen at the time.

They were on the shady side of the dune, out of sight of everyone. The two then sat together, and Timothy told him made-up stories while they hugged close until the shade felt too cold.

"Let's go swimming," Timothy had invited him.

"No, it's too deep."

"C'mon."

"No, I'm scared."

"It's only water."

He took David up on his back and waded out to the far sand bar, where, what seemed miles from shore, they stood in ankle-high water, Timothy pointing out faraway ships. David looked, but was more interested in touching the freckles on Timothy's back.

That night Timothy took him on a flashlight expedition to find a gnarled branch of driftwood. They dragged it to the porch of the cabin and decorated it with starfish, weeds, ribbons, and pieces of Sugar Pops boxes.

Christmas Eve, Curt and Timothy let David set off one of dozens of fireworks that sparkled like bright crumbs over the bay.

Before Curt and Timothy left for further adventures elsewhere, Timothy found a moment alone, took the little boy in his arms and gave him a soft kiss on the lips.

Months later, after Curt had completed his mysterious adventures with Timothy, the two rounded off their coast-to-coast road trip with a return visit to Ohio. David's mother welcomed them and David was thrilled when his father let them sleep in his bedroom. He slept on the couch.

The next morning, when told to go upstairs to wake them, David had crept into his own bedroom as if he were about to rob a jewelry store.

The lanky frames of the two men lay in his bed and a cot across the room. He was especially thrilled to see Timothy lying on his bed. David stood over him for a very long time, watching Timothy's lightly furred chest rise and fall, wanting to touch the beard-stubbled cheeks, or perhaps tug the sheet lower than the revealed stomach.

But from the cot, Curt coughed, and Timothy opened his

eyes, grinned sleepily, said, "Morning, little man," eased out of the bed completely naked, barely hid his morning boner, grabbed his shorts and sauntered into the bathroom. The day they left, David nearly screamed at his mother for changing the bed sheets.

"You going to visit my parents?"

Karen Hildebrand picked at a slice of pepperoni and mushroom pizza over the coffee table. David nodded, distracted by the television. In addition to Karen, who graciously let him sleep on her couch for a few days, a quintet of Spanish-speaking young men huddled over the kitchen table playing cards in her small Dallas apartment.

Karen Hildebrand was his aunt's daughter. She had lived in Serene a few years, a few times offering to deflower a fifteen-year-old David, who had embarrassingly passed on the offer.

"Well, when you do," she said, "just tell them how I'm doing. You don't really need to talk about Eduardo." Karen resembled a female version of her brother Curt, who David was hoping to see as he continued his aimless trip through Texas.

"Oh, okay, no problem."

David knew about secrets. He'd kept secrets with Karen since he was five when she was his first babysitter. There had been days where he'd been dropped off at her house to stay over while his own parents fought. He and Karen played Ghost in the Graveyard in the real cemetery near her home. They'd run over ivy and hopped around graves, careful not to step on top of the grass in front of headstones so as not to wake the dead. They liked to huddle under the doorways of stone mausoleums. Karen held his hand once while they watched an old man dig a grave in broad daylight. She tried to scare him by saying that there was a body under the tarp, but he knew it was dirt and even dared her to go lift it up. David and Karen had plenty of secrets, almost as many as with her brother Curt.

"It's just that my parents, as nice as they are, hate the idea of me dating a Tex-Mex." Karen glanced over at the men playing cards. "Curt's home down there, too, y'know."

"I know."

"He should be fun. He's had his share of mess-ups. But I'm sure he'll tell you all about it. He'll tell anyone who'll listen. You ought to stay for Thanksgiving, but it's not gonna be very traditional."

David glanced back at the TV.

"You know, Eduardo has a friend you should meet. He might be able to get you a job."

"Oh, you don't have to do that."

"I mean, if you want to stay, maybe even for just a few weeks."

"Really?"

"Yeah. Hon?"

As the poker game broke up, the men laughed and started on another round of beers. Eduardo, Karen's boyfriend, sauntered over, bringing a tall Black man with him.

"Hey, did you meet Cubano?"

Eduardo, a small feisty Mexican-American, thin with an equally thin mustache, introduced the tall, strikingly handsome man. "He just got off the boat. Don't speak English. Maybe you can talk to him."

"Hello."

The tall man grinned, awkward.

"Where's he from?" David asked. "Cuba?"

"No, man. He's Dominican. We jus' call him Cubano 'cause he lived there once."

David pulled his hand away, realizing he'd been holding the guy's large callused palm a moment too long. They sat while Eduardo rolled a joint on the cover of a Santana album. They had already gotten high earlier, but it seemed rude to turn down the offer. He finished rolling it before David even saw it happen.

"So, babe, why don't you take David to meet Rick? Maybe he can get some work."

"Oh, yeah, Rick." Eduardo inhaled deeply and passed the joint to David, leaning close. "You don't mind working in a gay bar?"

David nearly choked on the joint, but his high school experiences saved him. "Uh, no."

"Eduardo," Karen scolded, rolling her eyes, as if it weren't obvious. David wondered if it was. He noticed the other men, who were getting ready to leave, make a joke that seemed to be directed at him. "Cubano" seemed oblivious, but eager for a bit of the joint. He was also doe-eyed, coffee-brown gorgeous.

"Yeah, I'll take you tomorrow, eh? He works happy hour." Eduardo passed on the return of the joint, glancing at the television.

Eduardo stood. "I knew there was a reason I trusted you in the same house with my girlfriend," he said, grinning before leaning over, patting David's back, shaking his hand goodnight, then retreated into the bedroom with Karen.

Cubano looked perplexed. As the two got more deeply stoned, some process of cannabis logic, his one year of high school Spanish, and conversational attempts with the farm workers sparked a light in the man.

Cubano grinned as they shared phrases, and his real name, Rafael. He gestured, saying how he was working on a construction site twelve hours a day.

"Trabajo en un gran projecto de construcción. Hace frío. No me dan guantes." *I work on a big construction project. It's cold, but they give me no gloves.*

David commiserated, trying to explain his recently abandoned farm work.

"*Una granja de le* . . . pumpkins."

Rafael had no idea what pumpkins were, even when David hastily drew a cartoon of one. But when they compared calluses, they started out almost reading each other's palms. David felt something else.

Rafael seemed excited, relieved almost, that he had actually communicated with someone else in this road and skyscraper-clotted megalopolis that David tried to compare for Rafael to an old 1950s science fiction movie he'd seen on TV, *The Monolith Monsters*. That was pushing it. Rafael didn't get it.

David didn't know how to make a pass, but there was obviously something going on. This man was gay, and he also had a slight lisp. David wanted very much to kiss him, his lips were so full, his anxious frustration needed soothing.

Eduardo returned, took Rafael back to his home somewhere in East Dallas. He and David said goodbye like long-lost friends. But the real frustration was that neither had phone numbers or addresses to speak of.

David and Karen shared more childhood memories, then put the pizza leftovers in the fridge. She let him sit alone in the living room for a while.

Karen thanked him for befriending Rafael. "That's probably the first time anybody white ever talked to him like a human."

Eduardo made pot deals at stoplights, he was that cool. Driving David in his red Camaro through a mess of traffic under glaring sunlight, he seemed at ease. Just looking at the cigarette billboards a hundred feet high and zooming past made David a bit woozy.

David wondered how people didn't wreck their cars all the time from the glare; the buildings acted like solar panels. When they pulled into a mall parking lot and entered a bar, Magnolia's, on Cedar Springs Road, which on the outside resembled a fancy Taco Bell with no windows, he was temporarily blinded by the darkness and chilled by the overactive air-conditioning.

Eduardo led him to a small secondary bar where a young man's blond hair almost glowed under the bar's track lighting. He wore a not-too-tight T-shirt, just-tight-enough jeans and a too-tight black apron.

Eduardo introduced them, shared a few jokes, and then left to talk to someone else. He'd been a cook there and retreated to the kitchen to talk with his Mexican friends.

David attempted a quick conversation. "What's it like to work here?" he asked the guy whose name he'd already forgotten. He was too shy to ask for it.

"The guys are rich, obnoxious queens, some ultra-butch, others as nelly as a ruby pump. It's good pay and good tips and you meet a lot of nice people. You can also meet some generous older gentlemen, if you know what I mean."

"Not exactly." David didn't know what half of what he said meant.

"You know, rentals."

"Oh."

"Do you hustle?"

He was being scoped out, his scent discerned, one young buck preparing to rut against another. David didn't even qualify himself as a two-pointer yet, and he didn't like the feeling. "No, I don't."

"Oh. Well, you can still make good money. We need busboys," he said casually, as if it was on a shopping list below olives and Bloody Mary mix.

Driving back out on a main avenue, Eduardo relit the joint from earlier. David wondered if Eduardo was ever not high. David had been stoned since he met him.

"So, do you think you might wanna work there?"

"Maybe," he lied. Eduardo seemed eager to help David get a life, thereby getting him out of his girlfriend's apartment. David didn't take offense, but he wasn't planning on landing just yet, his migration still incomplete, its destination unclear.

Eduardo sucked another toke as he slowed at a stoplight. David opened his window a crack. A guy in a neighboring car signaled to him.

Eduardo nodded back cheerfully, waited for the light, pulled over, gave David the joint and hopped out of his Camaro, putting the car in park. That "Lunatic Fringe" song popped up again on the radio. David looked in the rear view mirror as cash and a small bag switched from hand to hand. Come to where the flavor is.

"You know you could work for me, if you wanted to," Eduardo said after returning.

David nodded, but he already knew that the opportunities presented in Dallas only made him want to keep driving.

The music at Magnolia's helped him ignore the persistent flirtations from patrons, and David found himself exhausted from a week of scooping up empty plates, mopping up spilled drinks, broken glass, and the occasional spray of vomit in the toilet stalls. He learned all the sassy comebacks from watching the drag shows, and almost connected with a few of the go-go boys, who frequently dared him to strip down and join them. "You'll make a lot more money than picking up beer cans," one of them taunted.

The other bars and a bathhouse advertised in the little gay magazine *This Week in Texas* tempted him as well. Yet he remained a bit distant, coldly removed from the invitations to go to brunch or two-stepping at the nearby Country-Western bar. He learned that he could make up stories and keep his memories of Serene—and Joshua—inside.

But what made the men at Magnolia's less tempting was Rafael, who showed up at the apartment one night. David managed to figure out an excuse to go for a walk, be alone with him, until they found a dark alley and let desire draw them together for an abrupt, clumsy, and utterly overwhelming near-hour of passion that left them both quivering, their pants down to their thighs, their pulled-up shirts sopped with chest sweat.

After that night, Rafael would visit or they set a meeting place, or he'd simply show up at the bar before closing time and wait outside by David's truck. They couldn't be choosy, humping and kissing in darkened alleys, a park, anywhere no one would interrupt their nearly unspoken couplings.

Rafael preferred fucking, and David tried to accommodate his girth in various clumsy positions in the truck, or, bravely, once, on its flatbed under the canopy, the metal ridges pressing into his back as Rafael thrust into him, more easily after he bought some Vaseline and sat on top. Sometimes, Joshua's face would flash in his mind and he'd grab Rafael's hips to thrust harder, as if to wipe the memory away.

They rented a cheap motel room a few nights, but that cost him a few nights' pay. "Eres tan bonito," Rafael whispered as he caressed David's skin. *You're so pretty.*

"Eres tan bonito grande!" he joked. "Es lindo, estar en una cama." *You're pretty big! It's nice being in a bed.*

A few days later, Rafael came to the apartment not for sex, but to say goodbye. He'd been hired to work in Baton Rouge on another construction project. Somewhat saddened, and as another form of coming out about their brief affair, David asked for a camera, and Karen dug up an old Polaroid. He saved that photo of the two of them, Rafael towering over David like a monument he'd conquered.

A few days later, despite the upcoming Christmas holiday, Eduardo subtly hinted about wanting his couch back, so David politely resigned his job at Magnolia's, bid Karen and her boyfriend farewell, and headed further south, almost relieved to be free of such hopeless passion.

Chapter 29

SEASIDE RENDEZVOUS

"WELL, WE FIGURED you'd show up sometime." Audrey Hildebrand's craggy familiar face nearly brought David to tears. She welcomed him in with an awkward hug. "I bet you're starving."

"Yeah." He'd been lost for about an hour since approaching Corpus Christi, since the roads were all rural. At every sign he had to slow down to figure them out in the early twilight. He finally called from a corner liquor store, where his aunt told him to look for the glowing plastic Santa on the lawn.

"Well, we just finished dinner, but I'll see what we've got left."

"Thanks."

"So, you've been roaming?"

"Um, yes, ma'am."

"Well, I hate to burst your bubble, but before I give you a plate of food, you're sitting down by that phone to call your father."

"But I can't go back yet."

"I'm not saying that. Just call him and let him know you're alive."

Audrey Hildebrand was supposedly some genius medical student who'd become frustrated when another doctor ripped off her thesis. She was a nurse now, and his uncle kept them well-off with wise stock investments and high-paying science work. In a word, they were cooler than his dad's side of the family.

"I heard Curt was here."

"Oh, yes," she called out as David sat on the sofa by the phone. "He's at a meeting. Pete's picking him up."

"Oh."

"Have you forgotten the number?"

"Dialing, Ma'am."

Having once again assured his father of his existence, the threat of violence upon his return unspoken but understood, David, deciding as he said it, told his father he would be staying in Texas through Christmas.

David filled up on his aunt's cooking, which was warmer and better than any Denny's or Stuckey's between Ohio and Texas.

"So."

Audrey Hildebrand sat across from him in what looked to be her chair, just like his dad had his own chair. "Is this just a little adventure, or do you plan on moving here?"

"Actually, I hadn't thought of that. I suppose I could stay a while, if I got a job."

"There's not much here," Aunt Audrey said.

The town had a population of about four thousand. Aside from nearby Corpus Christi, the only businesses were hatcheries and bait shops, other than the 84 Lumber he'd passed on his way in.

"I noticed."

"Well, we like it," she said. "It's not far from Pete's work," the latest of which was with a team of oceanographers calculating the rate of damage that humans were inflicting upon local sea life. They were getting busier every day.

His aunt's cigarette smoke curled around her like a pet. She had a persistent throat "a-hem" that didn't seem to stop her habit. David sympathetically lit up, but asked if he could open a window.

As if reading his mind, his aunt said, "We haven't heard from your mother in years. Last time was a postcard from Paris, of all places. I guess you got your wanderlust from her. But we have a few old photo albums with her in them, if you're interested."

"Thanks. That'd be nice."

"Now, don't think I'm harping on you for doing this. I'm just concerned for your father. He cares about you, even if he always was a jerk."

"I know." David turned away. He didn't want to get messy by talking about the years of abuse. Car headlights passed through the window.

"God knows Curt had his bad boy spells. Still does, at least until recently."

"Oh really?"

"Well, I'm sure he can fill you in. That must be them now."

They waited a moment, expectantly, while the footsteps approached, then the door opened. Curt's face beamed in almost mock surprise.

"Well, little Davey! I'll be damned!"

While Karen shared simple babysitter treacheries with David, Curt had other, deeper ones.

He and his high school buddies had gone to elaborate heights to entertain David when he stayed at their house. They'd staged backyard battles with garbage can lids and brooms. Curt had even staggered into the living room once, arm coated in ketchup, feigning a stab wound.

Curt had played Rolling Stones albums for him, damning his Archies, Kiss, and Monkees albums to a teen-hood rubble pile. He let David hold the steering wheel of his Mustang while they zoomed down township roads.

There had also been days spent skinny-dipping in a nearby lake, and going to the city pool, and snow sledding, often finding times to be alone together, changing clothes, depending on the season. David remembered the close nights spent together before Curt stopped letting him do that.

After Curt shipped out for Vietnam, David cried for hours until his father smacked him. Curt's return led to fights about other family problems, and before a year had passed, the family had splintered.

Now Curt was a two-years divorced, sober man attempting to get his life together.

The Hildebrands were building an addition to their house, which faced the Gulf. Curt was quite adept with a hammer, but had turned down two jobs after just a day on sites. Curt said it was because he should finish his parents' house first. His aunt told him it was because the men on the site were "practically Klan members."

That first evening together, David's heart felt pressed against his chest just to be near him again. He could barely speak.

Sitting on the roof, they watched the bay grow dark.

"Great back yard view," Curt said.

"Yeah. Nothin' like this back home."

"Hmm."

"So, Curt, how are you, really?"

"Well, I go to AA meetings. Met a nice girl. We might get engaged, but I'm at a difficult stage right now. Lost my driver's license after the last bust. Tryin' to get work. It's not that easy. Spend a lot of time up here, nights, just lookin' out at the bay, watching the freighters go by. See that yellow light? That's a bridge that crosses back to the mainland. That little white one is moving."

"Oh yeah?" David squinted.

"So, I'm just trying to relax and figure out what to do with myself."

"And I thought I could get some answers by coming down here."

"Hah. This place just grows questions."

David told of his own tales with The Seed. They compared experiences but David hesitated at any mention of Joshua.

"You ever hear from your mom?"

"No. She left so long ago. She sent a few postcards, one from New Mexico. I used to race to the mailbox when I was a kid after she left, but Dad found 'em and ripped 'em up."

"That's rough."

They sat a while longer.

"I remember the crazy things you used to do," David said, determined to change the subject.

"I'm trying to forget as many as I can."

"You'd been camping with that friend of yours, Timothy. He was so nice. He gave me a starfish from when you guys came back from California. I still have it."

"Wow. What is this, total recall? How do you remember all that?"

"I don't know. Some things tend to stick out."

"Oh, no. Here it comes."

"You tried to scare me into thinking you cut your arm up and poured ketchup all over your elbow."

"Oh, with Tim."

"That was so silly."

"Whaddaya' mean silly? It was convincing."

"It would have been if I hadn't smelled the ketchup first!"

They laughed loudly. A neighbor in the next yard, a bit late in hanging outdoor Christmas lights, looked up, waved them off, as if to say, I ain't complaining.

"Whatever happened to him?"

"Tim?" Curt looked at David, uneasy. "Aw, he died a few years ago. Fell when he was rock-climbing in Colorado."

David didn't know what to say. He looked away, down at his legs, a cigarette in his hand. How do you mourn someone so long gone, so slightly remembered? Curt wasn't drinking anymore, and David's bar work got him back into sipping a beer every now and then, but at the moment he craved a shot of Old Bob the farmhand's Night Train.

They sipped soda in silence. The freighter had traveled further across the bay.

"What was Tim like?"

"Oh, gosh, he was wild. Wilder than me, if that's possible." Curt stretched his arms. "Used to catch bugs and frogs and bring 'em to school. Did the same in 'Nam, catching weird bugs. Puttin' them in guys' pants."

"Did he have a girlfriend?"

"In school, yeah, but— Listen, I know . . . you're gay, aren't you?"

"Guess so."

"Well, it's funny you remember him, 'cause, when we were travelin' together, Tim told me he felt . . . like that too."

"How did you feel about that?"

"Well, I was surprised, but happy he was still my friend, even though I wasn't . . . like that. Is that why you wanna know about him?"

"I guess."

"Funny thing. He told me once, we'd just finished playing with you guys one day on San Padre. He told me he knew you were, too."

"How did he know?"

"I'm not sure. He just said he could tell."

David ground his cigarette out on the roof tile, held the butt.

Curt asked, "Did you . . . did you know that soon?"

David finally figured out how he did. "I still remember the freckles on his back."

Curt patted his shoulder.

"Must be tough."

"Oh, it's not so bad." David shivered from the cool night air and the sudden honesty he felt about himself. It wasn't so bad anymore.

Curt said, "I think you two woulda' made a nice couple."

"Get outta here."

"No, I mean it. You're what, nineteen? He'd be . . . twenty-nine?"

"Wow."

"Yeah. Anyway, I'm sorry to be so—"

"No, it's—"

"I mean, it's how he felt about you."

"It's okay."

"I'm sorry if—"

"It's okay."

The freighter out on the horizon was long gone. They both sat for minutes after that, saying nothing, as if they were both watching a silent movie of Timothy memories.

"Well, I'm beat," Curt sighed. "I'm gonna get to bed. You comin'?"

"Hmm? Um, I'm gonna stay here a bit."

He was beginning to remember things, some distant as the departing freighter, but they still shimmered, and he wanted to savor them before they slipped away.

"Okay, jus' don' go to sleep. Wouldn't want you fallin' off the roof."

A week later, after completing one half of the roof, David sat on the bank of the Hildebrand's back yard on the wooden dock. Parts of it were in the early stages of decay. David wondered if the Hildebrands would let him stay as long as something needed repair.

Curt approached and sat next to him, saying nothing.

"Let's go," David said from the middle of a long silence.

"Where?" Curt asked.

"San Padre."

"Why?"

"I kinda' need to."

"Is that why you came all this way?"

"I thought it was for you, but . . ."

Curt nodded.

"It would mean a lot."

David didn't have to say Timothy's name. Curt seemed to understand. "You're the one with the driver's license, little man."

The drive took a few hours. In between the radio songs they sang, David prodded Curt for stories about his friend.

The dunes were nearly flattened from the previous year's hurricane, the ocean tainted. An oil spill from the previous summer left remnants of black slits on the beach, a poor version of those brightly colored sand-in-the-bottle landscapes. There was no landscape here, though, just a few new glaring ugly hotel boxes. A married couple lounged under a huge beach umbrella, desperate to relax.

But at the beach on the rim of Texas, David just wanted to go swimming.

"Let's go in," he said.

"I didn't bring a swimsuit," Curt argued.

"We gotta' go in."

"Go ahead." Curt waved him off.

"You have to come in! We can't come all this way and not swim!"

"I can swim at home. Besides, even my dad could tell you this water's a mess."

When he saw David strip naked and dive in, Curt relented.

The kid may have been almost ten years younger than him, but to Curt, he seemed wiser and stronger as he yelled out, shouting happily for the first time in months, waist high in the waves, "C'mon! It's only water!"

The joy from their day clung to them like the dried salt water on their skin. They sang along to the radio, stopped at a shack of a restaurant for fish tacos, and bought jokey holiday gifts for everyone at a tacky trinket shop.

But they returned to see his stone-faced aunt and uncle sitting in the living room.

"What's wrong?" David asked.

"We got a call, from Serene."

David waited. The first person he thought of was Joshua.

She said, "David. Your father died."

"What happened?" Curt asked, filling in David's stunned silence.

"He got in a fight at a bar downtown and had a heart attack."

David turned, haltingly walked back outside and closed the door.

He kept on for a few blocks, past neighbors' sad blinking red and green lights, far enough to be alone, to try to bring up a ghost of a tear, but instead only muttered, "Well, well. What a goddam Christmas miracle."

Chapter 30

SLEEPING ON THE SIDEWALK

THEY ALWAYS WANTED show tunes.

Queen? No. Styx? Maybe, if they were in the mood. But mostly, the patrons at his second job wanted show tunes, so Joshua bought more sheet music.

After being ousted by Garrett, Joshua had settled in at a somewhat run-down apartment complex on Fountain Avenue with Margaret Blustein, a lesbian production assistant and aspiring television writer who needed a roommate. She plied him with lots of vegetarian food and relieved his sense of shock.

"You got away easy," Margaret said over a surprisingly delicious dinner of seitan noodles and vegetables as they half-watched the TV while sitting on the sofa. She'd been explaining the Moliere farcical roots of *Three's Company*, but Joshua seemed distracted, so she muted the volume as Mister Roper got a door slammed in his face three times.

"I mean, no offense, but gay guys can be pretty mean, especially to someone younger and more talented. Garrett's probably on to his next 'discovery.' You got a moment, and that's more than a lot of talented people get in this town."

"But what do I do now?"

"I could get you a production assistant job, but there's a line of kids willing to do that for free. You can scrape for an agent, go on auditions, get work playing anywhere that pays. Or you can go home."

"No, I can't. It's . . .." Joshua spilled out an abbreviated version of his year with David, the arrest, and subsequent rejection. Margaret listened patiently, shared her own less difficult coming out experience to her parents back in Michigan. "I'm lucky; I have two older brothers whose wives already produced grandkids."

Margaret also pestered him to call home the next day, which he did, awkwardly explaining his plans to stay in Los Angeles, "for a while," as his mother sounded like she was holding back tears and his father a reserved resentment or blame.

He did eventually find a job, thanks to a reference call from Garrett. Four days a week he walked down to Santa Monica Boulevard and took the bus to the El Capitan Theatre on Hollywood Boulevard, where, in an usher outfit that made him feel like a flying monkey, he sometimes watched a movie four times a day. Between sweeping up popcorn and mopping up the sticky remnants of soda and candy wrappers, the ornate décor lost a bit of its initial charm. But at least it was cool and dark on hot days.

Thursday, Friday and Saturday evenings, he walked a dozen blocks to play piano for a few hours at Cabaret on La Cienega, opening for drag pianist and chanteuse Rose Marina Del Ray.

Patrons sat and listened a bit more attentively to Rose's sets, which Joshua stayed for a few times. During her breaks those first weeks, as she sipped a cocktail and revealed tidbits about her life (and her real name), Ross offered tips and compliments like a jaded mentor.

"It's very artistic, what you do," Rose/Ross said in a husky voice, as if defending an argument. "Almost, a form of 'straight camp.' But the patrons who tip want to hear songs from *their* youth, not from yours."

Joshua knew that from seven to nine-thirty he was background music for early drinkers and the clear contrast of elderly gentlemen and younger somewhat-hustlers. Despite being below the drinking age of twenty-one, Joshua had charmed the manager by playing for free and getting smatterings of applause for his lounge versions of a few pop songs. He didn't drink alcohol, and the police had apparently been paid off for other indiscretions anyway.

Joshua played to polite applause and tips dropped in a glass jar by older patrons who didn't know they were listening to an acoustic instrumental version of "Heart of Glass." The twinks who knew such songs focused on cadging free drinks from potential tricks or clients. They didn't tip.

Other young men his age frequented the bar, but they were mostly talking to the older men. One gentleman, who bought him a soda after his set, seemed to not know he played piano. Said one, "I'm not into anything rough, and I don't ask a lot for my money."

"What?"

"Honey, how much do you charge?"

"Oh." He'd seen the gay magazines that had escort ads. One priced himself at "$100." That seemed a fair price, if he could only find out what they meant by In/Out.

"I'm not a hustler."

"Oh, honey, we're all hustlers in this town," remarked another.

"I get it, but I just play piano here."

"Oh, well, you could tickle my ivories any night."

He allowed men to flirt and a few times take him to their homes, but never his. Almost all of them wanted to fuck him, and that hurt, so he stopped doing that. He got pretty sick of the chit chat, the condescending tones that followed his admission of being from Ohio, the indirect gestures and catch-phrases to get him out of their apartments after the sex.

He stopped after a few awkward attempts at hustling: the tall and handsome high school coach who drove him all the way to Van Nuys, then cried after a shuddering orgasm; the wiry Latino in Silver Lake whose vigorous energy—and a nearly forced offer of poppers—exhausted him. They never offered a ride home, just extra "cab money" to get rid of him.

Getting back to Margaret's apartment, usually before midnight if he hadn't met a potential date, he often couldn't sleep. On weekends, the parties would start at one or another nearby apartment, the cackle of voices and low-playing disco bouncing across the courtyard. No one else seemed to mind. Margaret would be out or holed up in her room typing up her never-finished teleplays and projects. Some nights, Joshua just went for walks, hiking uphill along the small streets that snaked around more wooded areas. The night view in any direction over-whelmed him.

By September, he'd seen *Alien, Moonraker, The Muppet Movie, Rocky II* and *Apocalypse Now* a dozen times each. The usher job didn't pay half as much as the bar job, but he didn't have to work as hard, either.

Wildfires in the hills turned the sky into an orange hazy mist on the day Joshua thought he saw David Koenig.

Mid-song with his rendition of Elton John's "Tiny Dancer," he fumbled a chord as he saw a young man in combat boots, torn jeans, a flannel shirt with the sleeves ripped off, and a baseball cap leaning against the bar, ignoring his drink, and slyly smiling at Joshua.

Recovering his place somewhat, Joshua kept stealing glances as the guy occasionally adjusted his hat to show off a side-shaved scalp with what seemed an at-rest blond Mohawk.

Realizing it wasn't David, just someone who resembled him, Joshua finished his set a bit early, and the hidden-Mohawk guy approached.

"That was excellent," he shook hands. Joshua blushed. "You wanna go get something to eat? I got something I wanna talk about with you."

Joshua's defenses went up. "Are you hustling me?"

"What? Me? Oh, hell, no." He nodded towards a young man sidled up next to an older gentleman. "No offense, but that ain't my bag. I'm in a band. There's a fun old diner on Melrose. My treat. Looks like your tip jar's a little short."

"Right." Joshua clutched the few bills and his sheet music and followed his mystery man out of the bar before Rose had even shown up.

Zeff, as he called himself, rambled enthusiastically about his punk band, Unleashed, in between chomps of a burger and fries, and what sounded like a completely different world only a few blocks away. They shared stories: Joshua's home life, his brief bursts of TV fame, but no mention of David. Zeff's family down in Encino had kicked him out at sixteen when they caught him naked in bed with another boy. He'd fallen into homelessness and drugs, then sobered up and made a life for himself, found other kids into music, and had only a few months ago formed the band.

"I think they'd really like your stuff. It's like, sarcastic but real."

Joshua hadn't thought of his playing that way, but took it as a compliment.

"I'll bring some friends by. You play Saturday, too, right?"

True to his word, less than half an hour into his next set, a motley crew shuffled into the bar: plaid-skirted girls, boys with spray-painted skulls on their jackets. The manager, fearing them to be a gang, hassled them with extended ID checks, but they all bought drinks and sat or stood quietly as Joshua played. They applauded. They sang along. They tipped him between numbers. Suddenly, the manager liked this little herd.

Invited to walk down to a bar called the Anti-Club, Joshua, his sheet music stuffed into his shoulder bag, was surprised when Zeff hung an arm over his shoulder.

"You're gonna love this," he promised.

DJ'ed thrashing music filled the bar, with spray-painted slogans and frayed wooden benches along the walls. People stood posing and smoking with sour expressions, lightened by the group's entrance. Zeff introduced him to a countless array of oddly named people with gelled and dyed hair.

"Hold on. Lemme get Skip." Whoever that was.

Standing awkwardly for a few minutes, trying to get into the angry beat of the music, Joshua wondered what Zeff was up to until an older man in a black T-shirt and jeans was introduced.

"This is the guy I was telling you about. He's great."

"So, what, you play solo?"

Joshua nodded.

"You got a keyboard? We ain't got a piano."

"We'll get one," Zeff assured him.

"Fine. Next Wednesday, eight o-clock. You suck, it won't matter. Hardly anyone's here then. You bring people in, we bump you to later before the other bands. Nice ta meetcha. I gotta get back to work."

"What's going on?" Joshua asked after Skip left.

"I just booked you," Zeff said.

"Here?"

"Yeah, they don't just do punk. All kinds of performance art and wild stuff."

Half an hour later, they endured one such act, a screeching clown-faced "singer" who any place else would have been booed off the stage.

"What you said, about a keyboard?"

"Don't worry," Zeff patted his shoulder. "I know a guy. I work at Aron's Records down the street. There's always a bunch of flyers, people selling instruments."

As they waited for a band to set up, Zeff ordered them drinks, himself a soda and a beer, but as they moved away from the bar, switched them.

"I'm straight-edge."

Answering Joshua's confused look, he added, "Don't drink alcohol. No drugs, either. I quit all that."

Perplexed but a little relieved, Joshua sipped his beer and began to enjoy his new friend's energy, particularly as he goaded Joshua into the mosh pit in front of the punk band. The gentle shoving and circular stomping brought him to a sweat, and the sheer silly joy brought on by the music's angry tone left him exhilarated. Zeff's at-rest Mohawk became a flopping flag of hairy freedom.

Outside the bar later that night, he gave Joshua a friendly hug.

"I'll have flyers and stuff made up tomorrow. Don't worry. We'll get you a keyboard, buddy. And oh, I had an idea. Pick a few slow songs and make 'em fast, like, fake punk. That'd be so funny!"

His face glistening with drying sweat, his eyes wild with joy, he offered Joshua a friendly smooch on the lips. "I'm so glad I met you, Joshie!"

The endearment made him think again of David, but he let it pass.

"You need a ride home?"

"Uh, sure. It's just up the hill, but . . ."

They had to walk farther than that to Zeff's beat-up compact, and with three other friends packed in, it felt like a clown car. Joshua figured he wouldn't be sleeping with Zeff that night, if ever. He couldn't read where his affection would go, even after his little car glugged down the street outside his apartment.

They'd traded phone numbers and met up the next day to hand out flyers Zeff had made on pink paper cut into little squares: LOUNGE ROCK WITH JOSHUA LEE. The Anti-Club's address below it, and a chopped-up illustration of a keyboard.

"You forgot my last name."

"Oops. Sorry. I'll make different ones next time," Zeff said as he and Joshua hiked to Melrose, handing out flyers, sticking them under windshield wipers, stapling them on any café bulletin boards, and, at the record store, leaving a stack along with dozens of others near the cashier's counter.

"Let me play you some music," Zeff offered. He drove them to his cluttered apartment, which he shared with three other people, two of them his band mates. Zeff played Blondie and punk bands Joshua had never heard, then some old jazz and even a bit of classical. He was all over the place, sipping coffee and talking, until—was it during the Tom Jones album and after some leftover pizza?—Zeff plopped himself down on the bed where Joshua had been sitting and kissed him.

They kissed and touched and pulled their shirts off and Zeff licked Joshua's armpit and bit his nipples, but stopped short of getting completely naked.

"Let's save it for now," he said, grinning as if full-on sex were a prize they had yet to deserve. Joshua tried to settle down but pulled Zeff back for at least some more kissing. He spent the next days crushing on Zeff and eagerly anticipating his debut at Anti-Club.

A few days later, arriving half an hour before the Wednesday show, he found Zeff, his Mohawk stiff and upright with gel, setting up a keyboard as a bald guy in black jeans and a Ramones T-shirt set up a drum set.

"There he is." Zeff held his arms out as if presenting the electric piano on a game show. "Whaddaya think? Hold on." A few plugs, power on, and Joshua plunked down a few chords. The sweet clean quaver of the Korg made him smile.

"It's got a bunch of sounds, too, so organ or whatever. This is Butch. They go on after you."

"I hear you're some kind of lounge act." A cymbal in his hand, Butch surveyed Joshua with a curious look.

"Something like that."

Joshua felt that he had to prove himself all over again. He'd considered renting a tux, to be more performance-like, "ironic," as Zeff called it, but decided to dress like the patrons in a simple black T-shirt and jeans.

About a dozen people stood waiting as Zeff took the stage to introduce him.

From the first song, his ballad version of Devo's "Gut Feeling," he heard chuckles, then a few people sang along in muttered tones. A bit of applause, and he went ahead with a few more songs, each time feeling he might not be making the grand impression Zeff had expected.

His arch rendition of "My Sharona," revised to a florid Liszt style, got a few laughs. His reeling waltz version of Cheap Trick's "I Want You to Want Me" even inspired a few kids to partner dance for a few verses. But he felt their attention fading after a few less clever songs, and then cut ahead to his faithful version of "Bohemian Rhapsody."

Punkers and New Wave kids could be dismissive of more commercial music. But they got him. They understood the sly humor of his stylings. With that Queen epic, no jokes were needed. As with his other performances back in Ohio and in the TV studios, people calmed down and listened, then sang along. By the raucous last section, a few kids even moshed and nodded heads with a fervor. He ended with that, took a brief bow and left the stage.

"Fan-fucking-tastic!" Zeff grabbed him in a hug.

Zeff's friends gathered to congratulate him and offer compliments. Skip, the manager, presented Joshua with fifty dollars in cash and offered him a weekly Wednesday night gig.

Zeff spent that night at Joshua's apartment after a proper introduction to Margaret and a respectable period of chatting in the living room. Margaret promised to attend his next show and invite a few friends.

Joshua's "dates" with Zeff, infrequent as they were, mostly followed his shows at Anti-Club. He'd pick Joshua up, help him haul the keyboard in its case along with his own amp and cables. More people showed up each week, and the two spent more evenings out.

More of Joshua's fans showed up at his Cabaret gigs, and he noticed a visibly peeved Rose Marina Del Ray waiting impatiently by the bar when he performed one too many encores for his new crowd. He wasn't surprised to be dismissed under the ruse of his age being a problem. One thing Joshua learned from his brief time in Hollywood was to never upstage a drag queen. So he plotted to find more gigs, even opening once for Zeff's band, whose songs all seemed equally thrashy, loud, and interchangeable. Joshua withheld any critiques. Zeff had become his manager in a way, and he owed him.

And although he didn't owe him sex, he did feel a sort of trade had taken place. The energy of their shows, including Zeff singing onstage for a few songs to spice up his act, fueled their desire. Zeff didn't care for fucking, which was a relief to Joshua. He did, however, enjoy Joshua's butt, mostly with his tongue.

"Wow, that was amazing," Joshua sighed as the two untangled themselves from a sort of sixty-nine. A brief, glorious, rambunctious three months had passed. *In Touch* magazine (the gay version) had featured Joshua's act in a one-sentence mention as part of a round-up of New Wave and Punk acts in Hollywood, including a small photo of him playing next to a shot of the Circle Jerks.

But as happens so frequently in the land of dashed dreams, things changed.

"So, you're happy with the shows?" Zeff asked him as they cuddled after another abrupt bout of sex.

"Sure," Joshua agreed.

"You think you can go it alone for a while?"

"What do you mean?"

Zeff shifted in the bed, grabbed a T-shirt from the floor, wiped his crotch.

"You know I love you, right?"

"Uh, thanks?"

"But I never said, we didn't say it'd only be us, right?"

Joshua hadn't even considered dating anyone else. "No, but—"

"I've always wanted to go to Hawaii, and I met this guy, an older guy, a former Marine, remember I introduced you at one of our shows? And he was visiting, and he invited me, and I've always wanted to surf more, plus nature, you know? I'm just really thinking . . ."

"So, this is just—"

"It's been fun, right? You're famous now."

Again, actually. But he didn't correct Zeff. "What about your band?"

"Aw, they can get a new singer, and I'll be back, maybe. But you'll be fine. You're already on your way."

To what?

Joshua didn't fight or argue or plead. He nodded at Zeff's invitation to visit him in Hawaii some day. He looked at this wiry guy, saw how many of his thinner features didn't really match David's.

"It's all an adventure, right? You took a chance when you came out here, from fuckin' Ohio!"

Joshua nodded, listened. It was familiar. He knew how to be abandoned.

He kept calm, sulked, and spent a few days in and out of bed with Zeff.

Two weeks later, after a too-long goodbye, he returned to the Anti-Club, but couldn't find the energy. He would ask Margaret for a ride or take a cab, but after a few more weeks, he said couldn't do the shows anymore. Skip shrugged, knowing another act would show up, gave Joshua a parting tip of fifty dollars and wished the boy good luck.

With his only true friend gone, a simple fact assured his failure in the City of Angels.

He kept breaking even with money, and the only way to get more was to play in bars he no longer wanted to visit, banging out songs he no longer wanted to play, not even in his room on the electric piano with headphones on.

Margaret was very nice and let him not pay rent for a month, especially when he told her he'd probably be going back home soon. He just hadn't found the nerve to do it yet.

What set it off was the night he got drunk at a New Year's Eve party one of Zeff's remaining friends invited him to, who insisted on plying him with cocktails. No one noticed when he left. Stumbling to a bus stop, he found himself harassed by a street hustler clearly not up to making a new co-worker friend. "Face it honey, you're just fresh chicken around here. And the longer you're around here, the less fresh you are."

He walked the street, back and forth a few times, unsteady in his gait. He leaned against the brick wall of a building. A disco beat thudded through it to his back. He began to feel a flashback of his seizures, The Feeling, but it was sloppy, not as much fun as he'd remembered it. He felt sick.

Drunk on vodka, which he'd never experienced, he retreated off Santa Monica Boulevard to a quiet residential street. Dizzy, he searched for a dark place to vomit. He leaned against a cluster of flowering bushes, then his eyes glazed as he tried to focus on the small yellow blossoms. "Honeysuckle," he almost said aloud before the soured drinks hurled backwards up his throat.

Maybe he wanted it to happen. Maybe he tried to make it happen. Maybe he was just drunk and didn't see, but when he walked against the light and heard the tires screech, he didn't so much as look toward the car that blared its horn. He didn't even turn back until a heavy hand grabbed his shoulder.

"Hey, kid. Stop right there."

The uniform scared him in a way he'd never known. Back home they were just good ole boys who got their jobs from their brother. Here, this was a man who chose to be a cop. He looked frighteningly good in the uniform.

"Don't you know you almost got killed?"

"Oh, I'm sorry."

"There's a reason we have jaywalking laws, y'know."

"Yesshur."

"You're new in town, aren't you?"

"Pretty much."

"A hustler too, I bet."

Joshua bit his lip and felt nothing, then a wave of guilt and shame that made his eyes turn away and well with wetness. "Not exactly."

The cop nodded. "Where ya from?"

"Serene."

"What is that, an ashram, one a them cults?"

"No, it's where I'm from. It's in Ohio."

"Yeah? I'm from Lancaster myself."

"Pennsylvania?"

"Where else?"

"There's one in Ohio, too. I was there once. They got Amish families there, too."

The cop sighed. As Joshua watched the night glitter in his badge, the cop's body changed, his face softening, opening.

"What's your name?"

"Joshua Lee Evans, sir."

"Joshua, my fellow former farm boy, the best thing for you to do is hop on a bus and go back home for a while until your head catches up with your crotch."

"Yessir."

"If I see you hangin' out here again sellin' it, I'm gonna run you in. An' I don't wanna have to call your parents all the way back in Ohio."

"Yessir."

"Right now, I'm gonna take you to a pay phone, and you're gonna call a cab, and then you're gonna go wherever you're staying, and you're gonna call your parents and ask them to help you get home. Will they do that?"

"I think so." Yet he stood, wavering.

The cop eyed him with doubt. "You know what? I'm off in an hour. How about I park you in that diner," he nodded across the street, "and meet back with you. Sound good?"

"Okay." He was hungry. "Why?"

"Why what?"

"Why are you helping me?"

"Because I want to. I am going to help you get where you need to be."

Adam let him take a bath for two hours. Adam let him try anything in bed. Adam also had manners. He presented himself to a slightly astonished Margaret when he brought Joshua home, wanted to make sure she knew he was all right. Joshua began to spend more time at his apartment.

But Adam did not play music, owned very few albums except some Johnny Cash and Carpenters. There was something deep and sexual that helped Joshua find adventure and bravery in his sexuality. But there was something missing in Adam, the cop from Pennsylvania, something that paralleled that ignorance of music. He was a just man and sexually passionate, but as Joshua described him when showing me the pictures he sent, "a good cop, a great fuck, but not very musical, if you know what I mean."

Chapter 31

MOTHER LOVE

WITH HIS BRIEF career as party entertainment and nightclub novelty act finished, Joshua took Adam's advice to volunteer his piano services at a local hospital, where in a bland lounge he entertained seniors and cancer patients, mostly in wheelchairs. Although they didn't clap as loud or shout requests like bar patrons, he felt he'd found his most appreciative audience in months.

He took breaks as different groups were wheeled out and into the lounge. One day, a thin man in a bathrobe standing by the door as he held an IV tube on a rack looked familiar. One of the patrons at Cabaret? Joshua wanted to say hello, but by the time he'd finished his set the man had gone.

He even played on Christmas Day, deciding that, after a quiet dinner with Adam, it would be a good thing to do. Besides, Margaret had left town for the holidays with a new non-Jewish girlfriend for a week at what she called a "pagan women's retreat."

Into the first month of 1980, Adam welcomed Joshua into his home a few nights a week, sometimes inviting him for a daytime meal and a bit of sex. His shifts as a policeman were often long and demanding. Moving in was not discussed, which came as a relief to Joshua, who preferred to hole up in his room, dabbling with his own rambling compositions.

Joshua wanted to call home again. But the last time, he had refused to return home even with the offer to pay his plane fare, his father shouting, "Get yer bony ass back home where it belongs, young man!" So he hung up.

Joshua called a few old friends instead, as if to show off or to test the waters, see if anyone missed him.

He called Ed Wallenbeck, whose reactions made it seem like his television appearances were as impressive as a gig on *Don Kirshner's Rock Concert*.

"When ya comin' back, rock star?"

"I dunno."

"We gotta jam, dude!"

Ed's words encouraged him. Joshua then called David's ex-girlfriend Brenda Kruger. She was happy to hear from him, if not completely surprised. She also wanted to know when he was coming home.

"Soon, I hope."

"Maybe you can see Dave."

"What?"

"He's not with me anymore."

"I kind of figured."

"Well, you know he broke up with me for you."

"Yeah, listen, about that—"

"Joshua, don't worry. I got a gay cousin in Cinci. Took me out to the bars and stuff. Anyway, Dave."

"Yeah?"

"He took off to Texas to visit his relatives. But he came back. Course we hadn't seen each other for a while, you know after he got all creepy from that rehab place. I'm engaged to Luke Humerkieser."

"Oh really?"

"You have been gone a while, haven't you? Dave's father died. Got in a fight at The Night Owl down on Center Street and got so worked up he had a heart attack. Dave came back from Texas and moved back to his dad's farm. Just, lemme see, it was in the paper, I saved it . . ."

Joshua listened to the rustle of his hometown paper a few thousand miles away, the sound as comforting as her voice. He imagined lying on the living room floor of his parents' home, reading it himself. With the receiver crooked in his neck and shoulder, he waited for Brenda to find the article, but his hands had already begun flipping through the Yellow Pages for the Greyhound Bus station.

"Mom?"

"Joshua? Are you all right?"

"Yeah. Sort of."

"Do you want to come home?"

"Not yet, but soon. Um. I need to—"

"Let me call my mother. Would you like to go to San Francisco to visit her?"

"Maybe."

Sara convinced him to call back in half an hour, collect. Then she called San Francisco.

"I'm having dinner, Sara," Katherina DiGiorno said. "What is it?"

"It's about Joshua."

"Oh. Does he have his own television show now?"

"Mother, please."

"I'm sorry, dear."

"He's still in Los Angeles."

"Dreadful town."

"I was hoping he could stay with you for a while, just to see to him. He doesn't want to come home yet, but I thought you could—"

"I don't think that would be a good idea."

"But Mother, he really likes you."

"He's met me once, when I visited, and then he only spoke two words."

"He's shy."

"Not too shy to spill his problems on national television."

"Can't you just . . . I'll send you some money."

"I don't think now would be a good time."

"Why not?"

"Don't you people have newspapers out there that print anything but the farm report? It's pretty grim over here. Cults, riots."

"What are they rioting about?"

"The Mayor. An ex-cop shot the mayor and the gay supervisor. They let the guy off. Well, he was a horrible man, but my goodness, not even a jail term. I mean, I understand their anger, but the gays damn near blew up City Hall."

"But, that was last year. What does this—"

"Sweetie, I don't think this would make a good impression on the boy. In the state he's in he could become the next Che Guevara of the Gay Liberation Front. He's rebellious, like you were."

"Mother, I promise to come fetch him if you just let him stay with you awhile until I get there."

"Well, that would be nice. I haven't seen you in years."

And so, an accord was found.

The house seemed smaller than he'd imagined it. The only photos he'd seen, of a young Sara Evans standing next to his equally young father in uniform, were taken at a low angle, giving the house in the background a looming black and white appearance.

Joshua had taken a cheap flight then splurged on a cab since the various bus and train routes into the city confused him.

In a light yet chilly February rain, his driver, a husky Armenian man, offered a nonstop commentary about the wonders and horrors of San Francisco, finally landing at his grandmother's surprisingly small home in North Beach. Larger apartment buildings shadowed the Victorian, which was done up in subtle cream and light blue trim.

While his grandmother had been brisk in her opinion of

Joshua's misadventures in Los Angeles, she at least welcomed him in, standing at the top of the steep stairs as he lumbered up with his two duffel bags and the keyboard in its black case.

After a night of rest and a simple breakfast, with reference to a mysterious cat that still feared the new visitor, she encouraged him to play her baby grand piano whenever he liked. He learned to mask Led Zeppelin's "Kashmir" to sound like a lullaby. "That's nice," she'd say while petting her Siamese, who had finally made an appearance.

"If you want to go meet some of your kind, you have to take two buses. There's a map in a drawer somewhere."

He took her advice, found Castro Street, and warily strolled up and down a few times. He felt done with bars, and figured he'd get carded anyway. Men in mustaches and bulging jeans eyed him as he pretended to peer into shop windows and only snuck into a bookstore for a reprieve from what he figured were chicken hawks showing interest.

His mother, who arrived by plane a few days after he did, was not so brief with Joshua. After settling in and spending some quality time with her cranky mother, she was about to address her son when Mrs. DiGiorno announced that her brothers and their families would visit that weekend.

"Really, Mom? All of them?"

"When will we ever get a chance for a gathering like this? You never visit, and they all want to see you."

"They'll just make fun of our small town life and berate me for not being a Catholic anymore."

"You're still a Catholic, whether you like it or not. Besides, the boy needs to meet his cousins."

"All eight of them."

Joshua smiled, eager to please but a bit nervous at the prospect of such a gathering.

Sara sat him down in the living room, and for the first time that he could remember since that one talk about sex, the two of them shared a couch. "I want to have a little talk before the brood gets here." Then she let him have it.

"We're getting our phone number changed to a private listing," Sara started. "I have had it with the phone calls. Not that I'm blaming you. We may have to move. First the neighbors didn't say anything. Then the church freaks came. The Baptists want to save your soul. The Jehovah's Witnesses want to baptize you. And the Presbyterians want to invite you to play for their music group on Tuesday nights. I told them you'd be busy. I don't know how they worked it out so I only got one visitor a day, but young man, I will not tolerate another Bible-thumping inquisitor in my house. I have tried to raise you and your sister the best way I know how, but I am a transplanted city girl. I come from here, San Francisco. I only left here because I love your father, not because I love that pea-hole of a town. I know you want very much to move on and be rich and famous, and now maybe even someone more outlandish, but until that time comes, you are going to get along with those monsters and you are going to live near them. If I can adjust to living with them, so can you. God knows I'd rather just stay here for a while."

"But, Mom—"

"Now, I know you have very serious feelings for David. Don't try to think for a minute that I didn't see that. I let you do what you wanted. I let you indulge and come home buzzed too many nights, it seems, but if you expect to get out of Serene again, I want you to have some more education under your belt, not just a few TV shows. Whatever you do after that is your decision. We are not going to send you to that place like David's awful father did. If you don't want to go to college, let us know now, because we also have to get a new refrigerator."

"Okay."

"And the next time you plan on taking some glamorous trip to Hollywood, don't you dare think of going without inviting me along. You know damned well I would skin my mother's cat to find a reason to come out here for a time, and at least I have that now. I kept waiting for my mother to invent some illness just to give me an excuse. I could leave you here, but not yet. You can live here when you grow up. There are lots of people like you out here and they are living happy lives, I'm told. I just don't think you're ready for it all. But I think you have a reason to come back home, and I think you have a little more growing up to do. Now, have you eaten? There are some terrific restaurants here in North Beach where your father and I went on dates. And I can show you where the Beatniks used to hang out."

His mother and grandmother chatted about old times over their pasta dishes at Fior D'Italia, bought cannolis at a pastry shop, then brought his exhausted grandmother home in a cab. The next day, Sara took him out to visit Chinatown, then to other neighborhoods, parks, and museums.

On the night of the big dinner, his uncles and aunts drove in from Millbrae and Concord, squeezed him tight in welcoming hugs while his cousins offered wary greetings—each one, from the toddlers to the teenagers, as brown-eyed and brown-haired as his mother. Anthony, Angela, two Marias; he lost track of whose kids were whose.

Except for answering a few questions about his Ohio life, Joshua remained silent while an endless array of food, unpacked and reheated, filled his grandmother's house with savory odors. They all ate and shouted and joked, mostly at each others' expense. Joshua remained almost a cipher until, over coffee and desserts, the families filling the chairs, sofa, and floor, one of his uncles said, "So, your mother says you're a musician."

Joshua nodded.

"Play something."

"Okay."

"He's not a wind-up toy, Anthony."

"You said the kid's a musician. I'm just asking."

"It's okay, Mom," Joshua assured her as he got up, sat at the piano in the next room, and considered what to play.

There wasn't any doubt. His arty L.A. renditions of New Wave songs would befuddle them. Only his "hit" would do. Besides, they seemed like an operatic group. He played "Bohemian Rhapsody" with daring flourish, adding extra trills and glissandos, more comfortable in his grandmother's house to really let go than he'd been at any of his previous performances.

And as he bowed before his reconnected family, Joshua felt a sense of happiness, of safety, and hope. Not just because he'd toured the city with his chipper mother, who seemed filled with a sense of pride and energy he hadn't seen in years—in tears, actually, for having redeemed himself on her behalf in front of their relatives—but also because he knew that back home, David had returned to Serene.

Part 3

Into the darkness they go, the wise and the lovely. Crowned
With lilies and with laurel they go; but I am not resigned.

—Edna St. Vincent Millay, "Dirge without Music"

Chapter 32

LET US CLING TOGETHER

SAMUEL EVANS'S EMBRACE on the sidewalk of the Cleveland Airport had never been so tight. He couldn't remember his father hugging him so strongly, or ever showing a hint of tears. But there it was, his love, his regret at having let his son escape, possibly because of his own words.

As they drove south to Serene, he let Joshua chat with his mother about their adventures, returning to his stoic demeanor, a bit overwhelmed by their tales, particularly Joshua's, which seemed haltingly edited at the mention of bars and certain people.

Sara told him to take his duffel bags and electric piano up to his room, which he did. But she sensed his discomfort as he returned, sat on the sofa for a few minutes, not really watching the television, just a bit stunned to be home.

"Dinner'll be ready at five-thirty," she said as if he'd never left.

Five-thirty, just a few minutes after his father returned home, had he not taken an afternoon off from work at True Value. It was a moment ingrained in him, as familiar as a bundle of paired socks in his drawer or towels in the linen closet. But it was only three. His father had retreated to the garage for yet another project.

"Um, can I stay here?"

"Well, it all has blown over, I guess. Unless you want to find a place of your own. Let's not worry about that now."

His heart rose to a warmth he had forgotten to feel. His mother walked out to the kitchen, then yelled, "But one more visit from a church group and I'm getting a rifle!"

He laughed hard and followed her to the heart of the house, the warm familiar kitchen. The table was half set.

"You've got a bright future ahead of you."

"Yeah, I know, but—"

"And I know it's been very difficult for you, but I don't want you going off and running away whenever you can't talk to us."

Her eyes welled up again. He had to hug her just so he wouldn't have to watch her face get all crinkled up and soggy. He listened to his mother as he smelled her hair.

"And I know things are hard for . . . people like you. But there's a whole new decade coming. Things are going to change for the better. You just wait and see."

"Yeah, I hope you're right."

Joshua could smell dinner cooking. It felt good.

"Oh, and the school choir director called. I ran out of excuses, said you were on a camping trip. You went to the Rockies. You had a great time. Here's his phone number." She returned to finish some work before dinner.

So there he was, back home again. Might as well unpack.

But what did the choir director want?

"We'd like to use that song you wrote," Mr. Kinnick explained over the phone. "Mr. Rose thought it one of the best from his theory class."

"The Gregorian chant thing?"

"Yes. I had to make a few tonal changes, and fix up some of the Latin grammar."

"Oh, that's okay. I'm sure it'll be great."

"Good. I think it'll be a nice gesture. People always love local talent. You know, you can live here if you don't make a fuss."

Or get caught, Joshua almost said. *Or come out on TV.*

"Would you like to come to a rehearsal to hear it?"

"Sure."

"Wonderful. Wednesday, two weeks from now, that's when we start. It'll be for our Easter concert, so there's plenty of time."

Two weeks. So, he'd already prepared to perform the work whether he got Joshua's approval or not. But that wasn't such a bad thing, he realized; a sort of posthumous tribute without being dead.

He penciled the date of the rehearsal on a scrap of paper and tried not to get too excited about going.

But then he thought he'd ask someone else to go with him.

Joshua had begun taking things out of his bags and putting them in place.

"Where is it? Where is it?" he said out loud, as he dug into his belongings.

Inside a small box of trinkets and toys, he found the small envelope, the invitation to a wedding so long ago, and he took out the little paper accordion of pictures of David.

He was feeling very tired, but he returned to the kitchen. "Can I use your car?"

Sara Evans turned at the sink, surprised by her son's sudden appearance, that he really was home again. "Of course. The keys are on the table by the door."

"Thanks," he said, trying his best not to bolt out of the room and through the front door.

"You know where he is?"

He stopped a moment as if caught, like all those nights coming home late drunk or stoned or both.

"Yep. Thanks."

"I want you home for dinner."

"Yes, Mom."

"Oh, and you might as well invite him over. He doesn't have any family anymore, so . . ."

"Okay. Thanks, Mom."

As he drove along the familiar country road, he thought he should be nervous, worried, afraid even. But something else, perhaps a little imagined voice of a Claymation dog, told him that all his travels weren't the real adventure, that this moment was the true beginning.

287

Chapter 33

NOW I'M HERE

HE PASSED THE farm twice, once in each direction, pulled into an off-road to other homes and parked as he tried to calm his fluttering nerves. What if he was still the not-David, with that dead-eyed dismissive look in his eyes, that cauterized version of himself? And even if he wasn't, what if he'd found someone else, a man or a woman?

Finally parking by the house, which was coated in a dusting of snow, Joshua stepped out of his mother's car, approached the door, and was about to knock when he heard a clattering sound in the distance.

He walked out to the barn. He saw the old red Ford pickup parked just inside. David was bent over the front bumper, trying to reattach what looked like a giant shovel. Joshua walked across the yard past a pile of cut tree branches. Snow had begun to fall, tiny flakes melting on his shoulder and head.

He focused on the curve of David's back, huddled over the truck, knowing so well the smooth pale slip of bared skin under his coat, and where it led, down to the soft mounds. He felt a flutter in his stomach as David turned to see him. His hair and a wisp of a blond beard had grown out some.

As Joshua approached, David stood and wiped a palm on his jeans. He held a large wrench in the other.

"Thought you'd gone off to Hollywood," David said.

"I was. Now I'm here."

"Yeah, me too. Texas. And well, now I'm here, too."

Joshua stuck his cold hands in his pockets, unsure what else to say. "I'm sorry about your dad."

"I'm not."

"Okay. Is that a plow?"

"Yup. Uncle Joe lent it to me. Damn thing fell off when I hit a rock. I been shoveling snow for folks around, driveways, mostly, for extra money."

"Good timing." Joshua nodded back outside toward the gathering flurry.

"Hope so."

"Need a hand?" Joshua asked.

"No." David dropped the wrench to the ground.

Joshua's heart sank a moment.

"I need two."

Joshua would tell me, years later, that before hugging David, he looked at his own hands, so slender then, so full of talent, enough to fill concert halls if only things had gone differently. He would play the piano, but it would never be the same. He saw, in that moment, what his hands would become: callused, hard, chafed from the cold, browned with the dirt of a worthy sacrifice, to farm that land with David.

Despite the chill and the afternoon snowfall, the barn's shelter warmed them as the two boys, barely men, embraced, held each other close, shared a few clumsy words, blurted apologies silenced by more than a few kisses, until their hands crept under shirts and tugged down jeans. A car whooshed by down the road. David tugged Joshua farther inside the barn. In the darkened shade, out of sight, despite the winter breeze floating in through the wide open door, they touched, caressed, humped each other standing, took turns kneeling and bringing each other to bursts and loud unrestrained moans and gasps.

After they pulled their clothes together, with a pair of dopey satisfied grins, they kissed again.

"Maybe next time we can actually do it in a bed."

They laughed, embraced, pulled apart.

"You stayin' over?" David asked with a smirk.

"You inviting me?"

"That I am."

"I gotta get my mom's car back."

"I'll drive in, follow you," David offered.

"No, um. Stop by later. She invited you to dinner."

"So, I guess I'm part of the family now."

Joshua smiled. "If you want. Besides, I got some packing to do."

As simple as that, they understood. Distance would no longer separate them, not even across town.

As he watched Joshua drive off, David wiped his mouth and resumed work on the plow. Even though it was winter, there was work to do.

Maybe they didn't actually say that. Perhaps they told it like an old story, the way your parents describe how they met, with a wistful tone. After all those months apart, losing each other, finding themselves, they would finally settle together.

Those first few nights and days together, they rarely left the bedroom, save for bathroom and food breaks. Reconnecting, naked under thick layers of blankets, they touched and kissed, hands grasping and tugging, mouths exploring, but more pressing together, their heat almost filling David's drafty bedroom.

"I missed you so much," must have been uttered a dozen times as they told stories of their journeys apart. Regrets were shunted aside over toast and coffee, and they cuddled in silence, or whispering along to music, content simply to gaze at each other's flushed faces.

"Listen to it," David whispered on a bright cold morning.

"What?"

Naked except for a pair of thick socks, David slipped out from under the pile of blankets, stood by the window, pulled back a curtain. The bright whiteness of the world flooded the bedroom.

"That tiny little crunch of snow."

Joshua saw heat rise from David's body, the lithe back and firm butt and thighs that he'd spent days and nights caressing with a renewed rush of desire, now almost glowing.

"What do farmers do in the winter?" Joshua asked as he patted the bed, which brought David back under the covers.

"We wait. Most have to find jobs. My dad worked in a factory a few years until he hurt his back."

"Did you always want to be a farmer?"

"No, it was just what we did." David shifted to his side, his fingers aimlessly grazing Joshua's shoulder. "Remember when we watched the moon landings in grade school?"

Joshua nodded.

"I came home that day and said I wanted to be an astronaut. Dad laughed at me, but I used to go out in the fields and lay on the ground just staring up at the stars."

"We could do that again some night soon."

David shifted closer, clutched Joshua. "We can do everything together now."

Despite his mother's protests—"But you just came back!"—each night he spent with David, Joshua brought a few more clothes and music books packed into David's truck, leaving most of his childhood toys and other possessions at his parents' house.

Itching to play piano again after a few weeks, Joshua enlisted the help of his father, and, with David and his dad grunting as Sara Evans shoved furniture out of the way, they hauled that old piano out of the dining room, onto David's truck, and dragged it on carpet patches into his rarely used dining room.

"We gotta get this tuned," Joshua sighed, as he finished a rambling doodle at the piano.

"You need some fixing up here, you just let me know," Sam Evans offered, his polite way of showing disdain for the run-down house and, perhaps, his unspoken acceptance of their new domestic situation.

Over many nights, Joshua joined David for an after-dinner rest on the lumpy couch in the living room. The two boys shared their different tales, of Hollywood and Joshua's brief flare of fame in the nightlife scene. David told of the drag queens at Magnolia's and almost hesitated before mentioning Rafael.

"It's okay. We both had some wild oats to sow."

"Oats are a bitch to harvest," David deadpanned.

They slept together in David's small bed, becoming used to each other's heat and nighttime habits. Some nights, David would cuddle Joshua, awakened to see his fingers twitching, as if he were playing some song in a dream.

One night, on his way from the bathroom, Joshua opened a door that had been closed for weeks. Inside, a large rumpled bed and dresser with a few boxes lay dormant.

"That's . . . private." David appeared in his pajama pants and a T-shirt.

"Your dad's?"

David followed him in and pointed to a small square box. "My dad."

"His ashes?"

David nodded.

"You didn't bury him?"

"Been putting it off. Son of a bitch at least had a life insurance policy. Ain't much, but . . ."

Joshua reached around to David, hugged him from behind. For the first time since he'd heard the news down in Texas, David cried.

"Uncle Joe's wife, his sister, kept bugging me about it, said it was the Christian thing to do. Like he was any sort of that." He sniffled. "He was a good man, for a while. Took me hunting right out there. We never got more than a rabbit or two."

As they settled, Joshua walked to the dresser, touched the box, and looked around the room. "You gotta take care of this."

"Yeah, I know."

"No, now."

"What? It's almost midnight."

"You're calling the cemetery tomorrow. And this," he waved around the room, stepped over to a closet door to reveal clothes and shoes, "all gets donated."

David sniffled, nodded assent.

One of their many new freedoms of sharing the remote farmhouse included being able to stay up late, blast music, and be together naked in any room, any time they wanted. That night, they sorted boxes, saved photos, and even dragged the rumpled mattress outside to take to the dump the next day. Garbage bags were filled with clothes and left outside on the porch for later donation.

Joshua surveyed the nearly empty room with only a dresser and a stripped bed frame. "We'll turn it into a den, or a storage room, something." He shoved the creaking window open.

"What are you . . . ?"

"He needs to go," Joshua said as he led David out and closed the door.

A single marble square, ROLAND KOENIG marked the small gravestone with his birth and death dates. David had been adamant with the headstone engraver about not buying a larger "family" grave. "I am not spending eternity next to him," he'd said.

The service was a small one, held at the first thaw in March when ground could be cracked open, with the boys, Joshua's parents, David's Uncle Joe Kemp, and his wife Emily attending. Although Emily had been estranged from her brother and silent about his years-long abuses, she offered a few kind platitudes and invited them all to her home, where a modest meal of casseroles and soft drinks were served. Her children, excused from the service, hovered about the table set with too many dishes of food.

Conversation remained polite. Joe Kemp and Sam Evans discussed hardware and tools, a subject of common interest. Joshua's mother refrained from going on too long about her mother in far-off California.

The unspoken topic, and the most obvious reason for these two very different families having gathered, left Joshua and David mostly silent, sitting together and exchanging smirking glances, while their families ate slowly to avoid mention of the fact that the two were living together and more than friends.

But funerals, even delayed ones published in the local newspaper, give way to small gossip, from Emily Kemp to her church group, from a mechanic's son to a grocer's wife. The curious and unusual always set tongues wagging in any small town.

Chapter 34

DEAR FRIENDS

I OWE MY reconnection with Joshua and David to a can of creamed corn.

Spring of 1982, I think it was. Between semesters at Oberlin College's Conservatory of Music, I shopped for my mother at the local A&P down on Claremont Avenue, even though the new supermarket next to the Walmart out by the highway was much better stocked. The A&P was kind of a tradition, since it was only a few blocks away. While I usually greet anyone I know—it's good for the family's real estate business—I wasn't sure I wanted to speak with Joshua's mother when I saw her. I wanted to give her some space. Besides, I would not have known what to say. "So I've heard your son, whom I've had a quiet crush on since grade school, has come back to town!" It would not really have been appropriate.

But she had been trying to replace a can that fell to the floor, then looked up and greeted me.

"Why, Eric Gottlund. How have you been?"

"Mrs. Evans."

She knelt to pick up the can and placed it back on the shelf.

"I don't know why I even looked at that. We never eat creamed corn," she said, almost embarrassed.

We got to talking, the usual chit chat, me talking about my parents, college, and a few concerts I'd recently played.

And then out of the blue she said, "You know, you ought to visit Joshua. He's not in college anymore, but he's been keeping up with his music and I think you would probably have some good suggestions for him."

I must've become a bit flushed by the prospect of reengaging with the subject of my former fascination.

I told her I would stop by her house sometime, but she stopped me.

"Oh no, he's living out with David Koenig at his farm."

Matter of fact, just like that, she made no mention of them being boyfriends or lovers or whatever they were to her.

Before I could protest, she took out a little blue pad from her purse and scribbled the address and phone number.

Of course I knew where it was, where everyone visited when they wanted to get the best pumpkins, Indian corn, and decorative gourds each autumn.

I thanked her and promised her that I would do as she asked. I had no idea how to reintroduce myself to them. Was it simply because she suspected that I was gay, or because we were all "musical"?

Back home, I put away the groceries, my mother hectoring me for getting a few of the wrong brands. After every can, box, and bag of food was stored, I pondered the little note and the address out on the county road. How many times had I driven by that house years before on my way south out of town without thinking that this might become the center of their lives, of our lives, for a few years?

I let a few days pass, thinking that it would be proper, that Joshua's mother might call him to let him know that she had put us in contact.

Putting all my bravery together—after all, I have performed for thousands over the years at concerts, although this was clearly different—I dialed the number, which rang several times with no answer. I figured that David must be out in a field somewhere and perhaps Joshua was so busy playing he couldn't hear the phone ring.

David abruptly answered my later call that evening. "Yup?"

My fumbled reintroduction was met with enthusiasm.

"Sure! When you wanna come by?" David said. "Josh ain't home now, but I'm sure he'd love to see ya."

We made plans for the weekend before I had to return to Oberlin. I figured that would be the best, what with the work he had to do. Of course, farm work never ends. But David wasn't my reason for visiting.

By Saturday, I had selected a stack of sheet music and albums, then put some away, thinking he might be put off by my classical suggestions. What was he playing? What interested him? I had no idea.

When I pulled up the driveway to the house that day, I was met by an affable black and white border collie and Joshua and David standing amiably on the porch.

"What's his name?" I asked as I got out of the car with my satchel full of sheet music and records.

"That's Goliath," David said.

"An apt name," I replied.

"Good to see ya," Joshua said as he gave me a hug. He'd filled out, grown a semblance of a beard, his auburn hair contrasting David's fuller yet fairer facial hair. "We made lunch and everything."

The interior of the house was surprisingly clean and warm. As I appraised its value and the expanse of the property—a family trait—I knew it to be one of those sturdy farmhouses that could withstand a tornado. The interior was decorated with used contemporary furniture, the walls a light ochre in the living room and mint green above white wainscoting in the dining room.

"Mom came by last year and insisted on fixing the place up after David's dad died. She wanted some new furniture, so we got their old stuff." Joshua pointed at a sofa and chairs. On two living room walls, simple yet colorful patterned quilts had been hung up.

In the kitchen, I stood back as the two fussed over the table with sandwiches and side dishes and a pitcher of lemonade. From out the window over the sink I saw a flutter of red.

"Ah, must be our cardinal. They love the feeder Josh hung by the porch."

"And you said they wouldn't notice it," Joshua nudged David, who countered, "No, I said they wouldn't get any seed unless we greased the pole to keep out the squirrels!"

Their playful ribbing brought a flush inside me. That hint of a bond between them back in high school had blossomed, now open and free.

After a pleasant lunch where we caught up on the missing years, the boys both told me about their adventures in Los Angeles and San Francisco and Texas while I mentioned a few of my concerts in Oberlin and elsewhere. David announced that he had some work to do in the barn, and Joshua led me to the dining room, where a small electric keyboard sat next to an old upright piano.

While I had known him to be shy and quiet in school, once we got talking about music, Joshua seem to light up. I brought out some scores, music I thought he might like, a few of which he dismissed.

He practically demanded that I play first, and I dribbled through a Schubert passage.

I thought better than to ask for an encore of Joshua's solo version of "Bohemian Rhapsody."

He instead pulled out a worn copy of a Yes songbook complete with psychedelic artwork on the cover.

"It's really not as hard as it sounds," he said with pride as his fingers dangled over the keys. "Just a lot of repetition." While I admired his dexterity, I didn't really much care for the music.

Joshua spoke of his two semesters at Beekam College, where he enjoyed the studies, but the focus on scales and theory in the classical genre proved a bit overwhelming. "I might get back to it, but right now I'm just staying with my rock stuff."

It was as if we were musically trying to find a middle ground, somewhere between my better trained yet impassionate technique and his great enthusiasm marred by the occasional mistake. A few times the middle C and E keys stuck, but we plodded on.

I stole glances as he played, his hair longer, shaggy, almost covering his face and its bit of stubble.

"Sometimes when I really get going, David just leaves the house and finds a reason to work outside." Joshua shrugged, smiling. "Most times, at night, when I'm not down in Columbus, we hang out, get stoned, and even though the piano's a bit off-key from the record, it doesn't matter. Oh, hey, speakin' of which . . ."

I passed on his invitation to smoke a bowl of pot, considering I had a Ladies Auxiliary function that evening that needed a harp player. Instead, I segued back and asked him about Columbus.

"Oh yeah. I play in a gay bar, The Garage? They have a piano bar up front of the disco. Pretty good money. I just play for a few hours, don't drink so I can drive home. David went with me once, but he got hit on so much it made him antsy, so he just lets me go alone. Sometimes, we go together and stay overnight in a hotel. It's like a little vacation."

"And what about when *you* get hit on?"

"Ha! Oh, I just point at the tip jar."

Joshua's casual mention of the gay bar, which I had only visited once, seemed to push aside any question about our mutual sexuality, but also established the kind of brotherhood that would remain chaste.

"Forgive me," I said with a faux-hauty air that nevertheless implied the truth, "but someone of your talent is better than playing in bars."

Joshua shrugged. "It beats working at a hamburger joint. Winters, David's gotta do other work to pay the bills. I help him with the chores and, you know, at first I was all worried about my precious hands getting hurt. But I think they got stronger from some of the hard work."

He held up his hands, those little callused palms and stubby fingers. I resisted the urge to grasp them. I blushed, feeling a moment of clarity: the balance these two had found despite their prior separation and the potential of never having reconnected. I think I almost came to tears and had to turn away and make an excuse for more lemonade.

David returned, the sound of his boots clumping in before him. Goliath scuttled around him, then to a corner pad that seemed to be the dog's indoor bed. David stepped into the dining room and jokingly said, "You two still at it?"

I realized that hours had passed with both of us just sitting at the piano playing and talking. We hadn't even bothered to turn on any lights, the dusk settling through the windows.

Politely declining an invite to stay for dinner, I promised more afternoons or evenings together. David seemed to sense that the reason, or excuse, for my visits would always be the music. It wasn't as if I might chat with him about hybrid gourd seeds or fertilizer. But still, he seemed pleased that Joshua had found someone from his past to connect with, to chatter about notes and chords and symphonies he would never understand.

What I remember feeling as I drove home was that reconnection, that the social strictures from our high school years had been dissolved, and that more important than any of the cordial gossipy or impersonal relationships with others—elders, people selling and buying their houses, local cashiers, barbers and gas station attendants—I finally found two young men my age who made me no longer dread returning to Serene, Ohio: two young men who had overcome distance and odds and parents, and in one afternoon, as simple as that, became my friends.

Chapter 35

LOVE OF MY LIFE

REMEMBER HOW DIFFICULT things could be back then, how one crowd of people could sing your praises while another could strike out with hatred? How is it that our charming little town managed, for a time, to accept Joshua and David, knowing about them? In a way, it was the music.

Perhaps it was the silence that troubled us; the silence of sending kids away to camps, the girls gone missing through a pregnancy, the vacant desks after a fatal car accident down a winding county curve renamed in whispers after the names of its victims.

Joshua's foresight in knowing something might happen kept him closer to David, holed up, as it were. That, he would have said, led to his trepidation about considering another local public performance. He did occasionally volunteer to play lighter repertory at the local senior home. And David's amiable nature when selling pumpkins each fall was measured by working with his uncle. Certainly his uncle's workers, Zeke and Hector, didn't care, aside from making a few good-natured jokes.

Their occasional trips together to town remained untroubled. At the video store on Center Street, Joshua even found Giannis Bacchus's "Tunisian epic," but while watching it they fell asleep halfway through.

The bliss of spending every day together became peppered with joking arguments that turned into private catch phrases. "Tines down!" David would shout from the kitchen after poking his hand on an upturned fork left in the dish rack by Joshua.

"Hausfrau day!" Joshua would call out as he carried a load of wet laundry from the washer to a clothesline David set up in the back yard when the dryer conked out. David eventually bought a new dryer before first frost so they could avoid a frozen bed sheet dilemma.

As they watched TV, Joshua endured David's habit of spitting out unchewable bits of pumpkin seeds into a bowl, while David ignored Joshua's habit of silently fingering the piano parts of any music that played during a movie or sitcom.

They shopped together, attended the County Fair—David handed over the Big Mac pumpkin weigh-in competition duties to his uncle—with rarely a problem. The boys were locals, known but "passing," as the term goes. Young local men often traveled in pairs, and David could flirt with any ladies who cared to receive his innocuous attention. They didn't call attention to their relationship, and to the credit of most Serene residents, few people cared.

But perhaps an affectionate jostle between the two of them struck some other male of the species as too close, too obvious. We know all too well that the roots of hatred come from within.

Joshua recalled that he was discussing a possible concert at the college some day soon, David half-nodding as they lay settled on the couch, listening to their latest musical discovery, Tangerine Dream. Goliath the dog, curled up nearby on his bed, perked his head up moments before it happened, a loud smash at a nearby window, glass crashing to the floor. At the sound of a hoot from a gurgling car zooming off in the night, David nearly shoved Joshua off his lap to stand, stare out the window through the broken glass to see red taillights swerve down the road.

"Goddam motherfuckers," he stormed into the back of the kitchen, rummaged under a cabinet and extracted the rifle Joshua hadn't seen in months.

"What the fuck?"

"Stay here. Stay low." David shoved bullets in, spilling a few cartridges on the counter.

Joshua knew not to argue, sat panicked, then tried to calm Goliath's barking and keep him from running out the door to follow David, who rushed out in his stockinged feet, rifle raised, all the way down to the road.

He stayed out for more than an hour, waiting while Joshua shooed the dog away from the broken glass, cleaned it up and taped over the window with a piece of cardboard he cut from a box.

"Why would anyone . . . ?" Joshua asked when David finally returned, peeling off his wet socks.

"You know why."

"We should call the sheriff."

"No."

"What? Someone just—"

"You wanna call the cops? The same guys't hauled me off just a few years ago? They won't do a damned thing, except a possible illegal search and seizure."

Joshua let it go.

Their flares of affection took time to reassemble and find a balance with their newfound fear of the locals. Joshua discovered that domestic life wasn't all it seemed to be, considering they were both young and fractured in different ways. For several nights, David, bundled up in sweaters and a coat, sat on the porch with the rifle, sipping coffee, smoking cigarettes, staying up late. They never found out who did it, and the police would have discounted it as a mere prank, but the boys knew better.

David's paranoia had some logic. AIDS had been making headlines more frequently in the news. Anyone accused or, as with the boys, known to be gay became targets. Nothing could be done about it.

They pretended it wouldn't happen again, and fortunately, it didn't. Their visits into town became a vague guessing game. Was it him? Those guys? Teenagers? It had to be someone who knew they were gay, and even years after Joshua's little TV show confession, people talked because they had little else to fill their lives.

But David would get stoned a bit too often and find himself getting angry like his father when a crop failed, or the tractor's engine died, or the water heater broke, and the bills kept coming.

For several days, David and his Uncle Joe spent hours sitting at the dining room table, going over their accounts left in disarray by his father. Joshua made himself scarce with other work. Later, David explained the confusing financial situation of subsidies and market pricing and how many other farms were going bankrupt.

"Fuckin' Reagan," David growled. "Made all these promises, shows up in a cowboy hat on TV for a photo shoot in Iowa, then goes back to lyin' more."

On a mid-July Saturday that summer, Joshua managed to cheer David up a bit as the two hosted a viewing of the Live Aid concert aired by satellite from Philadelphia and London. With a massive bowl of popcorn, myself, Ed Wallenbeck, and a few of their other friends, we watched band after band play at a global fundraiser for famine causes. We partook of a feast of snacks, fried chicken, multiple bowls of herbal refreshments, and beer.

Joshua held back a giddy enthusiasm as Queen returned to the Wembley Stadium stage for their now-legendary twenty-minute set. For days afterward, Joshua dove back into playing his Queen favorites, leaving an amused David to dance along or sit back in the living room and enjoy it, an audience of one.

Some news that was both good and bad came to me in Autumn 1985 via Sara Evans. Her mother had had a stroke and died in her San Francisco home. She called me, requesting real estate advice on her mother's house. After offering my condolences, I made a few calls to agents out there, who strongly advised on keeping the property. My own small prescience concurred; the one thing that rarely decreases in value is a well-kept house in a growing city.

But Sara Evans seemed more interested in selling off the house than becoming a long distance landlord, and her husband agreed. So she and her husband and daughter flew out for the funeral, to handle her mother's affairs, and argue with her brothers about the alleged sizable inheritance.

"I still wish I'd been able to visit her again," Joshua said.

While several personal items ended up shipped back to their home in Serene, Joshua's sister claimed several pieces of furniture the brothers didn't want and hired a moving van that eventually brought them to her home in Cleveland. She'd dropped out of college to marry an older classmate who'd started a dermatology practice.

"I asked my mom about shipping that beautiful piano back here, but she was too upset about it all," Joshua said after it had been sold.

It turned out that his grandmother's will left a substantial amount of money to her daughter, and equal amounts of about $20,000 to both Joshua and his sister.

As they waited for Sara's mother's estate to be settled, Joshua contributed what he could to David's needs, driving to bowling alleys and bars and Kiwanis fundraisers, any place that would pay for a piano player who knew a few pop songs.

While David appreciated Joshua's contributions, he was also frustrated to have to take more from his father's insurance money to pay off bills. Joshua's absences began to bother him, but then his presence sometimes annoyed him, too, since the rickety upright piano had not been tuned for months. After a difficult day in the fields, David became suddenly irritated by the sound of Joshua practicing a song he'd heard too often unfinished. He waited until Joshua drove off for another night in Columbus. Then he drove his truck up to the porch. After trying to do it himself, he called up a farm hand in need of twenty bucks, and he and the hired hand hauled the piano out of his house and left it in the middle of the barn.

Joshua didn't notice the piano's absence that night. Having arrived home late, he foraged in the kitchen then up to bed. David feigned sleep.

The next morning, David heard Joshua's blurted profanity, eased downstairs and simply pointed toward the barn.

"That piano means a lot to me."

"I'm sorry but it's . . . old. I'm getting you a better one. It was a surprise. I still got some money from my dad's life insurance."

"We can't afford a better one, at least not yet," Joshua argued.

"Yes, we can. A new electronic one, with headphones." Joshua's used keyboard from Los Angeles had started acting up a year before and had been relegated to a corner in its case.

"Oh, so that's the point. So you don't have to hear it."

"No, it's— Ed said there was one on sale at the mall."

Joshua glared at David in a way he had never done, then put his coat on and, before walking out through the kitchen door, said, "You could have waited. My grandma's money could buy you a new tractor, too."

It has been said that their neighbors half a mile away could hear Joshua pounding away on that piano in the barn for days, that it chased away birds and squirrels. Goliath, however, liked to follow Joshua to the barn and often curled up nearby.

David finally presented him with a new electronic keyboard and headphones set up in the dining room. He also got the water heater fixed. But Joshua continued to play in the barn.

"You want me to haul this back inside?" David asked the next day as he leaned on the piano. Joshua had been playing for hours. The echo captivated him.

"Not just yet."

"Okay, well, supper's on."

"In a bit."

David walked back to the house, called back, "You know I love you!"

They learned to get along, enjoy their time together and not worry about random gunshots through their windows or old pianos. They learned when it was better to not be in the same room together too long except to watch TV, or to go out to eat at small restaurants out of town, or to hold each other in bed. David learned once again to enjoy listening to Joshua play on his new keyboard as he discovered new sounds and effects he could add to his music. They could have gone on to lead simple quiet lives, but a new creative spark in Joshua's mind was about to ignite.

Chapter 36

LILY OF THE VALLEY

"WHAT DO YOU really want to do to improve the farm? Something different?" Joshua asked as they sat in the kitchen, finishing another well-cooked dinner. Below them, Goliath gnawed on a ham bone with dedication.

"I don't know. Definitely not livestock," David asserted. "We could get bees, make some honey."

"Ouch. Bee stings."

"Aw, they're not so bad."

"I think you're forgetting something."

David's quizzical stare matched Goliath's, who perked up attentively for a random scrap of food.

"I seem to recall you mentioning a secret dream a long time ago."

David shook his head, shrugged.

Joshua quoted David from a stoned conversation they'd had at the mall when they were still in a state of mere flirtation. "'Who doesn't love pansies?'"

Joshua smiled wide, having made the toughened, bearded love of his life blush.

A week later, on a blustery spring day, David and Joshua set about staking out a flat rectangle of land behind the barn. Stacks of lumber and heavy wire frames had been purchased and hauled, as well as packets of thick rolled plastic and a bucket of nails.

Ezequiel and Hector stood among the stakes, surveying their project. Happy to be offered some other work in addition to the crop labors, the two men had joined in with a bemused enthusiasm. Goliath sniffed at the new objects with curiosity.

"Gonna be a piece a cake," Hector stated with confidence, a tool belt around his waist.

"What about you, Zeke?" David asked. "You gonna be okay with the saw?"

"Sure." Ezequiel leaned against the circular table saw. David had rented it from True Value with a special family discount thanks to Joshua's father, who said he looked forward to helping out on the weekend.

David surveyed the plans from a book he'd bought, *How to Build a Greenhouse*. "So, we start with the drainage ditch and the floor. I'd say, two weeks?"

Two days later, a small truck pulled up in the driveway, and a tall boy emerged and walked up to the project. He looked familiar to David.

"Remember me? From the school bus?"

"Toby Findley?" The two shook hands, patted backs. "You sprouted up quick!"

"My dad finally sold off the chickens, and I need the work, so you said I could work for you. I always did love pumpkins."

"Well, we don't start plantin' 'em till July, but we got something else going on right now. How are you with a hammer?"

"Pretty good."

"You know how to make a table?"

"Sure. You need one?"

"About a dozen."

As the men were introduced to each other, Joshua smiled proudly to see his investment being born and David's teenage dream of growing flowers becoming a reality.

If their workers knew or cared about their relationship, they never brought it up, except with a few mild jokes. It was a rare kind of polite indifference, or perhaps, in Toby's case, a kind of quiet admiration.

The boys never married since of course back then they couldn't. They could have traveled to Canada or Massachusetts or other places where it eventually became legal. But no Ohio court would recognize such a bond. So there wasn't any ceremony.

I like to think they wed in the pumpkin field, just holding hands and making quiet vows under an autumn sunset, with no guests but a few crickets, perhaps a late bouquet from the greenhouse blossoms.

On one of her visits "just to check" and bring some food or cookies, Sara Evans also brought a postcard from Hawaii, sent to Joshua's parents' address from his Los Angeles friend Zeff. The open invitation to visit enthused Joshua, who wrote back with the hope of a vacation.

But David, concerned about the expense, and perhaps a bit jealous, hesitated and put off such plans.

Instead, he began to treat Joshua to much shorter journeys that offered their own magic and an opportunity to revive their affections. With merely a radio, they danced slowly together in the barn, Goliath their only audience. On moonlit warm nights, David led Joshua through the cornfield where he flattened a few stalks as a sort of sacrifice before laying down a blanket for them to strip down and make love, the moon making their skin glow.

He also drove with Joshua on overnight mini-vacations to Columbus. They would visit me in German Village, where I'd moved after college. We'd enjoy a meal or drinks out, even a few concerts when I performed with the Columbus Orchestra. But they stayed in a hotel to enjoy more private romantic nights, one time even spending a weekend at a gay and lesbian Country Western two-step gathering where they danced the night away, arm in arm. David, surprisingly a better dancer, usually led.

Joshua still hoped for that Hawaiian vacation, but they never found the time.

The first hint of Joshua's illness—and David's, although less symptomatic—was his fatigue and a few days of almost uncontrollable diarrhea. Joshua sat on the toilet for hours, waiting for it to end. David drove into town to the nearest drug store for a few boxes of Imodium, which held it off for a day.

Dehydrated and woozy, settled into bed with a towel just in case, he looked up at David and said, "You know, there's a test out."

"For what?"

"You know. AIDS."

David tried to contain his anger. "No. That's not what it is. We're not . . . like that."

Joshua shook his head. "We both had our little adventures, you know. It's not like—"

"It's prob'ly just food poisoning."

"We always eat the same food. Davey . . ."

That cartoon Goliath voice. David sat back down beside him on the bed.

"Where would we go? We can't, not here in town."

"There's a place in Columbus. I heard about it at the bar."

David sat, gripping Joshua's hand, staring off at a wall. He wondered about Noel, the guy he met at the country-western bar, and Rafael, and that go-go boy from Magnolia's, then scolded himself for not thinking first about Joshua, whether he could have given it to him, or if Joshua had— No. He had to be strong.

"Okay."

The waiting room at Planned Parenthood in North Columbus, just a few blocks from the Ohio State campus, had a few young men and women, mostly students. The boys looked like them but felt worlds apart.

They took their turns stepping into a small room, had their forearms swabbed and punctured, the blood strangely darker and thicker than expected.

Back then, you waited for a week. Then you had to return.

You didn't get the results over the phone. The next week was fraught with a low tension. David had mysteriously gone out and returned with some weed and got stoned each night after working overtime in the fields. Joshua threw himself into a new book of early David Bowie songs. They ate, avoided discussing the test or what they would do afterward.

When they drove back to Columbus, each returned from their private consultations with a slow-speaking nurse who offered vague assurances of hope despite the diagnosis, stern instructions about safety practices, and a packet of condoms, as if it were a consolation prize.

"So, we're supposed to use rubbers now?" David hadn't spoken for miles.

Joshua took a cigarette from the pack in the glove compartment, lit one for David, who took it.

"I don't know why. We've already both got it. We might as well just—"

David swerved the truck, yanked it back as he almost hit a car in the next lane.

"What the fuck! What do you think you're doing?!"

"Fuckin' shit. Sorry. I'm just—"

"I know you're upset. I am, too. But we're not dead yet! Jesus, Dave!"

At the next turnoff, David pulled over, drove into a gas station, filled his tank, then pulled away and parked near a dumpster, shut off the motor.

"We ain't tellin' anyone."

"What about—"

"Especially your mom. Jeez, she'll be runnin' by every day like Nurse Hot Lips or whatever."

"You mean Florence Nightingale."

"Whatever."

"We gotta start takin' care of ourselves, of each other. Eatin' right."

"We eat good! I do most of the cookin'."

"And did the nurse tell you the same thing as me? These," Joshua grabbed the pack of Marlboro Lights from the glove compartment, "have gotta go." He tossed them out the window.

"What the fuck!" David stormed out of the truck, paced around it swearing, and picked up the pack, shouting, "Not yet, dammit!"

He stood away from the truck. Joshua stewed inside, watching as David repeatedly kicked the dumpster.

After he calmed down, they drove home in silence for a while, until Joshua stuttered, "Are you . . . ?"

"Am I what?"

"Are you scared?"

David scowled, shook his head. "Course I'm scared."

"Me, too."

"Well, I guess we'll just be scared together." He reached to pat Joshua's shoulder, kept it there, driving one-armed until their hands met and held on for the rest of the drive home.

The boys had to tell someone, and being their only out gay friend, and the only somewhat worldly companion, I got the news, took it in, offered my sympathies and a grain of hope.

I knew of a few men in other towns who'd become ill. They did make an appearance here and there, mostly in the cities I visited. They didn't discuss it, but one could see a thin pallor, a slower gait. Others remained in a state of fear, awaiting symptoms.

I recommended the services of a lawyer in Columbus who was neither wily nor particular about his clients' private lives. The boys were smart enough to go into business together, co-owning the house and the land, still mostly leased to David's Uncle Joe.

They didn't have many friends other than myself, Toby, and Hector and Ezekiel, plus Ed and a few classmates from high school. To anyone who didn't know or remember or care, they just became a couple of bearded guys who occasionally rode into town for groceries and supplies, the ones at the pumpkin farm who'd started selling flowers. That was all people knew, for a while.

Eventually, they had to tell Joshua's parents. Still struggling with the decision, their visits to Sam and Sara's, usually for Sunday dinner, lost the air of light conversation. Sara's maternal prescience eventually pried open their defenses.

"You boys have been pretty quiet."

"Just, you know, lots of farm worries."

"And other things." Joshua looked over the table to David for support.

"What other things?"

"How 'bout we talk after dinner," David offered. "Don't wanna spoil this fine roast."

A silence ensued as they ate until Sara declared dinner over, although no one left the table.

Sara stared at her son, knowing, needing to hear it.

"We both . . . we're both HIV-positive."

An expected stunned silence followed.

"How long did you know?" Samuel Evans glared at David.

"Couple months. We got tested in Columbus."

"So, you two have been . . . ?"

"Been what?" David asked. "We prob'ly weren't together when we got it."

"You have it, too?" Samuel Evans eyes flared.

David nodded.

"Goddammit."

"Sam."

"I never shoulda let you—"

"Dad, he didn't. We both had . . . other things happen when we were away."

"That's not the point."

"No, it *is* the point, Dad. We didn't know. Nobody knew just a few years ago. Do you think we did this on purpose?"

Sam Evans's anger quelled as his wife stood, leaned over her son, hugged him tightly, then did the same to David, who almost shuddered at her touch.

"None of that matters," she sniffed. "Are you okay now? Have you been sick?"

Joshua wiped the rush of tears that swept over him. "Just a little tired. Nothing bad—"

"Yet," David blurted.

"Well, we're just going to get you to a doctor, someone who can help."

"We've been to see doctors, in Columbus. There's nothing to do."

David cleared his throat, tried to stay objective. "They keep taking blood tests, talking about T-cells and stuff. They wanna track us, keep up with how we're doing."

Sara held her son's hand, refused to pull away. "We'll just wait and hope."

Sam Evans had been silent, his face covered by a hand. When he banged a fist on the table, exposing his reddened face and bleary eyes, the others, silenced, shocked, stared at him.

"We're not gonna let this thing take you away from us." He offered a sad look to his son, then to David. "Neither of you. Not gonna let this happen."

David's eyes welled up, unable to hold back tears as he looked at Sam as a sort of father-in-law, or the kind of father he wished he'd had.

Chapter 37

SOMEBODY TO LOVE

HOW TO MANAGE sex when you feel diseased, when you don't know if you've made it worse with every act of love or lust? How they held on and refused to let fear divide them remained mostly private. I never pried, but I knew that David would not stop kissing and hugging Joshua, would not stop holding him in bed, that every separation, be it across the field of growing pumpkins or across town to retrieve a tractor part, hurt more.

A single show of affection stirred up a bit of trouble that fall at the Serene County Fair.

The boys had spent most of the day admiring the produce, attending a cattle auction, wolfing down fried foods they shouldn't have eaten, and later met up with Ed Wallenbeck and his new girlfriend, Amy, where they all snuck back to the parking lot to smoke a joint before the demolition derby.

On their way to get seats at the grandstand, someone had told a joke, and while laughing, David leaned close, clasping his arm over Joshua's shoulder. An innocuous gesture, but given the whispered rumors, it caught the attention of a random idiot, some low class yokel they probably knew from school but had ignored until the word shouted across the way near a corn dog truck made them halt.

"Damn faggots!"

David turned and saw three men about his age, standing ready for a confrontation.

"You got a problem?" David stepped forward, fearless.

Joshua considered how he might carry out one of his surprise Bruce Lee moves from his playground days. But they were joined by Ed and his girlfriend, who shouted back more epithets than they could take in, and any sort of fight was cut short.

"I'll get you!" shouted the yokel. "I know where you live!"

"Never mind those assholes. I could take them on," Amy boasted.

"Glad you came to our defense, muh lady," David joked.

But Joshua turned back for a last glance, unsure if it was over, or that it ever would be.

A week before Christmas, Sara Evans stopped by the farm house bringing cooked dishes: lasagna, a pie, and even some canned goods, as usual.

"Mom, we have food. David's a real good cook."

"I know, dear. This is how your mother shows she cares. Give me that."

"Well, thanks anyway." He put the pans in the refrigerator, pondered the boxes and cans as they stood in the kitchen.

"Where's David?"

"Over at his uncle's, trying to figure out which crops to grow next year."

"Well, it's just as well. I need to tell you something alone, first."

"What now?"

"You know you're both invited to dinner for Christmas, all day, since it'll be early, like your father prefers. But your sister was asking about you, and I did feel I had to tell her."

"Tell her what?"

Her sheepish look of concern answered the question.

"Why?"

"She's your family. She deserves to know."

"Fuck."

"Joshua!"

"Mom. So, is she not coming, because of us?"

"Well, I did have to convince her, and even though her husband is a doctor, sort of, she's not the brightest bush in the barrel."

"That makes no sense."

"Anyway, I told her it's not contagious, casually, that is, and hopefully her husband can convince her."

"That's great. Just great."

"I'm sorry."

"You can't just go telling people, Mom. This town is not—"

"You'd be surprised. And no, I haven't told anyone about . . . it. But there are a few folks who've been very nice to me. They ask me about you and your piano playing and David, and how much their kids love to pick pumpkins here, as if you're just any other couple of—"

"The town queers. Terrific. Thanks for your diplomacy."

"Anyway, she's coming, with her husband and daughter. So if she can behave, you can too."

"Sure."

"Thank you." She enveloped her son in a tight hug. "Now, bake that lasagna at 375 for about forty minutes."

Despite Sara Evans's hopes, that awkward Christmas dinner of 1987 became the day one member of the Evans family induced a separation that lasted for two years.

The first problem started with the dog, Goliath. Familiar with visiting the Evans home, he had curled up comfortably in the living room after David and Joshua were welcomed inside by Sam Evans, who, usually reserved in his affections, vigorously patted the appreciative dog's rump.

Joshua helped his mother in the kitchen, adding his and David's side dishes to the ample array of food. Sam and David chatted in the living room as the stereo played Christmas songs on a low volume.

"Let's take a break," Sara wiped her hands, leading Joshua out to the living room. "Your sister called earlier. They're going to be late, so let's just do Round One of presents."

Socks and sweaters, a radio alarm clock, books, candles, and sheet music unwrapped and appreciated, the four of them and Goliath had almost settled into a balance of affection and appreciation of the day.

Until the late guests arrived.

Sensing an end to the calm, Sam Evans stood to open the door and sighed, "Here goes."

Goliath jumped up, excited to see Sister, her husband, and most amusing to the dog, their daughter, who squealed, "Puppy!"

"What is that animal doing in here?" Sister snapped.

"Sorry," David grabbed Goliath's collar, held him back. "He's just happy to see ya."

Sister clutched her child in her arms as if threatened by a wolf.

"I can't have her in the same room with . . . that."

"It's just a dog, honey," her husband's attempt at diplomacy was met with a glare.

"I'll take him out to the garage." David led a confused Goliath out through the kitchen as Sister and her family nervously removed coats, exchanged awkward hugs, and settled down.

Once David returned, Joshua nodded toward him and the two sat together on one side of the couch—too close, apparently, for Sister's approval.

A few more gift exchanges remained cordial if a bit stiff, as were conversational topics: the weather, the snow, the traffic, Sister's apparently busy life in Cleveland. At each veer toward David and Joshua's life together, however, she sniffed or coughed, interrupted, or sat stone-faced and silent.

The meal brought the next problem. Excellent as it was, the eager guests piled food on their plates, with one exception.

"Have some beans, dear."

"No thank you."

Her husband passed the squash. She also declined.

"David and Josh made those," Sara said with pride.

319

"I know that. I'm just not that hungry."

Her daughter, however, was and made a grab for the plate. Sister yanked it away and the child whined.

"Stop it."

"I notice you're declining the side dishes David and Joshua brought. They grew those."

"I know they live on a farm," her daughter scolded.

"Mom, please," Joshua whispered.

"No, seriously. Is something wrong?" Sara prodded.

Samuel Evans shook his head, sensing the oncoming cloud-burst.

Sister's face tightened. "It's just . . . shouldn't we be careful?"

"About what?"

"You know."

A fork clattered against a plate. Sam glowered. "If you think you can get—"

"Don't say it!" Sister almost moved to cup her daughter's ears.

"No, no, that's all right," Joshua interrupted. "Sis, since we got 'it,' we've been doing a lot of research, more than you, apparently. And although I didn't get my information directly from *The New England Journal of Medicine*, I'm pretty sure AIDS isn't transmittable via cooked vegetables."

David withheld a snort of laughter.

Sister gasped, looked to her husband for support.

"Actually, hon, he's right."

"I can't believe this! I'm trying to protect my child."

"Oh!" Sara mocked as she raised her nearly empty wine glass. "Like you invented motherhood."

Sister abruptly stood, shoving her chair out as she grabbed her daughter, who howled appropriately, then rushed out of the dining room and up the stairs.

"I think we better get going," David said, wiping his mouth with a napkin.

"No!" Sara almost shouted. "You sit right there. You are family, too."

Joshua pleaded, "Mom, don't."

"I'm going to have a few words with my daughter."

Left at the table, the men ate slowly in silence. The music changed to Bing Crosby's "White Christmas."

The argument eventually led to an early exit by Sister and her family and a distance that endured for holidays to come. Cards and phone calls would remain polite but perfunctory at best. Samuel Evans foresaw this. Some decades-old survival tactic from his Navy days may have clicked in as the argument between the women, accompanied by a howling child, echoed from upstairs. On one side, his daughter was strong, arrogant, and well cared for by a well-off husband and a usually adorable child. She would be fine. On the other side, his son and sort-of son-in-law, wounded and in danger, bravely endured scorn, even in his own home. He came to a decision.

"Pass me those beans, Dave."

Chapter 38

A KIND OF MAGIC

"BEFORE I DIE, I want to do something great in this town."

Such a resolute statement might be considered farfetched for anyone else, but when Joshua said it, David understood and helped him plan the now-famous concert in the barn. He knew why Joshua wanted to be remembered as more than "that kid who got on TV a few times and played 'Bohemian Rhapsody' at a school assembly."

But the real question about the barn concert is its inspiration.

The rumor goes, Joshua had a party of friends all sit down to watch *The Wizard of Oz* while he played Pink Floyd's *Dark Side of the Moon* at Brent Carse's 1988 New Year's Eve party. Someone else allegedly heard about playing *Dark Side of the Moon* while watching *The Wizard of Oz*. Joshua always shrugged off his role in deciding to play the Pink Floyd record, but did admit to playing along in an adjoining dining room. His friends drank and smoked, with David sitting beside him, entranced, their thighs pressing together.

Their friends drank beer and howled along all the way through the amazing vocals of "Great Gig in the Sky" like white farm boys impersonating a thousand years of Black suffering (even though the vocals were performed, of course, by the diminutive white British singer Clare Torry).

This was before YouTube or anything. Really, there was no way this idea could have traveled quickly. I know you've all heard about it years later on the Internet. But I tell you, I don't care what anyone says about it, it's merely a nice juxtaposition of song cues.

Anyway, I don't get all the underlying themes of how the Pink Floyd song goes with a scene from a family classic—give me Elgar any day—but, for instance, that spot where Almira Gulch appears and the bells and alarms go off, or when Dorothy trips out from the bump on her head during the tornado and the music gets equally woozy. The part where the music stops exactly where the film switches from black and white, and how "Money" starts the moment it switches to verdant green Hollywood Munchkinland. Well, that it is just too trippy for words, as the stoners say.

Anyway, Joshua once said that he and David thought it up first, but he later denied it. For me, now that it came up recently through some grapevine whose seed I am telling you I knew, it seems a perfect way to remember these two boys. They weren't Judy Garland queens. They weren't just stoner farm boys. They were something in between or both at once.

Even all that had nothing to do with Joshua asking me to help him produce a concert version of Pink Floyd's *Animals* in the barn with a seven-piece band, an invitation I could not refuse. His health had leveled off, albeit with a few days of fatigue, and David remained mostly asymptomatic and took care of the more laborious efforts.

As for the inspiration, I like to give partial credit to myself. Joshua used to say, at the last few years of parties they had, that I had inspired him to bring together all his musician friends to perform what he called the band's "most sublime" album. He'd not witnessed any of their concerts in 1977 (at Cleveland Stadium) or in Columbus for *The Wall*.

"I was afraid of that one," Joshua said. "Seeing it live would have broken me apart." He sometimes mentioned how the song "Comfortably Numb" eerily reflected his childhood seizures.

What he didn't say was that concerts had become a bit too

exhausting. And by then, after all they'd been through, if he couldn't go with David, he wouldn't.

His visit to a slaughterhouse might have convinced him to perform the *Animals* album, based loosely on George Orwell's *Animal Farm*. When Sam mentioned over one of their Sunday dinners that a client had opened a slaughterhouse, Joshua surprisingly expressed an interest in seeing it. So Sam brought his son and David out to the butcher's on the north edge of town, where a colleague of his had sold a plethora of implements for the carving up and the cleaning up of great slabs of half-split cows and pigs that hung in twenty-foot-high refrigerated lockers.

Although he became mostly vegetarian after that experience, Joshua claims it wasn't the inspiration for what became an amazing concert, of which, fortunately, a pristine recording exists. It was a peak moment, not a declaration, as his many "Bohemian Rhapsody" performances had been.

This gathering was, for David and Joshua, settling themselves in, or defining themselves, becoming part of a community before it was too late, despite the gossip and the discreet shunning.

What Joshua said truly inspired the concert was his visit to one of the homes my family's real estate company had for sale. Since Joshua's mother had done her decorating magic, the boys were not in need of new or used furniture. But Joshua was always interested in musical instruments and the remnants of town folks' lives.

I'd called to show him a home on the auction block, the small ranch house of a childless widow of ninety who had left a lot of unwanted yet immaculate furniture, including a petite yet usable electric organ.

"She played at the Presbyterian Church on Broad Street until her arthritis stopped her. She used to practice at home."

As I marveled over the widow's near-pristine 1960s kitchen in classic avocado, Joshua swiftly found the power and volume buttons on the organ, and his nimble fingers played the first haunting trill of "Pigs."

That afternoon, we placed the organ in the back of David's truck, flat on its back with a stack of blankets underneath.

Why *Animals*? Joshua was still enamored of Queen and many other bands, but it was as if he'd cracked their formula. He'd tackled Elton John, ELO, Yes, Bowie, even Genesis epics. But his hunger for more challenges continued. Performing Queen or more complicated music seemed impossible for a band without a stellar vocalist, and his solo versions had become so polished they were too simple for him, saved for his weekend bar gigs. To be a bit critical, Joshua had become a bit of a rock music snob.

It was the subtlety of Richard Wright's keyboards in *Animals* that haunted Joshua. He had to decode its beautiful simplicity. After playing solo attempts on the old upright in the barn, or up nights in the dining room on his new electric piano, he realized the keyboards should be played by two people. He had to gather company.

The organ was placed adjacent to the upright piano in the barn one warm spring day, and Joshua brought in his Korg from the living room. He played his parts and other parts, turning the barn into a cathedral-like studio. He played over and over as the score he'd bought became worn. Eventually all the guys he and I and David called just started showing up for jam sessions when they could.

Ed Wallenbeck on rhythm guitar offered a steady hand and brought two amps.

Matt Crodach, in between time with his new wife and their child, gladly signed back on as drummer.

I knew a fellow from college, Dwight Black, who could approach both Roger Waters' nasal twang and David Gilmore's thin reedy vocals. Dwight offered his vocal and cowbell talents. He kept his musical theatre training at a subtle coolness, as well as his preference for men.

As I sat across from Joshua those afternoons in the barn, I remember how in many ways he resembled Pink Floyd's keyboardist Richard Wright. His hair had grown long, and he retained his quiet demeanor anywhere away from rehearsals. But what I most recall is how, at rehearsals and on that night of the concert, he never stopped smiling.

By the time the flyers went around to a few stores and the local mall, the Sheriff found out about it. Yes, Elwood Crumrine, that same sheriff who'd hauled David off to jail years ago.

A few days before the show, Sheriff Crumrine puffed himself up in the driveway as Ed and Matt were unrolling some large carpets they'd pilfered from a home demolition. Sheriff Crumrine waddled into the barn and asked about the setup, making vague unspecified threats about safety. In the midst of the hemming and hawing, our lead guitarist, Danny Hager—whose band had just returned from a tour of Pennsylvania bowling alleys and bars—cranked out the first few bars of "Sweet Home Alabama." It so charmed our local constable he simply scolded us about installing buckets of sand for cigarette butts and posting No Smoking signs inside the barn. He even came back with two other officers to provide security and see the show.

The local college had been informed as well, and one student offered not only to air the show on the student radio station, but also record it on reel-to-reel tape. Copies of that have been shared in the fan club's newsgroups and remain the most popular of Joshua's recordings. You're welcome.

And Pink Floyd never hassled him or his estate—i.e., me— ever.

When I unearthed a dusty synthesizer from the college equipment storage, Joshua begged me to play it for all the high-end synthy sounds so he could focus on the widow's organ and the banged-up upright piano for "Pigs."

David took care of the electrical resources with a generator hooked up downhill and out of sight, with more backup power from the house via a one-hundred-foot extension cord. Their young friend Toby took the weekend off from his Agriculture studies at Ohio State and helped out with the sound mixer.

So many moments from this night were barely captured by the local newspaper's photographer or even by the beautiful tape recording. Soft lampshades warmed the stage area, the carpets, the dozens of folding chairs people brought on their own. Food appeared magically and tables-full were put out. Worn couches scrounged by David and his trusty truck from home foreclosures and garage sales transformed the barn into one big living room. Even Joshua's sister, so removed from her brother during those years, drove down from Cleveland with her husband, the wealthy dermatologist, and her daughter to witness the concert.

They didn't charge admission, but somebody passed a hat at some point and we all ended up splitting more than a hundred dollars. But what truly set this night apart, in my mind, were the satisfied looks the boys gave me, even a few years later, when we played the tape again for Joshua, by then blind but still playing songs from memory.

What always made us giggle while listening to that night were the taped animal sounds Joshua had collected over two days by visiting a few nearby livestock farms. While he did occasionally sing into it, Joshua's microphone had a more important purpose near the gaffer-taped cassette player atop the organ. He simply pressed play to add the howls, snorts, and baahs that made some giggle as well, at first. When Goliath perked his head up, sitting nobly up front on one of those carpets, we all shared a perfect moment.

Although a few of the stranger sound effects weren't perfectly recreated, we did enjoy a pray-along of sorts when the audience, on cue from Dwight, took out little sheets of paper with the song "Sheep"'s version of The Lord's Prayer and muttered along.

Ed Wallenbeck, who had seen the 1977 Cleveland concert replete with the giant floating pig, had shared his memory of the diminishing ending. Those who attended our much smaller concert may recall the extra thirty-two bars the band gave for the final twangy crescendo of "Sheep," closer to the studio album than Ed's recalled variations of the rousing double-time concert ending. We had explored a single final chord instead, but it was Matt who piped up from behind his drum kit and offered, "Do the slow version. Josh should close us out."

So it was settled. Our boy, our little Mozart of rock, left about seventy people inside the barn and another few dozen who had gathered outside—either late or simply drawn by the echoing sound over the hills—mesmerized, clapping along or in tears, or both.

We didn't want it to end, that jangling uplifting chord-play, the bass bouncing octaves. By then some of the kids had begun dancing a little jig on the carpet in front of the band, the dog jumping and barking with joy.

But we eventually wound down to the last slow ending. As Joshua placed his fingers on the widow's organ, all other instruments fading to silence, it connected us all, down to that last chord.

Perhaps Joshua's father remained standoffish before the show—mostly, Joshua's mother told me, because he hadn't been asked to help. But he must have known, appreciated that this was, in a way, Joshua's declaration of independence from his father. He was living proudly and doing what he wanted. And while he knew his father probably wouldn't appreciate the sound of the music, that his son had put it all together was enough. I think that's why his father's hug after that show made us all turn away as we took down the equipment: it was too sweet to see.

Fortunately, it wasn't Joshua's last recording or performance, but it was one of his best.

Chapter 39

BLURRED VISION

FOR A FEW months over the next year, I was away in Europe (yes, even people from Serene go away to Europe). The boys kept low profiles except for the sale of their pumpkins, gourds, and the expanding crops of potted flowers. Folks in the know visited the farm for a discount, where David offered begonias, violets, pansies and other floral beauties. But most people at the grocery stores and at the mall didn't know the decorative corn bundles and gourds came from David and his uncle's land. He'd handed off the retail duties to Toby, whose young face served as much of a selling point as the superior produce.

The boys stopped going to places that would allow too many personal questions. Mostly folks just wanted to be friendly, at least in person.

Now, you have to remember the time when all they had for treatment was AZT. I want you to think back a bit, and if you were too young to remember those days, let me tell you they were scary. People died quickly and terribly.

Joshua hadn't been eating much for a few days and had taken to wearing the cheap glasses he bought; sheet music wasn't the only thing he had trouble reading.

One night at dinner he sat at the kitchen table, listening as David talked about ordering a crop of sunflower seeds, all with the sort of determination one gets to spite losing hope.

Joshua pushed the mashed potatoes and a chicken breast around on his plate.

"I need to lay down," he muttered and shuffled to the living room to rest on the couch.

"You didn't finish. We're s'posed to eat right, remember?"

David put away the food, did the dishes and some other chores. When he returned, Joshua seemed to be asleep. He left quietly, went outside to the greenhouse, Goliath following him. He puttered away on a table of planters with seedlings for a few hours.

Upon returning to the house, Joshua still lay on the couch, shivering.

"Josh?"

"I think I . . . got a fever or something."

"Josh?" David swooped down, knelt before him, felt his damp forehead. "Baby, you're burnin' up. Why didn't you tell me?" Goliath hovered, concerned.

"I— Get a bucket."

He managed to hold off until David rushed to retrieve a cooking pot from the kitchen. Joshua's vomit spilled over, but mostly made it inside.

"Git!" David had to shove Goliath away from the pot. "I'm takin' you to the hospital."

"No, don't."

"I'm callin' your parents, too."

Sara and Samuel Evans arrived before they did, pacing inside the emergency waiting room. That night there were few other patients, just an older man with his arm in a makeshift sling.

It was a good thing David had called them. After taking Joshua into an examining room, the admitting clerk, a stout woman with her hair pulled back in a bun, handed over forms. "Are you related to the patient?" she asked David.

"No, I'm his . . . he lives with me."

"Does he have insurance?"

"Yes," Samuel Evans said.

"I'm his mother." Sara took the clipboard.

The clerk seemed relieved.

Sara and David sat down to wait. Joshua's father stood, arms crossed. Sara took David's hand. "What happened?"

"I dunno. He'd been feeling tired the past few days, wasn't eating, and then he just got all fevery."

Sam Evans said, "Don't mean to be rude, but were you boys . . ."

"What?"

"Smoking or drinking any."

"No, sir. We were eating dinner."

Sara Evans sighed, looked toward the closed double doors where, somewhere, Joshua lay waiting or hopefully being examined. She stood, paced, avoided her husband's outreached hand, asked the clerk how long they would wait, got a snippy reply, "The doctor is with him now," then sat back next to David, looking to him for answers.

"I've been taking care of him. You know that." He looked up to David's father, who only stared at him.

A while later, minutes that seemed longer, an older man in a white coat emerged through the doors.

"Are you the parents of," he checked a clipboard, "Joshua Lee Evans?"

Sara stood. "Yes."

"Your son has pneumonia."

"What?"

"It's not uncommon, but it can be for someone his age. I have to ask," the doctor stepped closer, lowering his voice. "Is your son, is he a homosexual?"

"What?" Samuel Evans almost shouted.

"Please be calm. We can step into my office if you need to—"

"How does that have anything to do with—"

"This may be a symptom of an immune system infection." He didn't say the word, but they figured it out.

David squirmed in the chair, wanting to scream it out. He waited.

331

"We're going to take a blood test."

"You don't have to. He's HIV-positive."

All eyes on him, David stood.

"Excuse me. You are?"

"I'm his—" David halted, lied, for the last time ever, he would recall. "His business partner. We own a farm together."

"I see. Well, your *business partner* is very sick. And we can't have—"

"What do you mean, you can't?" Samuel Evans took the charge. "This is a hospital. You take in sick people."

David growled, "It's not spread through the air. Even you oughtta—"

"We can't have—" The doctor stopped, lowered his voice. "We don't have the facilities for such a case. We can keep him overnight, put him in isolation, but you'll have to make other arrangements after that."

Sara Evans gasped. "Excuse me, but my son was born here. I gave birth to him and my daughter here."

"Honey, please."

"Sam, don't."

The doctor continued, turning to Samuel, as if a man would be more reasonable. "And we have two new mothers here now, with newborns. You really want us to take that risk?"

"You know, we have lived in this town all our lives," Samuel Evans started to argue, left it hanging.

"As I said, we are not equipped to handle this disease," the doctor restated. "I'll be back in a bit, give you some recommendations for clinics in Columbus and Cleveland." He walked away, leaving them to stare at each other in shock.

"This is an outrage," Sara fumed.

"How long has he been sick?" Samuel pressed.

"Just a few days, this time," David shrugged. "Look, we told you this might happen."

"This is just, just, oh god—" Sara muttered.

"You," Sam Evans glared.

David saw it, the flash of pure defensive anger, Joshua's father looming over him, fists clenched.

"What? This is my fault? My fault my dad sent me off to a boot camp? My fault he got sick, probably from someone in fuckin' Hollywood? Weren't you the one't kicked him out?"

"You son of a bitch."

"Sam. Stop."

"If you'da just let us be, none of this woulda happened."

"How dare you? I have been on your side for—"

"Sam, David. One of you go outside. Just stop." Sara shot a glance back at the admissions clerk, who'd heard it all.

"I'll go," David said. "But I'm gonna be right here, first thing in the morning."

He slept in his truck in the parking lot. Roused by dawn, he wandered the hospital halls to find coffee and a few dispenser snacks, then sat, disheveled in a waiting room chair, until Joshua's parents returned, looking clean and presentable.

How could they have slept soundly, only blocks away?

As Joshua's father filled out forms at the desk, Sara Evans took him aside.

"We're going to take him home, just for a few days."

"But I—"

"I had a talk with Sam. Just steer clear of him for now."

A nurse wheeled Joshua out, her face covered by a mask, rubber gloves over her hands.

"Really?" Sara Evans sniped as she helped Joshua stand up.

"Where's Davey?"

"I'm here, Josh."

The boys hugged, parted. Joshua stood weakly, eased into the Evans's car.

"But I live with Davey."

"This is just for a few days, until we figure a few things out."

Samuel Evans wanted someone to blame for his son's illness, and David seemed an obvious target. But after Sara Evans calmly explained what she'd read about transmission, and reminded her husband of their son's probable Los Angeles affairs, he calmed down. A truce of sorts was achieved, and David kept a respectful demeanor toward Joshua's father, or simply avoided him by visiting middays.

When he felt better, Joshua insisted on returning to the farm and Sara visited almost daily. If he slept during the day, Sara and David discussed and worried together downstairs or outside, where she'd join him in tending the greenhouse flowers.

Calls and more calls were made, and plans, and decisions.

A cough became a hack. A bruise became a lesion. The flu became more than a flu. His bad vision and fever was diagnosed: Cytomegalovirus retinitis.

Joshua became ill more often. It only took that one visit to the Serene hospital to grasp the underlying problem with our little town. Of course, you'd expect fear, but Joshua's mother knew better, even if the local doctors didn't. People talked; they made vague inquiries whenever Sara went shopping. A new plan took over.

The drives to Columbus then Cleveland Clinic for tests and follow-up doctor appointments brought them more understanding hospital staffers familiar with AIDS cases. It became a sort of quality time for Joshua and his mother and on weekends his father, if needed. David protested, arguing that he should drive, but Joshua's mother remained undaunted, leaving him alone sometimes for the day to worry while she drove Joshua to doctor's appointments.

I started visiting and the flow of months rode up and down a little more on Joshua's health than the weather. I had meant to visit between my travels, but like many in those days, postponing a visit to a sick friend became common. A few weeks of polite phone message tags, and then I'd be out of town.

After weeks of not calling back, I just drove out to the farm.

Joshua did not recognize me right off, but gave me such a hug, and we did not stop talking for hours. We didn't play the piano, however. I didn't press the point unless he wanted to play. Thinner and a bit distracted, he was obviously weakened.

The boys had me over for dinner on weekends after visiting my parents, and we had some very nice nights with piano duets and movies and pot, which I had not had in quite a while, but which unleashed the honky-tonk in me that hid behind the classically trained accompanist.

Joshua recovered mostly, but did lose his memory in bits, though not the details. He could no longer sight-read. But oh, when he had a good chord sheet and a burst of energy, Joshua played and played, and through his new keyboard, made recordings. You can hear them. I would later busy myself with getting them copied and turned into a CD collection for sale, forwarding all the proceeds to a local AIDS nonprofit. But they make only a few dollars a month these days.

The last large gathering was New Year's Eve 1989.

Out at Joshua and David's we could set off fireworks over the snow-blanketed fields and nobody complained. It was their land, and the neighbors lived too far off to care.

Back inside sipping eggnog, the holiday music dispensed with, a few folks departed, including Joshua's parents, David's aunt and uncle, leaving only half a dozen guests: the ever-cheerful Toby, Zeke and Hector, Ed and his girlfriend Amy, and myself. Basically, anyone who wanted a little New Year's herbal cheer.

Joshua sat at the piano, leaving us expecting a languid Christmas carol.

"This is a really different one," he smiled. "So if ya don't like it, step outside. I won't be insulted."

The piece of music Joshua played in the first hours of that new year stunned us all. It was nothing like we'd ever heard. I'd loaned him some Keith Jarrett and Charles Ives records and for-gotten them. Perhaps that was the influence.

He played on the electric keyboard with no score, no set plan, all improvised, switching tones and timbres with various knobs, playing some of the most haunting melodies and tritones, disso-nant at moments, clusters of chords riffed from other songs in his repertory; not exactly jazz, not rock. It was as if he'd created his own half-blind autobiographical genre, what he called "a terrific accident." People thought this might have been first-stage de-mentia, but I knew better once I heard the results. In his last year, despite his illness or because of it, he had ascended into the realm of genius.

Chapter 40

WHO WANTS TO LIVE FOREVER

THE BOYS AND David's uncle continued to grow the best pumpkins in the county. The legend of the Pink Floyd concert had swept away most of the town's hostility about David and Joshua, and it seemed like that had been his plan all along.

There weren't any more concerts, despite near strangers who hadn't attended but heard about it approaching David or Joshua, wanting another show. Joshua shrugged it off. "No use repeating perfection."

Instead, he focused on the simple labors of the farm, assisting David when he felt up to it. By autumn, they let kids pick their own pumpkins with scarecrows in the field, and corn and gourds and melons for sale most autumn days, the table maintained by the ever-cheerful Toby.

David always said, "It ain't work as long as the land ain't hard."

But things got hard. Half the state endured an early frost, and half the gourd crop rotted. Joshua's bar gigs were too exhausting for him to travel to alone, so he stopped going. David made the hard decision to sell off more parts of his land to his uncle. Not because of money issues; he simply couldn't supervise a crew while caring for Joshua and becoming increasingly ill himself. I advised against the sale, suggesting he lease more instead. But I wasn't his executor at the time, so what can you do?

Toby, when he wasn't at college, stayed in David's father's abandoned bedroom. He helped out around the house, labored in the field with the workers and Joe Kemp. With his seemingly boundless energy, he also grew accustomed to more intimate assistance: cooking and cleaning the house when no one else could.

Joshua and David got tired, together. That's basically the polite version of what happened in their last years. Sara visited more often, bringing food and vitamins or some new herbal supplement she'd read about.

But it was hard when Joshua's IV spurted out.

It was hard when David started smoking cigarettes again, just to make Joshua mad.

It was hard when David almost went mad.

It was hard the day Joshua stopped playing piano.

Of course nobody remembers the day they quit something, except maybe cigarettes. But that's not it, the thing. We all have a last day for some daily habit we've taken for granted.

Too late, my time has come. Sends shivers down my spine, body aching all the time . . .

We all cried. That needs to be understood. But why people cried is a different story.

Don't misunderstand me. People here are kind. Serene became a parade of cakes and pies and visits and tributes and polite obituaries that omit the cause of death. I have the clippings.

But you see, there's the time where it's messy and smelly and guests aren't the easiest things to handle when the shit is actually flying.

Three different homecare nurses quit visiting the farmhouse, despite their array of rubber gloves and facemasks. Joshua's dementia led to outbursts of anger at anyone nearby, David included. David gave up calling for any other nursing help until Joshua's mother, who'd been visiting almost daily, pressed him into letting her care for him at her home.

"She knows better how to take care of him, I guess," David said to me late one night.

My world travels on hold, I'd returned to my part-time position with the Columbus Symphony Orchestra as a harpist; not essential to most symphonies, but I had been a featured soloist for a few works, Bizet and Saint-Saens among them.

I was actually preparing for an upcoming concert when David called, his voice raspy from thrush, though he'd managed to quit smoking again. I told him to call any time he needed to, and that was usually on dark lonely nights, particularly when Joshua had been taken to a hospital again before being brought back to his parents' home.

"He still recognizes me when I visit, so that's a good thing."

I refused to placate him or offer hopeful aphorisms. Thoughts and prayers were like the two cats I'd adopted, both useless.

David didn't need to hear about the small AIDS fundraisers at The Garage for a local nonprofit, or that two acquaintances of mine in the local music community had died horribly, their families outraged in denial, their lovers' Columbus apartments ravaged by parents as if thieves had descended. Instead, I listened.

"I mean, I want to be with him. I stop by almost every day and call when I can't. His mom asked me to stop comin' by at night when that's all I can find time for, but he's asleep by then, so I just hold his hand or touch his face. When he's up, he likes to talk, or more listen while I talk, try to talk about the farm, and he pretends to care."

"He always cared."

"I know, but it's not his thing, and I don't know about music like you and him. I swear, I listen to his tapes all the time, but then I can't bear it, ya know? And his dad, man, he has become such a softie. He was so scared at first, remember? So angry, and now he's takin' days off, just being there for Josh, ya know?"

"Yup. He's a good man. How's Toby?"

"Aw, he's fine. Fixed up my dad's old room real nice. He's

foreman now, but his Spanish ain't for shit. It's a good thing
Zeke and Hector know what to do more 'n him."

"I still think Toby's got a little crush on you."

"Me? Hell, I look worse 'n my dad did, even my grandfather.
That's what I am now, a twenty-seven-years-old old man."

We laughed at that for a bit. We had to laugh sometimes.

"You taking your medications?"

"Aw, shit, that fuckin' AZT's worse than bein' sick. It's like
Uncle Joe's mom when she had cancer. She said the chemo was
worse. Gosh, that was a sad little funeral. I was just a kid, but it
seemed like it was all old people. Hey, you haul that harp all
over town for when you play?"

"Sometimes. With the orchestra, I usually leave it in the rehearsal room and practice there. There's a saying among
harpists. It either needs to be tuned or it's just been tuned."

"What, 'cause it goes outta whack from haulin' it?"

"Exactly."

"Well, I don't wanna be, like, morbid, but you have to promise me something, Eric."

"Anything."

"Promise you'll play at our funerals. Maybe one of those
classical songs, or, oh yeah, a Queen song. That'd be right.
You'll be like a little earth angel."

Stunned, I stuttered a promise.

"Good." And just as quickly, David changed the subject. "So,
when you comin' up to visit again?"

I told David about my upcoming concert, and that Sunday
would be the best day.

"I'll have Toby mix up some supper. I can't hardly hold a pot
up these days. He does wonders with all the preserves. We got a
whole shelf-full. Butternut squash up to our elbows."

I let David talk more, sharing bits of his life, his problems.
But I was silently holding back tears, imagining myself playing
in an echoing church.

People say, "What a lovely service" when their Aunt Edna passes at the ripe old age of eighty-one. They do not offer such contrived compliments when a young man is taken too soon.

The number of attendees surprised us all. David, frail and thin in a black suit he'd borrowed from Sam Evans, his arm on Sara as they took their front row seats, got a resentful glare from Joshua's sister as she coddled her daughter, then about five years old. The girl chattered away innocently, unaware of the reason for the gathering. She even blurted out, "Where's Uncle Josh?" As Sister abruptly attempted to quiet her, the child let out a wail in the middle of the pastor's homily, and thankfully not during my harp solo. Sister retreated to the back lobby for the remainder of the service to calm her daughter.

A sense of defensiveness pervaded Joshua's funeral that blustery Saturday in August. That crazy old preacher from *The Orin and Mabel Show*, still fuming his "God's wrath" spiel on the radio, had dared to accuse Joshua by name of "spreading a plague into our community." He'd even castigated the Presbyterian Church itself for hosting the service. No one knew if he might show up to fling a Bible.

He never did, but I could tell from my view by the altar, seated with my harp as I played "Love of My Life," that some of the attendees were mere looky-loos, reminded of the service by that vile man.

Certainly, Joshua's classmates, his father's coworkers and business clients, his mother's friends, and of course Joshua's piano teacher Helen Rose and her husband, had sincere affection for Joshua, or at least respect for his family. And although they'd met him only once, each of Sara's three brothers flew in from California to attend.

But some of the folks toward the back seemed merely curious, lured in by the opportunity to be this close to someone who had died from "that disease." I never heard it spoken that day, never outright saw it, but felt it through a sidelong glance, a refusal to touch or shake hands, all from people we didn't know in the first place, so why should we care?

Before the service, Joshua's mother had called in a panic. Donn Funeral Home, the only one in town, had hesitated to do their job. Her call to me included a bit of insight. It didn't take a discerning intuition to grasp that the funeral director was a "friend of Dorothy." My abrupt call, reminding him that I'd seen him lurking around the Columbus gay bars, convinced him to graciously change his mind. When carefully removing my harp from the back of my mini-van, I offered him no more than a stern glare.

During the cemetery burial, while David sobbed quietly, his father and mother did the same. I knew this had shattered them, the people closest to Joshua. But more, it angered them.

Geologists tell us that the Ohio Valley was formed by glaciers eons ago, thus giving way for the rolling hills and mostly flat lands that allow us to witness approaching storm clouds from miles away as they sweep along before operatically enveloping the countryside. Some took the next day's storm, the downfallen trees and mild flooding, as a sign. But I knew this was not Joshua's style.

Instead, on a visit to the farm to check up on David, he invited me out to survey short early sprouts of corn in a nearby field to, as he called it, "walk the rows." As I trudged behind him, overdressed and sweating in the humid August air, David checked the many bent and broken branches, with the untouched sprouts merely waist-high. He seemed casual in a worn T-shirt, jeans, and boots, his John Deere cap almost covering his face. I saw no visible grief, just a remote attendance, his stalwart observance of the natural destruction of his crop.

"Shouldn't be too bad," he surmised as he ripped up a bent sprout, checked its muddy roots, dug his fingers in, parsed out clumps of dirt, then dropped the branch.

"Good thing about pumpkins," he nodded towards the other field beyond us. "They just gotta sit and wait."

And then, the sign arrived, if it was a sign at all. A single white butterfly landed on David's shoulder. He didn't notice it at first until he saw my glance, then scooped it into his dirt-coated palm, where it nestled, crawled for a moment, then took off over our heads and above the field, into the sky.

Chapter 41

THE NIGHT COMES DOWN

TOBY WASN'T SURE how to react when David called him to the kitchen, where, expecting lunch on the table, instead he saw a rifle and a box of shells.

"What's goin' on?"

"Calm yourself," David sighed. "We ain't goin' huntin.' I know you hate that."

"But—"

"Sam's comin' over soon. I jus' wanted to have a talk first."

Toby had done everything he could to repay David for supporting him through his degree at Ohio State. But more, he took pleasure in helping out, even through Joshua's worst times, and now David's. The crops, the floral sales, laundry, even a few accidents David had in the bathroom—nothing tarnished his resolve to do right by these men for taking him in. But this, a gun on the table, scared him.

At dinner the previous Sunday at the Evans home, with Toby and Goliath along, David had casually mentioned the barn door having become stuck, either from the hinges rusting or the barn itself beginning to show its age. Without pause, Sam offered to help him fix it, despite Toby almost defensively saying he could handle it. Repairs became Sam's excuse for their time together without Sara quizzing David about his health.

David stood, felt a bit woozy, leaned back against the counter.

"I told you I could fix the door myself," Toby said.

"Never mind that. It's Sam's way of visiting."

"So . . ." Toby nodded toward the rifle.

"You have been so good to me, and to Josh. But . . . I wanted to say it's a gift, but the real thing is— You know how Josh went a little crazy toward the end, arguing, losing track of who we were?"

Toby nodded.

"Well," David gripped the counter's edge. "Sometimes, I think I'm starting to lose track of time. Like, I was just standing for a minute, but then I see an hour's gone by. And I get these thoughts."

"You ain't gonna—"

"No, I'm not. And that's the point. I won't. But I don't want this here in the house."

"What about if somebody comes by like that time you told me about?"

"Fuck 'em. Anybody comes by again, you can shoot 'em." David foraged in the cupboard for a hidden pack of cigarettes, lit one.

Toby scowled. "You shouldn't do that."

"I know."

"I'm worried about your health!" Toby shouted, a rare outburst.

David snapped back, "I'm gonna die soon, and you gotta face that." He instantly regretted saying it as Toby's face twisted into a red scowl of tears.

"But I'm not gonna kill myself. I ain't religious, but something tells me if I do it I'll never see him again, or go where he went, if he went anywhere but in the ground."

David sucked the last of the cigarette, searched for an ashtray, then dabbed it in the kitchen sink water and tossed it in the trash. "Take it, hide it, and know I'm gonna stick it out, because anything else would be too mean to you."

Toby, still pouting and teary, took the rifle and box of shells, and stomped out the back door with a clueless Goliath following.

David leaned out the doorway, "And don't hide it in the barn! That's the first place I'll look!"

Although he could hear Toby's footsteps in the yard, he didn't turn to look out the window. He waited, knowing he'd apologize later and that Toby would understand some day.

He sat down for a minute. Or an hour.

Even before the three light taps at the door, David knew Sam Evans stood waiting on the porch. Sam's repeated knocks stirred a flurry of emotions: his shame at having hurt innocent Toby's feelings, his conflicted admiration for Joshua's father, his yearning for Sam's dogged persistence in visiting for chores when he knew the visits were more personal.

He dreaded the space between conversations, the space of Joshua's absence. The entire house had become all about Joshua via his mother's renovations and, more recently, Toby's hopeful spirit. He couldn't pass the dining room without a winsome glance at the silent keyboard, and had even tried to plunk out a few melodies on a few lonely afternoons. He'd sometimes find himself staring out the kitchen window as a cardinal or blue jay returned to peck at the feeder Joshua had set up.

Smoking and drinking beer couldn't completely cloud his emotions, so he braved sobriety for days at a time, his solitude broken by Toby's supportive friendship, his energetic youth, and the occasional burst of tears.

But Sam Evans and his stalwart demeanor couldn't hide that empty space with Joshua invisibly between them. They would haul out the tool box, putter and hammer, oil and adjust, until a solution was found to make what was left of his life a little bit easier, be it a barn door, a stuck window, the tricky water heater, or a flat truck tire.

He could have stayed still in the kitchen, ignored Sam Evans's knocks, let Toby find him and the two carry on without him. But with a choked-back sob, he realized the visits were a way to connect to whatever was left of Joshua. Any story, no matter how brief, gave his parents another memory of Joshua, another day, another moment. He was all they had left, so he had to keep on for them. Somehow that made it easier.

"Suck it up, idiot," he muttered to himself.

Wiping his eyes on a dishrag, David walked past the dining room, nodded to the empty seat at the keyboard and its missing ghost, and pressed on to the front door.

"Hey, Sam. Good to see you," he said as he wrapped his slightly stunned sort-of father-in-law in a tight long hug.

Not long after Christmas 1990, a year after Joshua's passing, there was a day when I visited David, offered a meager present, remembered his baffled thanks. I thought he might be fine for a while. But a few days later, on some impulse I called and got no answer. Certainly there had been times when he would have been out working in a field or the barn, but this was not one of them. An unpleasant, un-Christmasy snow slatted sideways across the county road as I impulsively drove back to the farm.

After knocking for several minutes, I wandered around the house, saw a pair of footprints in the snow, and followed them to find David standing in the nearby field, facing the snow, a coat barely hanging from his shoulders. He was just staring toward the horizon with Goliath sniffing about.

"We played out here, like kids," he said as I stopped at his side, not even surprised by my presence, as if I'd never left days before. His face gaunt yet flushed from the cold, I saw the traces of his youth somewhere in his misty eyes. "Chasing each other through the corn field, like kids. Right there." He nodded toward the nearly bare field, cut-down brown sticks of corn stalks jutting up from the snow-laden ground. "And when he caught up with me . . . Well, you can guess what happened." His craggy face revealed a sly wink. "Hey, can you keep a secret?"

I nodded assent.

"I want you to do me a favor, some day."

He told me, and I kept that secret for a long time.

Eventually I led him back to his house and called the paid caregiver back to provide what I couldn't every day, the burden sometimes too great for Toby, or perhaps the tasks so utterly simple: to soothe him, to keep him company, to help him bathe, take his pills, and sleep.

Before I left, I found him standing in the dining room, trying to lean over to reach a few boxes.

"You oughtta take these," he said of the collection of cassettes and sheet music, the remnants of Joshua. "You know what they are. I can't listen to them anymore. It makes me too sad." His gaunt face attempted a smirk.

I understood, and even when he insisted I also take Joshua's old electric piano, unopened in its case after all those years, knowing I would also inherit the sadness of his memory, I accepted those gifts.

The new year did not fare much better. My father, nestled in his little twin bed at the Serene Senior Care home in the room he shared with my mother, died peacefully in his sleep, we were told.

While I was playing my harp at a Baroque music festival that summer down in Cincinnati, David's caregiver Emily called Sara Evans. They drove him all the way up to the Cleveland Clinic, where he'd had a few other visits, knowing the Serene hospital wouldn't know what to do, or even admit him, so backwards they were even then.

Sara had left several messages on my answering machine, and I must have waited an hour or so after loading my harp back into the house before calling back. Before driving to the hospital, I made myself a pathetic sandwich and sat in my kitchen as my two cats swirled around my feet. I tried to prepare myself for more death, forced myself to chew a turkey sandwich with too much mayonnaise.

After the long drive north, Sara had foisted herself on her daughter's hospitality. Sister reluctantly took her in but predictably refused to visit David. Yet Sara stayed there while I considered either getting a hotel room or driving back and forth to Serene.

It took several days for David to finally let go. He seemed to know we were there. I did decide to drive back home one day to collect what I thought might help: a few cassettes of Joshua's piano recordings and a little player with headphones. David didn't act surprised when he heard the music. More relieved, he heard it with pleasure, or perhaps as a map to where he was headed. He croaked out a joke, tubes in his arms and up his nose, the headphones cupping his ears.

"I feel like an astronaut."

David's funeral was a more subdued affair. Joshua's parents chose the Presbyterian Church again, despite David having attended few services. I took on the organizational duties. The pastor remained thankfully non-judgmental in his choice of Bible passages.

Once again, I was on harp as part of the musical service (a perhaps too-florid version of "Lily of the Valley"). Ed Wallenbeck then played a solemn acoustic guitar version of "Who Wants to Live Forever." The cryptic inside joke was lost on most attendees.

We delayed the service a week to accommodate the travel plans of Curt Hildebrand, who flew up from Texas with a new wife. He offered sympathies from his own parents and sister. At my request, he took to the podium and told of David's childhood and his trip down south years later, or what he knew of it.

It astounded me that Curt could travel thousands of miles to pay tribute to his cousin while Joshua's sister couldn't risk a two-hour drive from Cleveland, her daughter's conveniently timed illness preventing her presence.

Joe Kemp spoke of his nephew's stalwart work ethic, how he charmed shoppers on roadside stands and at farmer's markets into buying just a few more peaches or ears of corn, and how proud he was when David won Third Prize at the county fair's Big Mac Pumpkin weigh-in contest.

The remembrances, however, were spoken before mostly empty pews.

David had been adamant about not being buried anywhere near his father's grave, and fortunately a small plot was purchased next to that of the Evans family, which by then had only one engraved name. The director of Donn Funeral Home did not have to be strong-armed into accepting the burial request this time, although he did press for cremation—as he put it, "a more economical choice."

We accepted his opinion but knew the real reason. Once again, he didn't want to prepare the body. He also added a $300 "transportation services fee" from the hospital.

But the funeral director's behavior did not stir us to outrage. At the cemetery, those of us who knew both men had already been drained of our more vocal grief. And although no one mentioned it, the truth hovered. AIDS had become part of our community, and its losses, the "otherness," abandoned in quiet solemnity.

The one exception was lanky Toby, who barely stifled his sobs both in the church and at David's gravesite, while others remained quiet in their grieving.

His crying persisted even to the post-funeral gathering at the Evans's home, but shifted to an abrupt and surprising outburst of laughter when Sara and I reminded him, in conspiratorial whispers, of David's private pact, which we had secretly carried out. The contents of the urn buried in the grave were not David's ashes. Transferred and interred in his urn were instead a few ounces of his own farm's soil. Toby's glimmer of mirth, as if we had gotten away with a grand deception, helped us all get through that day.

The secret promise David had asked me to keep on that cold winter day months before was to spread his remains in the pumpkin field. In mid-September, a week before his church funeral, Toby, Sara and Sam, Ed Wallenbeck, Chuck, and a few other musicians from the barn concert gathered at the farm. Walking among the ripening orange gourds, we tossed his ashes amid the leafy vines, then returned to the house for food, drinks, and reverent versions of a few of David's favorite songs, me on the keyboard, Ed strumming his acoustic guitar.

Toby winced as we each claimed a few items as mementos, but that had been David's request: a framed photo, a knick-knack, a serving dish. Nothing that truly meant anything was taken. Toby had already hidden away David's worn John Deere cap and Carhartt jacket for himself.

Halloween was on a Thursday that year, so I drove over from Columbus to visit my mother and Joshua's parents. But the real reason for my visit was to witness, through a winding drive in David's old truck with Toby at the wheel, the hundreds of silently cackling, smiling jack o' lanterns on porches all over Serene. We knew that nearly every pumpkin had become, perhaps, a small part of David.

Our tour, however, was hampered by the well-remembered Blizzard of 1991, when snow and ice storms swept through the Midwest from Minnesota through Ohio and all the way down to Texas. Call it merely a natural occurrence, but I have other notions that defy logic.

And, a little more than two months after David passed, over in England in late November, that big-toothed gentleman Freddie Mercury followed him along the way.

Chapter 42

IT'S LATE

THE CRUNCH OF a John Deere extractor claw ripping through the wall of Bobbie Shoemaker's parents' house left a sad half-kitchen exposed.

Almost an entire long block was destroyed, leaving Sara Evans and two of her neighbors, whose homes faced the adjoining Center Street. Senior couples both of them, they simply refused to sell.

Each demolished house contained a personal story. Mike Kendall's home, where at a sleepover of tents in his yard we first heard David Bowie's *Diamond Dogs* played from speakers aimed out the window; Bonnie Rathborne and her twin sister Barbara, one known for her studious nature, the other as a consummate flirt; Ricky Bettancourt, who, as an enterprising teen, mowed lawns up and down the block for a few dollars.

They had all moved on, leaving their parents to cash out, move elsewhere: to Florida finally, or Zanesville, if they were less adventurous. Serene endured "renewal," a death of sorts, with a brash influx of residents unconcerned about the past.

The corrupt deal was exposed in September 2004 by Seth Pritchard, a Serene native and news writer for the *Columbus Dispatch*, whose summer visit to his parents' home three blocks away left him horrified by the sudden disappearance of half of his entire grade school paper route.

Pritchard's story was published soon after nearly all the homes had been sold and demolished, leaving gaping holes in the earth down through the basement, with only sidewalks and bulldozer-trampled lawns remaining before it was all flattened into a new parking lot for Beekam College, now a "University" through some other financial swindle.

The lies began with Arthur "Artie" Hinckle, the more ambitious son of my family's main real estate competition for decades. Artie told one resident that all his neighbors were going with the deal, offering to buy up the lower-to-middle-income homes for around $60,000 each. Then, when they agreed, he told others, until the aging parents of schoolmates decided to pack up for retirement homes or apartments in the newer section of town.

When the dust settled and that awful crunching sound abated, Sara Evans and her two neighbors' homes stood alone at the edge of the lot. Where for years Sara could admire her neighbor's oak tree and rose garden from her kitchen sink window, she now had to buy drapes to cut the evening glare of street lamps looming over the mostly unused parking lot.

Sara had given up cooking anyway since her husband died; a fall from a stroke atop a ladder. Samuel Evans had been "puttering" for years, making small improvements to rain gutters and cracked window ledges; anything to help forget the loss of his son.

Sara spent a good three years alone in that house, except for Sister's increasingly infrequent visits from Cleveland, sometimes with her husband in tow, more often with just her daughter.

And my visits suffered infrequency as more concerts in other cities took me away from Serene, until that summer when I happened to witness the destruction.

The college administrators could have spent half as much to build a two- or three-story parking garage on the campus's existing lot. But money from patrons seemed to flow like a geyser, until it didn't. The long-awaited new gymnasium stalled; the soccer fields on the other side of the campus were delayed when a majority of the residents in better homes told the college to stuff it. At least that neighborhood was spared.

By winter, without any neighboring homes or trees to block the wind, the windows of Sara Evans's home whistled through January snowstorms. Sara's daughter had pleaded, cajoled, and insisted she sell the house, probably in hopes of getting what she surmised would be her share of the payoff. But Sara Evans refused until she lost track of things: her checkbook, the remote, that book she'd been reading over and over.

By the time she gave in (and in this matter I agreed with Sister), Sara Evans understood her diagnosis of early onset dementia. She did finally agree to move into an independent senior apartment complex built only a decade before on the outskirts of Serene, out by the A&W and the YMCA. My own mother lives down the hall. They've become friends of a sort.

In her single room, decorated with small remnants from her home, Sara asks me about Joshua and David as if I, their friend and conduit in those difficult years, were still in contact with them.

Of course, in a way, I was, and remain so. She forgets that I've given her CDs of his music. Photo albums of the boys' years together would soothe but then irritate her. "Why won't he visit?" she'd grumble. Even in her pink pajamas, her eyes wider since she's grown thin and frail, holding her wrinkled arthritic hands, I see her as a most noble woman.

After wheeling her and then my mother out to the recreation room, I play the small upright piano for the residents, soft nice tunes, and they light up. Sometimes, Sara gets confused, thinking me to be her lost son. I have learned to not correct her.

Several times repeating my tales, I told her of my recent visit to San Francisco, and her eyes lit up. As a harpist, I keep up with concerts all over and got myself an invitation to perform at an annual Harp Festival. Held in nearby Walnut Creek in an austere auditorium with perfect acoustics, I played on a loaner; travelling by plane with a harp is not recommended, and damn near impossible.

But my visit had an ulterior motive, a sort of pilgrimage, where I flew first to Los Angeles to trace the ghost of Joshua's perform- ance venues. Then up in San Francisco. I stopped first at Sara Evans's childhood home, which she and her brothers had sold years ago for what most recently is estimated to be one tenth its current value. But who could have enjoyed that extra million dol- lars, save her otherwise indifferent daughter or distant remaining family?

Another part of my trip was to forage for something I couldn't acquire through unsuccessful eBay searches: a single copy of a specific issue of *In Touch* that included the photo and short article of Joshua performing in Los Angeles. A shop called The Magazine on Larkin Street proved a success, a place where a person could flip through dozens of used porn magazines with- out a shred of shame to find that one specific page, that locked-in talisman of memorabilia.

And, as an added surprise, while perusing the local gay newspaper, I noticed a listing for a Queen cover band performing at a leather bar; how truly San Franciscan.

Fat Bottom Girls, a quartet of gay bears in "swamp drag," their lead singer dressed in a chicken costume, inspired me to stay a few days to witness their talents. From "You're My Best Friend," to "Death on Two Legs," and the requisite "Bohemian Rhapsody," the band's cover versions pleased the San Francisco Eagle's few dozen clapping fans. Their joy matched my own as I sat by the bar, smiling as I recalled so much, comforted not to be the largest man in the room.

The edited version of my San Francisco visit told to Sara on returning home excluded my obsessive hunt for Joshua memora- bilia. She did enjoy my little cell phone videos of the chicken- suited lead singer belting out a few Queen songs.

So, instead of reminding Sara Evans of her son's existence and thereby his absence, I tell her stories until she fades into the past where stories don't end.

I have shared a few items on my blog, including some later news articles about Freddie Mercury and Queen, like the August 2006 article about a Zanzibari Muslim group that complained about Mercury's "flamboyant lifestyle offending Islam, bringing shame upon the island" where he was born.

When I read about a young teenager who, in a violent attack by his own classmates, was branded with HOMO on his back simply for wearing a Queen T-shirt, it brought tears to my eyes. The post I wrote about it still generates a lot of sympathetic comments, even years later.

I've also uploaded music and pictures of Joshua and David. I've got 234,094 hits. Where do these fans come from?

Joshua's sister got wind of my little online jottings and recordings, and I almost missed her inquiring emails in my spam box. I'd read so many stories of gay men's families swooping in to steal possessions from their surviving lovers. As I've noted, before they died, David Koenig, in a lucid state, had wisely agreed to draw up a contract naming Joshua as his business partner, there being no semblance of domestic partnership in Ohio at the time. After Joshua's death, he'd planned to give the land to his Uncle Joe.

Sister certainly couldn't get her hands on her brother's share of the farm, not even the house. David had specifically bequeathed the deed to Toby, who stayed on a few years before meeting a man who, after a brief online romance and visits back and forth, whisked him off to Oregon, where the two run an organic farm in Sherwood, just south of Portland. Toby, now Tobias, posts photos with his husband Chuck (married over the Canadian border years before the U.S. made it legal) and their son, named David.

And the farm, under Joe Kemp's vision, expanded to build more greenhouses and to sell more flowers, in addition to a small crop of pumpkins and decorative gourds. The pressure of full-on farming became a profit when he sold half the outlying land for the always expanding housing needs of Serene residents.

The barn is gone, torn down when it swayed and creaked too much and lost its usefulness to newer storage sheds. Before they hired the men to demolish it, Toby called me with his boyish voice, pleading for a new home for that rickety old upright piano. I couldn't resist and asked him to have it hauled over to my apartment, where a few neighbors helped drag it up the porch stairs while I hovered near doorways, thankful that I live on the first floor. As deft as I am with harp-hauling, a piano's a different creature, heavy with weight and memories.

Toby sold the house to Joe Kemp when he moved out. Joe converted it to a gift shop, renovated and expanded the porch, and replaced the house's front with wide windows and an accessible ramp. Inside, high school girls work at part-time jobs wrapping bouquets and offering sentimental cards, wooden goose lawn ornaments, and matching sets of floral print oven mitts and dish towels.

Sitting on the porch—a lone, feeble, and grayed sentinel—Goliath guarded the house by days, pleasant with visitors but standoffish to anyone after Toby left him behind. He stayed at Joe Kemp's during winters, but always returned to the empty house, even through his last summer, waiting for those who wouldn't return.

Behind the house, six rows of enormous tubular greenhouses wiggle in the wind but withstand our harshest winters, as inside row after row of floral beauties blossom. Every time I return to Serene, I buy a few planters and bring them to Sara Evans and my mother, because who doesn't love pansies? After attempting to tell a bit of the farm's history, I stopped when the salesgirl's eyes sort of fixed on me as if I were some babbling old aunt.

Recently, Sister pried and inquired again about Joshua's "music property" and hovered toward threatening legal action until copies of Joshua and David's wills were sent to her lawyer, along with my terse note explaining that there was no monetary value in a cassette tape of Joshua spiraling into a Keith Jarrett-esque New Year's Eve piano improvisation of forty minutes, no monetary value in David's souvenirs from Texas, nor in a flyer for one of Joshua's mini-concerts in a Los Angeles nightclub that is now a Starbucks.

No value, except for myself and his fans, these kids and older folk who show an electronic form of love that would have been nice to have while the boys were still alive.

They seem to connect with Joshua's music. Goodness, everybody's connected to everybody now. It's all so different, trying to keep up, but I have fast hands. A musical background can help with that.

I'm not making any money from the website. I don't need that. My orchestra job, harp lessons, and the occasional solo gig at weddings are my career. The bar in Columbus pays good tips, and I invite some of the cuter young men who happen to "friend" me online to come hear a few songs before entering the dance floor to spiral off into their romance of the night.

What I need is for people who never met them to know them, and not forget them and their possibility, their song cut short.

I still miss them both so very much, which is why I still return home to a town of people who never understood them and rarely appreciated them. Hopefully, they'll get it sooner or later. Gardening is much easier in this part of the country.

I still enjoy some time in the city. On a recent night, nearly midnight, I was about to finish my set at the piano bar when a pair of young men, one husky blond and his smaller brown-eyed friend, sat close by, actually listening. They asked for some of those old songs with a sincerity that touched me. I wanted to tell them who they resembled, how their affection for each other struck my heart. Instead, I merely smiled and played their requests. They thanked me, then walked out of the bar, arm in arm into the night.

ACKNOWLEDGMENTS

Enormous thanks to my editors Felice Picano and Louis Flint Ceci; to friends Stephen LeBlanc and Scott St. John for early enthusiasm; to my colleagues Mark Abramson, Jim Grimsley, Adam Tendler, Jack Fritscher, and Mark Hemry; to cover guys Lian and Kevin and photographer Dot; to Gregory Yee for musical wizardry; to my family for enduring my years of piano playing in the dining room; to my music teachers and the farm coworkers who inspired this story; and to my many concert-going pals. Thanks for listening.

ABOUT THE AUTHOR

Jim Provenzano is the author of the Lambda Literary Award winner *Every Time I Think of You*, its sequel *Message of Love* (a Lambda Literary Award Finalist), the novels *PINS, Monkey Suits, Cyclizen*, the stage adaptation of *PINS*, and the short story collection *Forty Wild Crushes*. He received a BFA in Dance from Ohio State University and an MA in English/Creative Writing from San Francisco State University. A journalist, editor, and photographer in LGBT media for three decades, he lives in San Francisco. Contact him at www.jimprovenzano.com, or through his blog, jimprovenzano.blogspot.com.